HEIRS
OF A
LOST RACE

DR. FRANCIS F. PITARD

ISBN: 978-1-961078-53-6 (Hardback)
ISBN: 978-1-961078-54-3 (Paperback)
ISBN: 978-1-961078-55-0 (eBook)

Library of Congress Control Number: 2024911219

This book is a work of fiction. Any resemblance to real places, events, or individuals, whether living or deceased, is purely coincidental. All characters, names, and incidents portrayed in this novel are products of the author's imagination.

Printed in the United States of America.

Springer Literary House LLC
6260 Lavender Cloud Place
Las Vegas, Nevada 89122, USA

www.springerliteraryhouse.com

CONTENTS

FOREWORD

Technical writing is my specialty, as a scientist and internationally known expert on sampling statistics. My hobby is archeology, and for many years I have been fascinated by ancient Polynesians, also called "the Vikings of the Pacific". So, writing a fiction novel about ancient Polynesians has been my dream for a long time.

Some archeologists, among them the famous, respected and inspiring Thor Heyerdahl, thought Polynesians came from the Andes in South America. We know now Polynesians came from the other side of the Pacific, as a logical and slow progression from island to island of the "Lapita" culture. Yet, something is missing at one given point in the history of this island people. From vocabulary similarities with some people from the Andes, and from old Polynesian legends, Thor Heyerdahl had the ability to open our eyes to one of the most intriguing pieces of the jigsaw puzzle making up Polynesian antiquity: Polynesians may not have come from the Andes, but they most certainly had contacts with people from the Andes. Who were these people from the Andes?

For reasons that are unclear, many years before Francisco Pizarro invaded the Andes and brought the Incas to their knees, a well-respected and peaceful people vanished. They were called the Viracocha's people. The legend says: "Viracocha took his people on rafts, and vanished at sea, following the setting sun. He would never return." So, it is conceivable that Viracocha had contact with the Polynesians and made a great impression on them under the legendary name of Kon Tiki. This would trigger a well-planned exploration of the eastern Pacific by the Polynesians, ending with a massive migration to their ultimate destination: Easter Island.

The following story is based on legends from the Andes, from Polynesia, and from Easter Island. It is indeed only one scenario out of many, but whatever the scenario, it must have been the root of an astonishing saga. It takes only a glance at this area of a world map to be convinced of the incredible magnitude of the undertakings of these early adventurous seafarers. It could never have been done without extraordinary will, abundance of unrecognized skills, appalling physical and mental suffering, and the loss of many lives. Yet, they did it, and this is an archeological fact. The remarkable civilization they developed on Easter Island is awesome proof of their courage.

In ancient Polynesian cultures, emphasis is placed on the values of peace and love rather than on warfare. Knowledge of peace and love was far more important and respected than knowledge of ritual. Polynesians had strong mottos, perhaps not expressed as what we should do or should not do, but expressed as who we are and who we should be.

For Polynesians, Tici, Teke, or Tiki is the sacred origin of all knowledge. In the Andes, Kon Tici means "Son of the Sun": What a remarkable coincidence! Kon Tici had the courage to live with a superb, unshakable ethic of peace. Along his breathtaking journey, he meets a young Polynesian woman, Hina of the Valley. Born with a noble heart, motivated by her tremendous respect for nature, self-reliant, and driven by constant love for her people, she matures quickly, and becomes a priestess second to none. Heirs of a Lost Race is the love story of Kon Tici and Hina of the Valley that should inspire, give a model of ethics, and provide hope and optimism. They are from different worlds, races, cultures and beliefs, leading to a breathtaking encounter. Within a microcosm of the South Pacific, forgotten values with universal reach are explored. Around the characters there is a constant powerful, spiritual and cosmic presence. The characters feel that presence, which adds a mysterious touch to their story and behavior.

ACKNOWLEDGMENT

I am indebted to many people who have supported my work, inspired me, and encouraged me to pursue, day after day, a complex piece of literature. I am especially grateful to Henri Forget for his effort to polish the manuscript. The novel is based on archeological evidence and inspired by the wonderful works of Douglas L. Oliver in "Ancient Tahitian Society" and Thor Heyerdahl.

I dedicate this novel to my family, my friends, to the children of this world, who dare to dream about peace, and to the Polynesian and Maori people, who can show us a different and attractive philosophy of life, with outstanding ancestral values. These wonderful islanders, with an untold story, may have wisdom that we may share and, in the process, benefit from.

FRANCIS F. PITARD

ABOUT THE AUTHOR

Francis F. Pitard is a consulting expert in sampling statistics and Total Quality Management. His hobby is archeology and anthropology of ancient Polynesians. Before becoming an American citizen he lived two years in Tahiti and six years in New Caledonia. The author believes that quality of life is essential to everyone. He is convinced that each of us holds the key to such quality, through peaceful ethics, self-confidence, self-respect, self-control and respect of the freedom of others. His novel is meant to fight the arrogance of those who want to rule this world. His fight is meant to transform arrogant leaders into peaceful ones who will protect people around them and inspire the ones far away. He was born in Normandy, France, during World War II, a few miles from the infamous invasion beaches. His great uncle Louis died in a concentration camp in Germany, and his wife, Aline, escaped from the Ravensburg concentration camp. As a young man, Francis Pitard was fascinated by his elderly aunt's stories about the French Resistance: He knows what war is all about, and how valuable peace is. His work often takes him to copper mines, high in the Andes, where it is easy to meditate along the fascinating Inca trail. At times he and his wife, Deloris, spend days hiking the rocky hills of Easter Island, preparing the sequel of Heirs of a Lost Race, which will be the inspiring Rapa-nui Settlers, by Choice and Necessity. He now lives with his family near Denver, Colorado.

He is from one world, high in the Andes. She is from another world, more than 5000 miles away, across the Pacific Ocean. Kon Tici had the courage to live with a superb ethic of peace. Along his breathtaking journey, he meets a young Polynesian woman, Hina of the Valley, born with a noble heart.

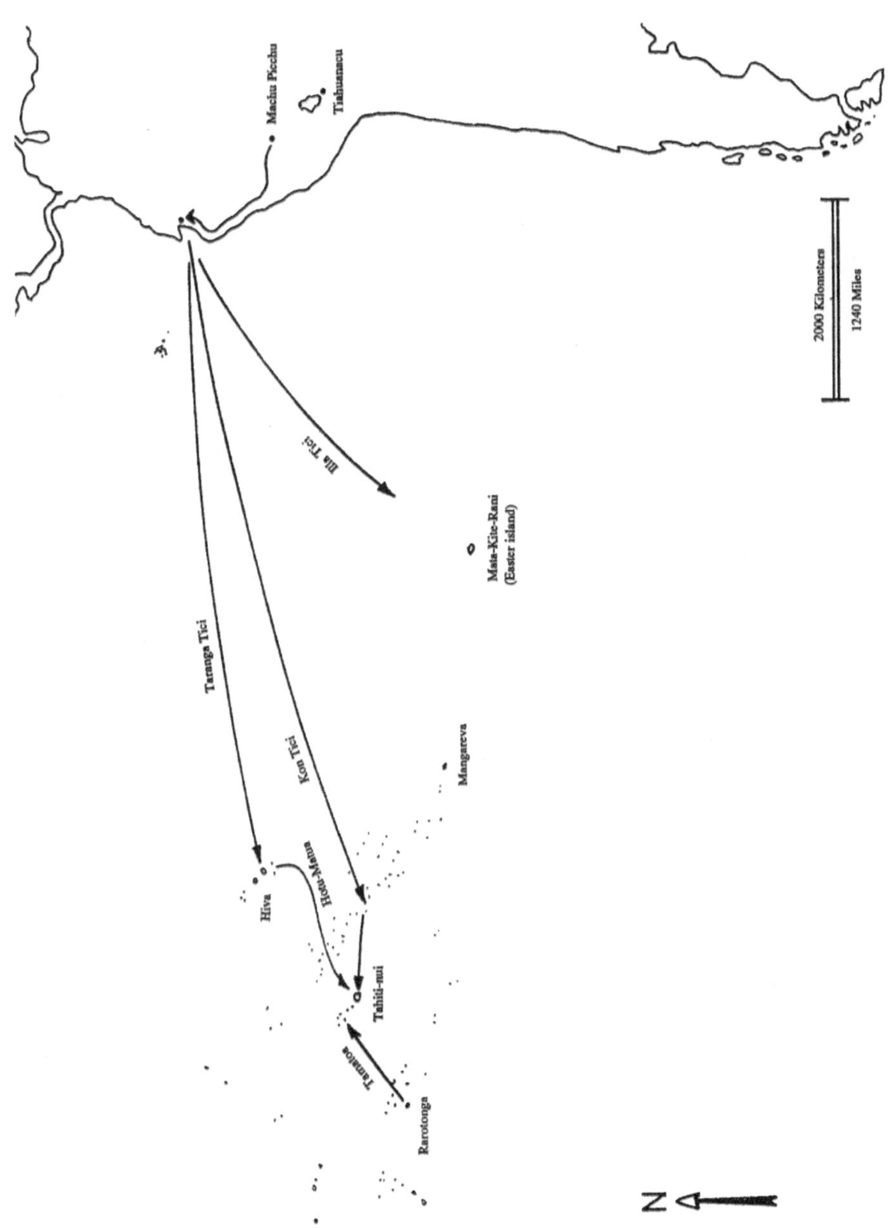
Machu Picchu
Tiahuanacu
2000 Kilometers
1240 Miles
Illa Tici
Mata-Kite-Rani
(Easter island)
Taranga Tici
Kon Tici
Mangareva
Hotu-Matua
Hiva
Tahiti-nui
Tamatoa
Rarotonga
N

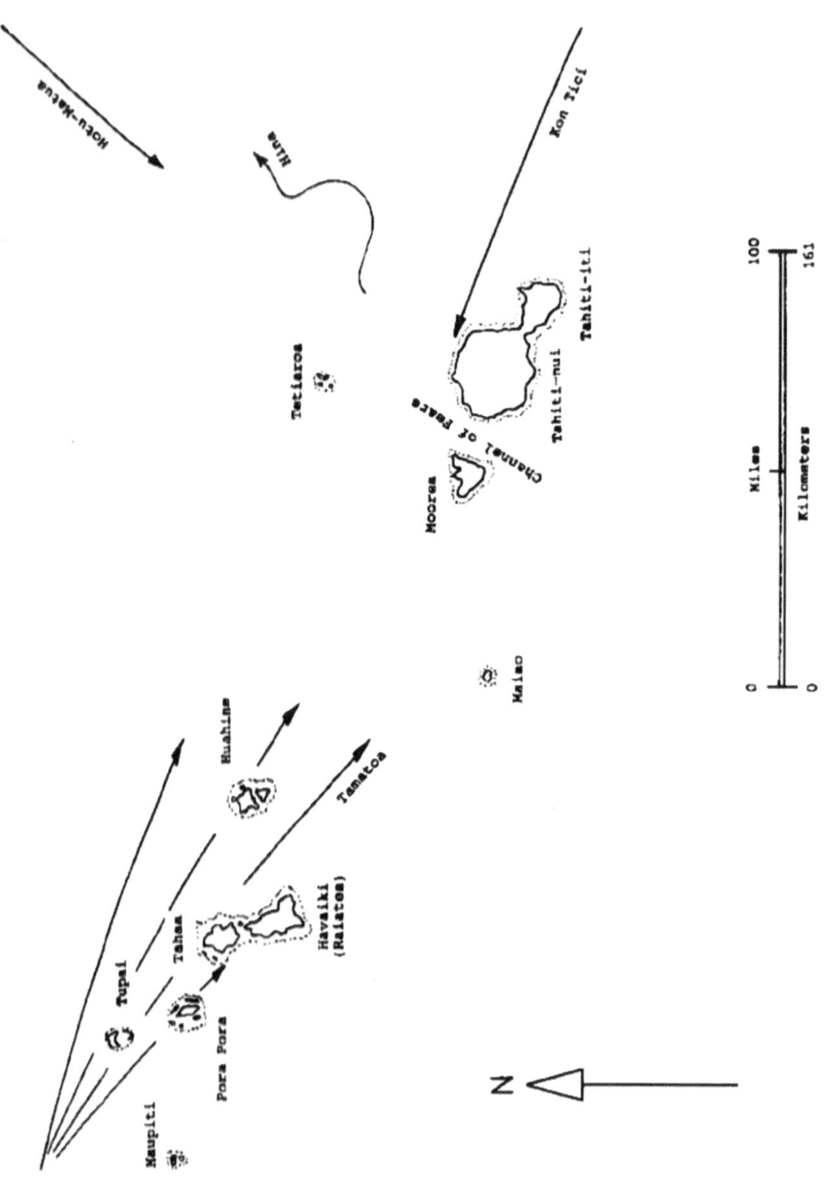

Hotu-Matua
Kon Tiki
Hiva
Tetiaroa
Tahiti-iti
Tahiti-nui
Channel of Paea
Moorea
Maiao
Huahine
Tamatoa
Tupai
Tahaa
Havaiki
(Raiatea)
Bora Bora
Maupiti
Miles
Kilometers
100
161
0
0
N

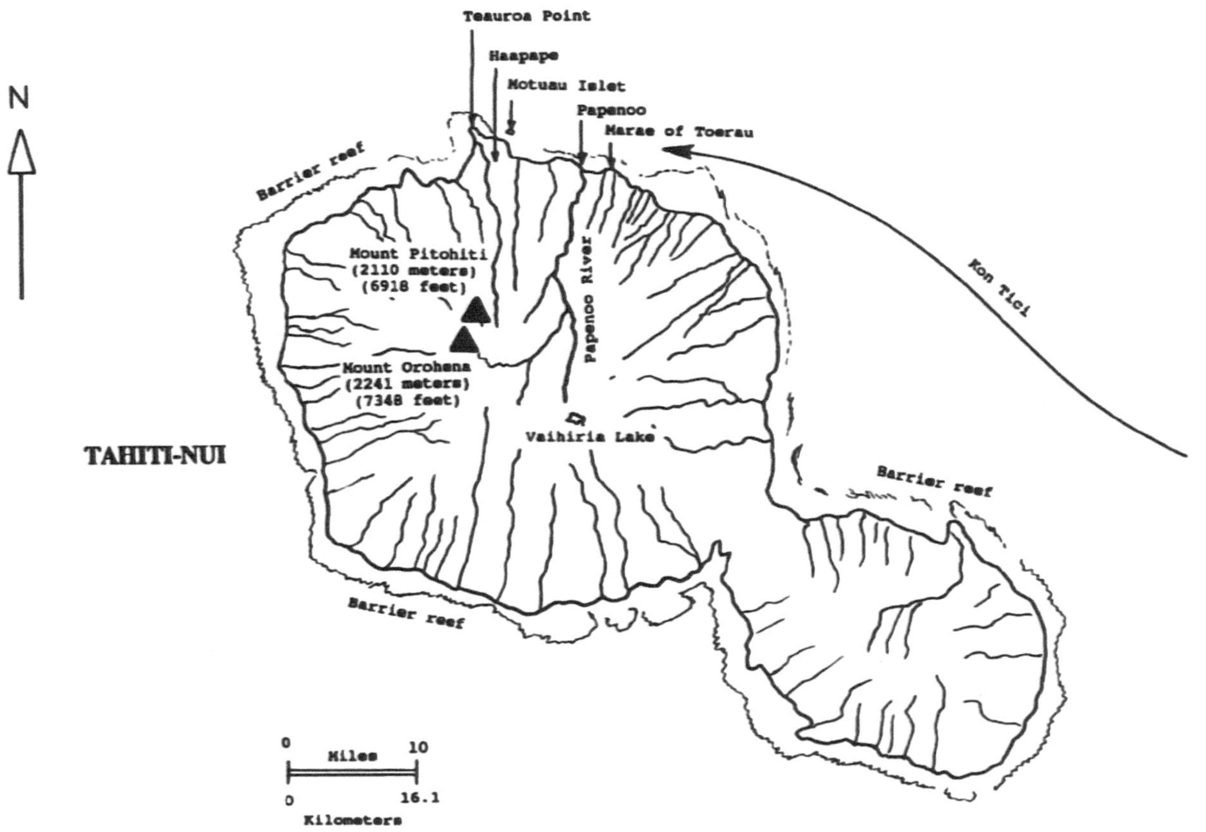

N
Teauroa Point
Haapape
Motuau Islet
Papenoo
Marae of Toerau
Barrier reef
Kon Tici
Mount Pitohiti
(2110 meters)
(6918 feet)
Papenoo River
Mount Orohena
(2241 meters)
(7348 feet)
Vaihiria Lake
Barrier reef
TAHITI-NUI
Barrier reef
0
Miles
10
0
16.1
Kilometers

CHAPTER 1

Sixteen hundred years ago, near Machu Picchu: "I shall not fight with my adversary. My adversary shall not become my enemy."

Kon Tici Viracocha

"I am the Light. I am pure energy. I am the past, the present, and the future. I am what is. Along my eternal journey, I had the privilege of meeting children who understood the Light: The following saga is their remarkable story. They shall inspire many others."

The distance between Kon and the Inca's warriors diminished rapidly. At any time, a spear could paralyze him in a river of blood. Despair invaded his mind. He knew his life had come to an end.

His older brother, Illa, ran faster. They would no doubt kill him too: It would take just a little longer. Kon heard the steps of the killers in the dry grass. From his left, he heard a spear whir through the air. It landed between his legs. He lost his balance, and tumbled into a dead bush. Before he could stand up, five warriors grabbed his arms and shoulders. Kon speculated on what the afterlife could be.

Earlier, at dawn, the Inca's legions entered the secret City of the Sun. By midday, they completed the massacre of all its peaceful inhabitants, except two young men, two brothers. Kon and Illa, hiding behind the pillars of a temple, were discovered by a patrol. The two brothers ran out of the temple and reached a long stairway leading to lower terraces. Still more warriors came from the terraces: They had nowhere to go.

"I want them alive!"

The order was loud and clear. It echoed against the walls of the city, and the surrounding mountains.

"... alive! ... alive! ... alive!"

Silence came back, implacable.

Kon never thought the word "alive" could mean so much. At this moment, it was the impossible word. At the high elevation where the city was built, voices could be heard clearly from long distances. The order came from the main temple, at the top of the city. It was the temple the Inca had selected for his headquarters, just after dawn. With their hands tied behind their back, the two brothers were taken to the Inca. Covered with dust, blood from multiple wounds, and perspiration, Kon thought about his forefathers. For generations, they had sweated in the effort of building gigantic cities in daring places, such as the City of the Sun, Tiahuanacu, and many others. They taught the people of all surrounding nations how to build roads, terraces for agriculture, and irrigation canals. With skill, they helped them to become self-sufficient for food, water, clothing, and tools. With good will, they inspired them to live in peace, to care about others, and to display good manners. All their efforts were suddenly lost, disintegrated into brutal reality. It was the reality of hate and jealousy, the reality of military and political leaders, the abysmal reality of arrogance.

Kon could not breathe well. It was not from physical fatigue, but from mental stress, anger, despair, frustration and mourning.

He looked at his beloved brother: Illa's face was cold as ice. His deep, slightly slanted, dark blue eyes reflected controlled rage. His long, straight black hair tied on the top of his head, fell around his strong shoulders. His beard reached his chest. His long, thin nose slightly curved up at the end. His lips were narrow. His chin showed pride and authority, and also determination and courage. His slender, well-shaped body was powerful. Illa was much taller than the Inca's men, and walked with commanding grace and self-confidence. Illa knew the Light, a Viracocha he was.

From a distance, Kon and Illa looked like twin brothers, but Illa was twenty-eight sun-cycles old, and Kon was twenty. Kon was almost the same height, but his beard was not as well developed. The high altitude sun had tanned their skin. When they were children, their ears were bored and the lobes enlarged until they could wear flat, gold plugs. Illa's plugs were three fingers wide. Because Kon was much younger, his plugs were only two fingers wide. As the precious disc-like plugs glittered all the time, it was a strong remainder to everyone that Illa and Kon knew the Light.

The brothers were dressed in flowing white robes, reaching to a hem just above the knees. A broad belt decorated with red suns accented their narrow waists. Their leather sandals, and white headbands woven with images of flying blue condors, were works of art. To the people of all the surrounding nations, Viracocha's sons had an imposing mien. Their grandfather was the great Taranga Tici Viracocha: Because of his wisdom, he was considered a living god who was in contact with the Light. When the Inca's army invaded Tiahuanacu one sun-cycle earlier, Taranga took his people far away into the jungle, near the seashore.

Kon and Illa's father was the great priest, ruler of the City of the Sun, who taught many unusual skills to his heirs. When Taranga left, the great priest stayed in his city, with a small group of men. He knew the old Inca well, and hoped to pacify him: He was wrong. The Inca was too old. The new generation, ambitious and well educated, waited, waited too long. The Inca could not control the new system established by the new generation. The Inca's position became only honorary: His son Ica had the executive power, and was determined to exterminate the Viracocha race.

"We should have left with Taranga, long ago," Illa said.

"Our father wanted to prove the City of the Sun was a safe sanctuary," Kon whispered.

"As a result, today, all of us are either dead, fugitives, or prisoners," Illa replied, with a sad face.

The eighty-sun-cycle-old monarch waited, seated on a large stone: He was the Inca. His skin was incredibly worn and chapped by the sun and the wind of high altitude. He had white hair, flowing in the gentle and cool breeze. His eyes did not express cruelty, but he had a sarcastic smile. The warriors bent in front of the respected ruler.

"Who are you, young men?" he asked in a gentle tone. "What are your names?"

Confused by the kind attitude of the old man, Kon looked at his brother, who answered for both of them. "I am Illa, Illa Tici, which means the Son of Fire. This is my younger brother Kon, Kon Tici, which means the Son of the Sun. Our grandfather is Taranga Tici Viracocha, who understands the Light. In our language, Viracocha means the Light."

Disturbed, the old man stood and walked around the two brothers. His face showed that he was preoccupied, and his smile vanished. He had never met Viracocha's grandchildren before. To have them both, right here, was much more than he ever expected. They were brilliant young men, well known and respected all around the land.

"Well, well! So, you are the direct descendants of the Great Viracocha. When I was your age, I traveled with him many times."

The Inca pointed a trembling, deformed finger toward Illa.

"Where are all the others? We found only a few men in the city."

"One year ago," Illa replied with annoyance, "after you massacred many of us at Tiahuanacu, they left to an unknown destination, somewhere in the jungle."

The Inca shrugged his shoulders and smiled viciously.

"Unknown destination to me, but certainly not to you," the monarch spat out with vehemence. "And you try to tell me that they went into the deadly jungle. This is a lie!"

The Inca was frustrated. He knew that Viracocha's children would never tell him where their people went. He knew that no torture, no matter how painful, would work. He knew they were capable of taking their own lives within the blink of an eye, if necessary. The old man recovered his calm, and sat on the large stone.

"Why did you stay here?" he asked with a soft voice.

Before replying, Illa took a deep breath, and stared at the Inca.

"This is our sacred city. This is the City of the Sun. This is where the soul of every man can find peace. This is where wisdom blossoms, closer to the Light. This is where we thought you would come in peace: You came to commit genocide."

Illa's face became tense. His shiny, dark blue eyes reflected his pride and intelligence. He was silent. Crickets sang in the ululating wind. The old monarch shivered, and felt something invade his body. He was paralyzed and fascinated by Viracocha's face looking at him, straight in the eyes. In this face he could see beauty, strength, secret grandeur, and above all, judgment. Viracocha judged him and his clan. The Inca's sense of guilt was intolerable. He turned his face away from Illa, and gave an order.

"Let them go. They are free."

A high dignitary, dressed as a military officer, came before the monarch and bent down. A slight, tired movement of the Inca's hand gave him the right to speak.

"We cannot let them go like this..."

"Ica, my son, I know your feelings," the old man interrupted. "I know I will die soon, and this rising empire will be yours. Then, you will be the Inca, and do whatever pleases you. But, for the time being, I am the Inca, and I shall do whatever pleases me. Let them go!"

Illa and Kon knew it was only a maneuver that would allow the Inca to follow them, until they found Taranga.

"We need to take some of our belongings in the main temple, before we leave for our journey," Illa told the military officer.

"Go, go!" Ica said, after untying Illa's and Kon's hands.

Since dawn, the Inca's men would not let anyone enter the main temple, but at this moment, they made a monumental mistake. They saw Illa and Kon enter the temple: They would never see them again. The two brothers walked into a crypt surrounded by massive stone walls. They laid their hands on one monolith near the foundation. They searched for the right spot under their fingers. They found what they felt for, then concentrated as they pushed. The giant stone rotated slowly. Warriors were coming. Kon and Illa entered into the dark slit. They closed the secret entrance. They were in a new world.

The two warriors heard a thundering noise coming from the crypt. They ran to find out what it was. They saw nothing, and the silence was absolute. They inspected each stone. They pushed on each stone. The noise remained a mystery, and they were not even sure the two brothers had gone into the crypt.

They searched more, and concluded that Kon and Illa had vanished. Confused, the warriors immediately reported the event to the Inca.

Some light came through a narrow slit between blocks in the upper part of one wall. Illa and Kon climbed tall stairs carved inside a colossal stone. When they reached the top, they pushed another block. They again entered into a dark slit. They closed the second secret exit. It was so silent that they thought time had come to a stop.

Illa held Kon's hand, and they walked in absolute darkness to the edge of a staircase going down. For a moment they sat on the top stair: They had to carefully plan their escape.

"They will never find us," Illa said with contentment.

Kon knew about the secret exit leading out of the city, but had never used it. In other times, he would have been thrilled about the unusual escape, but the loss of his father overwhelmed him with sorrow. It was a day of infamy he would never forget: He felt hot tears streaming down his cheeks.

"Viracocha, why did you abandon us?" Kon lamented.

"Because there is a purpose for all this," Illa replied.

The secret exit had two functions: Eventually, it could provide an escape from the city, but it was mainly a water drain, preventing torrential rainfall from damaging the many cultivated terraces. Anyone trapped in this passage during a rainfall would certainly drown.

They started the long descent. It was cool and humid. From time to time they felt air drafts coming from narrow slits leading outside: These were water intakes. Through some of them, they could see daylight. Suddenly, Kon felt something touching his shoulder: He knew it was not Illa, who was ahead of him. From fear, blood rushed to his head. With one hand, he grabbed the warm and soft animal, and realized it was a harmless bat they had disturbed.

They reached a place where several waterways converged into the main stairway. On their right, they saw a large slit. It was wide enough for a bat to pass through. This water intake was between two gigantic stones. They stopped and looked outside. They had a good view of the cultivated terraces and temples. Warriors were everywhere, searching for Illa and Kon.

"You can look for a long time," Illa said and smiled with satisfaction.

However, Kon's face expressed horror.

"Look at the sky!"

Dark clouds accumulated around the mountains. They both knew what would happen if it rained: It was indeed a highly effective drainage system.

"Let's go, my brother," Illa said. "Remember, it was our only chance, and we took it. There is no possible turning back."

They continued their descent. The slits leading to the outside became rare. There were no more beams of light. The stairs became steeper and slick, polished by the many cataracts of water they had sustained over time. Kon thought that some day, there would be no stairs left, therefore no escape. As they entered into the entrails of the earth, it was colder and so black that there was no hope for the eyes to adapt, which provided a sense of dizziness. After a journey that seemed an eternity, they reached a platform where new waterways converged onto the stairs: Each of them was a small stream of water. Kon kept thinking about what would happen if all these waterways were suddenly filled with water. It became an obsession. It was another kind of fear, that of man against nature. There was nothing he could do about it, except keep going as fast as possible.

"We are about one-third of the way," Illa said. "We will reach the river late during the night."

Kon did not answer. Illa's words were exactly what he did not want to hear. As they went deeper, the humidity rose. Water started dripping from inlets from all sides. At any time, they could slide on the slippery stairs, and start a fatal fall. At times, they bumped into piles of mud. Soon, the stairs became a running stream. Slowly, the water rose to their knees, pushing them forward. The stream became loud, to the point where they could no longer communicate by speaking normally: They were dealing with a potentially fatal waterfall.

Illa put his hands around Kon's ears: "Soon, it will not be as steep," he said loudly. Kon covered one ear, and pulled his brother's face against his other ear, and signaled him to repeat.

"Soon, it will not be as steep," Illa repeated. "But the water will be deeper. When we reach the level of the river, we will dive and find our way into it. Under water, let the current transport you, and keep your hands against the ceiling. When you cannot find the ceiling, you will be out."

These were Illa's last words. The noise intensified, and became intolerable. When they finally reached the level of the river, they were inside an immense room. They could not see it, but they could tell because of the frightening noise from all directions. The level of water reached their waists. They had difficulty keeping their balance. Suddenly, the stairs ended with gravel and boulders. The noise was incredible, and Kon thought his head would explode.

When Illa placed his hand around Kon's neck and pulled him

down, Kon knew it was the signal for the final dive. Illa dived first. He was gone. Kon felt apprehension as if the world behind him was some kind of unknown monster. He concentrated on what he had to do, and repeated Illa's words. He strongly inhaled and exhaled several times, until a slight sense of dizziness told him he had enough air in his lungs. Then, he dived into the unknown.

****

Far away, near a beach, in a modest hut covered by a vegetation roof, Kukara awoke from a horrible nightmare. Kama tried to comfort the child, then took her for a walk to the beach.

"What did you dream about?" Kama asked.

"The Inca killed my brother," Kukara answered, smothering a sob.

Kama was deeply disturbed. She knew Kukara's dreams had been accurate in the past. The old Taranga heard Kukara's words, and saw the distress on Kama's face.

"Something happened this morning in the City of the Sun," Taranga said. "But let's wait for the facts, and we will not know them before three moon-cycles from now."

"I cannot stop worrying about Illa, my husband," Kama said. "He and Kon were with Kukara's brother, all the time."

"I wish the world could be as beautiful as you are, Kama Tici Viracocha," Taranga Tici Viracocha said with a smile of infinite wisdom.

"One day, I would like to be as beautiful as you," Kukara said.

"You will be, and your adoptive mother will be an astonishing woman," Kama replied.

"But, since the Inca killed my parents, you are my mother," Kukara said with a frown on her face.

"For now, yes, I am your mother. But, the time will come when you will meet my sister from another world. When you see her, you will know, and you will remember my words."

Kukara shook her head: Kama's words did not make sense.

****

Kon did not need to swim. Instead, an incredible force sucked him, the underground river transporting him fast, and accelerating in narrow passages. He tried to protect his head by keeping his hands against the ceiling. The current became so strong that he no longer knew the difference between up and down. He bumped one shoulder against a sharp rock. He felt his head rub against the polished walls. He needed to breathe. Breathing became the only thing he could think about.

Suddenly, the current slowed and he found the ceiling again, then lost it: He knew he was out, at last. As he broke the surface, he coughed and breathed rapidly. He was in a pond, below a waterfall. Under the moonlight, he saw Illa swimming and waiting for him.

"We should stay in the river," Illa said. "They should not find our tracks anywhere."

The Urubamba River was strong, dangerous, and unpredictable. All night, Illa and Kon fought for their lives in the powerful current. The river continually battered them. At dawn, they were exhausted, cold, shivering and covered with cuts and bruises. Their garments were torn apart, and half-missing. Only their sandals were still in good shape. They found a bank protected by a steep-walled canyon. They crawled to some flat rocks, and immediately went to sleep.

Attracted by the smell of blood, a condor flew above Viracocha's grandsons.

****

Higher, on the plateau, the Inca's patrols were at work.

"I want every river, stream and trail to be searched," Ica ordered. "Furthermore, I want all legions, near and far, to be part of this search. I swear I will find them."

****

Late in the afternoon, Kon awoke. Nearby, on the top of a boulder, stoic and patient, two condors waited. Kon frowned, and suspected that flying condors could reveal their position to the Inca.

"Not yet! This is not carrion," Kon said, shaking his brother.

The two majestic birds soared toward the distant, high mountains, where the two brothers would have to face their toughest battle. The condor's instinct knew it all.

Kon looked at the current transporting skim, dead leaves, branches and trunks. In pain, he inspected his wounds. With sorrow, he thought about his father and Kukara's brother, killed the day before, and about his mother, killed a year earlier.

"What is wrong with us?" Kon murmured with desolation. "What is the driving force that makes an educated man a killer?"

There was no answer to his questions. Only the turbulent river showed the way. Everything seemed bizarre. Man was bizarre…

"We must continue in the water, as long as we can," Illa said, after describing a plan for their three-moon-cycle journey.

"What will happen if we don't reach Taranga in time?" Kon asked.

"They will leave on rafts, across the unknown sea, following the setting sun, without us."

They entered the river, and followed one bank. They stepped off the river only when absolutely necessary. Two days later, they found a large inlet they were searching for. It was a turbulent stream coming from the high mountains, toward the setting sun. They climbed sharp, deep gorges. Often, they walked through the jungle, past canyons and falls. They were wary of poisonous snakes. They endured hungry insects. Day after day, they were assaulted by the cruelty of the forest. Several times they went to a dead end, forcing tortuous turnarounds. Fortunately, food was no problem. They caught fish under stones, ate them raw, and found papayas and guavas.

At last, one afternoon they reached a transition zone where the trees were smaller. For several days, every afternoon they walked inside misty clouds rising from the hot jungle behind them. The insects and snakes were gone, and it became cooler. The vegetation became scarce, and gave way to the high-altitude, dry grass. Now, they were on friendly, familiar ground: the high mountains. Illa knew the area, and the location of a few isolated refuges built with moraine stones by fearless travelers.

Inside one refuge, they found a few old ponchos: They selected the best ones, and wrapped them around their shoulders. It was bitterly cold. They started a fire, with just enough wood to produce a few embers. They cooked four fish they had caught in the afternoon. Wrapped inside their ponchos, the brothers ate their first hot meal in a long time. Then, they went to sleep peacefully.

Around midnight, exploring rodents woke them up. The silent night sky was clear, with many stars. They went to the rivulet, and sat on large boulders transported long ago by the regressing glacier. From place to place, under the starlight, a few patches of snow were visible.

"We shall leave at dawn," Illa said. "We must pass the great divide before midday, when it is not too cold."

As they often did, they went into meditation under the starlight. Such communion with the Light was an intrinsic part of their life and their spiritual food from outer space and from another dimension. Silent, they became humble, with infinite pleasure.

After the brothers reached a trance state, the Light gave them a special power they called Mana. Illa saw a round boulder, went to it, and pressed three fingers on it: The boulder slightly rolled on its curved base. It would have taken several men to move that boulder. However, Mana's force was ephemeral. Its origin was unknown, and only Viracocha's sons knew how to reach it in the blink of an eye. The Inca resented such talents: they were a threat to his powerful political and military leaders. Without saying a word, Illa went back to the refuge. He rolled himself inside his poncho, and went to sleep. Illa Tici Viracocha was content.

Kon followed the stream to a small lake. He walked around the lake, then sat cross-legged on a flat stone. In the distance, a rodent whistled, or at least what he thought was a rodent. The sharp sound echoed in the high peaks. Then it was total silence again, a powerful silence. He listened to his heart pounding. Possessed by light coming from the stars, Kon's mind became infinite, his body forgotten.

A strange feeling invaded him, sending shivers along his spine. Someone was here, with him. The surrounding mountains became ghosts, talking to his soul. His eyes captured the splendor of the firmament, and endless questions came to his mind. He knew a supernatural force was around him. It was a forbidden force nobody could see.

"Are you the Supreme Creator?" he murmured, afraid to break the silence. "Why did You create me? Why am I here, listening? What does my life mean? Am I important to You? Am

I Your experiment?"

The word rang in his mind as if echoed by a surrounding ghost: experiment...experiment. He closed his eyes, trying to focus on the meaning of this word only Taranga had used once before. Then, he remembered Taranga's words, long ago when he was a child, near the giant Gate of the Sun in Tiahuanacu: "We humans are all part of a wonderful experiment that can proceed only if we are unconditionally committed to peace. If this commitment is broken, ultimately we will die physically and spiritually, leaving room for a new experiment, somewhere else. It is the inescapable law set by the Light. If we want to, we are free to enjoy the experiment. Indeed this would make the Creator happy. Young Kon Tici, look at this face staring at you on the top of the sacred gate, and never forget what it is telling you: Be the inspiration for your adversaries. Be their guide. Show them strength and good will. Show them love and wisdom. Then, long before they become your enemies, they will wonder why you are totally free of arrogance."

In the cirque swept out by a glacial breeze, Viracocha talked to his son.

Kon awoke, looked once more at the stars, and wondered how long he had been asleep. He was cold, and it was time for him to go back to the refuge. As he walked along the stream, he thought someone followed him. He stopped and listened. He heard only the running and lapping water in the stream. As he started walking, he clearly heard the steps of someone behind him. He stopped, and turned around. He saw nothing, heard nothing. He was alone, with the silence of the night. The fear of being ambushed by one of the Inca's patrols invaded his mind. By now, these patrols were probably crossing the entire country searching for him and Illa. Then, he thought he should never have left Illa alone at the refuge. Kon walked to the large boulder Illa had pushed earlier, went behind it, and crawled on the dry grass, until he could see the stream where he heard someone. He stopped and listened. He heard a few steps in the water. A bear cub was drinking with gentle laps. Relieved, Kon was amused by his naiveté. He went back to the refuge, rolled himself inside his poncho, and went to sleep.

At dawn the sky resembled glowing red embers. The snow and the glacier were pink. Illa found a few dehydrated potatoes inside the refuge. He went to the stream to reconstitute them with water. With two partially frozen papayas, and three guavas, it was all they had to eat.

They slowly started their journey toward the divide. In front of them was a formidable barrier of boulders, glaciers, snowfields and crumbling rocks. Once more Kon had an ominous premonition, and carefully scrutinized the vicinity for the Inca's warriors. Their torn garments covered by mildewed ponchos, wearing shabby sandals, Illa and Kon accelerated their pace. They knew the mountain. All their life it had been their ultimate sanctuary. For them, climbing was innate and an enjoyable game. They circled the main glacier. They struggled through wind-carved pinnacles of snow covering the ground everywhere. At the last stream they stopped, and drank its clear water. It was the last time they could drink before they would reach the same elevation, on the other side of the divide. They raced against each other, as a way to boost their resolve. From mutual understanding, they became competitors for a short time, but the mountain waited for them, immense, silent, and unpredictable.

At a short distance from the divide, Kon stopped and waited for Illa, who was far behind him. The sun reached its zenith, and its rays burned Kon's face. It was cold, but tolerable. There was no wind.

"You are getting too old," Kon said with a triumphant smile.

"Remember what you said, one moon-cycle from now," Illa answered with defiance. "You never made a journey like this one before, nor have I."

Quite sensitive to human disturbance, a condor left a rocky cliff. Kon admired the bird gliding above the glacier. The bird turned around and sailed straight toward Kon, and passed just above him at full speed. Kon could see the white collar around the neck of the dark gray sacred bird. It had white markings under the wings. Then, the condor circled to a very high altitude. In flight, it was a majestic bird. Birds fascinated Viracocha's sons. They had a cult for birds because they had access to what they considered the last frontier: They could fly closer to the Sun.

The condor circled down into the cirque, below the glacier. The bird knew this was the place. On the steep slope, between two boulders, Kon took a large step and held a sharp pinnacle for support. Some gravel fell along a narrow crack, and instantly paralyzed him: From experience, he knew what was going to happen.

"Illa! Get down!" he screamed.

A rock, about as tall as Kon, dislodged, and bounced right above Illa. More were coming. Kon rotated his body against the mountain, just before a colossal piece of the mountain slid, slowly at first, then gained momentum, until the entire mountain seemed to be falling to his left. He closed his eyes, felt a large rock rolling on his left hand. His thumb instantly felt numb. He heard each huge block bouncing on the ground, shaking the entire mountain. Several avalanches of snow, ice and rocks started in other places.

Kon opened his eyes and searched for his brother, but saw only a cloud of dust. The falling masses crushed small glaciers, changing the entire terrain. They pulverized everything in their passage. It was an awesome display of the force of nature. Finally, the giant boulders reached the other side of the cirque, and lost momentum, until they came to a stop. Some gravel still rolled from place to place. Silence reigned again. Somewhere, a rodent whistled. There was no trace of Illa. Kon slowly walked down the mountain, afraid of what he might discover.

"Illa! Where are you?"

"I am all right. By all the spirits in the Sun, I never dreamed of seeing something like this. Are you all right?"

"I am fine," Kon answered, rubbing his badly bruised thumb. "I also have a deep cut below my knee. It is not bleeding, but it is painful. And you, any damage?"

"Not a scratch," Illa replied. "Now, I am convinced luck is on our side."

Still in shock, Kon was pale, shaking and covered with goose bumps. They both ran to the top of the divide, as if they wanted to escape a catastrophe already part of the past. At the top, the cold wind coming from the other side slammed into their faces. Their perspiration instantly turned into ice crystals.

"Let's walk down fast," Illa commanded.

Kon looked at the flying condor checking the cirque for carrion.

"A few days from now, this bird may need to diet," Illa joked. "Let's go!"

This side of the mountain, with a gentle slope, was much easier to negotiate. All along the descent, they commented on those few instants of terror they would never forget. By sunset, they reached the first stream, and the first bushes below the land of dry grass. Both were very thirsty. Kon squatted and washed the deep cut below his knee.

"I smell smoke," Illa said, crouching near Kon.

****

Kukara heard the condor, then a thundering rumble. She turned around and saw the giant boulder coming toward her. She instantly awoke and sat on the mat where she was sleeping.

"One of those dreams again," Kama murmured in her ear, caressing the child.

"Before the stone reached me, the condor gave me a warning," Kukara said.

"This is why we wear woven condors on our headband," Kama said. "It is our sacred bird for many reasons."

"Tell me about the legend of the condor," Kukara said.

"The Sun, seeing that men lived like wild animals, took pity on them and sent a son and a daughter to earth. Viracocha's children were escorted to the Titicaca Lake by two golden condors. Then, for several days, the two condors circled the sky always at the same place, until the Sun spoke to his children: 'On this plateau, you shall build the most prestigious city on earth, and it shall be named Tiahuanacu. Every man and woman who enters this city must pass through the Gate of the Sun, then you shall teach them to live by my wisdom…' Ever since, the two golden condors circled the sky above our city, just to make sure everything went well."

****

At some distance below, they saw smoke: Someone was here.

"Probably a trapper preparing for the night," Kon said.

"Or, one of the Inca's patrols," Illa replied.

Cautiously, they came closer. They saw several people, including women: This was not a patrol. Five llamas grazed around a large tent.

"We should not surprise them," Illa said. "Let's call them from here. Hello!... Hello!"

Agitation and confusion were apparent in the group around the fire. Three people ran inside the tent. The llamas looked at the two brothers with nonchalant circumspection, their ruminating obviously a much more serious business.

One old, thin man came forward. He did not walk like the people from the high plateaus.

"Who are you?" he asked from a distance, in a language Illa and Kon knew well.

He was a Nazca, from the low land nearer to the sea.

"We are friendly travelers," Illa said.

The man stopped, surprised at first. Illa had spoken the Tiahuanacu sacred language. A broad smile invaded the old man's deeply-lined, wind-chapped face: He knew these men with long black hair, and dark blue eyes. Everybody knew them for their skills, wisdom, gentleness and peaceful trading culture.

"My name is Manco," the man said. "I am a trapper, traveling with my family. What happened to you? You are in terrible shape."

"Yes, we are," Kon said. "But it is a long story."

"Come share our meal," Manco said. Then, he called the other people hiding inside the tent. A middle- aged woman and two timid children came forward. "This is my wife, Mirza, my daughter, Nina, and my son, Macco."

"I am Illa Tici Viracocha; this is my brother, Kon Tici."

The man and the two women bowed their heads. Nina pushed her brother's head down. They were in front of the highest Viracocha dignitaries. They knew it. With respect, they were humble indeed.

"It is a great honor for us," Manco said, holding his wool hat with both hands.

Kon thought his modesty rendered him beautiful. They all saw the gold plugs in the brothers' earlobes, and the golden condor glittering on their chest. There was no doubt as to Illa and Kon's identity. Embarrassed in front of such nobility, they did not know what to do next, or what to say.

"Do not feel embarrassed," Illa said. "Your hospitality is most welcome. At this moment, we need you more than you need us."

Warming themselves in front of the fire, Illa and Kon summarized their misfortune. The two women went to prepare additional food, and listened to their story with interest. At times, they were all shaking their head in dismay. To Illa and Kon they were already good friends: They were the good people.

Manco pointed to the cut under Kon's knee. "This is a bad one," he said, turning his head toward the women. "Nina, clean this cut carefully with boiled water, then protect it with a bandage."

The shy young woman, maybe in her fifteenth sun-cycle, came and crouched in front of Kon. She inspected his cut. Disturbed, she went to her mother, asking for guidance. As Nina boiled some water in a clay cup, Kon looked at her face. She was not a beauty, but she was attractive. She had full, sensual lips. Many thin, tight braids of blue-black hair framed her plain face. Her nose was well shaped. She had thick eyebrows, and frowning was natural for her because of the brightness of the sky and the cold wind. The skin of her cheeks was already slightly chapped by the aggressive, continuous wind. Her eyes met Kon's eyes. They shared a gentle smile. She brought the cup of boiled water, and some bandages. She crouched in front of him. As she cleaned the cut, Kon closed his eyes, happy that someone else was looking after him. Her touch was delicate and cautious: She was obviously pleased to help him. She did not say a word. When she implanted four stitches with a bone needle and a thread, she was amazed that Kon did not show any sign of pain.

Manco listened to Illa's sad story. At times Manco's melancholy turned to anger, because there was not much he could do.

"Now, where are you going?" the old man asked, his eyes lost in the red embers of the fire.

"Far north, but I cannot tell you where, for your safety and ours," Illa replied.

Manco nodded with approval: "Are you going farther than the city of Chan-Chan? This is where we go next to sell my furs."

"Yes, we are going much farther than Chan-Chan," Illa replied.

"Then, let's travel together. I know the way very well. I also know that some Inca's patrols have been going north."

"What else do you know about the Inca?" Illa asked.

"I heard that the Inca's oldest son is taking control of everything. The old Inca does not have the necessary energy to command."

"Yes, I think we know that," Illa said with a sarcastic smile. "If we meet a patrol, you must swear that you don't know us. We came asking for food."

"Don't worry," Manco said, laying one hand on Illa's knee. "I know the way much better than they do, and I have reliable friends along our journey. It gives me pleasure to help you."

"Thank you," Illa said, looking at the sincere and reassuring face of a friend.

"Now, eat this food," Manco said, smiling to his wife with

devotion, and showing his decayed teeth. "Mirza is a good cook."

Nina was fascinated by Kon's long, black, straight hair, fastened above his head with a gold pin. His hair fell gracefully around his strong shoulders. She thought his short beard looked better than Illa's long one. His thin lips and dark blue eyes were new and mysterious to her. In her simplistic mind, Kon was like a fabulous living god. The light glittering from the golden condor on his chest added to her dream. She was not afraid of him. She even felt secure, and wanted to stay close to him. She felt attracted by a force she could not describe. It was not because she was a woman, and he a man. It was something else, his kindness.

When they finished their meal, the two brothers went inside the tent and immediately went to sleep. Nina covered them with warm llama furs. She looked at them as her living treasures of the moment.

Manco wrapped himself under the furs, and pulled his wool hat around his ears: Outside, the cold wind swept the dry land. Thinking about his forefathers, Manco could not sleep. He remembered the words of his great grandfather:

"Viracocha's children let us draw giant birds and animals on the surface of the desert plains, invisible to any traveler. They were signs for the Sun, so he could know the golden condors were at work, and everything was going well."

Manco did not understand these words, but he knew Illa and Kon wore golden condors, therefore they must have been in contact with the Light.

When Illa and Kon awoke, just before sunrise, Manco's family was packing all their goods. Already, three llamas were heavily loaded, looking at their masters with scornful tolerance. Mirza brought some food to Illa and Kon.

"Tonight, we will stop early," Mirza said, as if it was a

command. "Nina and I will repair your garments and sandals. Then, after you take a bath in the stream, it will be easier for you to travel."

Illa glanced at his brother, who looked away and giggled. Manco saw him and chuckled.

"If you want peace, you better listen to what she says," Manco joked. Everybody laughed with good humor.

It took them five days to cross the deep valley of the thundering Apurimac River. It took strong will and great courage to raft its waters. Then, they climbed the steep slopes of the last divide before the ocean. Near the summit, they stopped near a lake in the middle of the dry grassland. At some distance, they could see a glacier.

"It is always cloudy around here," Manco said. "Surprisingly, today the sky is clear, which means the night will be cold."

Long before dawn, Kon awoke and went outside for meditation: It was a clear night with light from the stars everywhere. He walked far away from the camp, to the glacier. He found a suitable boulder, and sat on top of it. His mind was consumed by the infinite display of light.

"Viracocha told us they were all Suns," he murmured, trembling with admiration.

"You created me, take me, talk to me; I am your humble servant."

Once more, he felt a presence in the emptiness of the high mountains. This time he knew someone real was behind him, looking at him. He turned around and saw Nina's outline in the dark. With a friendly sign he invited her to join him. Without disturbing the silence of the night, she sat by his side. As he put one hand around her waist, she laid her head on his lap. He was looking at the stars, and so was she. He laid his other hand on her head. She felt his long fingers caressing her hair, and took pleasure in it. She perceived a continuous flow of energy entering her body through his fingers. She felt the power of tranquillity. She felt possessed, but was happy about it. She slowly went into a trance, and saw light everywhere. With Kon Tici, she traveled where time and reality are meaningless concepts.

At dawn, when she awoke, two dark blue eyes were looking at her. Two large black eyes were looking at him, but Kon was still in a dream: The woman he was looking at was not Nina, but a magnificent priestess from another world.

"I am Hina of the Valley, and I was chosen by Kama Tici Viracocha to help you, serve you, and love you." Then the woman vanished, and he awoke. He smiled to Nina. She did not say one word; she was thankful. She turned over, looked at his knee, and removed the four stitches.

Ten days later, they reached the sea where birds of all kinds gathered. The travelers endured the barren dunes, the rainless days, and the endless cloudy sky until they reached the city of Chan-Chan one moon- cycle later. It was the last time they saw their Nazca friends. Kon and Illa had little time left. With determination and discipline, they walked northward, until the coast turned toward the setting sun, until they reached mangrove swamps and a broad river.

They saw several rafts crossing the estuary in both directions. On both sides were several villages near the banks. They could see only the vegetal roofs among luxuriant vegetation.

They talked to several people, but could not communicate. Their language was unknown to them. Amazingly, nobody seemed surprised by the unusual aspect of the two brothers, which Kon found suspicious: Perhaps they were accustomed to seeing similar faces. They were friendly, with a touch of indifference.

They saw a raft paddled by six naked men. At the bank, they unloaded their cargo. Three colorfully dressed men came to meet the paddlers. Illa went to them, and in sign language tried to explain he was looking for people like him. One man seemed to understand him, and went to the naked men on the raft. They exchanged a few words. With no further discussion, one paddler invited Kon and Illa to come on board. Then he pushed the raft away from the bank. They went slowly, upstream. For the first time in many moon-cycles, Illa and Kon felt hope.

As they glanced at each other, a premonition brought a smile to their faces.

Halfway across the river, they saw they were heading for a village. At some distance from the village, there was a fleet of huge rafts aligned on the beach. This time, at last, they knew they had found their brothers and sisters. In joy, they hugged each other. The six naked men remained emotionless.

On the beach, as every day, the young girl waited. She had long, shining black hair. She had large, candid, slightly slanted eyes: They were marine-blue, ringed with long black lashes. She had fair, smooth, very clean skin. She wore an elegant white robe, with a large belt around the waist. The lowest part of the robe was embroidered with coral-red Suns. She wore sandals, and a white headband. There was no doubt: She was a Viracocha's child.

She stared at the coming raft for a moment, and suddenly ran away behind a wall of vegetation. At some distance, between trees were many huts, roofed with woven palm-tree fronds. Instants later, she came back with the entire Viracocha's clan. A tall, old man, with white hair and white beard, dressed like the young girl, led the way. He held her hand. He was Illa and Kon's grandfather. He was the great Taranga Tici Viracocha.

Both brothers ran to him. Trembling and his eyes wet with

emotion, Taranga hugged his grandsons. Before they could say one word, Taranga put his fingers to their lips.

"Don't tell me," Taranga said. "In my dreams, I saw everything. My heart hurts, but today it will be tolerable."

A tall woman of remarkable beauty, made her way across the crowd. Illa saw her, ran to her, and took her in his arms. "Kama, my wife! I missed you so much. I love you so much," he murmured with passion. She could not say a word. She looked at him, sobbed and put her lips on his. They closed their eyes, and for a moment in this life, there was justice.

Behind them, three children were politely waiting for their turn. Ku, Illa's first son, was six sun-cycles old. Kane, his second son, was five. Kura, his daughter, was three.

"They grew up so much," Illa said, taking two of them in his arms. "And you Kama, you are more magnificent than ever."

"I took care of myself, and Kukara knew you were coming."

Taranga was still holding Kukara by the hand.

"Where is my brother?" she asked Kon, pulling on his garment.

Kon glanced at his grandfather with distress. Then he took her in his arms, hugging her head against his shoulder.

"He is gone for a long journey, with the Light," Kon said, his voice in dismay.

"Will I see him again?"

"Yes, you will," Kon replied. "When you will be very old. From now on, I am your brother. Your brother was my best friend."

She kissed his cheek, and sobbed inside his hair. She understood perfectly the subtlety of his words.

"Could you also be my father?" she asked, her heart in agony.

Kon closed his wet eyes, wondering where justice was.

"Yes, I will, if you tell me your full name. I know you are Kukara."

For the first time, she showed a weak smile.

"From today forward, my name is Kukara Tici Viracocha."

Kon was devastated by Kukara's need for love. Never before had he felt his heart so totally broken. Kama came to welcome him, and kissed him.

"Now you must find a mother for her," she said, winking at Kukara.

"How old are you?" Kon asked.

"She is six," Taranga replied for her. "She is a brilliant child. Every morning she went to the beach, since she had a bad dream about her brother. She did not find him, but she found you. You committed yourself to her at an important time in her life. You know such noble commitment shall never be broken, under any circumstance."

Compelled by the warm strength of Kon's arm, the child looked at the river with melancholy: There was no other raft; the river was empty. She knew she had to look ahead and survive. She was a survivor, and now she had an anchor. With him, she would triumph against the odds.

"When we left Chan-Chan, the Inca's patrols were looking for us everywhere," Kon said.

"This is what I was afraid of;" Taranga replied. "All the rafts are ready. We must leave within three days. Come, I want to show you the rafts."

"These rafts are huge," Kon said. "How many are there?"

Taranga opened his hands five times.

Each raft was made of giant balsa beams, attached side by side. On the top of them, was a deck made of smaller balsa beams, and huge sections of bamboo filled with drinking water. A long cabin built of cane, covered by a roof of woven coconut-tree fronds, would provide living quarters. All around the raft, stakes and ropes provided a double railing for safety. A bipod mast, with a boom hanging near their top, would support a sail that would push them toward the sunset. For now, the sail was rolled around the boom. Vertical boards between the balsa beams were rudders, with which they would control the direction they would travel, to some extent: Sailing against the wind was impossible. The following day, when the tide was high, they pulled all the rafts into the river. Then, for two days, men, women and children loaded their cargo. The last evening before their departure to the unknown, Taranga gave his last recommendations.

"Illa, Kon, Rangi, Hiti, ..." Taranga called. "As you already know, each of you is in charge of one raft. We shall go straight toward the sunset. Many of us will get separated. I have no idea how long our journey will be. I only know that the longer it will be, the more likely we may lose contact with one another. These rafts are made to sustain the sea no longer than three moon-cycles. One day, we will reunite, maybe!"

At dawn, the fifty rafts left the estuary. For people onshore, it was an imposing, once-in-a-lifetime vision. The rafts had to cross the strong current coming from the south. Taranga had told them not to drift northward, under any circumstance. All men and women paddled for two days and two nights before the

current slowly turned toward the sunset. At this stage, many rafts were already unaccounted for, but from now on, the memory of the Inca would fade away. Facing a new destiny, they sang in praise of liberty. In front of them, the ocean was waiting, beautiful, unpredictable, and awesome.

****

Far away, in the ancient city of Tiahuanacu, the old Inca awoke. He had experienced a dream, and looked at Viracocha's face on the Gate of the Sun.

"Yes, I know! You are judging us," he said to himself. "Your sons left the continent. This is the biggest mistake the political and military leaders of this land ever made. You are an incredible loss for mankind."

He laughed without joy.

"Leaders hated you, because you were so powerful. The people loved you, because you were so kind. Ironic, isn't it?"

It was the dawn of the colossal military empire of the Incas.

****

CHAPTER 2

"A long time ago, a falling star devastated our land. Beyond the sea, there is a new land on which my heirs shall study the Light coming from the stars."

Illa Tici Viracocha

At dawn of the third day at sea, far in the east, the fading dark outline of the continent was still visible under the red-amber sky. The sea current was strong and westward.

Kon dropped a few wood chips into the sea, and watched them disappear behind the raft: They were on an irreversible course, pushed by the current and wind. He observed the men and women around him. They knew the mountains, but they did not know the ocean. They were terrified by the sea swells, but for everything he would do or say, they would watch or listen. On board were: Kon, Kukara, three young couples, four children, one elderly couple and two single men named Ra and Ilo, who had a bizarre destiny awaiting them.

Kon climbed to the top of the mast, and sat above the boom holding the sail. The increasing distance between the rafts concerned him, but he was in the middle of the fleet, right on course. Five rafts were trailing him. Taranga's group was farther to the north. Illa's group, the largest, was on the south side. They could identify each raft from colorful drawings woven on the sail.

Kon's sail was white, embroidered with a coral-red sun: He was the Son of the Sun. Illa's sail was also white, with red flames: He was the Son of Fire. Taranga's sail was golden, with a white star: He was in touch with the Light.

Being in the middle group, Kon decided not to worry about his course. He went down on the deck where Kukara was waiting for him. They sat cross-legged side by side and ate a few fresh fruits: a luxury they might not have for a long time. Kon renewed a recommendation that became an obsession to him.

"Kukara, make sure you always stay away from the edge of the raft. Anyone falling in the water would be lost. The raft cannot stop or turn around."

"I know," she said shrugging her shoulders, "I can take care of myself. It is boring around here. Can you tell a story?"

"What kind of story?"

She looked at the huge sea swells, then looked at him with her magnificent dark blue eyes. Kon thought she was beautiful, and remarkably mature for her age.

"Several times I listened to the story of our origins," she said. "I like it, but I don't understand it."

"You are right, there are parts that are difficult to comprehend. But, we only know the facts," Kon replied.

The four other children came near Kon.

"Can we listen, too?" a little boy asked, politely.

"Yes, you can," Kon said, "sit around us."

In the background, a few adults were also listening.

"Many generations ago, we were a seafaring people, and builders of monuments made of giant stones. We came from the north where the land is cold. Where the deadly eastern jungle grows now, we found a wonderland where happiness was taken for granted.

One night, the thing came, a thing nobody knew could exist. A huge ball of fire appeared in the western sky. It was so bright that nobody could look at it. It crossed the entire sky, going east at an incredible speed, emitting a sputtering wheeze. For a moment, the darkness of the night became the light of the day. It disappeared behind the horizon, leaving a long pink tail across the sky. Then, the night came back. A moment later, a mysterious sound came from the earth, like a plaintive melody from another world, a thing nobody had heard before. A tremendous earthquake followed. Some temples fell and people ran in all directions. They all knew what an earthquake was; they also knew this time it was something different: They all immediately connected the thing they had seen to the quake. Terrified, they waited for what would follow. It did not come right away. It was dawn when they heard a rumble in the east. Under the dawn light, unusually red, the awesome thing was coming, crawling with force beyond imagination. It became so big and so high that everyone was paralyzed. They all knew it was the end of time. They hugged one another, accepting the horrible reality: The entire ocean was coming above the land.

Along the sea, everywhere in the world we knew, there were no survivors. But, several tiny colonies isolated in the mountains managed to survive. The water came all the way up to the site where we built Tiahuanacu, which at that time was not our homeland. These ancestors were traveling, exploring or trading far away from home to which they never returned. They saw new volcanoes forming everywhere. They sustained earthquakes they had never dreamed of. Many died under crumbling stones, landslides, pouring lava, boiling water streams and food poisoning.

For more than two moon-cycles, there was no daylight. The

sky was dark with terrifying clouds, half water, and half ashes. Then, the thing was still here, invisible but omnipresent, striking anyone at random. You knew it was around when your hair would become attracted toward the sky. Then, a dark purple lightning would crawl everywhere around you and annihilate everything it touched, like a deliberate hunt.

It rained continuously for many more days, and more people died of starvation. Slowly, the rain stopped, the water regressed to its original level, and the thing vanished. The few survivors regrouped themselves after many years of frustrating search. Our ancestors were so affected by this cataclysm that they took it as the starting date of time. Ever since, our people lived in the high mountains around Tiahuanacu. Many times, daring explorers went to the east to find out what was left from our forefathers: They never found a trace. Above the ancient wonderland, a deadly jungle grew."

Frustrated, Kukara looked at the sea swells.

"I still don't understand. Does that mean water is more dangerous than fire?"

"Perhaps it is," Kon replied.

"Could it happen again?" she asked, looking at him.

"It can. But we don't know when, where or how. There is nothing we can do about it."

"If so, what are we doing on the sea, now?"

Kon smiled. Her logic was good. Taranga had been right, she was a brilliant child.

"We are taking a chance, for the best or for the worst," he said with eagerness, looking toward the west. The next morning, Kon climbed to the top of the mast. Taranga's group was far ahead, in the northwest, and he could barely see the sails above the horizon. The weather was clear, and five rafts were always trailing him, among whose passengers he recognized Rangi and Hiti. Then he looked toward the south. There was nothing: Illa's group had vanished. He stood up above the boom to see farther: His brother was gone.

Kon faced a dilemma. If he shifted to the northwest to get closer to Taranga, he would lose his brother. If he shifted to the southwest to get closer to Illa, he would lose his grandfather. He had a perfect course, and he thought they might try coming back to a westward course. Therefore, he decided to do nothing for now.

Increasingly concerned for his brother, in the afternoon he slightly changed his course toward the southwest. When the other rafts behind him tried to do the same thing, he became puzzled by their erratic behavior. It seemed to him that everybody was still going westward, but sideways. He was not sure. He carefully observed the crystal-clear water. He slowly set a wood chip on the sea. Surprisingly, the chip was moving almost at the same speed as the raft. Furthermore, the raft was following the same course as the chip: Both were going westward, but sideways. Then he knew the current was strong, and the wind in the sail did not make any difference. Again, he observed the water, and saw tiny plankton particles following a laminar flow westward, which was further proof that the current ruled their destiny.

Kon closed his eyes, and speculated about the behavior of this current on a large scale. It was not long before a frightening thought crossed his mind. He stood up, and went to the front end of the raft.

"What if?" he asked himself. "What if the current starts diverging in all directions? The rafts are heavy and massive. The current gives them much more momentum than the sail. I am in the middle. Then I go straight westward. Taranga is on the north side. Then he goes toward the northwest. Illa is on the south side. Then he goes toward the southwest, and there is nothing anyone of us can do about it. If this is the case, after one moon-cycle, we could be tremendous distances apart from one another."

Furious, he slammed one hand against the cabin. They all looked at him. Silent, they waited for an answer. It was rare that a Viracocha's son would lose his temper, so he owed them an explanation. With patience and precision, he described his findings, and with dismay they agreed with his conclusion.

"We were told to go straight westward, so westward we must go," he ordered. "Don't try changing our course. Tonight, I should study the position of the stars."

Frustrated, Kon climbed the mast, and sat on the boom of the sail to meditate.

"How far could the land be? The longer this trip, the farther apart we will be. How large is this ocean, and how far does it go?"

Because never had anyone come from the west, deep inside, he had the premonition this ocean must be awesome. He spent the next night memorizing the exact rising and setting positions of the stars, and their path across the sky: He wanted to establish a reference point. He knew many of the stars by name and noticed that their position had not changed since they left the continent: So, he knew he was heading straight west. He also noticed the stars were much farther to the north when he was at the City of the Sun: This was a good reference for which he was content.

The next morning, as usual, he inspected the clear horizon. Illa and Taranga had apparently vanished for good, and only two rafts were trailing him. He felt powerless against this new, mysterious force of nature, the force of attrition. As a result, his anger grew, and he could not help talking alone.

"By all the spirits in the Sun, I will find you, my brother, even if I have to swim to you with this raft attached to my feet, I will find you."

"Are you mad again?" Kukara asked, looking up at him.

Amused, he smiled, went down and took her in his arms.

"No, I am not mad. I am trying to understand our destiny."

"I brought you some warm potatoes," she said, pointing to a wooden plate. She ate with him, and he was happy for her peace of mind.

"They are all scared," she said, "but they won't tell you."

Later at night, the breeze was cooler than usual. The crew sat inside the cabin, listening to old legends and laughing at a few jokes. In a corner of the room, lying on his side, Kon listened and observed the group. In a gold cup an elderly woman burned small spongy wooden balls impregnated with vegetable oil and resin. Before each ball died out, she would light a new one. The smell was agreeable and reminded them of the cold evenings on the high plateaus. It provided sufficient light to see. Taking their tour of duty, two men were outside, on the lookout for the unpredictable.

Kon's thoughts were lost among shadows of people dancing against the walls and the ceiling, like silent phantoms. His eyes looked at one upper corner of the room, where a tiny spider rested in its web.

We have one passenger I was not aware of. He thought, your web is your only territory. You have no idea about the other world outside. Probably, it is better that way. This immense ocean is of no concern to you.

He remembered his meditation in the high mountains, and the mysterious force entering his mind.

We are not alone, he thought. Someone beyond our

imagination is watching, the same way I am watching the small spider. Perhaps, this is just the beginning of a deliberate adventure. Perhaps, someone wanted it to be that way.

The thought gave him courage. He curled up near the wall, closed his eyes, and listened to the lapping of waves under the deck. His mind wandered far away until he went to sleep. The lapping of waves against the shell of the outrigger was the only sound he could hear. Ahead, he could see the golden reflection of the full moon only, on the quiet sea. Behind him, someone in the outrigger was paddling. Slowly, Kon turned around and saw the magnificent woman with long black hair and black eyes he had seen before in a vision when he was with Nina.

"My name is Hina of the Valley. Do not be afraid; I protect daring travelers lost at sea. My home is the moon, and my best friend is this green pigeon." The pigeon on her shoulder cooed.

Kon looked around, wondering where he was. They were alone, on the awesome sea. The woman wore bark cloth around her hips only. Around her neck, she wore the same golden necklace he had around his neck. On it, he recognized the sacred condor. He tried to talk to her, but could not. He tried to come closer to her, but she stopped him.

"Do not touch me," she said, as if she was afraid of something. As she was paddling, he clearly saw tiny purple sparks at the tip of her fingers, which clearly told him she was not human. Yet, she was so beautiful, so gentle, and so attractive that he could not resist coming closer to her. With his finger, he pointed at a small scar on her wrist.

"This is the mark of the great blue shark," she said. "It is a reminder that at another time, in another place, I mixed my blood with Taaroa's blood."

Who was she, and who was Taaroa? Once more, he tried

to touch her. This time, she stood up, and vanished into an ephemeral vortex of wind.

When Kon awoke, it was already daylight. He sat, and reflected on his dream for a moment, and thought it had been incredibly clear. From past experience, he knew it was not a dream. It was a vision with a message, and he would have to wait to understand it. He went outside, where children were running around the deck in a most unusual excitement. Flying fish were landing on the raft from all directions. It was a most unexpected food bonanza, and wonderful entertainment.

One moon-cycle went by. The sea was always empty. There were no birds. There was no rain, and the current became slower. Now, the wind in the sail was the main force pushing the raft westward. Kon took the opportunity to change their course toward the southwest.

They became accustomed that the raft was their only universe. At the beginning of the journey, they had a tendency to leave things unkempt, but now everything was exactly where it belonged. With care and gentleness, everyone tried to make all the others as comfortable as possible, but the amount of drinking water was diminishing fast.

What if we stay another two moon-cycles at sea? Kon thought. It is time to take action.

Reducing the daily allowance of water for each person was an answer, but Kon did not like it. It was not enough, and he searched for another solution. Several times he drank a cup of seawater. The taste was horrible, but it did not make him sick.

"Why are you drinking seawater?" Kukara asked.

"May I ask you to try something with me?" he asked, ignoring her question.

"Yes, what do you want me to do?"

"During the next ten days, you and I will mix one part of seawater for every two parts of fresh water we drink. If the idea works, it may save our lives."

"Do you think we don't have enough water?" she asked.

"If it does not rain, I am afraid so."

Kukara accepted the challenge with joy. Thereafter, he explained his project to everyone. When Kukara drank her first cup of the mixture, she looked at Kon with a grimace on her face, rolling her eyes upward. The other children roared with laughter.

"This is terrible," she protested. "Are you sure I have to do this?"

"I need to know if this idea is all right for the other children."

"All right! It was not that bad." She smiled, proud that he had selected her for the experiment.

To everyone's surprise, after ten days, the two healthier persons on board were Kon and Kukara. They never showed any sign of dehydration, and were much less thirsty than the others. Everyone started drinking mixed waters. The good news was transmitted to the two other rafts on the first occasion they got close enough.

Forty-five days went by. They caught more fish than they could eat, and found out that plankton was good for them. Many times, they watched sharks circling the raft, feeling fear at first, then curiosity, and at last, amusement, but their favorite show was the dolphins. Sometimes, the skillful animals would stay around the raft for two days. They also noticed that there were no sharks when the dolphins were around.

The sea became increasingly warmer, and the travelers developed a new game. When the dolphins were around, everyone was allowed to dive into the sea under two conditions: Only one person at a time was allowed to swim, and he or she had to be attached to the raft with a rope around the waist. It was healthful, and it relaxed their bodies and minds. It helped to keep their morale up.

Kon found that the stars rose and set at the same place as at the City of the Sun. Therefore, he decided that he had gone southwestward for long enough. It was time to go westward again. The next few days brought sudden changes. The sea was of a different color, darker. The swells were larger, taller and often covered with white caps. The wind was stronger. The sky became cloudy and rainy at last. The precious rain was collected on the top of huge, tightly woven square covers. One person would hold and pull at each corner. A hole in the center of the cover drained the water to a wooden tank. When the tank was full, the water was transferred into the bamboo containers underneath the deck. The amount of drinking water was of no more concern.

They all took off their clothes and washed their skin burned by the sun, the wind, and the salt. Their arms raised toward the sky, they found how good and sweet the warm rain could be. Feeling clean and free of salt was a new definition of luxury. In the evening the rain stopped, and in the west the sky was clear with no clouds. Right after sunset, everyone scrutinized the western horizon, looking for a dream, looking for an unmistakable dark outline, but day after day, the horizon remained empty, and their dreams were unfulfilled. Nevertheless, they had that feeling that every day they were one step closer, and closer, to a new land.

One night, the wind blew fiercely, and they were forced to roll part of the sail around the boom. The sea swells became larger than they had seen before. Once more, they were frightened, but Kon remembered his grandfather's words: "The raft can handle any kind of waves. It is a wood chip on the ocean, which simply goes up and down. You may get seasick, but do not fear the swells. However, beware of the land. The waves can slam the raft on the coast and kill you all."

Kon had another source of concern, something he had observed day after day. It was something everyone had observed, but no one had talked about. The raft was sinking slowly, but surely. Huge quantities of seawater had permeated the heart of the balsa beams: They had had their time at sea. It was becoming urgent to find land, any land. By measuring, day after day, how much balsa was remaining above the surface, Kon knew the raft would never float for another moon-cycle. The two other rafts did not look better. Something had to happen soon.

It came suddenly, and unexpectedly. One morning, Kon climbed the mast, and sat on the boom as usual. In the west, the horizon was clear, and there was no land in sight. Rangi's and Hiti's rafts were trailing him as usual.

Kon felt swift air turbulence above his head. At incredible speed, a large bird he had never seen before passed just above the mast. The bird had an impressive wingspread, and was a powerful glider capable of keeping its wings perfectly still all the time. Using ascending air currents, the bird soared very high with no effort. It turned sideways looking like a giant sword, then dived directly toward the sea and disappeared behind the large ocean swells. The next instant, it emerged at full speed just above the tip of a wave behind the raft. Everybody was startled by the unique acrobatic display. The body of the bird was about the same size as a condor, but the wing span was far more impressive. The wings were grayish and brown on the top, with black tips. The bird had a powerful, long yellow beak: There was no doubt it was a fish hunter, and it looked and acted as the monarch of the ocean's birds. So, there was land somewhere, but Kon had no illusion. He knew birds very well. By observing this bird at flight, it was obvious it could travel considerable distances in a short time. The land could still be many days away. Nevertheless, it was the most entertaining show they had seen for a long time. The bird remained in the vicinity of the raft for most of the day, then disappeared toward the west before sunset. Once more, everyone peered intently for the first outline of land, but they remained baffled by a confusing and puzzling destiny: There was no land in the west.

When the horizon became too dark, they went inside the cabin as usual. They were mute, hoping the next day would bring good news. That night, Kon and Ilo stayed on the deck, looking for the unpredictable. Somewhere on the south side, Kon thought he heard something, and placed a finger on Ilo's lips.

"Maybe it was the wind, or the tip of a wave," Kon murmured.

The night was so dark that they could barely see the other end of the raft.

"Listen!" Ilo said. "I also heard something."

Both men stood up, went to the front end of the raft and placed their hands behind their ears, listening toward the west: They distinctly heard some distant rumble. Kon went immediately inside the cabin.

"All men and women out, with paddles, and paddle backward. Ilo and Ra, roll the sail up around the boom, now!"

The rumble was more intense, slightly on the south side. Kon drove the rudders into the water. From the changing position of the stars, he knew the raft was turning north, but the rumble became stronger, frightening, everywhere: It was too late.

Between two swells, the raft went down, and Kon saw the reef on the south side of the raft. Another swell rose up, huge, and broke on the reef with thundering force, then the raft seemed to recede from the reef.

"Paddle, paddle strong!" Kon ordered.

The next swell came, the raft went down and this time they all saw the reef, which loomed like the deadly jaw of a giant. The raft slammed against the barrier of corals. On one side, two large balsa logs separated. The mast broke, and the boom with the sail around it fell on the cabin. The next serie of swells was small, and they could see the white foam on the reef nearby.

"Paddle north, faster!" Kon said, looking at the pass. "This is our only chance."

The raft slowly entered the strong current coming from the pass. When the next swells came, they were back at sea. Slowly, the rumble vanished in the south. Shocked by the violent encounter, they kept paddling, and tried to repair the deck and the mast. The tremendous crash had done considerable damage to the raft, and Kon considered if it was worth trying to save it. At dawn, after the repair they had done all night, he choose to save the raft.

Rangi and Hiti were at some distance on the northeast side, and they saw that Kon's raft was in trouble. Slowly, they came closer, until they could talk to one another.

"Anybody hurt?" Rangi asked.

"No, but we were lucky to be near the pass," Kon replied.

"We found land," Kukara joked.

"I know," Kon said with a grin on his face, "and I am not inclined to smile about it."

"What kind of land was that?" Rangi asked.

"There was no land," Kon answered. "It was only a crown of reef, barely above the sea level."

The three rafts stayed together until Kon's crew completed all the necessary repairs. Then, Kon decided to remain on the raft with only Ilo and Ra. All the others would be taken on by Rangi and Hiti.

"Kon, I don't want to leave," Kukara said with distress.

"You have to," Kon replied, "we will be together again, soon."

Reluctantly, she jumped on Rangi's raft. Then, the two other rafts left, half of the sail rolled up to keep the same speed as the crippled raft. Afraid of the reliability of the mast, Kon used only half of his sail. They were sailing westward again.

Kukara kept her eyes on Kon's raft for as long as she could. Once more in her life, she was anguished. However, she had also developed a sense of premonition. Something was telling her that she would not see Kon for some time. She even wondered if she would ever see him again. He had been good to her, and he was her only family. She loved Taranga, but he was gone long ago. She also loved Kama, but she had vanished with Illa toward the south.

Kukara's long hair flowed in the breeze. Her large, dark blue eyes were sad, but not afraid. She was no longer afraid of anything. She had courage and will, and she was very young. She had a lot to learn, and she would with remarkable skills. She was a Viracocha's daughter, and she was proud of it.

"I will find you again, Kon Tici Viracocha," she murmured. " Have a safe journey, my beloved father."

In her sorrow, as she glanced at the sea swells and the coming dark clouds, she managed a mocking smile, as if she wanted to challenge the force of the awesome sea.

Kon could see Kukara standing on the deck of Rangi's raft, her long hair flowing in the wind. Her white robe contrasted with the dark background of the coming storm. He knew she was looking at him. He knew she was talking to him. He felt pain in his chest, being perfectly aware that they would become separated, perhaps for a long time, even forever.

"I will, ... I will find you again," she sobbed.

In the afternoon, the wind became so strong that they rolled the sails. The sea swells became enormous and covered with large whitecaps. It started raining, and within no time it was pouring, reducing the visibility to practically nothing. Inside the storm, the three rafts became isolated, wandering at random with the swirling wind. Before nightfall, the sea became a fury, forcing Kon, Ilo and Ra to attach themselves to the crippled raft with ropes. Kon's only fear was to smash into another reef: At that time, it would signify certain death.

All night, the three men stayed attached to the raft, while they were looking at the sea with despair, and waiting for the reef.

"I think you made a mistake," Ilo said, staring at Kon.

Kon looked at him, but ignored the comment. His silence said more than any words. Kon knew he had made a mistake. They should have left with the two other rafts. There was no sense trying to save this one. It was only one step further in the attrition process that plagued them. Now, it was only the three of them. Kon was perfectly aware that at dawn the two other rafts would have vanished.

The storm calmed down just after daylight, but the waves were still enormous. There were still low, dark clouds, but the visibility was good. The sea was black and empty. There was no land in sight, and no other rafts. In spite of the waves, Kon climbed to the top of the repaired mast on which he had a difficult time to keep his balance. After a quick inspection of the horizon, he saw no trace of anyone: As he had expected, the other rafts had vanished, but something was new, something he could not believe, something he had feared for some time.

The entire southwest and western horizon was a solid, white

line of foam. From place to place, the foam climbed very high in the air, giving a clear picture of the thundering power with which the sea slammed the reef. They had to change their course toward the north, fast. They tried, but it became increasingly clear that they would not go north far enough.

Now, they could see many coconut trees above the foam. There was land, but it was a very low land. They heard the rumble. The rumble became loud as thunder. The three men could not paddle anywhere. They were on an inescapable course toward the reef. They had been at sea for ninety-seven days. This day they reached their goal, finally reached land, but they also had a rendezvous with death.

"Hina of the Valley," Kon murmured, "if you are indeed protecting lost navigators, help us now."

****

CHAPTER 3

"We found a land. It was a paradise of remarkable beauty, for fish, shells, and birds. Yet, for good reasons, it was a no-man's-land."

Kon Tici Viracocha

Kon looked for a pass through the barrier of coral: There was none. The three men knew they had to concentrate on what would happen when the raft would be crushed against the reef. As long as they were alive, they would hope for any opportunity.

Several waves blasted the barrier. Each time, the raft got closer. A series of six small waves came, during which the raft drifted above the barrier. Then, the seventh wave came, huge and awful. The sea receded from the barrier, opening the mouth of a monster, in which the raft was swallowed. They saw the reef descending into the abysses. Then, the formidable mass of water rose, pushing, lifting and tilting the raft. Ra fell into the sea. Ilo held the broken mast. Kon grabbed onto the cabin, his hands passing all the way through the rigid bamboo canes.

The bow of the raft got caught inside a broad rift. Kon thought the raft would turn upside down, and he was ready to jump into the sea, but when the raft emerged from the rift, he changed his mind. Instantly, the raft came back to the horizontal position. With incredible force, they were propelled above the corals. The water slowed down, stopped, then with the same force receded toward the barrier, but the next swell was already coming, almost as powerful. Kon smiled; he knew the raft would not return to the barrier. The thundering mass of the white foam lifted the raft like an insignificant wooden chip. The raft tumbled sideways making it impossible to remain on it any longer. Ilo jumped into the roaring foam, but Kon waited until he was sure he would not get trapped between the raft and the reef. He jumped into the water that was already slowing down, and quickly swam away from the raft. Just before the water started receding, he dived and tried to grab on to anything. To his surprise, he found a soft, rubbery coral, and clutched its foot with his arms. At first, he could easily resist the receding water, but the momentum of the water was powerful: He used Mana and concentrated all his energy in his arms. He thought the giant polyp would tear apart, but it did not. The next wave came, and he let himself go with the forceful foam. As soon as the water slowed down, he searched for another anchor. He found a round, brain-like yellow coral and grabbed it as hard as he could. This time, he could resist the receding water much better, but he realized the surface of the coral was made of many tiny blades lacerating his hands and arms. He did not care. Every step toward the beach was a step forward to safety and survival. As soon as the next wave came, he started swimming as fast as he could. Suddenly, there was not enough water to swim. He started running, but under the foam he felt something plow into his legs, then he immediately collapsed through crumbling coral. The next wave pushed him inside a field of branch-like corals, in which he remained trapped like a fly in a spider web. It was impossible to swim or walk. He would have to wait until a larger wave reached him. The foam was coming, fast and thick. He felt his body transported. Hard coral branches scratched his legs and his back. As soon as the water receded, he grabbed some branches but they instantly broke. He grabbed more of them, and finally succeeded to come to a stop. He felt sharp pain along his legs speared by multitudes of bristling sea urchin spines. The next wave sent him to a sandy area, a short distance from the beach. He recovered enough energy to stand up and walk. Several times he fell, because of the waves or because of the crumbling substratum under the sand. When he reached the beach, he wandered like a sleepwalker covered with running blood. Vaguely, he felt his feet push some vegetation. His instinct commanded him to collapse on the ground. He could not move. He could not see. He could not think. This spot was good enough.

When Kon awoke the sun was high in the sky patched with thick clouds. He sat, looked around him and chased flies away from his bloody legs. He ached everywhere, and recalled that in comparison the turbulent Urubamba River had been a pleasure. At some distance on the south side, he saw a shapeless hillock of what was left of the upside down raft, which had been pushed almost to the beach. The tide was receding, and the sea was much calmer. Then, he wondered about his companions.

Where are they?

With pain, he got up, and saw Ilo on the beach, his face in the sand, lifeless. Limping miserably, Kon went to him, and rolled him on his back. Ilo was breathing. Kon took him in his arms and laid him on the dry, warm sand at the top of the beach. Ilo coughed several times, and opened his eyes. As soon as he saw Kon, his face became clouded with anger. He hated Kon for what had happened the last two days, and would never forgive him for his mistakes. Kon tried to help him sit, but only sparked a vehement reaction from his wounded companion.

"Don't touch me!" Ilo sputtered. "Stay away from me. You

and Illa think you are clever, you are nothing."

Kon could not believe his ears. How was it that a Viracocha brother would hate him? With dismay, he walked away from the madman, and searched for his other companion.

He went to the raft and found no trace of Ra. He walked back and forth along the beach without success. Then, he went back to the raft and tried to imagine what its trajectory could have been. Halfway between the raft and the barrier, he saw Ra's body among coral branches. His face was under water. There was no chance he could be alive. Struggling a second time through the crumbling coral, Kon went to him and brought him back to the beach. Ra's body was mutilated beyond recognition. Without saying a word, the two men buried their long-time friend. They covered his grave with large blocks of dead coral. Ra faced the west and would watch the sunset for many sun-cycles.

For the time being, Kon choose not to argue with Ilo, whose mind was not rational. Instead, he searched for the others.

"Where are we?" he asked himself. "Where are the other rafts?"

He walked between the coconut trees, to the area where the land went down to the water. The island was a very narrow strip, a circle, like a giant crown. When he reached the beach, he was startled by the calmness of the shallow water. He looked all around, following the line of coconut trees. He noticed that they were almost on the north side of the island: It would not have taken much to miss it. He recalled that Rangi and Hiti were sailing farther north. They could have missed the island, but how could he be sure?

Kon tried to estimate the size of the lagoon. It would have taken three or four days to walk all around the island. It would have been easy if the strip of land were not cut by deep passes, leading to the ocean. Kon knew he would not take the risk of swimming through a dozen of these passes, against strong currents, without good reasons. He was also aware that they were ideal passageways for large predators. Furthermore, he was in terrible physical shape. He tried to climb a coconut tree to have a better view of the bizarre island, but he found himself clumsy and abandoned the idea. Then, he thought about a fire: This was the solution to attract attention. If there were any people on the island, they would see the smoke during the day or the flames during the night. If Rangi and Hiti were on the island, they would answer by also making a fire.

Kon thought about the children, and what could have happened to them if they had landed the same way as he did. He thought about Kukara's possibly fighting for life in the powerful foam, and deeply wished they had missed this island. Somewhere else, maybe, they would have a better chance. He collected all the dry wood he could find. He went back to the raft, and found a way through the balsa logs to what was left of the cabin. He found a basket full of sharp obsidian knives and two pieces of flint, but everything was soaked with water, and it was impossible to start any flame from the sparks. He collected a few dead leaves from coconut fronds, placed them on the warm sand, and let them dry under the sun. Later in the afternoon, he finally succeeded in starting a fire. Quickly, there was a huge amount of smoke that could be seen from anywhere around the island. No one could have missed it.

Patiently, Kon waited until dark, but never saw any other smoke. Also during the night, he did not see any other fire: They were alone.

The next morning, Kon went to the raft looking for drinking water. He found only three sections of bamboo that had not been broken. Their water supply was quite limited. Soon, they would rely only on coconuts, which were unlimited. He brought some fresh water to Ilo, who fought a fever. Many of his wounds were infected. Ilo took the cup of water without saying a word. To a lesser extent, Kon had the same problem with his wounds and cuts. He concluded that many of these corals must have been venomous. With sharp bone needles, both men spent half the day removing most of the sea urchin spines from their legs. Yet, some of them were too deep and could not be removed. Their bodies would have to work them out. It took ten days before their bodies started healing. Meanwhile, their water supply was consumed. From now on, their only beverage would be the milk from green coconuts, or the rain. The meat of the more mature nuts provided nourishing food, and they used the buds of germinated nuts as a vegetable. With their obsidian knives, they could cut the muscle of large clams living in the coral. These colorful bivalves were their main source of meat.

Ilo gave no sign of concession and refused to talk to Kon. Several times, he disappeared for an entire day. Kon knew he went to explore the island by following the narrow land strip. Kon's main concern was to find a way to get off the island. As his body was healing, he thought about it many times, and had concluded it was impossible to repair the raft. The only solution was to build a smaller raft with the material available from the wreck. It could take a long time, but it was their only chance. Kon was ready to work. However, he had to convince an uncooperative companion. He thought he had waited long enough, and decided to confront Ilo's problems.

Kon laid one hand on Ilo's shoulder. Ilo had not seen him coming, and glanced at Kon with surprise.

"Sit down; we need to talk," Kon ordered.

Ilo was on the defensive, but sat, to Kon's surprise.

"We need to build a new, smaller raft," Kon said, "using whatever is left from the wreck."

"You do whatever you want," Ilo answered with disdain. "I came here to die, and here I will die. Because of all the manipulative fantasies of you and your clan, my parents are dead, my brothers and sisters are dead. I had a girlfriend, and she is gone with her parents and Taranga. Now, please leave me alone."

"Perhaps, you don't want to find out if your girlfriend is still alive," Kon replied. "Perhaps, you prefer to feel sorry for yourself, and die in this no-man's-land. Well, I will not stay here. With or without you, I will build a new raft. When it is finished, you will be invited to come on board, and go west."

Angry, Kon left, then turned around.

"I am sorry for everything that went wrong," Kon said. "I never meant to hurt you or anyone. I am hurt about all the others, and I don't know where they are. But, as long as I have running blood left in my body, I swear I will find a way to reach them."

Kon went to the wreck and searched for what he could use to make a small raft. He decided he would start dismantling the needed pieces at dawn. Right now, he was infuriated and needed to take a walk. It was early in the afternoon, so he decided to go to the first pass on the north side. He followed the beach on the ocean side of the land strip. The sand was hot, and gravel inside his sandals irritated him. He removed them and kept them in his hands. It was a very hot day, and there was no wind.

Unaware of their presence, he disturbed a couple of white terns. They were elegant birds, with the top of their heads completely black. They took off, expressing their displeasure with loud, grating calls. One of them flew toward Kon and passed just above his head. Surprised by such aggressiveness from a tiny bird, Kon bent down, and walked away. Discovering new birds always gave him pleasure.

Before reaching the pass, Kon observed that the land strip was lower, with no vegetation, and looked like a battlefield of gigantic blocks of dead coral. He stopped, put on his sandals, and wondered where these blocks came from. There was only one answer: They came from the barrier, and had been detached by awesome sea swells. Tidal waves could have done it, and the thought upset him. This was not the right place to be during a hurricane, and it confirmed his desire to leave as soon as they could.

At some distance, he saw a blue pond looking like a giant hole inside the barrier. Around it the water was shallow, below Kon's knees. At the edge of the pond, he stopped and admired its crystal-clear water. In spite of its deep water, he could see everything. Colorful fish of all kinds were quietly wandering from one coral to another and from one hole to another. Between cracks, he saw two lobsters with impressive antennae. The bottom of the pond was patched with white sand, which looked like a fascinating blue because of the depth. He could not resist, removed his clothes, laid them on the top of an isolated coral and gently slipped into the blue pond.

He swam to the middle, when he saw a massive, dark shadow crossing the pond. He felt his blood flush his face and his heart pounded. He swam as fast as he could to escape the pond, and had the horrible feeling that something was following him, swimming much faster, closing in on him. When Kon escaped the pond, he was totally panic-stricken. Back on safe ground, he looked into the deep water and saw two sharks, twice his size, gliding from one side of the pond to the other. They also seemed disturbed, but not aggressive. He could have been an easy prey.

Kon dressed himself, and walked back. This time, he followed the beach on the side of the lagoon. At the top of the beach, he saw a magnificent nautilus shell entangled within the roots of a strange-looking tree. Protected by the roots, the shell was perfect. He took it, and would give it to Ilo, who had a passion for attractive shells. Then, he saw a sandpiper running on the beach. From place to place, the shorebird probed into the white sand, feeding on tiny animals. Kon was familiar with this kind of bird, and observed it without paying too much attention, until a vision suddenly crossed his mind. It had been like a quick flash. He stopped and concentrated on the bird. He closed his eyes and saw the sandpiper running on black sand. He opened his eyes. The sandpiper was running on white sand. Thus, the image went away from his mind. Tired, he sat in the shade of a tree, and took a nap.

Kon watched the sandpiper running after a receding wave, on the black sand.

"The bird has no fear of powerful waves," Hina of the Valley said, with a gentle voice.

Startled by the vision of the magnificent woman, Kon stood on his feet and tried to say something to her. He could not.

"Follow me," she said, "but this time do not attempt to touch me."

He followed her to a small village. He encountered a few people he had never seen before, and they all ignored him, as if he did not exist. She entered a dwelling house where several dignitaries were obviously waiting for her. She wore a long, narrow white dress, with a belt of shells around her waist. She had a white band around her head, with a few green feathers held between the band and her forehead. She sat on a large stone, and raised her arms, facing the audience. They all stopped talking, respectful. Kon sat on the ground, and listened.

"In the beginning of this world, there was only Taaroa," she said, in a charismatic way. "Taaroa had no forebears. He created himself and all first beings and things. Taaroa was, is, and will be. Taaroa is light to each of us. Taaroa existed alone, traveling in space and darkness at incredible speed, within egg-like shells. Wearying of his solitude, he broke out from his shells. One shell became his house, which contains the world we know: the sky, mountains, valleys, rivers and the sea. Another shell became trees, birds, fish, men and women. Within Taaroa were all the values we know: memory, thoughts, observation, knowledge, bravery, and..." She paused and looked at Kon. "And above all, kindness, and liberation from arrogance."

They all looked at Kon. She walked to him, and pointed a finger at his face.

"Kon Tici Viracocha," she said loudly, "in due time, you shall meet the great Taaroa."

Then the vision vanished in an ephemeral vortex of dust and light. Kon awoke and heard the sandpiper on the white sand: "Kee-wee..."

Greatly disturbed by the consistency of his visions of Hina of the Valley, Kon went back to the camp without noticing anything around him, until he saw Ilo.

"I found this and brought it for you." Kon said, after he laid the magnificent nautilus shell on the sand. He did not wait for any word from Ilo, and left.

Ilo inspected the shell for a long time: It was the first time he saw an unbroken nautilus. He wondered why Kon brought the shell to him, after all he did to make him angry. Deep inside, Ilo started feeling guilt. Was it possible that he had been wrong and unfair? He shook his head, rejecting the idea and thinking he was becoming too soft.

It took two days for Kon to remove all the valuable equipment from the wreck. Then, piece by piece, he dismantled the mast, the deck, many ropes... He was especially careful to keep ropes in good condition.

Six days later, he had dismantled the entire raft. Only the large balsa beams were left: Deeply impregnated by seawater, they had no further value for Kon. The most valuable pieces were the smaller balsa cross beams attached on the top of the large ones, making the deck. He had many of them, and they were in excellent condition, as they had not been continuously exposed to the water during the trip. They were very heavy, and he would have to transport them all the way across the strip of land near the lagoon, where he wanted to build a new raft. He attached a long rope around the first beam, and pulled it, little by little, to the beach.

Kon had been thinking about the safest way to leave the island. There was only one solution: He had to build the new raft on the other side of the land strip, on the beach facing the lagoon and the west. By doing this, they would not have to sail around the island. They would cross the calm water of the lagoon, then exit through a pass, on the west side, when the tide receded. Then the current would push the raft westward with no danger of being projected on the barrier. He thought nothing could go wrong with this approach.

Using Mana, he was able to drag the first beam a very short distance at a time. It took him more than half a day to pull the beam all the way across the land strip, and he did not rush anything. It was essential for him to remain in good physical condition.

The next day, as he was halfway across the land strip with the second beam, Ilo came. He did not say anything, but smiled to Kon, and helped him pull the log. To Kon's surprise, Ilo was in a good mood and actually found pleasure in working with him. It made a tremendous difference. In two days, they moved all the beams across the land strip. Now, they had to build a new raft. It was late in the afternoon, and the tide was low. The lagoon was quiet, with not a single ripple on its surface. The incredible beauty of the blue lagoon tempted them.

For the first time, they took a walk inside the lagoon. For a long distance the water was shallow, barely coming above their knees. Between isolated blocks of coral, the coarse, white sand provided a comfortable support on which they could walk with no effort. Both men were fascinated by the varieties of coral, their colors, and their beauty. It was an endless collection of yellow, orange, green, red and violet. It seemed that each color was specially selected at its best. The purple would outshine the prettiest crystals Kon had ever seen. The green would make the rich emeralds from the continent pale in comparison. The blue gill of partially open giant convoluted clams outshone any blue they had seen before. It was an ocean garden of unimaginable beauty, inevitably humbling the visitor.

Between coral blocks, a myriad colorful fish swam in peace and harmony. Some coral was made of delicate golden branches, surrounded by a crowd of tiny, dark blue fish. At the first alert or unusual noise, they would disappear inside the branches. Then, slowly, they would come back to their original position. Both men were amazed how the fish were familiar: No man had disturbed them before. The two men's curiosity culminated when they found their first live shells. Ilo followed a long track at the surface of the sand, reached one end, dug with his hand, but did not find anything. Then, he went to the other end, dug again, and found his treasure. It was a spectacular, white miter, circled with bright red-orange dots. Ilo stared at the living marvel, shocked by his discovery. With thrilling joy, he showed the shell to Kon, who was equally surprised.

Kon followed another track, reached the end, and saw a small moving bump on the sand. The shell must have been there, under the sand. He dug, and could not believe his eyes. It was a perfect, white screw shell, circled with black dots thoroughly aligned. It was longer than his hand, and extremely sharp at one end. He had never thought that the sea could hide such beauty, perfection and complexity. He was overwhelmed.

Kon saw a large purple coral, and bent down to look at the tiny organisms that were carrying the amazing color. They were five-side polyps, from which long, fine, whiskery tentacles explored the surrounding water, hunting for food. He disturbed a few with one finger, and they instantly went inside the polyp, but they came back, and adhered to his finger. These translucent, purple tentacles were alive. The entire coral was alive. He felt a slight burn on his finger. Now, he understood why their cuts and wounds healed so slowly. All these tiny tentacles could sting their prey with poison and paralyze it, which was the way they caught the microorganisms swimming in the water. Transposed into another dimension, Kon thought this strange world was a terrifying battlefield. He was right. The calm and magnificent lagoon waited. Its charming beauty hid its implacable cruelty. It was a paradise capable of becoming a place of torment in the wink of an eye, and the inexperienced visitor was the ideal prey.

Kon looked at the peculiar island, and an incredible thought came to his mind. The entire island was made of dead coral. All the large blocks were coral. All the stones were coral. All the sand was coral, dead coral. All these tiny animals were building islands on a huge scale. He instantly drew a parallel between all the stars in the sky, and all the polyps in the ocean. Once more, he was astounded by the ingenious power of his Creator.

"You are the Light," Kon said, looking at the sun already low on the horizon. "The purpose of your creation is unknown to us, but something is sure: Life must proceed, at all cost, on all scales, with no mercy for the weak."

In their excitement, they went where it was deeper, until the crystal-clear water reached their waists. Ilo saw a shiny object sitting on the top of a large, circular block of yellow coral. On one side, a dark hole large enough to accommodate his entire body, led to the unknown below the reef. He was so attracted by the lustrous shell resting inside a narrow crack, that he forgot to watch for anything else. He was magnetized by the glowing cowrie, and did not see the large moray eel nearby. When he tried to reach for the shell, the eel slowly emerged from the reef. The predator, about the size of Ilo's leg, snaked forward. He took the cowrie, and marveled at one of the best jewels of the ocean. The giant eel crawled on the sand to his feet, and opened its powerful jaws. At this moment, Ilo vaguely saw a moving shadow near his legs. Then he saw the jaw exhibiting long, needle-sharp teeth. Terrorized, he jumped back and fell in the water, then ran away to where the water was shallow.

To satisfy Kon's curiosity, Ilo agreed to go back and show him where the animal was. The moray was at the same place, and did not move. Kon took a dead branch of coral and slowly brought it in front of the moray. He pushed the branch closer to its jaw. The impressive animal would not attack, but would not back up, either. Then, he touched the jaw with the branch. The moray grabbed the intruding object with incredible force. Kon could feel for an instant the strength of the animal for whom he was no match. He thought he had pushed his luck far enough, and let the animal go with the branch of coral. Finally, the moray swam slowly toward the dark hole and disappeared.

Kon took the shiny cowrie and gave it to Ilo, who had not recovered yet from his terror. The red sun was halfway behind the horizon. They went back to the land strip and searched for some food.

At the same time, far away in the west, a young girl followed her father's steps to a legendary lake, where a giant eel lived.

"Father!" Hina said. "Where does King Vaihiria come from?"

"A long time ago," her father replied, "the most beautiful and tallest coconut tree of the island lived near the shore of this lake. Everyone came to admire the tree at least once in a lifetime. One day, the wind was so strong that the sacred tree fell into the lake, which was filled with waves. Then, through the waves, everyone saw the tree crawling like a giant eel. Since that day, everyone is convinced that King Vaihiria was born that way."

"Are we going to see the king?" Hina asked.

"Yes, these fish in my basket are for him."

At dusk, they sat near the quiet water of the deep lake.

"Now is the time," her father said, giving a shrill sort of whistle.

Immediately, a few waves came to shore, and at some distance, a dark mass broke the surface of the lake.

"Do not be afraid, my child."

Hina was startled by the awesome eel, which had moved about the surface of the water. The eel came with confidence and ate out of her father's hand.

"You can caress his head."

Hina bent forward, and put her fingers just above the eyes of the formidable animal: It was cold and slimy, but she was not afraid.

"This is King Vaihiria," her father said.

Around midnight, Kon awoke and wondered what could have disturbed his heavy sleep. He listened and heard Ilo snoring in a most unusual way. He did not even remember hearing him snore before. What could be wrong with him? Then, the unexpected question came.

"Kon, is that you?"

Startled by Ilo's voice coming from another direction, Kon jumped to his feet and went to Ilo. Now, both men wanted to know more about this. The night was clear with a full moon. They carefully listened to determine where the noise came from. They saw a thick bush at some distance, which seemed to be the only possible place. As they approached, they heard the bizarre snoring sounds again. When they pushed the branches aside, something moved under the bush, and they heard weird groans. Awkwardly, two shearwaters ran between Kon's legs and disappeared into the night. Kon and Ilo looked at one another, and burst out laughing. It had never occurred to them that two peaceful seabirds could produce this cacophony. As they tried to go back to sleep, at times they were still giggling. Then, silence again pervaded the night. In the east, the rumble of the waves falling on the barrier reminded Kon that the sea was giving life to billions of polyps.

The next day Kon and Ilo started to assemble the new raft. First, they laid a thick carpet of coconut fronds on the inclined beach facing the lagoon. The fronds would prevent three rollers placed under the raft from sinking into the sand. They set one row of nine beams, above which they set another alternate row of ten beams, giving the raft a comfortable thickness. They built a deck and a cabin with the bamboo they had saved. They raised a small bipod mast, a boom, and cut a sail of the appropriate size.

Finally, they installed a centerboard behind the raft that would be used as a rudder. After one-half moon-cycle of hard work, the raft was completed.

Just before dawn, when the tide was high, they decided to launch the raft. They cut the rope holding the raft to a coconut tree. They pushed on the raft that gently rolled on the three beams, into the water. They embraced one another, savoring their first victory in quite awhile. Then, with a long rope, they anchored the raft to a block of dead coral.

They spent the morning loading the raft with what they saved from the wreck. They took great care of the extra clothes and sandals that had never been used. They took enough coconuts at various stages of maturity to survive about one moon-cycle. They would leave at dawn, when the tide started receding. Ilo built a box with the bamboo they had not used, in which he placed each valuable shell they had collected, wrapped in a small piece of fabric. As the odor of the decaying shells was overwhelming, he attached the box under the deck, so it would remain in the water.

Then came the time when their destiny would suddenly change with appalling brutality.

At midday, the tide was low. Both men took their obsidian knives and went on the reef. Once more, they ate convoluted clams, and saved a few for the next day. Ilo still looked for shells with passion, and reached a flat table of dead coral. He wondered if he could find some cowries under it. He lifted the heavy coral from one side, and turned it up side down. Two bright orange cowries sat together. He took one and was astonished when he saw the violet color of the lips around the aperture of the shell. He waited until the water cleared up where the dead coral had been sitting: Perhaps, another cowrie could have fallen into the water. He saw the white sand appearing, and a cone shell of unusual, striated pattern, which reminded him of the skin of a snake. It never occurred to him that the animal could be dangerous. He took it, and placed it on the top of the stone he had turned over.

He went to another table, and turned it over. There were no cowries on the back of the stone. He waited until the cloudy sediments settled, and saw another cone. This one was different, larger, with a more fragile shell. The animal was very active, crawling fast. It was a hunter, and an awesome killer. Its striated shell was not as perfectly designed as the other cone. Nevertheless Ilo took it as a unique specimen. Then, he took the other cone. The men walked back to the land strip preparing for their last night on the island.

Ilo displayed the shells he found, and they both studied their shape and their splendid network-pattern of brown, white and orange. Interested by its unusual behavior, Kon took the more active cone that was about the same length as his hand. The animal did not seem afraid, and its long and colorful siphon was still searching at the front of the shell aperture. Kon had no idea that the animal could strike at any time with its long poisonous spear hiding inside the shell. The injected poison would have been ten times more powerful than the poison of the most deadly snake he knew of. He laid the shell on the sand, and Ilo took all the shells and went to the raft, to place them in his box.

When Ilo came back, he sat near Kon, and rubbed his left hand.

"I don't know what is wrong with this hand, it is all numb."

"Perhaps you touched some venomous coral," Kon answered.

"No, I think it was when I took the shells to the raft. The active cone stung me here, where it is swollen."

Then, Ilo tried to forget his hand. Besides, he felt no pain. They talked, anticipating what the next few days could bring.

Ilo got up, and immediately collapsed to his knees, to Kon's surprise.

"What happened, are you ill?" Kon asked.

"I don't know, I am dizzy."

Ilo turned his head toward Kon, and tried to look at him.

"Kon, I don't see you. Where are you? I don't see anything."

Only then, Kon understood what had happened. He tore a piece of fabric from Ilo's wrap, and constricted it around his left arm. Then, with his obsidian knife, he made a small incision lengthwise across the swollen area of Ilo's hand. With his mouth, he applied strong suction, several times.

Ilo's eyelids drooped. His words did not make any sense. He could not breathe. Slowly but surely, he lapsed into a coma.

"Ilo!" Kon screamed. "Don't go like this. Fight back!"

It was wishful thinking, and Ilo soon stopped breathing. His pulse raced. An instant later, his pulse came to a stop. Ilo Viracocha was dead. The quiet and beautiful lagoon had struck in a cruel and unpredictable way. The most powerful predator of the lagoon was not the shark, or even the moray. The greatest danger on the atoll was not its currents, or the awesome swells thundering on the barrier. For the inexperienced visitor, the most formidable enemy was a tiny, colorful and attractive cone shell.

Everything had happened so fast that Kon was in total disarray. He kneeled near his companion, and buried his face in his hands. Kon was shocked, humiliated and incapable of any clear thinking. It took him a while to recover from his pain. Then, and only then, he listened to the island. He could only hear the gentle breeze in the coconut fronds, and the ocean swells giving life to the barrier. He heard the loud grating of a tern. He was in another world, and would fight no more for the others. From now on, he would fight for himself: Kon Tici Viracocha was alone.

****

CHAPTER 4

"I love this island which is mine. Its clear rivers are my comfort, its blue lagoon my joy, its deep valleys my home, and its high mountains my soul."

Hina of the Valley

Hina was twelve years old, and Tupua's youngest daughter. Tupua was a respected king on the island of Tahiti-nui, which was divided into seven kingdoms. Because of his kindness and wisdom, other kings often consulted Tupua for advice. He was also praised for his talented high priests: The current high priest was Vana. Tupua's house, which was Hina's home, was located on the north side of the island, in a colorful village he had named Papenoo.

The young woman, still a child, walked on the long black sand beach. On a sunny morning, walking alone gave her pleasure, and she enjoyed the wet sand rubbing and cleaning her toes. Behind her, the waves erased her tracks. She was taller and thinner than the average Tahitian girl of her age. She was a well-educated and fine example of the Tahitian aristocracy, intelligent, capable, and self-reliant. She had large, solemn black eyes, and instantly charmed everyone. Her long, straight, blue-black hair hung elegantly to her hips. She had a tiny mole on the lower part of her left cheek. Her skin was clear golden-brown, pure, soft and well maintained with vegetable oil perfumed with fragrant flowers.

With majesty and calm, Hina looked out upon her small world. She believed only in what she could see, or verify with facts. Her greatest talent was her natural good disposition toward the people that needed assistance. All infants and elderly people were filled with wonder when Hina held their hand and talked to them. With patience and a few kind words, she would make them content with their life.

Tupua deeply loved his young daughter, and she was his favorite child. He was proud of her ability and willingness to learn anything. However, she had a character of her own, and for the king she was not an easy child. Among other dignitaries, she could become daring. More than once, she had been sarcastic with priests, when she did not believe their stories. Her questions, observations and convictions confounded many priests. Nothing irritated her more than a military leader showing mediocrity in judgment, and absence of magnanimity. For her, being noble was the ultimate favor given to those able to serve the people, and not the other way around. She was a wonderful dreaming child, with a noble heart. Her father and Vana, the high priest, thought she was gifted but often out of touch with reality.

The favorite hobby of Hina's mother and sister was to make colorful and opulent shell necklaces. Hina did not care for the craft, but found pleasure in collecting and cleaning the shells for them. She was a fervent shell hunter. When she was in the mood for meditation, Hina would walk or sit on the beach. Usually, two thoughts haunted her mind: What kind of land and people could live beyond the few islands she knew, and how she could, one day, walk to the summit of Tahiti-nui. She looked at the formidable Mount Orohena, grandiose, sacred, mysterious and never violated by man. The mountain was feared, and inhabited by supernatural forces. Because it was taboo, Hina was strongly attracted by Mount Orohena: She wanted to know its secrets. Only on rare occasions, the priests would allow skilled climbers to approach the summit, where a sacred duck lived on the cold waters of a tiny lake. The red feathers of the bird were used for war rituals. Many climbers had lost their lives before reaching the crater lake, but no man had ever climbed to the summit. According to the legend, those who tried never came back. Hina had been told that the name Orohena referred to the dorsal fin of a sacred shark, whose shape was the same. Mount Orohena was a giant fin that could be seen at sea from incredible distances. In Hina's universe, it was the highest mountain, and the ultimate challenge. She wondered what kind of spirit the mountain could host. She had often heard the great priest telling frightening stories that did not make sense to her. Nevertheless, as a learning child, she had a doubt about what to believe or not to believe. She consistently refused to accept the existence of spirits, but she was also afraid of being wrong. She sat on the warm, black sand and drew a shark fin.

"Tonight, I shall go to my father," she said to herself. "He may have an explanation for Mount Orohena's secrets."

On a nice day, she would walk to the nearest village, Haapape, located on the western side of Papenoo, near the beautiful Teauroa point where she often played in the sand dunes. She also loved bathing in the clear and fresh waters of the Vaipopoo River reaching the lagoon at the Teauroa point. In Haapape, she had many relatives and friends with whom she would often socialize, but Hina liked the Teauroa point for two other reasons: The lagoon around it was the best place for hunting seashells, and the view on Mount Orohena was most impressive. When the tide was low, she would swim to the barrier of coral. Enchanted by the incredible beauty of the reef, she would offer it to Orohena.

On her way back, she admired a charming islet named Motuau, at some distance from the beach. She had often wondered if she could swim to this uninhabited paradise, full of coconut trees and pandanus bushes. The bright white sand beach circling the islet impressed her. She had gone to it many times with her sister, using her father's outrigger canoe. However, she had never swum to the islet because she had been told not to. This was another taboo because the islet was not inside the lagoon. She had been told that a great blue shark often hunted around the islet. She sat on the top of a coconut lost on the beach, and studied the islet. It was a delicate garden planted on the surface of the blue sea. She was fascinated by its beauty and fully understood why it was a natural tribute and matter of pride to keep it clean. The only evidence of human presence were some footprints on its white beach. Still, it was prohibited to make more footprints than the seabirds would. In Hina's world, harmony with nature was an important matter.

In the evening, when she came back to Papenoo, she went to her father. As he often did, he was sitting on a coconut tree trunk which had fallen on the beach during a storm several moon-cycles earlier. It was his favorite place to meditate before dusk. She sat, cross-legged on the sand, in front of him. Tupua was in his fifties, overweight, but always well dressed and disposed to listen to anyone who wanted to talk to him. It always gave him great pleasure to chat with Hina. Because she sat cross-legged, he knew she had important matters to discuss.

"Father, I am strongly attracted by Mount Orohena, but the reasons are obscure. Did you ever feel the need to visit the sacred mountain?"

Tupua frowned when he heard Hina's question.

"My child, you know well that the mountain is taboo. Only selected warriors are allowed, during wartime, to visit the lake near the summit, where the red ducks live. But no one should ever attempt climbing to the summit."

"I know that, but why is it taboo to climb a mountain?"

"You can climb any mountain you want, except Mount Orohena."

"But why, what is so special about it?" she inquired.

"It is taboo for your own safety. I observed the summit from the lake when I was a good climber, many sun-cycles ago. Near the summit, Mount Orohena is very steep, covered with crumbling stones, and gravel. There is no vegetation to hold your steps. Losing your balance would lead to certain death."

"I see, now I understand better," she said, disappointed. "Would you be mad at me, if I climbed to the lake?"

Tupua looked at his daughter with surprise, and wondered if she could dare do such a thing. He knew her too well. If she contemplated such an idea, it was not in vain.

"It is far too dangerous for a girl like you to climb Mount Orohena. Yes, I would be mad at you, and it would greatly offend our great priest, Vana."

"Father, I am not talking about climbing to the summit; I want to go to the lake," Hina said, losing her patience.

"But, the lake is sacred, also. Only those with the sacred motive of collecting the red feathers from the duck are allowed to visit the lake."

"Well, I am motivated!" she exclaimed, with a triumphant smile.

"No, you will not go to the lake," Tupua roared.

"Even the daughter of the king cannot visit the lake," she

said.

"Yes, even you. The great priest would never grant your request; it is far too dangerous. Only a few men have been there; some never came back."

"Killed by the spirits, I suppose," Hina whispered. "I don't believe in these spirits Vana is always talking about."

She looked at the distressed face of her father.

"I am sorry, my father, I do not want to hurt you. You know I love you."

Tupua put his arms around his daughter and caressed her long hair.

"It hurts me when you talk like this about Vana. He has been my good friend since I was a boy. Promise me you will be careful about what you say to him. He is a respected priest, and I don't want you to embarrass him with incisive questions about Mount Orohena's spirits. There are things going on there that nobody understands."

"I promise. Besides, I don't talk to him very often."

Both noticed thick clouds above the northeastern horizon.

"It looks like a bad storm," Hina said.

"Yes, but it is too early in the season," Tupua said.

Hina looked at the rainy clouds and wondered about Mount Orohena's spirits. She imagined the wind blowing on the sea, in the trees, in the valley, and on the mountain. Maybe these spirits were only the effect of a game between the swirling wind and the rare ferns growing on the high cliffs. Maybe the wind would push some gravel that would roll down the steep slopes, sounding like awakening spirits. Or, perhaps the rain between stones would do the same. There was no spirit living in the mountain, they existed only in Vana's imagination.

The wind gained momentum, then it started raining. Hina

watched her father giving orders to remove all the outrigger canoes from the beach, to protect them from the large waves pounding the beach during storms. Then, she went home, where she found her mother, Atea, and her sister, Fenua, preparing the evening meal. Both women looked at Hina with irritated eyes.

"Where were you all day?" Atea asked. "We needed you to help clean the shells. I don't understand why you are always gone when we need you most. One day, you will have to work hard for your mate and children."

"I don't want a mate," Hina replied with a warm smile. "I want to remain free, and to become a priestess."

Atea and Fenua glanced at one another, astonished by Hina's words.

"A priestess needs to walk, meditate and learn about nature." Hina continued. "This is why I often go to the beach, to the barrier reef, or in the valley, where I can see, smell and listen. Now, what can I do to help you?"

"Did you talk to your father about what you just said?" Atea asked, with concern and dismay. "A girl does not choose to be a priestess, she is told by the king or the great priest, only if she is gifted enough."

"No, I did not ask father or Vana." Hina replied. "It became my destiny the day father chose my name, and I intend to honor this."

"Fine, but never say you don't need a man," Atea argued. "They do things we cannot do, as we do things they would not do. A woman without a man, or a man without a woman, always misses the greatest things life can give. So, if you become a priestess, with a man you will be a better priestess. Some day, you will understand my words."

Hina did not answer immediately. She ate a banana first,

sat near the shells displayed on the ground, flipped her long hair behind her back and stared at her mother.

"I comprehend your words very well," Hina said. "I just never met a man that I would be willing to share my life with. I want to learn many things first, then after, maybe. But, I will not take the mate I am told and give him children. I will do it my way, or not at all."

Hina took a piece of soft bark-cloth and polished the cowries Atea and Fenua had cleaned. Fenua was disturbed by her young sister's words, and sat by her side.

"This morning I fished with Aru," Fenua said, gently. "I don't like him because I was told he would be my mate. I like him because he is strong, and a future leader our father can rely on. We caught three lobsters and five parrot-fish for the meal tonight. Did you know he could carry his outrigger canoe from the top of the beach to the water all by himself? I could not believe my eyes. I love him."

Hina smiled at her sister, without answering.

My poor sister, you are attracted by muscles, she thought. That big boy has more muscle than brain. I would not love such a man. I would want him intelligent, knowledgeable and capable of teaching me new things, always. I would like for him to be superior to me."

"What are you thinking, my sister?" Fenua asked, trying to read Hina's mind.

"Nothing important, I guess. I think you and I are very different. We love one another a great deal, but we cannot love the same kind of man."

Alarmed by the increasing strength of the storm, the three women went to the patio, just as Tupua came in.

"This wind may damage the roof," Tupua said. "I want all

stays solidly attached around the house."

Swirling dead leaves and rain entered the house, forcing them to close all sides with coconut-frond panels especially saved for these rare occasions. Then, the night came, loud and different. During a storm, it was a tradition for the members of a family and friends to gather inside one house. The oldest man or the priest would recite ancient legends, and everyone would listen to him, away from the outside violence. Staring at the red embers in the fire, they would vicariously live the legend. Children would be astonished, the weak would be afraid, the strong would be inspired, and so the priest would transmit the sacred words to the next generation. It was their way to kill time, when there was nothing else they could do. The smoke climbed to the top of the vegetable roof, and escaped from the house through a wood deflector. Atea, Fenua and Hina sat on one side of the fire, while Tupua and Aru, Fenua's friend, sat on the other side near Vana. They were all prepared to listen to the great priest.

Vana was a skinny man, in his fifties. Half-black, half-white hair fell to his shoulders. He was dressed in simple white bark-cloth, and wore one lei of green feathers around his neck. Only the great priest could wear the feathers of the sacred green pigeon of the valley. Around his waist, he wore a large belt decorated with tiny white cowries naturally circled by a delicate golden ring.

He was the king's best friend, and they shared lifetime memories. To many, Vana was simply part of Tupua's family.

Hina came closer to Vana, and attentively listened to his words. She enjoyed a large piece of baked, steaming breadfruit. Several times she shook her fingers, burned by the hot fruit. She loved breadfruit, and could make a complete meal of it, if it was not for her mother, who forced her to eat other food. Hina liked all fruits, but did not care much for fish: She ate some only because she had to, and because everybody did.

The wind attacked the village with force, and the entire house shook on its foundation. Rain poured from the sky, and water found its way through the thick roof of woven pandanus leaves. Everyone ignored the elements, and found a comfortable spot. Vana was ready. At first, his words were slow. He saw Hina eating her breadfruit, and thought she was not paying attention to what he was saying. He tested her by asking a question without mentioning her name or looking at her.

"This is good for you." Vana said. "You seem to enjoy this kind of food. Do you know the origin of breadfruit trees on Tahiti-nui?"

"I never heard of it," Hina replied immediately, without looking at the priest.

Vana smiled. The girl was listening with a casualness that was only an appearance. He wondered if it was a natural attitude, or a calculated play, so he changed the subject.

"Vana, please, tell us about the origin of the breadfruit tree on this island," Hina asked, with a charming smile he could not ignore.

Tupua, who was not listening at first, was most surprised by Hina's sudden kindness toward the priest.

With mystery in his eyes, Vana related the legend of the breadfruit tree.

"A long time ago, when very few people lived on Tahiti-nui, a family was established near our village, close to the Papenoo River. They had come as solitary navigators, and they stayed here a few moon-cycles, having nowhere else to go. Then, a long drought occurred and, soon, there was nothing to eat.

The small colony included the old grandparents from the mother's side, the parents and seven young children. The drought was especially hard for the old couple and on the youngest infant that was only four moon-cycles old.

One day, the mother came to her husband. She was crying because her baby was dying of malnutrition. In a desperate move, the husband took his family to the mountains. They walked for several days, deep inside the valley, until they found a small cave near the dry riverbed. They took a rest and found enough water under a few surviving tree ferns.

Before the sun sat behind Mount Orohena, the husband took his wife for a short walk. As he gently held her hand, he told her something she could not comprehend.

"My dear wife, these ferns are not good for our children, they are not nutritious enough. I am going to end this famine by doing something you shall never forget. Tomorrow, at dawn, I will exit the cave while everyone is asleep. When you will wake up, I want you to come right here, where we are now. You will see my hands becoming large leaves, my arms, my legs and the rest of my limbs becoming a large tree, and my head and my heart becoming the most wonderful fruits you ever saw."

She smiled at him, and kissed him with warmth for his generous kindness. She thought he was only trying to comfort her heart.

Early in the morning, when the mother woke up, she found that her husband had left. She remembered his words and went to the place where she had kissed him, and saw a huge tree. It was a kind of tree she had never seen before, majestic with large leaves made of long pointed lobes, in which she could wrap the food and cook it. It was a healthy tree with rich bark round the trunk, with which she could make soft and solid cloth of a quality she never thought possible. It was a productive tree with heavy fruits whose nutritive properties were most extraordinary. It was the breadfruit tree.

The mother took a fruit and sat on the ground. For a long time, she caressed the fruit, and now she understood her husband's words. To save his family, he had changed himself into a tree of life. Tears slowly found their way down her cheeks. They were tears of happiness because all her children were safe. They were also tears of sorrow because her husband had gone onward.

Sometimes, life is a compromise. You may have to pay a dear price for the security of those you love most."

Hina was fascinated by Vana's story, and she held his hand in a sign of warm recognition, but now she was ready to ask questions.

"That man was a good man," she said, gently. "But, do you think it really happened that way?"

Tupua glanced at his daughter, apprehensive of her unabashed inquisitiveness, but Vana did not seem to object to her question.

"I don't really know, Hina. Legends are legends, and people repeat them from mouth to ear, many times over many generations. I am sure the exact original story could have been different, but I repeat it the exact way I heard it."

"How can you be sure if the story is true or not?" Hina asked.

"It is simple to answer your question," Vana replied. "Legends carry a moral or a lesson. As long as the living message is not lost, then the exact way facts happened is irrelevant. Legends are a teaching tool, that is all."

"I understand," Hina said looking at the embers in the fire, her thoughts running through her mind. Vana knew she would ask other questions. She had challenged him many times before, and today would be no exception. Then, she looked at him straight in the eyes.

"May I ask another question?" she said.

It was an anxious time for her father, who worried that the priest would become impatient or offended.

"Hina, Vana has other stories to tell," Tupua said with infuriated eyes, "he cannot answer all your questions."

"No, no, my friend," Vana objected, "I want Hina to ask her question."

"The breadfruit tree lives right here in the village," Hina said, "close to the sea, or sometimes slightly inside the valley. But, in your story, you mentioned it lived deep inside the valley or even in the mountains. There are no such trees in the mountains. Am I wrong?"

Vana looked at Hina with enlarged eyes, fascinated by the accuracy of her question. He thought the memory and analytical power of the girl were extraordinary. His dark eyes became shiny and enlivened with pleasure. He came closer to the girl, and placed one arm around her shoulders.

"A relevant question!" Vana exclaimed. "There are indeed such trees in the mountains, in the deep forest where you have never been. They are rare and sacred trees, called haamas, and they are the original breadfruit trees. The kind we have around here is domesticated, giving much larger fruits. However, these haamas yield fruits much more nourishing."

"What would you do..." She stopped when she saw her father. Then, she put her hands around Vana's ear.

"What would you do, if someone ate the haama fruit?" Hina whispered.

"It depends," Vana said. "If there were a famine, it would be permitted to eat the haama fruit. Indeed, we keep the haama for our survival. Also, sometimes, domestic trees develop diseases, and may disappear. In such a case, the priest would go to the original haama and develop a new generation of domestic breadfruit trees."

"Thank you, Vana," Hina said on a respectful tone. "Now, I think I understand."

Later in the evening, when Vana's stories put most people to sleep, the storm calmed down. Vana told the king what a fine girl Hina was.

"Her questions are good," the priest said. "I used to think she was too distant with everybody, but I was wrong. Hina is not challenged enough, that is her problem."

"But, she asks too many pertinent questions," Tupua said, overwhelmed by his friend's words, which were never complimentary without good reason.

"That is good," Vana said, raising his arms. "We don't have enough people like this. I often regret that everybody accepts what you or I say. Many of us are too simple, and take things for granted. One day things may change, and too few will be prepared."

"What do you mean?" Tupua asked, surprised by Vana's subtle implication.

"I don't know, my friend. It is just a premonition, and indeed things may change. We will need smart people around here, if we want to survive."

Vana went to sleep, eventually. Tupua was lost in his thoughts, did not see Hina come close to him, and jumped when she put a friendly hand on his shoulder.

"Father, may I ask you a question?"

"Now, it is my turn," Tupua whispered, amused. "Sit here. I am listening, but don't make it too complicated, I am only a king."

Hina giggled, then quickly regained her solemnity.

"Why did you name me Hina?"

The unexpected question had a stunning effect on the face of the king. There was indeed a good reason why he named her Hina, but how could she even suspect there was a reason? He had never shared his secret with anyone, but Vana. He knew Vana could not have told her. Therefore, he concluded that she just guessed there was a reason. Suddenly, he was compelled by her cleverness, and took her hands.

"My dear daughter, I am going to tell you the reason. Just before the night you were born, I had a dream, a beautiful dream. Still, it was a strange and disturbing dream."

He caught her attention. Hina stared at her father with puzzled eyes: She wanted to know more.

"I dreamed that my youngest daughter would be the mate of an extraordinary man. Because your mother and I were already too old to have children, I assumed your mother was carrying her last child. Then, I said to myself: If this last child happens to be a girl, I shall give her a beautiful and legendary name. I shall name her Hina."

"Who was that man?" Hina asked, her eyes bright with anticipation.

"I have no idea who he was, but I often thought about that vision. He was tall, not like us. He was strong but slender. His skin was clear, and his face like someone I had never seen before. He had long black hair, long ears, a long, thin nose, and thin lips. Above all, he had amazing dark blue eyes, giving him an impressive and enigmatic look. He was calm, kind, assessing everyone and everything, and seemed to irradiate a mysterious force."

"What does that have to do with the name Hina?" she asked, confused.

"Because I thought this man must have been someone

very important. Therefore, he should mate a woman equally important. If this woman should come from Tahiti-nui, if she should be my youngest daughter, thus I wanted her to be named Hina. Hina is a respected legendary princess in our old tradition. Giving a child this glorious name is an important matter, and the great priest must approve it.

"Did Vana approve?" Hina asked.

"Yes, he did, but only after I told him about my dream."

"Did he think your dream could be true?"

"He told me it was not a dream. It was much too detailed to be a dream, and must have been a premonition. He insisted that such a sign can become true many years later."

"Did you have any of these premonitions that became true, in the past?"

"Not really, but I know some people to whom it happened. It happened to Vana, for example."

"Of course!" Hina whispered, partially asleep.

At dawn, the storm was gone, and Hina wished she could walk along the beach looking for shells. She had always found new and unexpected shells after a storm, but she had to stay at the village with her mother and sister, cleaning around the house: Many plants and trees needed their attention. To her surprise, during the day, she thought several times about her father's dream. She tried to think about something else, but could not. For some reason it seemed important to her. So, on the evening of the same day, she went to her father.

"Do you think a man with blue eyes could exist?" she asked with perplexity.

"I don't think there is such a man," the King replied. "However, when you travel across the seas, you never know whom you may find."

"Are we going to travel?"

"No, but who knows, someone may one day, travel to us."

Hina looked at the sunset, and planned for the next day.

"Father, do you think I can walk to the Haapape village tomorrow? I know I will find many shells after the storm... Please."

"Of course, you can. The village is back in order now. But, you better leave early, at dawn, because other people may just do the same."

When Hina left Papenoo, the eastern sky barely showed a narrow pink strip along the horizon. The tide was low, and the sea very calm. A few stars were still shining, and she saw a shooting star: She thought it was a good sign for her day.

"I should walk directly to the Teauroa point," she murmured to herself. "It is the best place for nautiluses."

Several times, she ran on the black sand. When she arrived at the Teauroa point, the sun was not far behind the horizon, and she had already two nautilus shells in her hands. To her delight, their shells were not broken, as was often the case: They were perfect. She glanced at the sea. Behind the barrier of reef, she saw a dark spot, drifting.

It must be a fisherman with his outrigger canoe, she thought. But, this is an unusual place...

Several times she looked again at the drifting object, and saw it was not an outrigger canoe. It looked more bulky, like several tree trunks attached to one another. Finally, she saw nobody, and paid no more attention to it. She went inside the dunes where the waves had reached during the storm.

Here is another nautilus shell. It is beautiful, and larger than the other two.

She took the shell, and looked at it with excitement. Then, she walked to her favorite place. It was an old sand dune, farther inland, surrounded by tiare bushes. She stopped and collected a few of the strongly perfumed flowers just starting to open with the sunrise. The tiare was her favorite fragrant flower. It was a pure-white, majestic flower, made of seven slightly spiraling petals, about half the size of her hand. She knew several places to find tiares, and each day she would place a new flower on her ear. She sat on the black sand, as her mind traveled along the spectacular jagged peaks leading to grandiose Mount Orohena. Already, the sun lit its summit. The air was so clear, she thought she could touch the mountain. She could see details of the distant tree ferns near the formidable cliffs.

"My name is Hina," she murmured. "It is a special name given to special women. One day, I will become Hina of the Valley, who will be remembered because she was the only woman to climb to the lake where the red ducks live. Furthermore, Hina of the Valley will climb the forbidden Mount Orohena, something no man has ever done."

She felt a light breeze blowing at her side. She turned around and saw a vortex of fine black sand climb the dune, stop near her, and vanish. For the first time in her life, she considered that spirits might truly exist.

****

CHAPTER 5

"When the white-tailed tropicbird came to me, astounded I was. Overwhelmed I became, when the majestic bird showed me the imposing mountain."

Kon Tici Viracocha

At night, Kon buried his last companion. Ilo and Ra would rest, side by side, on this atoll lost on the awesome sea. Hopeless, miserable, and shivering, Kon swallowed his despair. He looked at the stars, but they were meaningless. His destiny was a dark hole in which he could not see, comprehend or endure. For some time, he would have to rely on instinct alone.

At dawn, he stepped on the raft, released the anchor and raised the sail. Pushed by a gentle breeze, the raft drifted westward across the atoll. Kon looked at the marvelous undersea garden with no joy. The dazzling display of beauty did not move him. His eyes could see, but his soul was blind.

Close to the other side of the atoll, an automaton paddled the raft into the current leading to a pass. Two hammerhead sharks visited the drifting intruder, but Kon did not see them and did not care. The tide still receded, and the raft exited into the open sea with no problem.

The Son of the Sun looked behind him. Faraway, he could

see the coconut trees shading his companions. Never again he would see these trees. The force of attrition had disseminated the last of Viracocha's sons. Would they regroup some day, or were they a total loss? Kon did not know the answer. With melancholy he looked ahead, thought about Illa somewhere on another raft and about Kukara, who had been through a similar devastating destiny. With courage, she had survived. The idea that she could be alive, somewhere, gave him renewed determination to pursue his journey toward the west.

Several days went by. He saw many seabirds, and once he saw the top of a few coconut trees above the southern horizon. He chose to ignore the island. Now, the birds were rarely seen. One time he saw a colony of terns and a few frigates. Two days later, he saw an isolated booby. Then, the birds totally vanished. Kon wandered on the calm sea for about one-half moon-cycle. By looking at the sun during the day and the stars at night, he knew he sailed northwestward.

With time, his mind healed, and fought his state of depression. Little by little he struggled through the visions of what his destiny could be. Many times he thought about Hina of the Valley, who created hope. He found pleasure in trolling the few lines he had saved. He caught bonitos and voracious needlefish, which gave him more food than he could eat. Kon Tici was well, and his resolve strong again.

One day, as he rested inside the cabin, he heard the characteristic loud grating call of a tern. Kon hurried outside, and bumped one shoulder on the entry of the cabin. He saw the bird fly away. He followed its direction toward the south, but there was no land. His eyes circled the horizon looking for a miracle. There was nothing. However, the northeastern sky was covered with massive, black clouds. Already the wind raised larger sea swells, and a heavy front of rain reached the raft. He collected some of the fresh water, and prepared for a new experience.

He took some ropes and attached everything he could to the logs under the deck. Afraid of being drowned at sea, he saved one rope for himself and secured it around his waist. Because the storm looked particularly violent, he rolled the sail down, and waited.

Gusts of wind suddenly slammed the raft. Kon took refuge inside the cabin, and tied the rope around his waist tighter. He just had enough length to walk freely from the cabin to the centerboard that he used as a rudder. The rain was so heavy that the visibility became nil. He felt the waves growing. From stress, he felt his heart pound, and he deeply hoped he would not collide with a reef.

It was not long before Kon experienced symptoms of something he had successfully escaped so far: seasickness. The more he thought about it, the more the sickness invaded him. The motion of the waves and the raft going up and down made him nauseated. Everywhere he looked, something was moving. He walked outside the cabin and let the rain and the wind slam on his face, washing the expulsed contents of his churning stomach. Never before, had Kon Tici felt so sick, and with an empty stomach the sickness became worse, literally plowing his entrails. He looked for a coconut, and managed to open one and drink its milky juice. He ate its fresh meat with no appetite. Still, the recovery was ephemeral, and his stomach was empty again. Soon, he gave up and lay on the deck, inside the cabin, hanging at one end of the rope.

Half-dead, Kon lost all sense of danger and time. He crawled outside the cabin, almost fell into the sea, crawled back to the cabin, sat in one corner and held the bamboo canes of the walls with both hands, his head hanging on his knees. Outside, the waves were more than three times the height of the mast. They were hills of water with titanic power, but the raft went up and down these hills like a small wood chip.

At times, Kon opened his eyes, and wished he was dead. Suddenly, he glanced at the entrance of the cabin and thought he was hallucinating.

"What is this? I don't believe it!"

He could not tell if the vision was a dream, the beginning of a new life or the impossible reality. A magnificent white-tailed tropicbird awkwardly walked into the cabin, looking for a shelter. The bird shook the water out of its feathers, and looked twice as normal for a short time. He looked at Kon, not even surprised. Kon reached the bird with one shaking hand. The bird, obviously very tired, crouched on the deck and did not object to the warm contact with the man.

Kon forgot his sickness for a moment. He knew that species of bird well and had observed them many times on the rocky coast of the continent. He had always been fascinated by the inaccessible places the bird selected for nesting, usually spectacular cliffs. This meant a lot: There was land around here, possibly with mountains. However, the night was coming. Furthermore, the storm was becoming a hurricane.

"By all the spirits in the Sun, this is my luck," Kon said with anger. "Every time I have come to a land mass, it has been at night. I shall not sleep, and be prepared."

Nonetheless, Kon had no illusion. With such sea swells, any collision with the coast would have meant certain death. He would have to wait, fear and trust his unknown destiny. Kon Tici refused to believe that he had made this trip to die here, in a storm. There must have been something else waiting for him. For the time being, the only thing he could do was to ignore the storm. Between unwanted sea showers, he chose to study the bird. Being able to look at this rare bird so closely was a golden opportunity as, after all, it might bring him good luck. The tropicbird was a large bird, as long as Kon's forearm, not counting the tail. Its pair of long white tail streamers was even longer than its body. Mostly white, the bird had black eye stripes and light black streaking on the wings and back. The tips of the wings were black. The beak was powerful, sharp, and bright red, as long as Kon's fingers. The bird was streamlined in appearance, but most of all, its tail was spectacular. Its very short legs, much too close to the tail, made its walk awkward: The bird was designed to fly, dive and swim, nothing else.

The white-tailed tropicbird walked behind Kon, came out on the other side and crouched. Kon tried to caress its head, but this time the bird clearly advised him that it was here only for convenience, and that it should not be touched. Its powerful beak attacked Kon's fingers with surprising speed and accuracy.

"Ouch! Silly bird, look at what you have done."

Kon retrieved his speared, bleeding fingers, and smiled. He liked the bird anyway. Its presence was a break in his loneliness, and hope for the next few days. He suddenly felt better, crawled near the entrance of the cabin, and looked outside. The gigantic whitecaps seemed to peak abruptly, instead of tumbling over in the direction of the wind. Kon concluded that the current traveled against the wind. Just before the storm, he remembered the wind came from the northeast. Therefore, it was possible that the current was coming from the southwest, which was most unusual. Kon was deeply disturbed by his observation. Something unusual was happening. Something was changing.

Suddenly, between two sea swells, the raft spun several

times. Kon immediately deduced that there were several currents converging upon one another. The only explanation for the phenomenon must have been the presence of one or several islands nearby. Still, visibility was poor in the dark night. More than ever, fear invaded him. He was terrified by the idea of battering the reef. He looked at the bird sleeping peacefully, and wished he could do the same.

Several times, mountains of water splashed on the raft, flattening the cabin on Kon's back, but the raft went over the tip of the wave every time. Once, there was so much water over the raft that Kon could not breathe, and the bird would awake and swim. As soon as the water drained between the logs, the bird crouched and went back to sleep. Kon knew he could not survive an encounter with the reef, but the bird most certainly would and its instinct knew this.

By midnight, the strength of the wind diminished rapidly. The waves were still enormous but longer, and the whitecaps not so imposing. Kon relaxed, though his fear of the reef was still real. He looked at himself, at the bird and at the tiny raft. He thought he was part of the elements of nature, and in the same way he was part of a mysterious plan. He had not slept for two days. Slowly his body gave up and collapsed on the deck. Curled up, Kon went to sleep. The tropicbird and Kon Tici traveled through another dimension.

Just when the sun rose, Kon awoke and heard the calls of many seabirds. He saw the tropicbird walk awkwardly outside. The sea was much calmer, and the visibility apparently good. The pink sunlight entered the cabin. The tropicbird took flight, sending a loud, rattling cry into the warm air. Kon went outside, and followed the bird that slowly turned westward. With no warning, Kon was suddenly overwhelmed by an astounding vision. His mouth dropped open. He rubbed his eyes, staring at the impossible dream. The entire southwestern horizon was filled with mountains reflecting the rising sun. To the south, there was a sharp summit, which was apparently the closest point relative to the raft. In the southwest, the island was separated into two halves by a low isthmus. The main part of the large island was to the west, culminated by a formidable summit, whose shape reminded him of the cliff-top of the City of the Sun. This was not by chance, he thought. Kon Tici knew immediately this island was the place for his destiny. He respectfully knelt on the deck, removed the rope from his waist, and reached out for the island with both arms. With tears blinding his eyes, he finally found reason for hope and happiness.

"This island resurrects my soul," he said. "From this place, I shall rebuild our future; I shall perpetuate the peaceful message of Viracocha's sons."

He kissed the deck.

"Powerful Creator, I thank you!"

He admired the beauty of the island. It was no ordinary island. He looked at the sharp cliffs, the deep valleys, the majestic falls, and the deep green cover of luxurious vegetation. From the sea, all the way up to the summits, there were no barren rocks. He could recognize the tiny outline of many coconut trees circling the coast, but he was not close enough to see beaches or the reef, if any.

Kon trembled from emotion. He tried to calm down and concentrate on what he had to do next. He checked the direction of the wind. It still came from the northeast, therefore it would push the raft toward the island. Then, he checked the current by looking at the crest of the waves. The crests tumbled slightly to the west, while the waves headed southwestward, in the direction of the isthmus. Therefore, the current ran parallel to the island, toward the west. All conditions were perfect for a smooth and straightforward approach. Kon smiled at last good luck was with him. He raised the sail and adjusted the centerboard to approach the island at a westward angle. By night he would be close enough, and would make his final approach in the dark.

Kon was too far from the coast for anyone to spot the sail, but many questions came to his mind. Was the island inhabited? If so, who were the people there? Where did they come from? Were they friendly? What was their culture? Were they primitive or advanced? He was alone, and could not afford to make a mistake. He took his time to carefully study the morphology of the island. Nothing indicated any human settlement, but he knew he was still too far to draw any accurate conclusion. He knew that someone up in the hills could eventually see the raft, so as a precaution, he rolled the sail halfway down. He was in no hurry: He needed to memorize the island for later, to think, and let the sea calm down. For a long time, he scrutinized every detail of the mountains, and memorized their sharp cliffs and vertiginous falls. He mapped the island in his mind. The thick vegetation reminded him of the great jungle of his homeland, and he wondered if it was as dangerous. He could see that the access to the valleys was not a simple matter. However, because of the many falls, he guessed there were many rivers that might simplify the access. He decided that he should reach the mountains without being discovered. In the mountains, he would be at a tremendous advantage. The experience of Viracocha's sons in the mountains and in the jungle was unsurpassed by anyone they had met. He would go to the mountains, recover, observe and find out who they were. Then, and only then, he would find an appropriate way to contact them.

By midday, Kon was just north of the isthmus separating the

two parts of the island, and much closer to the coast, but he could not see the beaches or the reef. The island was larger than he had imagined earlier, which added more dimension to its fantastic summit. Then, something new answered one of his questions. Not far from the isthmus, smoke billowed upward between the fronds of coconut trees: The island was inhabited, so he would not approach the island before night.

A crown of clouds developed around the summit. He wondered if there were other islands nearby. He scrutinized the horizon and saw none, at least from this side of the island. He thought these islanders must have been navigators, and maybe, they were traveling from island to island all the time. Indeed, they could have been excellent seafarers, and the thought troubled him. What would happen if he met some travelers, or fishermen? Kon feared his plans could be ruined if he continued approaching the island before dark. He changed his direction toward the northwest.

Along the main part of the island, not far from a majestic waterfall, the mountain seemed to plunge directly into the sea, with no place for a beach or any settlement. There was, however, a deep valley in which he could see gigantic trees. Before dark, he saw a few islets at some distance from the shore. They were characteristic clusters of coconut trees encircled by white-sand beaches. The barrier of coral was scattered at different distances from shore, often nonexistent or dismantled under the surface of the sea. He thought he was still too far from the tall mountain, whose summit was so attractive to him. So, he decided he would sail farther to the west, following the north side of the island during the night.

Right after sunset, the moon rose above the eastern horizon and he knew it was the time for a low tide to take place. Therefore, he knew the tide would be low again at dawn. The idea pleased him because the sea would be relatively calm then. The last thing he wanted was a repeat of a deadly collision with the reef. It was a must for him to remain physically strong. Later, he saw a few lights near a beach. The fires gave him an idea where people concentrated most. He quickly concluded there were many people, and mostly settled near the sea, never faraway from the line of coconut trees. During the night, he saw only two fires deep inside the valleys, and none in the mountains, the thought of which pleased him.

The sea was calm, and the night very clear, under the moonlight. A small breeze was strong enough to push the sail. The current was consistent, going west. Kon could accurately maneuver the raft with the sail and the centerboard, and he came closer and closer to the shore. Then, he wondered if someone could see him in the moonlight, something he had not thought about until now. It was too late to wonder about this, and he decided there was nothing he could do about it.

Some time before dawn, Kon sailed in front of a widely spread village. There were a few fires, and he could see the top of some vegetal roofs between trees. The houses seemed scattered, far from one another. They were not clustered like villages he saw before on the continent. He could also distinguish the phantom-like, formidable mountain. It looked like a sleeping giant, guardian of a seafaring race. This was the place where the enigmatic summit was nearest to the coast. He would have to land soon. He saw another islet. Then he heard the gentle rumbling of small waves dying on the reef, which circled a long point. After the point, there was a large bay. Kon decided to land at the point. Just before the point he saw a few sand dunes, then what looked like the mouth of a small river. He would walk up the river to avoid leaving visible footprints.

Kon unloaded the raft of all food, coconuts and water. With his knife he cut enough ropes to make the raft look like a wreck on which no one could have survived the storm. He took a large, heavy bag in which he had all the goods he wanted to save, and slowly went into the water. He swam to the reef on which he could walk with relative ease. He crossed it, them swam through the lagoon. In the east, the sky was already pink. Kon thought he would reach the river just at sunrise.

The lagoon was not deep. At times he could walk with water only as high as his chest. At other times, it was easier to swim above the crumbling branches of coral he knew painfully well. Slowly, he approached the mouth of the river. Nobody was on the beach. As far as he could see, there were no people.

Finally, Kon stopped swimming and walked into the river. The flow of the river was very slow, and its water was cool. Kon's body was no longer accustomed to unsalted water, and he found the contact delightful. He also noticed that the sand dunes and the beach were made of black sand and recalled his visions of the sandpiper and Hina of the Valley. Behind the dunes he saw a few dark green bushes covered with occasional white flowers. He smelled the strong fragrance of tropical flowers. He could not identify the perfume with anything he knew. Beyond the bushes were many coconut trees and other large trees he had never seen before.

After walking for awhile in the narrow river, there was enough vegetation on the banks for him to walk outside the water. He stepped outside the river, and for the first time in many moon-cycles, Kon Tici Viracocha walked on land. For him the atoll was no land. He felt his heart beat inside his chest, and there were many reasons for his emotion: He came here alive, it was a new land, there were new people and there was an impressive mountain. Kon thought that conditions were right for him. They were indeed right, beyond anything he could have imagined. At some distance, he saw a vortex of sand swirl and die on the dune. He stopped, recalled his visions, then pursued his journey.

****

CHAPTER 6

"I placed my life into Hina's hands as her inheritance,
so she might receive it, honor it, add to it,
and one day faithfully hand it to the people of Tahiti-nui."

Kon Tici Viracocha

Sitting on the black sand, behind the tiare bush, Hina smelled the fragrant flowers. She leaned back, closed her eyes, listened to the breeze, the gentle waves, the awakening birds and someone walking in the Vaipopoo River.

Caressing the delicate petals of a tiare flower, she wondered who could be walking in the river so early, and so far from the nearest village. She looked under the bush. A soft gasp escaped her, then she remained silent. Stunned, she observed the tall man. She closed her eyes and her mind spun between what could have been a dream or the unbelievable reality.

This is impossible, she thought. This is the man of my father's dream.

She opened her eyes and looked at him walking away. He stopped, looked around, showing his long beard. His skin was lighter than hers, though her skin was lighter than the average Tahitian. His garments were unusual and torn. She could not see his eyes, but his long hanging earlobes astonished her. She was paralyzed, unable to do anything, her large black eyes wide open.

The land seemed totally unknown to him. His legs were bleeding: She thought he must have been swimming and walking across the lagoon, but why should he swim through the lagoon? Then, she recalled the strange tree logs she had been puzzled by, instants earlier.

"He came on this raft," she murmured. "He came from another world, and he has survived this terrible storm."

She wondered why he looked at Mount Orohena so often, and what could have been his interest for the sacred mountain. Could it be the same interest as hers? She decided to follow him. Carefully, she pushed her three nautiluses under the bush and covered them with sand. She would come to take them another day. After he left the riverbed, the man stopped and looked behind him, concerned by his footprints. Why should he be concerned about his footprints? Is he afraid of us? Questions flooded her mind, but never once did she wonder if the man could be dangerous to her. Nevertheless, she followed him with extreme caution. She wondered where he would go, and what could be so heavy in his large bag. At times, he had to set the bag on the ground and rest. When he reached the first hills, he turned east, crossed the Tuauru River, went over another hill, and crossed the Aohu River. He admired the thick ferns, the flowers and the trees. Then, he turned in the direction of Mount Orohena, and followed the ridges from which he could see the valley of the Papenoo River.

Hina knew the land well, which made her pursuit easy. The man was obviously tired, still he was capable of walking fast, effectively, with a well-planned path. She thought he must have been familiar with mountains and forests.

It was about midday when the man took a break. He squatted among a cover of short ferns, and looked at the sea and the Papenoo Valley. He pushed his heavy bag under some large ferns, lay down near the bag and rolled under the ferns. The ease and silence of each of his movements impressed Hina. If she had not seen him roll under the ferns, she would have lost him. Where he was, no one could find him. She had been right; he was tired and was going to sleep under the ferns.

It was a nice sunny day, but Hina did not know what to do next. She thought she should let him sleep. If he went to the mountains, he would not find much food. She had seen him drink in the rivers, but he had not eaten anything. He must have been hungry. This is what she would do: go to the valley, collect a few fruits, and some medicine plants for his wounds. Then, she would come back, but what if he had left in the meantime. She would never find him again. He was too skilled at blending with the vegetation. It had been only by chance that she had found him. She also knew the man did not want to be discovered, and she knew he could remain elusive as long as he wished in the deep valley and the mountains. Would she take the risk of losing him? She pondered what to do, then decided to go to the valley. He was asleep, and she would not be gone very long.

Carefully, she walked away. As soon as she thought she was far enough, she ran down the valley, until she reached a narrow trail she knew very well. She put a stone on the side of the trail and looked at the trees, to remember the place on her way back. She forgot about the fruits, completely lost in her thoughts. She suddenly realized she had never been afraid of the man. Was it because of what her father told her, or was it because the man looked peaceful and gentle? He was strong, tall and impressive. Yet, he seemed to be a kind man. Or, was it wishful thinking, as she knew nothing about him? She shrugged her shoulders, leaving the answers for later. She thought about his long hair, his beard, and his enlarged earlobes, which made her laugh. Still, there was something about the man she could not explain, as if he had been filled with peace mixed with confidence and strength. She was puzzled, beyond anything she had ever imagined. She thought about her father's vision. How could such a thing be possible?

Her eyes happened to scan in front of a banana tree. Only then, she remembered she had come to look for fruits and medicine plants. The thought of losing him pushed her to activate her search. Quickly, she selected a few bananas, taros and sugar canes. She wrapped them inside banana tree leaves, and tied them closed with long grass she found near the stream. She made a loop, so she could hold the package like a basket. Then, she looked for some medicine plants, on which she was not an expert. She wished Vana could have been with her, to counsel her. In a small meadow along the creek, she found a tree the priests protected. It was called a tamanu, and was often grown around temples. She knew about the healing properties of its yellow seeds, enclosed in a round shell. She took several shells, and ran back to the hills. She rapidly found the place to leave the trail, and followed her own tracks through the thick cover of ferns. She hoped the man had not left. Her heart pounded, both from her uphill run and from the idea of meeting the man of her father's dream. She wondered if he could have blue eyes.

At some distance from the man, she stopped to recover her breath and think about the best way to meet him. She did not want to wake him up from too far, as he might run away from her. She came a little closer to make sure he was still under the ferns. She saw he was still asleep. She waited for awhile, smiling at the idea she was going to scare him: There was no other way.

She walked straight to him, as if it was natural, and as if she had always known him. As she approached, she could not help laughing in a childish way. The man sat up and came out of the ferns, looking at the girl, and glanced around to see if she was alone.

Hina instantly stopped laughing, kneeled in front of him, her lips trembling with emotion. She looked at him straight in the eyes, dropped her bag, stunned by their deep blue color. Indeed, he was the man of her father's dream. So, it had not been a dream, it had been a vision of the future. The man looked around again. She understood his concern and tried to reassure him, but he did not understand what she said. With some gestures, she managed to explain that she was alone.

She kept looking at his dark blue eyes, and thought they were as beautiful as the deep blue lagoon. His eyes were slightly slanted, his nose was long and narrow, and his lips were thin. He looked younger than what she had thought. Surprised and magnetized, she gave him a warm smile. Kon saw peace, innocence and tenderness in her large black eyes. There was something familiar about the girl, and he thought he had seen her face before. A flash of humor crossed his face, which made her more comfortable. He reached for her trembling hands. They were soft, warm and well maintained. The friendly contact with the man's hands clearly showed Hina she could trust him. She was not afraid, she stared at him, waiting in silence.

Kon knew the girl would not understand him. Just to be sure, he tried several simple words in five different languages he had knowledge of. She understood none of them. He took her hand, and let her touch his chest. At the same time he pronounced his name.

"Kon."

He repeated the gesture, and his name several times. Hina

understood immediately. She placed her hand on his chest and pronounced his name perfectly right the first time.

"Kon!"

He smiled and seemed to approve. She took his hand, and let him touch her chest. At the same time she pronounced her name.

"Hina."

The man opened his eyes wide, and seemed deeply troubled by her name. Exactly as he did, she repeated the gesture, and her name several times.

"Hina," Kon said.

She gave him the warmest and most enchanting smile he ever saw on the face of a woman. She was the woman of his visions. She was Hina of the Valley, but some years younger. Suddenly, a path for his destiny germinated in his mind. Then, he tried his full name.

"Kon Tici Viracocha"

"Kon Teke Viro..., Kon Teke Vichacora, Chacoravi..."

Both laughed with joy. He tried several times again, then gave up with teaching her to say Viracocha. He also noticed she could not pronounce Tici correctly. It seemed the sound did not exist in her language, but she was consistent with saying Teke.

"Kon Teke," she said victoriously.

For him, it was close enough. She opened her basket and showed him the food she had brought. She started eating a banana and invited him to do the same. They ate together, and Kon was indeed starving. He wondered how long she had been following him. Kon went to a small creek, washed his hands and drank the fresh water coming from a nearby waterfall. He squatted where some sand had accumulated during rainfalls. He invited her to sit near him. He took a stick of wood and drew on the sand.

She understood he was trying to explain something.

Interested, she concentrated on his drawings. He drew many people at the bottom of a hill. Then, he drew one large and one small person at the top of the hill. She understood the people at the bottom of the hill were her people. The ones at the top of the hill were he and she. What was he trying to tell her?

Kon pointed to her people, he placed one hand on his chest, then one finger on her lips, as if he wanted to close her mouth. She understood. He did not want her to talk about him. He wanted him to be her secret.

Hina seemed to object to the idea. She explained with gestures that she would take him to the village. Then, she took the stick and drew. Among her people she drew a larger man with what he thought to be a sun around his head. She drew a few people bending at his feet. Kon understood he must have been the chief, or the king. Then, she drew a woman and two children near the king. He understood the woman was the king's wife with his children.

"Tupua," Hina said pointing at the king,

"Atea," pointing at the woman,

"Fenua," pointing at the tallest child,

"Hina," pointing at the smallest child.

He looked at her, surprised. He looked at her drawings. Could it be possible that she was the daughter of the king? In such a case, she could be a tremendous asset to him. She was an aristocrat, cultivated, initiated, and well informed about everything. This was one more reason why he wanted to take his time, learn her language, her people's culture and traditions. Kon showed the king with the stick, then placed one finger on her lips again, and made sure she understood he did not want her to talk.

Hina realized he understood her message, but his mind was set. He did not want her to talk about him to anyone. She closed her mouth with her fingers: She would not talk. Kon smiled, and caressed her hair in recognition, wondering if he could trust her. She seemed to have a character of her own, and somehow he thought she would not talk. He also knew he would see her again.

Kon understood she wanted to show him something. He took his bag, and they walked to a valley heading deep into the heart of the mountain. She pointed to a cliff at the end of the valley, where he saw a dark, narrow opening. It was the top of a cave entrance. With gestures, she explained he could put his bag in the cave and sleep there.

Hina went back to the creek, and made more drawings from which he vaguely understood that nobody would come to this valley or the cave. After a few more efforts, she finally made clear that in this area Kon would be safe, and nobody would ever suspect his presence. She also explained to him that they would meet at the place where they drew on the sand. He thought she was a clever child in the ways she tried to communicate.

It was late in the afternoon. Hina explained she had to go back to the village, but she would be back in the morning. He understood. They looked at each other a long time, then she pronounced his name slowly, with a gentle and soft voice.

"Kon Teke."

"Hina," Kon murmured.

She left, and ran downhill, without turning back. He looked at her going away until she disappeared among the large ferns. It had been an unforgettable day. Kon was happy, puzzled and elated. He took a needed bath and relaxed in the cool stream. In the morning, he would honor the young woman by showing her the real Kon Tici Viracocha.

Kon took Hina's bag with the few fruits left inside, put it in his bag and walked to the valley. The access of the cave did not seem to present major difficulties, except for a thick cover of vegetation. He walked uphill, admiring the luxuriant plants, and thinking about Hina. He noticed there were very few insects, and no snakes, which pleased him. The variety of ferns was astonishing to him. There were all kinds and all sizes, from small, silky hair-like capillaries to the giant tree ferns with imposing feathery fronds, to intriguing fiddleheads. Many ferns grew on tree trunks and branches. It was humid, with a strong smell of humus. He stopped and looked around, intrigued by the silence and a totally different world.

He reached the cave when the sun disappeared behind the western mountains. There was no sign of any recent visit. He wondered how Hina knew about this forgotten place. He entered the cave and found the answer. In front of him, in the darkness, was an outrigger canoe covered in dust. Inside, a mummy rested in perpetual silence. The body was wrapped inside tight layers of a dusty white, felted bark cloth, like Hina's garment. On the forehead, tattoos were still visible on the dried skin. After a brief inspection of the canoe, Kon deducted the burial was not very old, two or three generations at most.

Tired, he sat at the entrance of the cave, where he had a fantastic view of the valley, all the way to the sea. The main river meandered along the valley, and was the recipient of many tributary streams. Then, he reflected on what Hina had done. There was no doubt the cave was a sacred burial, where no one had the right to go. She knew this, and it was the reason why she selected that place for him. Furthermore, because of her father's rank, she probably was one of the few persons who knew about the place. This resting mummy could have been one of her forefathers. Still, to protect him, she showed the forbidden place. Without knowing anything about him, she had been thoughtful and compassionate. For an unknown reason, she had acted as if she had always known him, or as if she had been waiting for him. Freedom and safety invaded his mind. He knew he could trust Hina: She would not betray their secret as long as he wished. She was a child of honor.

He thought she could have seen him as he swam from the lagoon to the river. Could anyone else have seen him? Not likely, or at least Hina was not aware of it. He recalled several instances when he had the impression that someone was following him. Each time he had thought it was only fear, but he had been right: Hina was following him. Then, she let him sleep for a long time, went to collect some fruits for him, came back and made sure they would meet. He thought her behavior and logic had been superb. With natural simplicity she was direct, precise and very effective. She was a clever girl.

He took Hina's basket, unwrapped it, and found a few nuts among the fruits. He broke one nut, chewed the seed, and immediately spat. It could not have been food, and he would ask Hina in the morning. He ate the tasty fruits he had never seen before, looking at the sky becoming dark. Very high in the sky, he saw some birds come back from the sea, and head for the distant cliffs. He recognized the long streamer tail characteristic of tropicbirds. He walked away from the cave entrance, and tried to follow the closest bird. There was no doubt, it was a white-tailed tropicbird heading toward the huge mountain at the end of the valley. They were going home, where no man, or very few, could go.

Kon cut large and coarse fern fronds. With half of them he prepared a bed. With the other half he would cover himself during the cool night. He found the ground in the cave remarkably dry, in spite of the storm that had hit the island two days earlier. Kon

Tici was at home in the cave of Hina's forefather. Peacefully, he went to sleep and shared dreams with the wandering spirits from beyond the known world.

At some distance from Hina's village, near the river and under a very old banyan tree, a shadow left a decaying house. The place was feared by everyone on the island, and was inhabited by the living remains of an old great priest. The shadow went to a swamp full of reeds, and remained still until the night invaded the valley. The shadow saw Hina coming from the valley, going back to the village.

"Hina of the Valley," the shadow murmured, "you are mine, because you have been chosen."

Hina felt a little breeze at her side, stopped and looked toward the river. She saw the old banyan tree and the swamp full of reeds. Near the swamp, she saw what she thought to be a vortex of dust like the one she had seen on the sand dunes. However, it was already too dark, and she was not sure. She also felt as if someone had spoken to her. She shrugged her shoulders, and left.

Along the river, she saw a tamanu tree. "I forgot!" she said to herself. "I completely forgot about the wounds on his legs. Tomorrow, I will show him how to use the seeds."

She wondered what she should bring to him, besides food. She would give him a bark cloth to cover himself during the cold nights in the mountain.

She reached the village and went straight to her father's house. At the entrance, she saw Vana, Tupua and some other men involved in a passionate discussion. What could they be talking about? She approached the group, and instantly felt a chill in her back. They were talking about the raft they had found behind the reef at the Teauroa point. Could they know about Kon? Could they know he went to the mountain? She listened carefully, pretending innocent interest.

Her father wanted to know if someone had been on the raft, and swam to the coast. If it was the case, he wanted no harm to the travelers, but he wanted to know who they were and where they came from. Vana philosophized about the possible origin of the trees with which the raft was made. There was nothing like them in the world he knew. His conclusion was clear: The raft came from a very distant place, unknown to him, somewhere in the east. Most puzzling to him was the part of the sun so nicely embroidered on the sail that, at some time, had been cut to a smaller size. Whoever those people were, they worshiped the sun. Awakening to the fact that Tupua was not listening, Vana explained that no one could have survived the storm with a raft that was a total wreck.

"The wreck drifted here on its own," Vana said, "long after its passengers died."

For Tupua, Vana's words were good enough. Hina felt relief. Nobody would ever suspect the presence of Kon in the mountain cave, but why did he want to stay alone? She went to the beach and sat on the black sand. Kon did not know anyone but she. He did not know her language. His motive was simple: He wanted to learn about her people, therefore he had to learn her language, and with her he would. She drew a hill on the sand, several people at the bottom, and two at the top. She smiled and erased her sketch.

"Who are you, Kon Teke?" she murmured.

Back at her father's house, Hina had a difficult time suppressing her excitement. Her mother noticed her unusual behavior, similar to an excess of joy.

"Did you find any shells, today?" Atea asked.

"Yes, I found three nautiluses, but I left them at the Teauroa point under a tiare bush. I found a friend, we walked all day together in the valley, then it was too late for me to go back to get them."

"It is unusual for you to spend an entire day with a friend. Is it a boy or a girl?"

"It is a boy," Hina answered, "but don't be afraid, mother, he is no ordinary boy."

"Well, I am not afraid, but remember your rank. You cannot play with any boy unless he is from a noble family."

"I know, mother," Hina replied with irritation. "But people can also be good friends. My main interest was in visiting the deep valley with someone who likes it. I enjoyed it, and I will most certainly go back to the valley very often. On my way back, I saw a lot of birds returning from the sea."

"Did you see any tropicbirds?" Atea asked.

"Yes, there were tropicbirds," Hina said. "I am fond of their tail feathers."

"I remember when I was your age, I often went high in the valley with your father. From the foot of a waterfall we could see the tropicbirds nesting very high on the cliffs. At that time there were both red-tailed and white-tailed tropicbirds."

"I did not know we could find red-tailed tropicbirds on Tahiti-nui," Hina said.

"They often change their habitat," Atea said. "Some years you may see many, some other years they nearly disappear."

"How can the men find them, and take the feathers from their tail?"

"On lower islands it is much easier," Atea replied. "But here, only outstanding climbers can reach a few nests, which are always built on dangerous cliffs. The nest is vigorously defended both by the chick and the parents."

"Do they have only one chick?" Hina asked.

"Yes, it is a sacred bird that needs to be protected."

"I would like to have some of their feathers, they are so beautiful."

"Sometimes, they fight between themselves, and it is not unusual to find a feather at the foot of the waterfall I was talking about. However, most of the time they are feathers from the more abundant white-tailed tropicbird."

Hina's father came in the house. Hina gave him a warm hug, and told him she had had a very good day. She wanted to tell him about Kon so much that she could not find anything to say, but she had given her word to Kon, so she would not tell anyone about him. In the morning she would go back to the valley, and nobody should become suspicious. She chose a direct attitude, so everything would look more natural.

"Tomorrow, I want to go back to the valley with my friend. I will be gone all day. I am the one who would take the food for both of us. Maybe we will find some tropicbird feathers at the bottom of the cliffs mother mentioned."

"Do you remember?" Tupua said with a boyish smile, and looking at his wife. "It was a long time ago, before we mated."

Atea's entire face spread into a smile: Tupua remembered.

"Who is your friend?" the king asked his daughter.

"This is my secret for now," Hina said with a furtive grin, "but don't worry, my Father, I am aware of your rank. I will never become a disgrace to our family. On this you can trust me."

"I trust you for everything," Tupua said, caressing her long hair. "It is wonderful to have secrets at your age. It gives you freedom to experience all the wonders of this short life."

That night, Hina could not sleep. She always saw the face

of the man she met, his beard, his long, thin nose, his thin lips, and his dark blue eyes. Never before had she seen so enigmatic a face, filled with powerful peace. He was no ordinary man. She remembered the skill with which he could explain himself with sketches or gestures. He had always found a way for her to understand his message at his first attempt. She had much more difficulty to make herself understood. She thought the man would be fascinating to her father and Vana. In due time, they would meet him. Then, she thought about her father's words: "I dreamed that my youngest daughter would be the mate of an extraordinary man." Could it be possible? The thought was unbelievable to her; still, she liked him, she admired him and she protected him. Her large black eyes opened wide, looked at the moonlight through the doorway; she wanted to know more about him, much more. Her eyes were far away in space. For the time being, her body was forgotten, and she became the legendary Hina of the Moon.

A long time ago, on the island of Havaiki, Princess Hina sailed with her brother Ru for a great voyage of discovery. For many days, Hina and Ru raced side by side in their respective outrigger canoes. One evening, when the moon was full, Hina sailed off on her own to visit it. She liked it so much she set her canoe adrift and stayed there. She became Hina of the Moon, guardian of daring seafarers. When the moon was bright, she could be seen making bark cloth from the numerous branches of the banyan tree, the shape of which could be seen in the shadows on the moon. On one occasion, she broke off a branch of the tree with such force that it swirled through space and landed as a powerful whirlpool near the Papenoo River. At this place, a giant banyan tree took root and became the first banyan tree in the world. Since then, the banyan tree had been protected, and looked at only from a distance. When the sun was low, priests gathered at the tip of its shade and told stories to the distant people.

At dawn, Kon squatted at the entrance of the cave and studied every detail of the valley. He heard the loud "kwack" of what he thought to be a bittern near the river. Slowly, life awoke in what seemed a paradise. Would Hina come? He knew she would, but how difficult would it be for her to vanish so often from her people without raising suspicion? He understood she might not always be able to do what she wanted. He unpacked his bag, and dressed himself with a new white robe covering his body from his shoulders to his thighs. It was the characteristic dress of Viracocha's sons, showing simplicity with class. He attached a white belt around his waist, embroidered with two parallel blue frets with red suns between. He tied a new pair of sandals around his feet. He placed the gold disks in his enlarged earlobes, and circled his wrists with large gold bracelets. On one bracelet a sun was carved, on the other a gliding condor. He attached a gold necklace around his neck, supporting a large gold coin pendant on which symbols of the sun, water and mountain were carved. Above the mountain representing the sharp cliff-top of the City of the Sun, was a magnificent gliding condor. He attached his long, straight hair above his head with a gold hairpin. His hair fell gracefully around his shoulders. Finally, he placed a white headband around the upper half of his forehead, embroidered with the same blue frets and red suns as on his belt. Then, he took his knife and cut his beard shorter. This was the real Kon Tici. He smiled at the idea that Hina might not even recognize him.

Kon walked to their meeting place, sat near the stream and ate the two bananas he had left. Not long after the sun rose above the eastern range, he heard Hina walk up through the ferns. She reached the place where she had surprised him the day before.

She did not see him sitting cross-legged in the shade, near the stream. He threw a small stone near her. She turned around and saw him stand up and walk toward her. For an instant she became paralyzed, as if she was meeting him for the first time again. She laid her basket on the ground, hesitated with conflicting emotions, looked at his dress, and finally saw the glittering objects. She could not keep her eyes away from his necklace, earplugs, bracelets, and hairpin, shining as the sun. They were made of material she had never seen before. She touched the large gold coin hanging on his chest, was shocked at its weight, and shook her head with amazement. As she recovered from her surprise, she gave him a radiant smile. She took some of his hair in her hand and looked at it closely. The day before she had seen his black hair, but had not noticed the auburn glints under the sunlight. She thought his hair was most unusual.

Kon took her basket and they walked to the cave. She held his hand, and did not say a word until they approached the cave entrance where she realized she was trespassing a taboo. With signs she explained she did not want to enter the cave. Kon smiled, put his hand around her shoulder, and invited her to come in the cave with him. Reluctantly, she walked with him to the outrigger canoe. She bent down and drew on the dirt a man with a child, three times.

"Hina," she said, showing the child on the far right. Then, she showed the man on the far left and pointed at the canoe. He was her great-grandfather. Therefore, it was a royal tomb. She explained that he could stay in the cave, but she preferred keeping out of it. Kon respected her wish, took her hand, and they exited. With signs he asked her where she wanted to go. She took him to the nearby cliff and showed him the deep valley of the Papenoo River, ending in front of a sharp range of mountains. She pointed at a part of the valley turning toward Mount Orohena, but they could not see the end. Hina explained they would go to the end of the part of the valley they could not see, but he could imagine the fantastic view of the mountain they would have at this place where the sacred giant was plunging straight down to the valley. He was thrilled with Hina's idea.

As she walked ahead of him, he observed her. Her dress was simple, like a single piece of white bark cloth wrapped around her body from the upper chest to her thigh. Still, she was elegant. Her hair was magnificent, blue-black, slightly waving all the way down to her waist. She showed only very early signs of womanhood. She wore a fragrant white flower above one ear, which added to her charm. She must have covered her body with fragrant oily perfume prepared with the same flower. The odor was strong, but pleasant. Her sandals were made of coconut husk. It was a clever design, but not as reliable as his leather sandals. She was thin, but solidly built and energetic. Her steps were precise and her balance good.

By midmorning, they reached a small river that Hina called Vaitamanu. The forest became increasingly thicker and darker. At times, through the top of gigantic trees, Kon could glance at the formidable mountain rising into the sky. He was puzzled that they could come so close to it, yet never climb anything. Along the way Hina taught Kon the names of plants, trees, ferns and birds. Several times he took her hand, and would ask for the name of something unusual to him. He would ask her to repeat what he had already forgotten. They learned each other's key words such as: river, water, mountain, sun, sky, clouds and so on. They were so involved in learning that they did not realize they were approaching a meadow. They left the dark forest. They looked up, silent, in total ecstasy. There were no words to describe the scenery. The river became a small stream, and the tiny trail became steeper, until they reached a majestic waterfall ending in a clear pond framed by a spectacular rainbow. The mist from the falling water refreshed their faces. Kon looked at Mount Orohena. It was here. It was everywhere. Its powerful presence obliterated everything else. It was undoubtedly a silent force. They were at the foot of an awesome wall of volcanic rock covered with ferns, incredible cliffs, narrow ledges and waterfalls. It was a breathtaking sight Kon had not seen anywhere else. For him it was a powerful incentive for a fascinating journey. The mountain was full of mysteries, and no matter how imaginative Kon could have been, he would have never envisioned what he was going to do on this mountain.

"Orohena!" Hina said, pointing at the summit straight up in the sky.

He looked at her. She was a beautiful girl. Her sparkling black eyes circled with long black eyelashes, showed happiness and care. How could she have known so soon this was the most important place for him to be? She knew she would give him pleasure by coming here, and that was the reason she looked so happy. Why should she make him happy? Why should she care so much about him? He did not know the answers, but he knew that nobody could explain those forces that may tie durable bonds between two people. For Kon and Hina, the Creator was at work.

As he looked at her, she saw his heart and his tenderness. She knew he liked her, and she liked him. She was still a child, but as he looked at her face, her soft cheeks, her charming nose, which was a little too wide, her full lips, and her cheekbones and delicately carved chin, he knew she would soon become a beautiful woman. Intuitively, he knew she would become important in his life, just as he knew the mountain would be. Both looked at Mount Orohena. A dense, tropical vegetation, mostly ferns, covered everything except the steepest cliffs. It was obvious that only the hardiest of souls would dare penetrating the secret of the sacred mountain. For Kon, climbing the mountain was a must, and discovering its secrets was a promise, but he would wait. Today, Hina introduced him to a new world.

They sat, cross-legged, above a cover of fragile ferns. Hina unwrapped her basket. She took out a white fruit that resembled a coconut. She took Kon's knife, looked at its curious shape, split the fruit in two halves, and gave him one. To his surprise, the fruit was still warm: It had been cooked and peeled. Its taste reminded him of the sweet potatoes from the continent, but it was richer with more flavor. Hina seemed to love the fruit, and she ate it with a voracious appetite: For that he teased her, and they both burst into laugher.

Hina looked at the gold coin hanging on Kon's chest.

"Orohena?" she asked, pointing at the cliff-top of the City of the Sun.

He was amused by her innocent naivete. She was right, there was a striking resemblance between Mount Orohena and the cliff-top of the ancient city. Kon himself had made the same observation, the morning he had seen the mountain for the first time.

Suddenly, they heard the loud, rattling cry of a tropicbird above them. They stood up and followed the bird's swirling path in the ascending air current. It was a white-tailed tropicbird coming back to its nest, far above the waterfall, on the vertical cliff. Hina jumped with joy, and she explained she wanted the long feathers from the bird tail. Moved by the girl's joy, Kon explained he would climb to get the feathers for her.

First, she smiled at him with surprise, then her face became hard. It was the first time he saw her frown. She shook her head with disapproval, trying to explain it was too dangerous, but he insisted he would climb and his mind was made up. Sadly, she realized it was impossible to stop him, and he was already climbing. She deeply regretted having shown so much eagerness for the long feathers. Next time, she would have to think twice before asking something from Kon Tici. Now she knew he was a calm man who did not fear the most dangerous challenge. He was a man with high goals, regardless of the price.

Twice, he slipped over the natural stairs under the waterfall. He looked at the rock closely, then selected a more secure path where the ferns would help him to maintain his balance. With apprehension, two large black eyes followed his every step. As he reached the first major obstacle, she expected to see a man somewhat hampered, but with precise steps and very little help from his hands, he overcame the cliff with remarkable ease. Admiration succeeded her fear, yet the worse was to come. Kon accelerated his pace with increasing ease and skill. Obstacles became more and more difficult, and the mountain rapidly became a forbidden wall, but Kon Tici progressed, smooth, confident, and unchallenged. Surprise succeeded her admiration, yet the cliffs headed into the sky with appalling steepness. She recalled looking at the climbers from her village. She remembered Aru, her sister's friend; he was the best climber. Still, she had never seen him climb as well as this man from another world. She deduced that he must have been living in the mountains before. She wondered what such a world could look like. Was it conceivable that higher mountain than Mount Orohena existed?

Ahead of Kon, the wall became vertical. He stopped and scrutinized all possible paths, all rifts, and all ferns. Then, he attacked the last barrier before the tropicbird's nest, with the same ease and skills. Nothing seemed difficult enough to stop his progress. Hina sat on a stone, fascinated by a display of mountaineering skill she had never thought possible. Her fear became confidence, and admiration supplemented with respect. Hina knew Aru could climb the same cliffs, and her surprise was not the fact that Kon could climb to the tropicbird's nest, but the lightness, precision and confidence of all Kon's movements surprised her most. He made the dangerous climbing look simple and safe.

Kon finally reached the nest where a female sat on one egg, and pulled the two long feathers from its tail. The bird screamed and vehemently complained with its powerful red beak. Kon heard Hina applaud, and waved at her with the feathers in his hand. Hina thought Kon would come back. She never suspected what would happen next. Kon studied the mountain above him. Far above, he saw another nest with a larger bird sitting on it: It was a red-tailed tropicbird. He placed the two feathers between some ferns, and continued his journey up.

This time, Hina's mouth dropped open. She looked above Kon, and saw where he was heading. Her head spun from confusion and disbelief.

"No! This is impossible," she murmured to herself. "If I would tell this at the village, nobody would believe me."

Slowly, cautiously, but steadily, Kon escalated a cliff where no man before had dared. There was no place to put his feet or his hands. Still, Kon Tici found enough tiny cracks, ferns, and protuberances to discover the inner secrets of the mountain. He worked with toes and fingers. For Hina, it was like magic, and she rubbed her eyes to make sure she was not dreaming. She felt a chill on her back. Who was that man? She suddenly realized how little she knew about him. Was he a man, or something else?

She felt overwhelmed by too many mysteries. Then, she became even more determined to learn his language and teach him hers. She watched him reach the nest of the red-tailed tropicbird and could not contain a question that came again, and again.

"Who are you, Kon Teke?"

She had the premonition that the more she would know him, the more she would be puzzled, and wider would the gap between herself and Kon Tici would become. Now, she understood the reasons why Kon wanted to learn her language before contacting her people: He was afraid to shock them without being able to explain the reasons for his actions.

After exchanging a few vigorous arguments with the bird, Kon succeeded to pull out the two long, red streamers. However, he did not see a new threat coming, fast, determined, and deadly. Suddenly, Hina gasped, then screamed.

"Kon!"

Alarmed, Kon glanced around and saw another red-tailed tropicbird plunge from great height directly at him. The bird was on a suicidal mission to protect his nest. The powerful red bill was coming at the speed of a hurled spear. Kon raised one arm, and hit the bird under the chest. Deflected just in time, the bird crashed among ferns growing on the top of a narrow ledge. It took a moment for the bird to regain consciousness and start attacking Kon again with his snapping wings: The bird was angry. Kon climbed on the ledge, and walked away from a territory where he did not belong. He found a place where he could sit and contemplate a breathtaking view of the valley and the mountain. He waved at Hina, and smiled at the thought she had saved him from serious injury. He had not anticipated the ferocious attack from the bird.

He looked at the ledge curving toward the north. Not too

far above it, he saw the dark shadow of a cave entrance. Because of the ledge in front of the cave, it was impossible to see the entrance from the valley. It would have been equally impossible to suspect the presence of the cave from the top of the mountain still far away in the sky. The size of the entrance was quite large. Suddenly, in the blink of an eye, he thought he had seen a shadow moving across the entrance of the cave. It had been so quick that he was not sure, or perhaps it had been a large bird. He thought he should visit the cave, but Hina waited. Soon it would be time for her to go back to her village. Reluctantly, he started his long and hazardous descent, after glancing one more time at the intriguing hole leading inside the mountain.

It was mid-afternoon when he reached the pond under the waterfall, where Hina waited. He gave her the four feathers. With admiration and almost afraid to touch them, she took his present and looked at him with modesty. He understood her confusion about him, the man she had met only the day before. To comfort her he put his hand on her shoulder and hugged her gently. She did not know how to thank him, so she tiptoed and kissed him.

Hina walked to the pond, and with signs invited him to come. Then, she did something Kon had not expected. She removed her cloth, innocently revealing her delicate, golden young body, and she dived into the pond. She swam under water until she reached the waterfall, and she let the falling water run down her face. Again, she invited him to do the same. Amused by her natural act, he undressed and dived in. They played for awhile, splashing water onto each other's face. Hina jumped on Kon's back, pushed his head under water until he suffocated, then she swam away. He tried to follow her, but she was much faster: Against a seafaring islander in water, he was no competition.

Hina showed him the sun. It was time for them to leave. With stones she crushed the Tamanu seeds she had saved in her basket. She formed a thick oily paste, and applied it to Kon's old wounds. Now, he understood what those seeds were.

On their way back they recalled all the words they had learned. When they reached the cave, she stopped, looking at him with expressive eyes. Then she looked at the feathers.

"Thank you, Kon Teke," she said, with a glint of humor in her eyes.

He kissed her on her forehead. She turned around and disappeared between the giant ferns. Kon sat on the ground, reflecting on the long day he had shared with Hina. It had been one of the most pleasant days in his life. The reason was simple: It had been filled with rare simplicity and sincerity, and they did as they willed with freedom and honesty. They had had a wonderful time because they had followed each other gladly. Each felt that he or she did not set out to dominate, but always simply wished to be useful. Kon thought Hina was great. Was she representative of her people?

The sun was low on the horizon, when Hina passed nearby the sacred banyan tree. Under it, in the dark, the shadow waited. The shadow saw the red-tailed tropicbird feathers in Hina's hand.

"You reached the forbidden place," the shadow murmured. "You will never be the same again."

Hina went straight to her father's house, and found Tupua and Vana engaged in telling old fishing stories. When they saw her and the feathers they became silent. In their eyes were many questions.

"Who gave you these feathers?" Tupua asked.

"My friend and I went to the valley, and he climbed to get them for me," she said, pleased with herself and the surprise she gave them.

Tupua and Vana looked at each other, wondering if they heard her words right.

"Who could this be?" Tupua asked. "The best climber is Aru, who was with Fenua all day. Nobody else can reach the tropicbird nests."

"Who told you we had to climb all the way to the nest to get these feathers?" Hina asked, teasing them. "Yesterday, I told you I had a secret."

She gave one red feather to her father, and one white feather to Vana. They were honored by her gift. She kept the two other feathers and walked to the beach. Tupua looked at his old friend, then at the feathers.

"What is going on?" he wondered aloud.

"I am not sure," Vana replied with a puzzled grin.

They both went to the beach. Vana looked at the sunset, then scrutinized the tip of both feathers.

"My friend, these feathers have been removed from the birds today," Vana said. "You see the fresh blood on the tips. Obviously, these feathers did not fall on their own. Besides, when someone finds tropicbird feathers, usually it is not a pair, or two pairs. Furthermore, climbing to the red-tailed tropicbird's nests has not been done in my lifetime."

"I must find out whom she was with," Tupua said, annoyed.

"No, my friend, don't!" Vana recommended, looking at the sea. "Let her have her secret. She does not play enough, and this worries me. I think it is important that you allow your daughter to harbor a secret. In time, she will come to us, and she will tell us. You have my word on that."

Tupua approved of his friend's wisdom. They both looked at the red clouds circling Mount Orohena. Vana raised his arms calling upon the mountain's spirits.

"I have the vision that a new era is coming," Vana said. "Too many events have been happening recently. We shall prepare our minds."

"What are you talking about?" Tupua asked with authority.

Vana placed one hand on his friend's shoulder.

"I am talking about a cross between a gentle butterfly and a powerful moray eel," Vana said with amusement in his eyes.

Sitting on the black sand, Hina caressed her cheeks with the two long feathers. She heard a short, sharp whistle to her left. While feeding, a sandpiper ran down the beach following a receding wave, and ran away followed by the next wave. She smiled at the skill of the fragile bird, confidently withstanding the brutal force of nature.

****

CHAPTER 7

"When I climbed the mountain, no wealth in the world could have given me nearly as much joy. We were two great and pure human beings, with fine ideas and noble deeds."

Hina of the Valley

The next fourteen moon-cycles brought steady changes around Tahiti-nui. Everyone was living in a world of mysteries. Cracks, voices and elusive shadows haunted the deep valleys. Fires had been observed in the high mountains during clear nights. Climbers went to those mountains to find the reasons for these fires. They never found anything - no tracks, and no ashes. One evening, all the people around the island witnessed smoke at the top of Mount Orohena. Some priests claimed that spirits living on the sacred mountain would bring devastation by fire, followed by starvation and war. Some claimed that the same spirits announced the arrival of a powerful invader, because from the high summit they could see far away to the sea. Some thought spirits were bored and played games with the weak mind of the living and the shadow of the dead. Many insignificant details assumed dramatic proportions, and simple stories became legends. The transmission of the truth by word of mouth became a virtue of the past. Priests were confused, leaders concerned, and the people fearful, but, with time healing all things, these mysteries became part of day-to-day life. A new order took place, where the power of the priests became stronger. In many ways a local high priest would not hesitate to turn unknown phenomena to his advantage.

The great priest of Papenoo had been the only one wise enough to remain stoical, lucid and patient. Many details suggested to him that soon, Hina would explain everything. The magnificent young woman was also a mystery, like the valleys and the mountains. The spiritual force inhabiting her astounded her family, and fascinated Vana and the other priests. She could learn everything they told her, and she could speak combinations of words unknown to them. Only her calmness and beauty equaled her wisdom.

Because Hina was so good to the people of the lower class, she rapidly gained admiration and respect. The arrival of a monarch in distant villages was always marked with rituals, but the arrival of Hina was marked by popular joy: Vana quickly saw and appreciated the difference. Aware of it or not, Tupua's young daughter planted the seeds of a new social system. Hina could also inadvertently create many jealous enemies, and Vana liked her too much to remain inactive. One day, he took his old friend the king aside.

"Tupua, I want to talk about something I have kept to myself for too long."

"By all spirits, what could that be?"

They sat on the old coconut trunk, which lay on the beach.

"Your daughter has the class of that a great priestess," Vana said, "and enough wisdom to be loved by the people. But, I have no idea how she became who she is."

"My older daughter, Fenua, was always carefully guarded, as are all girls of noble birth," the king said. "But, we never succeeded to lock Hina under such a guardianship. Since she was a young girl, she always violently rebelled against it, and found ingenious ways around the rules."

"It is true, and the last few moon-cycles she has mastered her art to perfection." Vana said. "Yet, she is smart enough to save your honor, and even add to it."

"This is because she has royal blood," Tupua answered proudly.

Amused, Vana left toward the river.

"Maybe, or maybe not," he murmured to himself, looking at the sea. "I wonder if this dismantled raft we found long ago has something to do with all this. It was right after the raft arrived that so many things became odd. It was right after that when Hina came back with the tropicbird feathers. It was right after, that she became increasingly clever."

Vana looked at the sacred mountain.

"Where was she, the day we found the raft? She was at the Teauroa point a long time before anyone else. She found three nautiluses, and brought them back two moon-cycles later: How unusual of her!"

Suddenly, a spark of light crossed Vana's mind. Of course, everything was so simple.

"Amazing Hina," he murmured with a grin on his face, "your secret is alive and well. Your secret goes far beyond what we all naively imagined. Young woman, I have respect for you; you have more audacity than all of us put together."

It was a sunny morning, and Hina rested with serenity on the warm black sand. Now, she was a young woman, and almost fully grown. Physically, she was a "vahine" at her best, and many young men were fond of her, but she was of royal blood. Any man from humble birth who would have outraged her would have been beaten to death. Beautiful she was, but most of her beauty was in her mind, inaccessible to most people. After fourteen moon-cycles, she became a harmonious blend of two very different cultures. One culture reflected ingenuous simplicity, sensitivity, sensuality, and strongly earthbound happiness. The other culture was the ultimate achievement of the human mind: disciplined, boundless, profound and capable of drawing out fascinating ideas from a vast source of knowledge. Nevertheless, both cultures had several things in common: Bravery, sociability and eloquence were appreciated qualities. Hina was the living proof that contact between these two different cultures could result in something good for both, and Kon knew that already. The key for Hina's success had been simple: She and Kon were willing to learn from one another, with honesty and determination, but above all without prejudice.

Hina was delighted and amazed at how fast and well Kon learned her language. She learned his, but with difficulty, and what she could learn from him was endless. The more she learned, the more she realized she knew little, and the more she wondered who Kon Tici was. He taught her about birds, plants, stars, his land of birth, his people. He taught her unusual skills, such as reading signs in the sky, understanding the secret life of the forest, listening to the noises of the night and how to find strength in calmness. He taught her how to walk in the forest, remain unnoticed and leave no tracks. He taught her how to climb the mountains, and she taught him how to swim better and how to dive.

Kon witnessed Hina's physical transformation, and became increasingly attached to her, and more dependent. She became a necessary part of his life. The idea that he might one day lose her became inconceivable to him. Never before had he experienced the deep feelings he had for her. He was almost ready to meet her people. He had traveled everywhere on the island, knew all the mountains, saw from a distance the deep lake Vaihiria, where enormous eels lived. Once, he went to the top of the forbidden Mount Orohena, and visited a fascinating range of mountains resembling a gigantic diadem. He went to the least known part of the island around what Hina called Mount Mauru and the plateau of Viriviriterai. However, he never returned to the tropicbird nests and to the large cave he had seen once from a distance. At times, Kon's mind was still haunted by his people he had lost.

Vana walked back to the beach and saw Hina laying on the sand. By the way she was frowning, he knew she was thinking about something important.

"Hina, may I talk to you?"

"Of course, Vana, sit down."

She thought he looked at her in a gentler way than usual, which put her on the defensive.

"I was thinking about you," Vana said. "I thought a long time about your secret, and I finally realized what it is."

Surprised, she looked at him straight in the eyes, her large black eyes openly amused.

"Then, tell me what my secret could be," she replied without flinching.

"Fourteen moon-cycles ago, you found a few nautiluses at the Teauroa point." Vana said, looking at the sea. "They are important to you. Yet, you forgot them for two moon-cycles."

"How do you know this?"

"Your mother told me."

"So, what is unusual about this?"

"Because, that morning, you met one or several travelers

from another world."

Her face blushed, and her long black eyelashes flipped several times. "There was only one traveler," she said with a wide smile on her face. "He was a man. But, how did you figure this?"

"Pure deduction, after much meditation. It was a game for me. The only thing I cannot figure out is why you kept this a secret all this time."

"I don't want to talk about this, unless my father also listens."

"Would you wait for us, if I go looking for him?" Vana asked.

"Yes, I will wait. I think he is at our house."

Vana left, walking faster than usual. She smiled at his apparent excitement, then looked at the waves receding on the beach. She had been successful in keeping her secret for a long time. Now, she owed her father and her people an explanation, and she would tell the truth. Then, she would have to explain what happened to Kon. She quickly sought a strategy. She had to find a way to talk to Kon before she would tell too much. Vana was her only hope to handle everything the right way: She had an idea.

Moments later, Vana came back with Tupua, awakened from a nap. Vana looked as excited as a young boy with a new toy. Both men sat near the young woman.

"Vana told me you were ready to give up your secret," Tupua said, yawning with laziness.

"Yes father, I am, because Vana found what it was all by himself. However, because I was taken by surprise, I have a favor to ask you both."

"I am listening," Tupua said.

"You have been waiting fourteen moon-cycles, and I thank you for this. Now, I am asking you to wait two more days before I will tell you more. And, I am asking Vana not to talk about what he found before I do it myself, two days from now."

"Hina, what kind of game is this?" Tupua grumbled, dissatisfied.

Determined, Hina felt a stream of warm blood rising to her head. She stood up, and suddenly found a reason why she was royal blood.

"I, Hina, tell you that for the sake of what is best for our people, I need two more days before I shall reveal a secret that will change the entire destiny of this land. Furthermore my father, for me and for you, it is a matter of honor."

"What could be so important?" Tupua asked, disarmed by Hina's strong words.

"Something that will bring you cheerful joy, my father."

Vana looked at Hina, embarrassed and puzzled by her statements. He clearly understood she was trying to buy time, but she was swift, and she did not wait for his words.

"Vana, you have part of my secret, but you don't have it all. Even for you, the best is yet to come. You are our respected great priest. Therefore, I am asking you to consider my secret as a taboo that nobody should talk about during the next two days."

"What do you mean a taboo?" Tupua said.

"It is a taboo for both of you," Hina replied. "As you told me once, a taboo is not made for the sake of making it but for the common good. Can you trust me?"

Both men glanced at each other. Vana smiled and placed a hand around Hina's shoulder.

"We will wait," Vana said, "we will wait until the time is right for you."

"The time will be right the evening of the day after tomorrow," Hina said. "I will leave the village tomorrow at dawn. No one shall attempt to follow me. I will be gone for two days. When I come back, I will have no secret."

Tupua yawned again, and nodded his head with approval.

"My little girl, sometime I forget that you are no longer a child. You spoke with honesty, so we will obey the rules of your game."

"It is not a game, my father," Hina said with quiet firmness. "Two days from now, you will understand."

She left, and both men kept walking on the beach.

"Hina is a born priestess," Vana said. "She can learn anything from anyone, make it part of herself, and use it when the time is most appropriate."

"My daughter, a priestess," Tupua murmured, looking at the lagoon.

"Remember, you named her Hina. There was a reason, as you know. But, with such a name, it should not surprise you that she is remarkable."

"I know," Tupua replied. "Did you notice the firmness of her words?"

"Yes, this is a side of her I noticed long ago. However, recently it became her way of speaking at all times. There are ways of saying things that make them happen, which is a rare talent, and she has it."

"But you are the great priest, and I am the king," Tupua stated, finally awaking from his nap. "Should she be allowed to talk to us like this?"

"Yes! Why not? She has royal blood. Besides, Hina knows better, and she would never talk like this to us in front of other people."

"Maybe you are right. But, as the king, I must make sure everyone lives by following some basic rules, including my young daughter."

"Don't be angry with her," Vana argued. "What she will bring is good for all of us. Remember, I have always been good at reading premonitions."

"Premonitions!" Tupua glared. "Do you know what I can do with your premonitions?"

Vana smiled, shrugged his shoulders, and left his friend, who kicked a coconut and hurt his foot.

"Premonitions!...   Honor!... Taboo!..." Tupua repeated, spitting in the sea.

It was long before dawn when Hina heard the first rooster. Discreetly, she left the house for her two-day trip. However, her sister was awake and followed her.

"Hina, where are you going?" Fenua asked.

"Don't follow me," Hina replied, more surprised than angered. She hugged her sister and kissed her with affection.

"I am leaving for two days. Father knows about it. Make sure nobody follows me."

"Do you have a boyfriend?"

"Yes, I do. If you do what I say, you will meet him a few days from now."

"I knew it!" Fenua exclaimed. Satisfied, she went back to the house, with a radiant smile on her face.

"Fenua! It is a secret until I come back. Don't give me trouble, my sister."

Fenua looked at Hina from a distance, agreeing by nodding her head.

The sun was barely above the eastern range when Hina surprised Kon in the cave. Never before had she been so early. She was not behaving as usual, and in no mood for a smile.

"Hina, what is upsetting you?"

"We have to talk, and I am going to stay two days with you."

He looked at her with surprise. Her restlessness and solemnity added to her beauty. She felt an eager affection coming from Kon, but he knew her mind was somewhere else.

"Explain what is happening, " he said gently.

"You cannot stay here anymore. Vana figured out that a traveler from another world was haunting the island. There was no use in me lying to him. However, I did not explain who you are. I told Vana and my father I will give up my secret tomorrow night."

"But, Hina, I cannot... I am not ready."

"Oh yes, you are!" she exclaimed with anger. "You were ready the first day you came. Why should you stay away from my people? They are humans, they are good and they deserve to know about you."

She sat on a carpet of fragile ferns, and put her head in her hands. Silently, a few tears blinded her eyes. It was the first time he saw her weeping, and suddenly realized the difference she had made for him. She had been helping, patient and reliable. Now, he was being unfair to her, to her people, and maybe to himself.

"Would you come soon to Papenoo with me?" she said, trying to control her sobs.

He sat close to her, wiped her tears with his fingers, and kissed her cheek.

"Yes, I will, but let me prepare myself before we leave."

She looked at him with surprise, and pleasure instantly found its way through her tears.

"No! Not today," she chuckled.

She saw his confusion and was amused about it. He looked at her large black eyes, and was as much astonished by her beauty as by her answer. Slowly, she regained her composure.

"Before going to Papenoo, I want to climb Mount Orohena

with you."

He stared at her, amused and puzzled.

"Mount Orohena is too difficult for you, and it would take two days to make the trip."

"This is why I told you I was going to stay two days with you. Tonight, we will sleep in one of Mount Orohena's many caves."

"Come, let's prepare ourselves," she added, taking his hand firmly. "Today and tomorrow, we will be Orohena's children".

Happy and filled with energy and will, she knew the next few days would bring her victory. With Kon, she would reach the top of the world. She would introduce him to her people: the man she had taught, the man she admired, and had learned so much from. A look of triumph was on her face, so she would not stop talking, until she saw him folding two long ropes around his shoulders.

"What is this for?" she asked.

"None of us would be able to climb Mount Orohena safely without these ropes."

Suddenly, she realized that climbing the sacred mountain was much more difficult than she had thought. She had not seen Kon use ropes for climbing, and the idea disturbed her somewhat. She shrugged her shoulders and chose not to think about what they could do with ropes. They packed food, clothes and two bark blankets. Then, they left the cave toward the upper ridges.

She was so excited that she would not stop talking, so Kon accelerated his pace until she became short of breath. She understood his trick, and raced after him laughing like a child. He stopped and hugged her for an instant.

"Save your energy," Kon said. "You are going to need all of it before the day is over."

All morning, they slowly progressed through the giant

ferns growing along a narrow ridge heading to fantastic heights. Wheel-shaped orb spider webs, like gracious silvery nets, were often major obstacles. The ridge was a narrow blade of volcanic rock, on which it was difficult to keep one's balance. On each side, it was a free fall toward the deep valleys. They reached the point where Hina had not been before. She stopped, looked behind, and gasped at the giddy vision of her world far below. Then, she looked ahead, humbled by the grandiose majesty of the mountain.

"I look forward to meeting your father," Kon said.

"You are going to like him, and I have so much to show you in the lagoon."

"My memories from the lagoon are not all good ones," Kon replied.

"I know, but let's assume you know nothing about the lagoon. Can you see how beautiful it is from here? Where it is deep, it is the same blue as your eyes, and it is an open door to intriguing life forms."

Suddenly, she saw Kon's hand reaching a sharp rock. In the shade, where his fingers were clenched, a long brown creature crawled.

"Kon, watch it! Remove your hand from that rock," she screamed.

Kon felt the large centipede crawl about his fingers and understood immediately.

"I am accustomed to these insects. On the continent, in the great jungle, they are much more dangerous than here. A few days ago, one bit me in the cave as I was sleeping. My foot swelled and I had fever for two days. Then, the pain and swelling vanished."

"Yes, but if this one had bitten you, our trip to Orohena would have been over."

"I am still amazed how clean and pleasant this island is. In the great jungle it is difficult to remain alive and healthy."

"Is this the reason you lived high in the mountains?"

"It is part of the reason. One day I will tell you the other reason."

Soon, there was a dramatic change, as they reached the bottom of Mount Pitohiti, a major obstacle before Mount Orohena. The only way to climb was by following the same ridge they were on, but it seemed an insurmountable barrier, straight up. At the sight of the giant, Hina felt shivers down her back.

"Pitohiti is Orohena's son," she said. "Can we stop a while?"

"Let's eat something," Kon said, "before this great challenge."

"I see, and I am not sure if I like it. Yet, it is so exciting," she said, with a tight smile.

"We must reach the top before dark."

"It is much cooler here; I am glad you took all these clothes. Do you see all these clouds forming, high in the valleys? I hope it will not rain."

"It will be all right," Kon said. "Before dawn, you will see more stars than you ever saw in your life."

"Why is that?"

"High in the mountains, the sky is purer before dawn, free of this afternoon moist air."

"Do you mean there will be no air?"

"There will be less air, but still enough to breath," Kon replied, amused by her question.

"How do you know all these things?"

"We lived in high mountains for many generations. You know more things about the sea than I do, because you are a seafarer."

She smiled more broadly this time, relieved by his gentle

modesty. His kindness, combined with his knowledge, made him the pleasant and powerful master of her mind. Without objecting, she found she had no control over the influence he had on her. As a free islander, she found the feeling most charming.

Kon attached one end of the longer rope around his waist, then secured the other end around Hina's waist.

"What are you doing? Does that mean if I fall, you will fall too?"

"That means if you fall, I will save your life. Follow my path, exactly."

She stiffened her body as a sign of amused obedience, and they started climbing along the ridge. For each step, she had to explore the thick cover of ferns with her foot. It was a long process, but she was determined to go forward. Above her, the sharp, jagged cliff disappeared behind clouds. She glanced at the emptiness growing behind her, felt her head spin and wished she was already in the clouds.

"You are doing well," Kon said. "Take your time, breathe deeply and do not look down. Only what is ahead is relevant. Courage, sister!"

She stopped, secured her feet and stared at him with a hint of disapproval.

"I am not your sister. Furthermore, I don't want to be your sister."

They looked at each other with amused eyes, and started laughing. Deep inside, Kon knew she would be much more than a sister. Deep inside, Hina knew her complex feelings for the man, something she had not experienced before.

"Kon, I have vertigo. It is like being attracted by the emptiness below."

He stopped on a narrow ledge and gently pulled the rope,

helping Hina to reach him. Her hair covered her bowed face. She reached the ledge, flipped her hair backward and sat near Kon. They were just below the clouds. Nearby, a giant fern unfurled new pink fronds, facing the drama of the cliffs plunging to the rain forest of the valleys. Far away, the deep blue of the sea blended with the sky, showing no horizon.

"The sea and the sky are the same," Kon said. "It is a world where the venturesome traveler can discover eternity and its timelessness."

"It is a barrier for the soul," Hina replied. "Yet, the entire world is beyond this."

Patiently, they pursued their journey. The mist of the clouds cooled their faces, which were covered with salty perspiration. Hina followed Kon's steps with complete trust, and each step became the conquest of a giant stair. She was silent, concentrating on one flank of the cliff. Sharp rocks and dead ferns scratched her legs. Still, she found enough energy to glance at the surrounding magnificent plants hanging between every crack of the mountain, and wondered how all these ferns could survive and grow with so little soil. Each time she pulled on the long fronds, she did it with respect for the plant, trying to minimize bruises and wounds to its delicate pinnules. She stopped, and looked at Kon trying to find his way between two large rocks welded to the mountain by insecure bonds.

"These blocks could fall on us," she said, with a timid tone.

Kon did not answer immediately, and thought about that distant day, when the entire mountain collapsed under his feet. He recalled looking for his brother inside a cloud of dust. How lucky they had been, and it had been his mistake.

"Kon, when you don't answer, does that mean yes?"

"No, it is all right, they are well attached to the mountain, but

I have been wrong once before. One day when you expect it the least, the force of nature may teach you an unforgettable lesson: This is the mountain."

"This is Orohena," she replied, as with the mountain's own words.

The wind blew in Hina's hair. Her body was covered with mud, gravel and vegetal debris. Cuts bled along her calves, thighs, and forearms. Her lungs hurt from the lack of air. She could not breathe fast enough to give her muscles the necessary energy. Every part of her body ached, but not once did she think about complaining. She was determined to go forward, and forward she went. She followed her master, who was considerately waiting for her. At this moment, she fully measured the ease with which he could climb the mountain. For him, it was a skill he had perfected all his life. She was unable to hear his breathing, and could not even see a single scratch on his legs or arms, or any sign of weariness on his face.

"You are not even tired," she murmured to herself.

Kon reached the top of Mount Pitohiti, sat and pulled on the rope to help her. She finally grabbed his ankle and collapsed against the ferns. She was too tired to look, too tired to appreciate, too tired to fear the formidable emptiness spreading into the deep valleys, but it was her first victory, and she was well aware of it. Her face rested against the wet rootstocks of ferns, her nose lost between young fiddleheads; she bit her lips and giggled with pleasure. Nobody except Kon could share or understand her joy. It had never occurred to her before that so much pleasure could come from physical agony.

"People without soul would say you just became a conqueror of a useless empire," Kon said, protecting Hina's shoulder from the cold wind with a bark cloth. At last, she gained enough energy to make two more steps, and sat near him.

"Do you know what I say to people without soul?" she asked. "I say, suit yourself with the mediocrity you glorify."

Silently, they watched the valleys unfold as the cloud slowly vanished, pushed by the evening breeze. Now, they could see majestic Mount Orohena waiting for his children. Its mysterious spirits could be heard in the wind. Only few adventurers daring to become part of its wilderness, could see its splendor.

"I never saw it from so close," she said with a mixture of joy, contemplation and fear.

However, Hina knew she would never turn back. With Kon she would trespass the taboo of her forefathers. In her mind, there was no taboo for the people of Kon Tici Viracocha, because they were pure wisdom.

"Look at my legs," she said with dismay, "they are shaking all over."

"Let's walk along the ridge; it is easier for awhile." Kon said. "There is a cave not far from here, in which we should rest and spend the night."

"I am ready for that," she said.

"I am proud of you, Kon said, putting his hand around her waist. "There are very few people who would endure what you did today."

"Hina is a legendary name for my people; an ordinary woman Hina cannot be," she whispered, struggling to maintain her balance between the sharp rocks. She looked around and noticed that ferns were scarce here. Halfway between Pitohiti and Orohena, they descended a little on the north side of the ridge, and reached a cave whose opening was obscured by a thick cover of ferns. Under the cave, the mountain plunged into the abysses of its forbidden flanks where no man had put his feet. Far away in the valley, a few birds chirped before the silent night would overtake them.

"The sunset behind Moorea is unbelievable," Hina said in ecstasy. "I never saw anything so spectacular."

The entire western sky was purple, as the sun dressed in red, slowly disappeared behind the distant curvature of the ocean. From place to place, the phantoms of Moorea's peaks, the nearby island, propagated their dark shadows against the burning sky.

Kon and Hina entered the cave. Tiny ferns covered the ground, and spider webs crossed the cave in all directions. Kon took a fern frond and collected all the webs. Hina installed the large bark-cloth blankets on the ground. The place was dry and large enough to protect four or five people. However, the cave's ceiling was not high enough for Kon to stand upright. Hina could, but her hair touched the dusty, crumbling ceiling.

They went outside and walked to a spring dripping silently along the mountain before plunging into endless falls. They drank its clear and cold water. They undressed and washed their dirty bodies. Then, they went back to the cave and ate with little appetite. At the entrance, Kon managed to activate a small fire, but there were very few things around for fuel. Within a short time, no more dry ferns could be found, and the warmth of the fire vanished. The western horizon was still red, just enough to bring a little light. Finally, the night came. Kon and Hina sat side by side wrapped in bark-cloth blankets. The wind moaned gently. The spirits of Mount Orohena were speaking.

"How strange it is," Hina said. "I enjoy listening to the wind because I feel secure with you. If I were alone, I would be terrified."

"What should you be terrified of? Are you afraid of the dark? Are you afraid of the silence? Or, are you afraid of being alone?"

"None of that, I am afraid of the unknown. Many of my people would keep a fire burning all night to keep from being in the dark. They believe that spirits travel at night, but I do not believe in spirits. Nevertheless, their stories make me uncomfortable. With you, everything is so different, so I can live every moment, and enjoy things I would be afraid of otherwise."

"Listen!" Kon said with a tone of surprise.

"What is it?" she replied, scared.

"I think there is a bad spirit coming outside."

She looked at him through the dark, her mind congested with doubts. Then, she pushed him down, sat on the top of his thighs, and clamped her hands on his shoulders.

"You are going to pay for this, Kon Teke."

She bent down toward his face. She caressed his lips with hers. He raised himself and returned her kiss. Hina was surprised at how gentle and careful he was. It was nothing like her sister had described. He wrapped his arms around Hina. She relaxed and sank on top of his chest. Keeping her locked in his arms, he rolled her on his side. They remained silent, enjoying the warmth of one another. Aware of the deep emotion of the young woman and her overwhelming urge to pursue the mutual attraction much further, and fighting his own desire, Kon sat up on the ground.

"Hina, your body is not ready for this. You are still a young girl."

She objected by kissing him passionately.

"Because of my bondage to the rank of my family, I cannot do what many girls already do at my age. To them, I look like a retarded woman. Therefore, I don't agree with you."

After she partially removed her clothes, he pulled on her shoulders until she lay by his side. He caressed her hair and her back, and whispered in her ear.

"Hina, it is not our way to do this with a woman so young. Please, understand me, and be patient. Our time will come. And, because of what you just said, I think it would be a good idea for me to meet your father and your people first."

She caressed his lips with her fingers, then his long ears, then buried her face against his beard.

"Kon Teke, I love you. When the time comes, I want us to come back here, because this is the place where I want us to share our most intimate secrets."

She continued to undress, completely. She pulled the large bark-cloth blankets above Kon and herself. Then, she wrapped Kon's arms around herself. He felt her warm body, hard to resist, and almost regretted his own words. Silent and tired, they slowly slumbered. Orohena's children were at rest, inside the jaws of the sleeping giant.

Long before dawn, Hina awoke. She slowly moved away from Kon, put her clothes on and walked out. Kon heard her, but let her alone: She obviously needed to explore by herself.

She sat on the ferns at the entrance of the cave. There was no moon. The night sky was clear, illuminated by countless stars. She looked at the unknown, astonished and mute. Her mind was overwhelmed by the infinite display of the universe. She saw a shooting star and felt a shiver race up her back, yet she was not cold. From the sea level, she would never have imagined that there could be so many stars. Right here, she received an answer: There are no such things as spirits. If there had been, then they would have much more to do than to worry about Hina's limited world. For the first time, she had a feeling about the immense power of nature. The mountain was the limit of her universe, but now, she realized how small was the mountain. There was much more. She filled herself with the light from all the stars, as if they were talking to her mind. She looked at their unmistakable presence, at their brightness, at their timelessness. She suddenly became aware that she was nothing, and knew nothing. The thought came to her mind, with the flashing force of lightning, and never again would she be the same. Now, she started to understand the vast resources of Kon's people, who spent so much time studying stars. She looked up, and could not help murmuring a few words.

"Kon Teke told me there was a great Creator of everything. If so, you made all those stars. Who are you? What do you want from us? How can we understand your goals? I sit humbly at your feet. If you are listening, have good will and be kind to your tormented children."

Kon heard what she said, and she felt his hands around her shoulders. Both stayed silent for a moment. Kon knew the slow process evolving in Hina's mind was a priceless gift. It was a fragile message to her soul, entering through her eyes.

"My eyes are the gate between the stars and my soul," she said.

Kon did not comment. There was no need for words, as silent facts were self-explanatory. She understood that the vast majority of humans could not listen to this message, did not want to read it, or even wish to learn about it, but for the few who were gifted to receive its meaning, they would walk across the world with majesty and grace, beyond the pettiness of mediocrity.

She felt a current of energy entering her body. She glanced at Kon's arms around her chest, and she saw stars glittering in his gold bracelets. From his arms, something entered her body. The feeling was pleasurable. It went away and she thought it had been her imagination.

"It never occurred to me that there could be so many stars," she said. "What are they?"

"They are faraway suns."

"Suns! Impossible! And, how do you know?"

"Our ancestors told us."

"You will have to discuss this with our great priest," se said with a smile on her face. "I can see him turn into a sleepless man not able to look at his feet when walking at night."

Hina's smile deepened into laughter. The eastern horizon became pink. Once more, Hina looked up in amazement.

"Who could be the Creator of all this?"

Kon caressed her cheek with his long fingers, turned around and pointed to four large stars appearing close to one another, low on the horizon.

"When we attempt to understand something we cannot penetrate, when we struggle to appreciate the profoundest reasons and the most radiant beauty which are only accessible to our mind in their most elementary form, it is in this emotion that we, humans, become evolving intelligence."

She looked at him, shook her head and opened her mouth in a sign of confusion. He saw that she only partially understood what he had said. He smiled to her, then pointed to the eastern horizon.

"Only exceptionally high-minded people can go beyond the naive conception of spirits. The reason of our failure is because we give them a human image. You should not think of the Creator in human terms. If you work hard, making your mind travel among stars, one day you will make one step beyond the foolish world of the uneducated. That day, you will find that the Creator is what is, and your soul will become the humble picture of Himself."

Hina sat down and looked at the glorious rise of the new dawn. For her it was a different dawn. It was the dawn of a young woman, whose master taught her for the first time to read the beauty of nature using her soul instead of her eyes. A spark of light crossed her mind, and she realized how rich she was. The concepts of birth and death started to fall into place and to make sense. Between these two earthbound limits she was Hina. There was an immense universe above her, but inside her was another universe. Inside her was an immense universe she could not see. Today, at dawn, she looked through the gate that led to her soul, and she felt that she became a different person. She looked at Mount Orohena with different eyes. The spirits of the Mountain were gone forever. She looked at the distant valleys, the peaks and the sea. She listened to the morning breeze and stared at Kon Tici Viracocha. He was silent with an enigmatic smile, aware of what was happening inside her. All that time, he had been at work and skillfully manipulative.

She thought about the physical desire she had for him before they went to sleep, in the cave. Only then, she understood the words he had said. She measured how right he was when he said that their time would come. She had a long way to travel before she could deserve this man from another world. Yet, he deeply cared for her and was willing to wait. She realized how strong was her love for him, yet she did not know who he was. However, at the dawn of this new day, she discovered he was a fascinating sculptor of the human soul.

They ate, packed their goods and placed their bags between rocks at the top of the ridge: They would take them on their way back. They took the two ropes and started climbing. Filled with the energy of a new day, they looked at what would be the ultimate challenge for Hina.

"Do you see that pond ahead?" Kon said. "I noticed there were beautiful red ducks living around it."

"They are called mooraura," she said with excitement.

"Moo... Yes! I think you are right. What did you say?"

Hina pushed him as he started laughing.

"They are mooraura, and their red feathers are sacred. They are used during war ceremonies, as a sign of strength."

"War! Sign of strength! Do you recall the sky before dawn?"

"Yes, I know now. These things are stupid to you. Often, I thought they were stupid too, but there is nothing we can do about them. There are times when war is something we have to face."

"I strongly disagree. Leaders of war always lead to more war. In war you always have two losers, and what we call a winner is a caricature of an ephemeral success. Going to war is the ultimate defeat of those who prepared it. It is a cry from man saying loud and clear: 'Sorry, I was not capable of anything better, I had no choice.' There are always ways to prevent war: As humans, we shall find them."

"You are going to have fun explaining these things to my people. I warn you, your ideas may not always be well received."

"I am aware of that, but we shall see, in due time."

"Here is one duck swimming," Hina murmured. "Look how pretty it is."

"It is a male, look at its bright feathers."

"What do you mean?" Hina said, looking at her chest. "You think I am not as colorful as you are."

They looked at each other and burst out laughing.

They were not far from the summit, but there were no more ferns, only crumbling volcanic stones, and slippery gravel. Hina looked down at the abysses and immediately understood why the mountain was taboo. She stopped Kon with her hand.

"There is no sense to go through with this, it is too dangerous."

"It is going to be all right if you do exactly what I say," Kon replied.

He solidly anchored one of the two wooden posts he had brought with him. He attached one rope, the shorter, around Hina's waist, and tied the other end to the post. "You stay here, holding the post at all times, until I give you the signal to remove it. Then, you shall bring the post and use the long rope behind me to climb to the place where I will wait for you. Only one of us at a time shall move; the other one will watch."

He attached the other rope, the longer, around his waist and tied the other end to the anchored post.

"These ropes shall remain attached to us and to the post at all times."

Slowly, he started climbing among the crumbling rocks, as Hina watched him with fear. She held the post and the two ropes. She looked down behind her, and her head spun instantly from a dizzy vertigo. She closed her eyes, trying to convince herself not to look back. In a way, she felt secure because Kon knew exactly what he was doing, and it was not his first visit to Mount Orohena.

Kon reached the point where the longer rope had been stretched to its full length. He selected a safe spot to anchor the second post, removed the rope from his waist, and tied it to the post.

"Now, you can come. Hold the rope tightly, whatever happens."

She struggled to remove the post, rolled the shorter rope around her shoulder, and attached the longer rope around her waist. Then, she started her journey among the dangerous rocks. Several times she slid on gravel, and watched loose stones flying into the valley, but she held the rope well, and took all the time she wanted. When she reached Kon's hand, he lifted her to the narrow ledge where he sat. He untied the longer rope from her waist, attached it to the post in the ground, and tied the end of the shorter rope to it.

"You did well. Now, we are going to repeat exactly the same operation, until we reach the summit. Simple, isn't it?"

"Sure! It is great. Why am I doing this?"

"Because I like it, and because you like it as well," Kon said with a grin on his face.

She glanced at him with a cool frown, saying nothing.

"Well! Remember, it was your dream," Kon said, "ever since you were a young girl."

"Wait until we will be in the lagoon, Kon Teke," she said with a mocking smile, raising her eyebrows. "Seriously, why are we doing this?"

"Remember, some people would say we are the conquerors of a useless goal. I would say to them: For us it is a relaxation for the mind, a sanctuary where our soul can rest, a refuge against the storms of life, a place where nobody else can steal our freedom and pleasure."

With blisters on her hands, cuts under her feet, scratches on her legs and sweat all over her body, Hina climbed the mountain. The tensing of her face betrayed her pain, but being so close to the summit, she seemed to enjoy her struggle.

Kon already sat at the top and slowly pulled the rope to help her. With amazing determination and courage she made the last steps with all the power her legs could produce. She clenched her hands on the last piece of rock. Her white teeth were tight behind her half-open lips. Her long black hair floated in the cold wind. When she sat near Kon, she looked at him with savage, glowing eyes. Suddenly, it was over. They were at the summit of Hina's world.

With her forearm she removed the sweat mixed with the brown mud running along her cheeks, and kissed the man she loved. Then, she looked at the island, all sides at once, for the first time.

"I don't know if I will ever come back here," she murmured. "But, as long as I will live, I will remember everything I did today. This was not betraying the taboo of my forefathers. This was the very reason why they made it a taboo, because we were meant to be the only ones to come here."

Honored by the strength of her words, Kon removed the gold necklace from around his neck, and passed it over Hina's head. On her chest, the golden rising sun and the flying condor witnessed the dawn of a new era.

"At times, look at this pendant, because now it is yours," Kon said. "It will remind you that the Creator chose you to carry his message. Men and women, whoever they are, are all sacred. You have no enemies. If we fail in our mission of peace, we will all perish: It is the law coming from the stars, and there is no way around it, Hina of the Valley!"

****

CHAPTER 8

"If you think you have enemies, be kind to them. Make sure they understand the reasons for your kindness. In return, do not ask for their kindness. But, wait and see. The result will be a measure of howhonest you were."

Kon Tici Viracocha

Long after the sunset, Hina passed the old banyan tree, along the river near Papenoo. She felt as if someone was watching her. She glanced at the sacred tree but saw no one.

"Orohena is glittering on your chest," the shadow said. "Go to them, Hina of the Valley, and be a living legend."

Hina heard only the wind in the upper branches. Being tired, she went straight home. Sitting on a slab, Vana saw her from a distance, but did not seem to notice anything odd about her. Either he was not paying attention, or he was lost in his thoughts.

Tupua recognized her daughter's steps and raced outside the house. When he saw Hina, he barely recognized her.

"It is very late... What happened to you? You look terrible."

"I am fine, father. I had the most beautiful days of my life, looking at the red ducks on the lake near Mount Orohena."

"You did what?" Tupua asked, wide eyed.

"We spent the night in a cave, not too far from the lake."

The king grabbed his daughter with his powerful hands.

"What do you mean when you say we? Who was with you?"

"If you don't calm down, I will tell you nothing," Hina replied.

The monarch raised his hand to slap her face.

"Tupua, no!" Atea said, stopping him. "You never did this to Hina; you shall not now."

Atea politely dismissed a few guests, and went back to separate Tupua and Hina, who were already at one another's throat. Atea beat on a drum near a pillar, which instantly silenced father and daughter.

"Both of you, sit down, and talk intelligently," she ordered in a commanding tone. Then, she looked at Hina.

"Why are you telling a lie to your father?"

"Mother, I have never lied, and never will," Hina replied.

"She did not lie," Tupua said. "This is what makes me angry. It was planned for a long time."

"Whom were you with?" Atea asked.

"I was with a man from another world. I met him fourteen moon-cycles ago, when you found the raft at the Teauroa point. Vana knows about all this."

At Hina's words Tupua became outraged.

"You went with a stranger for fourteen moon-cycles without telling us. Girl, you dishonored my name."

He raised his hand toward Hina, who slipped aside. Atea took a bucket full of water and splashed the face of her husband. Shocked, the king sat down on the ground and started laughing.

"So! You support this girl," he said with sarcasm.

"No, I don't. But you are the king, and you shall treat your daughter accordingly. I will not tolerate the sight of you acting like a man from the lower class," Atea said, her fists on her strong hips.

Her words always had a positive effect on Tupua. So, he looked at Hina and smiled to her, and so did she.

"Tell me your story; I promise I will stay calm," the king said.

Hina sat, cross-legged, in front of her father. She knew she had to say something that would soften his negative attitude. With a few words, she had to be persuasive.

"The man comes from a world where the sun rises," Hina said. "He his a peaceful man, tall, with clear skin, long ears, and dark blue eyes."

Tupua stared at his daughter, wordless. He stood up and invited her to follow him to their private garden filled with fragrant flowers. Tupua sat near his favorite hibiscus bush, while Atea fed the embers of a fire they had made earlier.

"Hina, would you repeat what you said?" Tupua asked with a cool voice.

"The man I met has been traveling at sea for many moon-cycles. In sea storms he lost his people, and he has been here alone ever since. He is the man of your dream."

Tupua opened his eyes wider, his hands shook, and he could not hide the emotion on his face.

"Are you telling me the plain truth?" he asked, his body stiffened in shock.

"Father, when was the last time I lied to you?"

"Clear skin, long ears, blue eyes,... That is impossible," Atea murmured.

"It seems impossible," Tupua said. "But, Hina is telling the truth. Who could that man be?"

"If you wish, tomorrow you can meet him. I will take you to him."

"Fourteen moon-cycles, with a stranger,... in the mountains," he added with a frustrated tone.

"His name is Kon, Kon Teke. His people call him the Son of the Sun. He did not want to come to you before he could speak our language. So, I taught him our language."

"So, that was it," Tupua said looking at the ground. "I remember that raft we found, and nobody knew where it came from. But, why did it take so long for us to learn about this?"

"He had to learn our language," Hina repeated. "He did not know if we would be friendly. Barbarians killed many of his people. Outnumbered, they left by sea, their only chance for survival."

"Then, he is a weak man," the king said. "If you run from your enemies, you are weak. Sooner or later, the weak die without honor."

"I disagree; Kon is not weak, he is good. There is a difference," Hina argued.

"Why should I go to him? He should come to me," Tupua said.

"Father, don't make things difficult. I told him I would come with you, tomorrow morning. You will meet him in the valley."

Hina hesitated a little, then looked at her mother, and bent her eyes toward the ground.

"I care for him a lot," she said with a soft, timid tone.

"Did he ever abuse you, or touch you?" Atea asked with suspicious eyes.

Hina looked at her mother with silent humiliation. Tears escaped her eyes and rolled on her cheeks. Her face hardened.

"Both of you, you are unfair. You don't have trust in me. Yet, once I wished to make love with him. But Kon Teke is no ordinary man. He always respected me. He always respected you, even without knowing you. If you don't believe me, my mother may inspect my body."

Tupua put his hand in front of Hina's mouth.

"Don't say things like this, child. We know you are telling the truth, but we were not prepared for these events."

Tupua thought about Vana's words. Maybe, Tupua's dream about the man, long ago, was a good omen after all.

"We should talk to Vana," Tupua suggested.

"Father, every part of my body hurts."

"If you went to the lake on Mount Orohena, yes, I believe what you say," He said and smiled.

"I want to clean myself in the river," Hina said, "then, I will join you at Vana's place."

"I go with you to the river," Atea said.

Tupua went to Vana's house, and found his friend waiting for him.

"Come in, I saw Hina a while ago. She looked terrible."

"She went to the lake on Mount Orohena."

"So, she went to the prohibited place, without my permission," Vana said with a sad smile.

"You have not heard the best part yet."

"I know! I know! She went with that man from another world."

"You knew!"

"She told me the other day."

"Did she tell you what the man looks like?"

"No, she did not. Remember, she was supposed to tell us more today."

"Then, you know nothing," Tupua said.

Vana glanced at Tupua with a puzzled face.

"What do you mean?"

"Do you recall that dream I had, long ago, before Hina's birth?

Do you recall the man in my vision, with clear skin, long ears, and blue eyes? This is the man who has been in the mountains for fourteen moon-cycles."

Silent, the old priest frowned, and looked at his friend with amusement in his eyes. He took the tropicbird feather Hina had given him. All the strange events of the last fourteen moon-cycles passed through his mind.

"Tupua, may I ask you a favor?"

"Yes, of course!"

"The next time I talk about premonitions, don't kick coconuts."

After they came back from the river, Atea helped Hina dress with fresh, clean clothes. Then, Hina looked for something in the bag she brought back from the mountains. She took the gold necklace Kon had given her, and passed it around her head.

"Look at this, mother. Did you ever see anything like it?"

Atea's black eyes widened. Fenua's mouth dropped open. Hina's sister touched the pendant and was astonished at its weight.

"He gave it to me this morning, and told me I should keep it forever."

"The more you are telling me about this man, the more I wish I could see him," Atea said, still stunned.

"I must go," Hina said, "father and Vana are waiting for me."

Hina promptly left, leaving the two women in total confusion. They looked at each other, speechless. Atea shrugged her shoulders in a sign of acceptance.

"Where is he from?" Vana asked.

"Hina said from a large land very far in the east. Judging from the raft we saw, I think the navigation skills of these people are rather primitive."

"Well! What we saw was not the original," Vana commented.

"What do you mean?"

"What we saw had been constructed with the parts of something much bigger, which makes me think that man is a survivor."

"Hina said he is peaceful, and he had been respectful of her. She taught him our language."

"He is peaceful because he is self-confident, isn't he?" Vana asked with defiance.

"I don't know," Tupua replied.

"Amazing Hina," Vana murmured with his hands clasped behind his back. "She taught him our language! Do you realize how clever your daughter is?"

"She wants to take me to the man, tomorrow morning. You should come with us. And, something else, I think she is in love with him."

"Hina! You are telling me a joke. She never looked at boys, and does not like them."

At the same instant, Hina entered the house, and looked at Vana, amused.

"Kon Teke is not a boy, and he is not the kind of man we can find around here."

Her confidence and the authority with which she interrupted them surprised both men, but as she came closer, they became startled at the sight of the shiny gold necklace.

"By all the spirits, I never saw anything like this!" Vana said, wide eyed.

Tupua took the pendant between his fingers.

"Did you notice how heavy it is?"

"I never heard of such a substance," Vana said, astonished. "Indeed, this man comes from another world."

Both men admired the glittering object, almost forgetting Hina's chest under it, which made her burst into laughter. Then, Vana recovered from his surprise.

"I understand you went to the lake where the sacred ducks live, without my permission," Vana said.

"Yes, we did, and after we climbed to the summit of Mount Orohena."

The thin, old priest glanced at the king. His fingers shook, and his face became clouded with anger.

"It cannot be!" he exclaimed with blazing eyes.

"Without Kon Teke, I would never have done it. But, with him it was not difficult, and it was safe. He lived in much higher and much steeper mountains. Mount Orohena has no secret for him."

"Do you know what it costs to trespass a taboo like this, young girl?" Vana asked with bitterness.

"In some instances, it could mean death for me and Kon," Hina replied with cool eyes. She was unafraid.

"And this does not affect you!" Vana fulminated. "Who do you think you are? Were you naive enough to think you would get away with this?"

"Mount Orohena is a taboo because it is meant to be visited by Kon and me, alone. As such, I do not feel guilty for anything."

Hina looked at her father seated on a block of carved precious wood, his face resting between his hands. His eyes seemed to follow some ants traveling on the ground.

He never saw the ants, however, felt like a destroyed man. Hina looked at Vana and understood she was in trouble, but she was resourceful. She would not allow anyone to tarnish her soul because of rules she did not agree with.

"Both of you, listen to me," she said firmly. "Look at all this with an open mind. Kon Teke is no ordinary man; he is wise, and has no taboo. Meet him first, then you will recall my words."

"A group of warriors will come with us in the morning," Tupua said. "I want to teach that man a lesson."

"Then you will never find the Son of the Sun," Hina replied, "and will never meet the extraordinary man of your dream. You will betray your daughter's honor and yours as well."

Tupua's anger flared again, until Vana raised both hands in front of him.

"Do not be angry, my friend. Remember Hina in our legends. She had no taboo to obey. She was the goddess who cherished our blood and made it better."

Tupua remained silent, and looked at the darkness outside.

"I have to think about all this, until dawn," The king said. Then, he left Vana's house, and Hina followed him. They did not utter a single word. When he entered his house he ignored his wife and his other daughter and isolated himself on a woven mat. For a long time he watched the wall in the darkness. He knew he was a prisoner of his anger.

Early in the morning, Kon prepared himself for a very important day. First, he removed everything he had stored in the cave of Hina's great-grandfather. Near the stream where he had first met Hina, he searched for the best clothes he had in his old bag. He found a dark blue robe, which extended halfway down his thighs. He tied a white belt embroidered with red suns around his waist. He tied a white band around his head, embroidered with a flying condor on his forehead. He wore his last good pair of sandals. He carefully polished his gold ear plugs and gold bracelets. He kept his long, black, straight hair in place with a gold pin, so his hair would fall gracefully on his back and shoulders, which made him appear taller. His beard was neatly trimmed. Kon Tici Viracocha was ready for an overdue encounter. He sat, cross-legged, on the top of a large boulder near the stream, and waited. In his mind, he saw Hina coming with the king and the great priest. In his hands, he had two long red feathers from the sacred tropicbirds. They would be gifts to his distinguished guests.

When Hina, Tupua and Vana left Papenoo, the overweight monarch was still in a bad mood. The crowd wondered what could be the occasion for the king and the great priest to wear ceremonial clothes.

"Nobody should follow us," Tupua ordered, with an irritated tone. "I want all of you here when we come back."

The mysterious behavior of their leaders made the people even more curious, and everyone left their usual occupations. They all gathered in the village, waiting and speculating. Atea and Fenua knew much already, and they barricaded themselves inside their house. Both women were somewhat confused.

Hina led the two men. Tupua wore a red feather cape and a tall hat made of thick bark-cloth decorated with rare cowries. His hat was topped by long, dry grass fibers, so no one would or should be taller. Vana wore a white feather cape and a helmet covered with white feathers and decorated with a few green pigeon feathers. Both men had long, carved walking sticks made of precious wood. They stopped several times, as the king was often out of breath. By midmorning they finally reached the place where Kon waited. Hina saw Kon sitting on the boulder, turning his back to them. With her hands she stopped Tupua and Vana. Alone, she walked toward Kon.

"Kon, are you all right? Do you want to meet my father and the great priest?"

To her surprise, he did not answer, and kept looking in the

opposite direction. Tupua and Vana came closer. Hina put her hand on Kon's shoulder.

"These two men are Tupua and Vana," she said gently.

Kon stood up and slowly turned his head until his eyes met Tupua's eyes. They stared at one another for a moment that seemed an eternity to Hina. She was so worried, wondering if the two men would like each other, that she squeezed Vana's arm very hard. To temper her emotion, the priest put his arm on her shoulder.

Tupua came closer to Kon and looked carefully at the man who was much taller than he, if it had not been for his royal hat. He looked at his clear skin, his long ears, and his deep blue eyes. He was indeed the man of his dream. Impressed by the charismatic stranger, he smiled and put one hand on Kon's shoulder.

"You are welcome on this island," the king said in a ceremonial tone. "You should have come to us long ago."

Kon smiled, and in return put one hand on Tupua's shoulder.

"You are Hina's father; your name is Tupua, king of Tahiti-nui. I am honored, and I thank you for your understanding and hospitality."

"Where do you come from, and who are you?" Tupua asked.

"My name is Kon Tici Viracocha, which means Son of the Sun. The awesome sea separated me from my companions. I reached your island, alone. Hina calls me Kon Teke."

"Kon Teke, let me introduce the great priest of my kingdom," Tupua said. "His name is Vana."

As Kon put his hand on Vana shoulder, the great priest felt a strange current of energy entering his body. Never before he had felt such a thing, and he instantly knew the stranger had great powers. Kon gave one red tropicbird feather to Tupua, and another one to Vana.

"This is not much," Kon said. "But it took some time to find them."

"Did you climb to their nest?" Vana asked.

"Yes, I did, several times."

"Then, these feathers have great value; they symbolize the courage that is needed to get them," Vana said.

"How did you learn our language so well?" Tupua asked.

"Hina is my teacher," Kon replied, putting one arm around Hina's shoulder. "She has been kind and patient with me. With your permission I would like for her to remain my guide."

Tupua glanced at Kon's arm. The gesture obviously irritated him.

"Among your people, what was your social rank?" Tupua asked with eyes challenging the stranger.

"My grandfather is the physical and spiritual leader of all of us, and he vanished far away in the north. My father was cowardly assassinated before we left our land. My brother vanished in the south. He and I are the only successors of the great Taranga Tici Viracocha."

"So! You are royal blood," Tupua said. "Then, you may stay with my daughter. You shall learn our rules, and obey them."

"What is that substance?" Vana asked, taking Kon's hands and caressing his bracelets."

"Maybe you never saw this before," Kon replied with a smile. "On our land, it is commonly found in rivers. You can melt it with fire and mold it into any form you like. It is very heavy and remains shiny for eternity."

Vana looked at one bracelet very closely, saw his face in it, and burst out laughing.

"How many people traveled with you?" Tupua asked.

"Not many. We are the only survivors of an ancient race. At

this moment, I think we are a lost race."

"What were the greatest achievements of your race?" Vana asked, pointing one finger on Kon's chest.

"Huge cities, made of walls as tall as these gigantic trees, so they would survive the most powerful earth tremors."

Vana glanced at Tupua. Both were disturbed by Kon's words. They did not know if they should believe him or not. Yet, he looked like a majestic, well-educated, and honest man. Vana immediately understood Hina's interest in him, because he knew her curiosity and thirst for learning. It became clear that she had learned a lot from this man. Her prodigious transformation was the living proof that this man knew many things they did not. Vana was also clever enough to know that the man would not be a threat to him as a great priest, and as such he was the most appropriate interlocutor for Kon.

"What did you do all that time you were alone in the valleys and the mountains?" Vana asked.

"I visited the entire heart of Tahiti-nui. I know every part of it. I meditated and thought about better ways of life."

"I don't believe this," Tupua said, looking at Hina and laughing. "Those two are already meditating. Soon, they will look for omens in the sky."

"Do you know what is Tupua's favorite game when I look for omens?" Vana asked, with a mischievous grin.

"No, I don't," Kon answered, puzzled.

"He goes on the beach kicking coconuts."

They all laughed with good humor. Tupua put one arm around Hina's shoulders in a gentle manner.

"Hina, forgive my behavior. Last night I was unfair to you."

She looked at her father, with tears in her eyes, and laid her head on his chest. Vana and Kon were talking, near the creek.

"I love you, my father, and I knew you would like him. He is going to be good for all of us, and especially you."

"We shall see," Tupua said. "Let's go to the village."

"What are you going to say to our people?" Vana asked. "There is a crowd waiting for us."

"Don't worry; I will handle it," Tupua replied.

They saw the first sightseers long before they reached Papenoo. With his hand, Tupua told them to follow. At some distance from the village, near the old banyan tree, Kon suddenly felt a spiritual power enter his mind. He stopped, and looked in the direction of the river. In the shade of the old tree, he saw

something but could not tell what it was. Pushed by the whispering crowd, he went on, but tried to memorize the place for a future visit.

Some fearless children touched Kon's garments, pulled on his bracelets and Vana grumbled at them. Clearly, children were free to do anything they liked. However, at one point in life, they were told to obey some rules. Viracocha's children were intensively tutored when they were very young; then and only then, as they grew older the pressure of rules would be progressively alleviated, and freedom was a reward for their self-discipline and proper conduct. For those who could be taught such principles, freedom would never be a pretense, and mutual respect would blossom. Viracocha's leaders were not authoritarian. They established a system of competence first, to which they would add liberalism.

When they reached the king's house, everyone gathered around a hillock of stacked boulders, from which Tupua was accustomed to address his people. With majesty, he walked to the top. Vana took a large coconut, and kept it in his hands.

"Today is a very special time," Tupua said. "It is still early, and I want this day to end with joy, songs, dances, and of course...

and of course... What! Nobody knows?"

"A good meal!" the entire crowd screamed.

Kon was startled by the enthusiastic and warm disposition of the people. Then, Tupua pulled on his belt with both hands.

"Well! I will get a little heavier. But, I don't care because Atea told me I was beautiful like that."

Everybody laughed in sheer joy. Then, the silence came, long, ponderous. The monarch frowned. Respectfully, they all listened. Drums rumbled gently. Then, the silence fell again, and Tupua raised his arms.

"My friends! We have a visitor coming from far beyond our land, where the sun rises every morning. His name is Kon Teke; you shall remember that name. He is our friend. He is my friend. He is Hina's friend."

Everyone murmured to one another. Immediately, the drums rumbled to restore order and discipline.

"Yes! You heard well. He is Hina's friend. From the omens, it was meant to be that way since her birth."

Inadvertently, Vana dropped his coconut on the ground, and Tupua looked at him infuriated. Hina could not suppress a giggle. Immediately, drums silenced everyone."

"Do you know who I am going to kick this time?" Tupua said, as Vana's eyes glowed with amusement.

"I was telling you that Kon Teke..."

The king kept going, and it seemed he would talk until the end of the day. Hina came closer to Vana.

"Where did he learn all that stuff?" she whispered in the old priest's ear.

Tupua glanced at his daughter and the drums rumbled.

"In a few days, I will have another important message to announce. This will concern my daughter Hina."

The surprise was as great among the crowd as on Hina's face.

"What does he mean?" she asked, looking at Vana.

"Don't ask Vana," Tupua said, enjoying his own words. "He does not know yet. Until the time will be right, it will remain a secret, my secret. Now, we should rejoice."

All afternoon, great activity transformed the village for the evening festivity. Kon spent most of his time speaking with Vana and Tupua, at the king's house. Hina, Atea and Fenua silently listened. When Kon told the story of his long trip through the ocean, the excitement of the two Maohi leaders reached its peak: They were indeed seafaring islanders, and lovers of the sea. Then, Vana came out with the unusual question.

"You said you were the Son of the Sun. Who were your forefathers?"

"They came from the far north, many generations ago. They were traders from another distant land. Many died when a star fell in the ocean. My forefathers had always been builders of monuments made of huge stones, uncut stones at first, then well cut afterward. Many of the stones would not fit inside this house."

Tupua and Vana looked around and stiffened in shock. Fenua whispered a few words in Hina's ear, and both left the house.

"Now, what are your plans?" Tupua asked.

"I want to find my people again. Do you know if there are many islands, north and south from Tahiti-nui that they could have reached?"

Vana glanced at Tupua, who understood his thoughts. Tupua hesitated, then put one friendly hand on Kon's shoulder.

"Yes indeed, there are many islands, but they are far apart from one another and easy to miss. However, nine moon-cycles from now, you will have your chance."

Kon looked at the king with inquisitive eyes.

"On the island of Havaiki, not far in the northwest, a religious gathering will take place," Tupua explained. "It is an important event for good friends and distant members of a family who take this opportunity to see each other after many sun-cycles of separation. They will come from many islands, some of them from so far away that they will stay two moon-cycles at sea. If your people have been seen somewhere on these islands, you will quickly find out."

Kon exhaled with contentment, and his eyes showed a glint of hope. He did not say a word, but the two Maohis understood his gratitude was immense.

"It will save you time to wait here until the gathering," Vana said.

"In the meantime, I will try my best to become one of you," Kon said with humbleness.

"You are already one of us," Vana smiled. "Stay who you are. I want to learn from you."

"Hina told us your people have great wisdom, and never fight," Tupua said.

"For us, every man and woman, whatever the race, is sacred," Kon said. "We shall not kill humans. It is our belief that those who prepare for war always live in fear, while those who prevent war live with courage."

Tupua and Vana shook their heads with a mocking smile, showing their complete disagreement.

"I don't like war," Tupua said. "But, sometimes it is inescapable. Either you defend yourself, or you die."

"You have no enemies," Kon replied. "You may have challenging adversaries, and there is nothing wrong with this. Most of the time, an adversary becomes an enemy only because of a misunderstanding or the unwillingness to carefully share this wonderful world. The Viracocha people have no hate nor do they feel any need for revenge against those who killed our brothers and sisters."

Vana frowned in exasperation and pointed a finger at Kon.

"But, you left the land where you were living, isn't it so? In fact, you are fugitives, isn't it so? You ran away from your enemies, isn't it so? How can you say they were not your enemies?"

"I know how you think," Kon answered, with compassion and no anger. "You think in terms of the present. But, we think in terms of the past and the future. Conquerors of the past left nothing good to future generations. They are remembered only for the battles they won or lost, and for the flow of blood they created. A victory today makes you blind, then you fall tomorrow after you misused the resources of your land and of your people, which ultimately creates people with no soul. Those who killed many of us were not our enemies. Among them, many did not agree with what happened. For this reason alone, it is our conviction that we should respect them, and it was up to us to peacefully change the course of history. In that respect we failed."

Vana went to the entrance of the house, laid one hand on a pillar. His thoughts were lost among the fronds of coconut trees waving gently in the breeze.

"So, you did not run away from your adversaries," Vana said. "You simply left to protect your families from their madness. What was the reason for their madness?"

"Their people liked our wisdom and skills, so we became obstacles to ambitious military leaders," Kon replied.

"Your ways of thinking are noble," Tupua said. "But, in real life, your ways of thinking are suicidal."

"Like many, you miss what is most important," Kon said, looking the king straight in the eyes. "If the human race continues to prepare for war, we are all doomed, by law from the stars. So, what difference does it make to win or lose today, if in the process you kill the land and the soul of its children?"

Tupua put one hand on Kon's shoulder.

"Anyway, we like you," the king said.

"How can you transport such large stones to construct your cities?" Vana asked.

"We use Mana's power."

Vana glanced at Tupua, then looked at Kon.

"Who is Mana?"

"Mana is a powerful force living in your mind," Kon replied. "It takes years of training from masters, to meet, understand, and use Mana. It is a spiritual force that makes you physically stronger."

"Fascinating!" Vana said. "You will have to teach us."

"Did you use this Mana for things other than transporting stones?" Tupua asked.

"I use it to climb mountains, when I am ill or when I meditate. With Mana, my mind can travel without my body."

"I have heard enough today," Vana said, with a broad smile. "Remember, we have a ceremony soon. I expect all of you to be at my place when the sun will touch the horizon."

Hina came back from the garden with her sister.

"Father, may I take Kon to the beach for a short walk?"

"Sure, but don't be too long."

The tide was low, the lagoon quiet as a mirror, and the sun was just above the mountains of Moorea. Two sandpipers hunted for their evening meal on the peaceful black sand beach. Kon took some sand in his hands and recognized the alluvium coming from the river: Slowly, the mountain returned to the sea. The sandpipers kept their distance ahead of Kon and Hina, while the entire island of Moorea and the sunset reflected on the lagoon.

"What a paradise!" Kon exclaimed.

"It is my home," Hina murmured gently.

They watched the sandpipers run up the beach in front of a small, isolated wave, then run down following the receding wave while feeding.

"Do you see how they take advantage of the force of nature?" Kon said.

"They have Mana," Hina replied.

"It is simple, yet many humans cannot take advantage of these things."

Hina laughed at the birds. Disturbed, the sandpipers flew some distance ahead, and repeated their endless search for tiny animals living under the sand. As the sun touched the horizon, Kon and Hina recalled they had to go to Vana's place.

To Kon's surprise, the surroundings of Vana's place were drastically different from those of the king. The high priest's house was modest, but part of a larger complex. On both sides of the house, terraces decorated with walls of upright coral-slabs extended to a dwelling house. Behind the walls, tumuli made of unpolished stones from the river must have been graves, on top of which old skulls and carved wooden divinities stared at the living. The dwelling house had no walls and an immense vegetal roof. All pillars were built with trunks of coconut trees. To enter the house, Kon bent down under the well-cut rim of the pandanus roof under which a large volume of fresh air circulated. He admired the well-crafted carpentry. It was an ideal place where people convened, especially during the hot period of the day or during frequent heavy rainfalls. Like Tupua's house, the floor was paved with nicely cut and polished stones whose cool contact under the feet was agreeable.

Suddenly and without notice, Hina vanished. Tupua noticed Kon's concern and offered him a beverage in half a hard coconut shell. As Kon was drinking the sweet and tasty concoction, he watched young women coming near him, looking at his blue eyes, and going away giggling.

"They are going to be around you like flies," Tupua commented.

"They look nice and kind," Kon replied. "But, none of them has Hina's grace."

"Of course! Hina has royal blood," Tupua said with pride.

Sitting cross-legged on the cool slabs, the two men looked at each other. Kon wondered what was in the king's mind.

"What do you like most about my daughter?" Tupua asked with inquisitive eyes. He thought the question would be rather embarrassing for Kon, but the reply came fast, clear, with certainty.

"Her high chin shows pride when she looks at people, because she has royal blood. But, at the same time, her smile reaches people's mind with goodness and she makes everyone feel that she cares. Your daughter's soul is pure and worthy. She has class, and this is what I like most in her."

Tupua stared at Kon, rocking forward and backward on his knees. He was thrilled by Kon's words.

"You know Hina well. You may even know her better than anyone else, including me."

Tupua stood up and went to a group of men and women, exchanged a few words, then came back to Kon.

"Welcome, Kon Teke! Be our friend and one of us. You may live under my roof as long as you wish. The many sun-cycles ahead shall bring you joy through discovery."

Then silence fell. It was amazing to Kon how everybody

knew exactly the critical moment when it was essential to cease talking and make no move. In many ways it added weight to what the speaker would say. A few parakeets argued in the surrounding breadfruit trees. Everyone looked at the entrance of Vana's house. The great priest appeared, dressed in an amazing costume made of shiny, white tapa. He wore a large hat of red feathers. The makeup on his face made it difficult to recognize him. Around his neck was a colorful, heavy necklace made of the prettiest cowries. The largest cowrie was all bright orange, and must have been a very rare and prized shell. Vana stood in front of Kon, in the middle of the dwelling house, and raised his arms inviting everyone to sit on the cool slabs.

Kon glanced at Tupua, and wondered who of the two men, the king or the priest, had more power.

"Today is a very special day..." Vana said, repeating Tupua's earlier words. Then, he took Kon's hands and made him stand up. Tupua stood up immediately, afraid of being overshadowed by the tall man. When Vana raised Kon's and Tupua's arms, Kon noticed the priest carefully kept the king's arm higher and concluded that it would have been wrong if someone stood higher than the king.

"This man is part of our village, part of the king's family. Therefore, you shall treat him with the respect due to your king's family. Never forget that Kon Teke is of royal blood. By our tradition, I give a name to the new members of our community. I, Vana, declare that the name of this man shall remain Kon Teke, Son of the Sun."

Surrounded by all the high dignitaries, Kon had plenty of time to learn about each of them and quickly understood that Hina's society was highly structured. A good balance of power was maintained between

Tupua and Vana. They were not in competition. They were complementary. The two men had deep affection for each other. Kon's hosts were friendly, honest and without malice.

Suddenly, the drums rolled. Someone else was expected. With surprise, Kon saw Atea coming, holding her daughters by the hands. Hina and Fenua were dressed in beautiful skirts of long, dry grass falling to their calves. Magnificent leis made of flowers covered their naked breasts. Hina's lei was made with her favorite white tiares, and Fenua's lei was made with her favorite yellow frangipani. Both young women had tall, white feather hats. On Hina's hat, two long white tropicbird feathers were attached and made a long curve far behind her head. Fenua was attractively and solidly shaped, while Hina was taller but still on her way to full womanhood. Atea placed a crown of delicate forest ferns on Kon's head and kissed him with obvious warmth.

"Welcome, Kon Teke, " she said with shiny black eyes.

The drums rolled, and this time it was different. Some people found something to clap with, and many started singing. At first the song was slow-paced and melancholy, almost sad, but by small increments, the rhythm took momentum, and the song became joyful. The two sisters started dancing, keeping movements with the music in a skillful way. The dance tempo accelerated. Hina and Fenua gracefully swayed with their hips, keeping their arms above their heads. Kon admired their suppleness and beauty. The rhythm accelerated even more, and everyone became more involved and excited. Even the king stood up and started dancing. More were clapping with increasing energy. It was a combination of rapid calls between sharp sounds against split bamboo, loud claps against house pillars and trees, and the deep rumbling of the drums.

Hina and Fenua swayed so fast that their skirts parted

revealing their perfect legs. Faster and faster, they reached a speed that was breathtaking. Yet, it was not the climax. The two women had their eyes closed from pleasure and pain. Kon's mouth was wide open, as he never thought that such a rhythm was possible. Finally, swaying, clapping, drumming and singing reached their crescendo. Then, everything stopped at once. There was no music, no song, no talk, only the waves of the sea pounding on the far barrier reef. Covered with perspiration, Hina was perfectly still in front of Kon, her arms frozen above her head.

Fenua came toward Kon and put her lei around his neck, then she kissed him with passion. Hina slowly removed her lei and put it around Kon's neck.

"I love you, Kon Teke," she said firmly. "These flowers are good luck for you. Do not lose them. Many years from now, when they will be dry and very old, you will remember this moment. These flowers are a symbol of beauty, and they are always given with love. They are the jewels of this island, and this island is the jewel of the world. Now, you are part of this island, and you live in our hearts."

****

CHAPTER 9

"Promote harmony by helping those who need you most. Give them all your energy until you are bonded. Rewards will come as events that will enlighten your life."

Kon Tici Viracocha

A few days later, in the king's garden, several high dignitaries listened to Kon's words about Mana's power. They were all thirsty for facts.

"Show us simple examples where you would use Mana," Vana said.

Kon searched for two identical pieces of wood, about the length and size of his arms. He placed one piece on the top of two flat stones slightly apart.

"Try, with one hand, to break that piece of wood by hitting it halfway between the stones."

Everyone looked at the piece of wood with circumspection.

"It is impossible," Tupua said.

"Try," Kon replied

Several times Tupua hit the piece of wood with force, but the wood was just too hard. Vana called Aru, Fenua's friend, who was the strongest man of the village. He tried to break the wood, without success.

"Now, let Kon try," Vana said.

Kon squatted, facing the piece of wood and put his right hand on the top of it. With the sharp side of his hand, he gently hit the wood at regular intervals to test its response. He closed his eyes, and concentrated on his objective. He opened his eyes and stared at the wood, perfectly still. Then, his hand went up and down so fast that the wood snapped loudly, to everyone's astonishment. Tupua took the two halves and looked at the clear cut.

"Remarkable," he murmured.

Following Kon's example, they all tried with frustration and no success.

"What bothers me most is that you did it relaxed, with no apparent difficulty," Vana remarked.

"The secret is training," Kon said. "Each of you can do it with proper training. There is nothing magic about this."

However, they wanted to succeed, to do something on their own. So, Kon felt he had to encourage them.

"There is another exercise for beginners that is much easier. I need one big, fat man, and four weak women."

They all giggled at one another, thinking he was not serious. Kon did not smile, and waited. Hina ran away to find her sister and two other young girls. Then, Vana glanced at Tupua.

"I think I found the man who can volunteer," Vana said with amusement.

The king looked at the high priest with suspicion, offended.

"Would you dare to insinuate that I am fat?" Tupua asked, restless.

"I would say it another way," Vana replied, spitting in his hands. "I would say you are perfect."

"What are you laughing about, all of you?" Tupua demanded, indignant.

Hina came back with her sister and two other young women.

Atea followed, curious about this new development. Hina looked around; her eyes stopped on the king.

"Father, would you volunteer?"

"I told you he was perfect..." Vana burst out laughing. His laugh was hysterical and catching. Then, everyone's smile deepened into laughter. Vana found refuge inside the house, half laughing, half crying. Kon himself could not resist the healthful joy of the Maohis.

Instants later, Vana came back, still chuckling and wiping tears from his eyes. Tupua sat down on a wooden stool, and complied with the experiment, now in a good mood.

"These four women can lift this man, by using only two fingers." Kon said.

Everybody murmured and giggled.

"But, let's practice first without Mana," Kon said, by placing each woman at her place around Tupua. "Now, join your hands, and place your forefingers against one another. Two women shall lift Tupua from under his knees, and the two others from under his arms, all at once. Now, try lifting this man."

The four women tried to lift the monarch with a lot of effort and commotion: His massive body never left the stool.

"I am not sure I like this game," Tupua said. "As a king, I never thought I would have to endure something like this."

"Don't say that, father," Hina said. "I know you like to have four pretty women around you, taking good care of you."

"Now, girls, do exactly what I say," Kon insisted. "At all times, you shall believe the king is light."

Tupua glanced at Kon with anxiety, and Vana was ready to burst out laughing again.

"Put your hands on Tupua's head," Kon said. "Close your eyes and concentrate on only one thought: You shall lift Tupua.

Think only about this... Think!... Think!..."

One girl opened her eyes and looked at Kon.

"Don't look at me. Close your eyes, concentrate, think,... You are going to lift that man."

Finally, everyone became silent. The four girls succeeded in relaxing and concentrated on what they had to do.

"Now, you are ready; remove your hands from his head, slowly, and lift Tupua. Lift him!"

The four girls placed their forefingers under the monarch, and this time he went up in the air, light as a feather. Everyone was astonished at what they saw. However, Mana was ephemeral, and the king came down much faster than he had gone up. Surprised, Tupua started screaming at the four girls, who could not stifle their giggles. Atea sat on the ground roaring with laughter.

Vana raised one finger: "That, that was..." he began but he could not finish.

"That is what?" Tupua asked with fulminating eyes.

"That, that was Mana going up..." Vana said, mimicking with his fingers.

Tupua started laughing himself, while Vana lay on the ground, pounding on his chest: "Enough for me,... no more,... pity!"

In sheer joy, the great priest choked with tears, and so did everyone else.

Later, the same day, Kon took a walk along the river. At some distance he saw Fenua, Hina's sister, collecting frangipani flowers.

"Why are you walking so far to collect these flowers?" He asked. "They are everywhere around your house."

She looked at him with a timid smile.

"We gather flowers with thanks to the earth, and respect for the plant," she replied with a gentle voice. "We never strip all flowers from a plant, and we never take the whole plant. We leave enough flowers for the plant to continue its natural development. Flowers allow the plant to generate itself. Because the plant is a friend, we remove the dead flowers and the dead leaves. If a plant struggles, we do not cut its flowers, even if it means we have to walk far away to find more healthy plants."

Kon was surprised and fascinated by the young woman's explanation. She was less superficial than he had thought. With simple words, she told him these seafaring islanders had deep respect for their environment. They were willing to struggle for the one-day life expectancy of a tiny flower, a detail which said much more about Mahois than any long dissertation. Fenua's answer was revealing, and persuaded Kon that Viracocha's sons had at last met another race sharing their views.

Fenua took a frangipani flower and placed it on Kon's ear. Then, she smiled at him and left.

Kon walked farther along the river, into a dark meadow surrounded by gigantic banyan trees. Their long, horizontal branches sent out shoots to the ground and started new roots, which would one day become new trunks. The area was dark and the air humid. The silence was broken at regular intervals by cracking sounds within the trees. Beyond the largest banyan, Kon saw a small house made of bamboo. The opened entry faced him. Inside, from a distance, everything seemed black as night, but he felt a presence, a great spiritual power. Kon came closer and noticed the ghostly profile of a shadow looking at him. When he reached the entry, the shadow went away, and a croaking voice froze his steps.

"Don't come here, nobody comes here; this place is taboo."

Surprised, Kon backed up, afraid of trespassing one of the

numerous taboos ruling the people. The voiced echoed sadness among the cracking banyan trees and the afternoon breeze. Disturbed by the mysterious encounter, Kon started back to the village looking for Hina.

"You will be back," the shadow murmured, looking at Kon going away.

Kon found Hina with her mother, polishing cowries.

"Hina, who lives in the isolated bamboo house under the banyan trees near the river?"

"Oh! You cannot go there," Hina said with a chill in her voice. "It is Taaroa's house. He used to be the great priest before Vana, and he is a distant cousin of my father. A few sun-cycles ago he caught a rare disease from some distant islands. The disease has terrible effects, and people are afraid to catch it. Those who catch it are isolated forever; there is no cure."

At some distance, Vana heard the conversation.

"Travelers coming from the far northwest brought the disease long ago," Vana said. "Taaroa tried to cure them and caught the disease. There is no hope for poor Taaroa. If you are infected you loose your face, your fingers, your toes, and slowly become a monster."

"I think I know this disease," Kon said. "It is contagious only from wound to wound. This man is in misery, needs you and you fail to give him proper care. Don't you see his soul's immense distress?"

Vana looked at Hina and Atea: They were lacking arguments.

"The misfortune of someone should not be a burden for those who are healthy with a long life ahead," Vana replied gently.

Kon frowned at the priest. For the first time they saw anger on his face.

"Once, this man was your great priest." Kon said with

accusing eyes. "Once, this man gave you all he had. You owe him respect and kindness. If you betray a beloved brother, your life is not worth anything."

Tupua heard Kon's remarks and came to the rescue.

"It is sad, but there is nothing we can do," the king said. "We cannot gamble with the good health of others just because of his misfortune. Besides, Taaroa himself agreed to stay isolated. His place is taboo."

"It is not a must to isolate Taaroa," Kon replied. "He can live among you without touching you, but his isolation as someone you are ashamed of is intolerable. Your so-called taboo shows crude disregard and humiliating disgrace."

Kon stepped back from the group and pointed a finger at them.

"Because of his misfortune, this man suffers a physical torture. Worse, because of your attitude he is mentally decaying through lifetime damnation. Because of you, his mental agony is far greater than his physical pain. When you should give him your best, instead you curse him terrible turmoil."

The force of Kon's words compelled everyone. They knew he was right, and for the first time they realized who Kon Tici Viracocha was. For the first time they feared this man for whom they had so much respect. It became clear to them he was going to change their ways. He was a formidable defender of humble, hopeless and struggling human souls. He could stand above taboos for what was right, regardless of consequences. He left, going back to Taaroa's house. Hina and the others followed him from a distance.

When Kon reached the humid meadow, Hina knew he was going straight to the ill man. She ran to him and grabbed his hand.

"No, you cannot go, please," she said in despair.

Kon looked at her with a cynical smile.

"I am going to see this man, talk to him and pull him out of his misery. For that you shall not stop me because nothing will. Also, I suggest you remember the meaning of what hangs on your chest."

Never before had she seen that kind of smile on his face. Shocked, she sat on the ground, took the golden flying condor in her hand, and fought back tears. The others were behind her.

Kon entered the house and heard someone running away in the darkness.

"Don't come here! My illness is contagious."

Kon ignored the warning, and slowly approached the man, who was visibly trembling. Taaroa was in the corner of the room, hiding his face under a white, felted bark cloth.

"Do not fear. My name is Kon Tici, and I am from another world. I know about your illness and its terrible effects. I am also aware that under some circumstances it could be contagious. Be unafraid and look at me."

Kon saw the devastated hands and feet of the leper. Slowly, he uncovered the poor man's face, the left part of which was covered with round tumors. However, his nose, eyes and lips were untouched. Except for his illness, Taaroa was still physically strong. He was thin and tall, and his skin was mummy like, encrusted by ulcerous sores. Most of his hair was gone. He must have been in his sixties. Kon did not touch him, but sat on the ground and invited Taaroa to do the same.

"Why are you doing this?" the old priest asked. "Don't you see that I am finished?"

"This is precisely the point; you are not finished. You need them, and they need you."

"How could they need something like this?" Taaroa asked, showing his fingers and toes.

"They don't need your body, but they still need your mind. They are not aware of this yet, but in due time they will be."

"What do you mean?" Taaroa asked with a broken voice.

"As I said, in due time you will find out. In the meantime, you must live under the sun, near the sea, away from this rotten place."

"They will not let you do this. I am doomed and I shall die under the banyan tree. You should leave before it is too late for you."

Kon stood up and looked Taaroa straight in the eyes.

"As long as I live in this village I will try to take you where you belong. I have plans that will transport you to the climax of your priesthood. Give me the honor to guide you."

Taaroa's black eyes widened. In Kon's words he recognized the unmistakable touch of those gifted with great knowledge. The man facing him was also a priest, from another place. His goodness was equaled only by the halo of mystery attached to his message. Taaroa's knew his pain and the sluggish, irreversible course of his illness were suddenly secondary. Inside Kon's glittering golden bracelets, he could see the deformed features of his face, but he also knew he would not die as a hopeless wreck. Before making the ultimate voyage, he would have to do something important.

"In a few days, I will come back," Kon said. "I will take you to your new home. I will restore your high priest status, and in due time, you shall learn about your destiny."

Kon left swiftly, passed in front of the crowd, ignored everyone and walked toward the riverbank.

Taaroa was alone again. He sat on a large stone, under the banyan tree, and for the first time in many years he noticed the quiet song of the yellow warbler of the valleys. He knew the magnificent bird well, but for a long time he had not seen it, he had not heard it, he had not cared. Now, suddenly he cared about the tiny warbler. Why?

Taaroa looked at his decaying body, at his terrible skin, at the deadly process in which he was trapped. Yet, somehow, the small bird of the valleys reminded him that his soul was intact. Why had he never thought about this before? Why did the short visit of this mysterious man make such a difference? Who was he? Taaroa's eyes, behind his hanging brows, followed the warbler from branch to branch. As a child, he had always been puzzled by how familiar the gentle bird was. The warbler flew onto a branch very close to Taaroa, and extended its head and long beak parallel to the branch, perfectly mimicking its environment. For the bird, Taaroa was no discovery, but for Taaroa the bird was a revelation.

The yellow warbler flew to a patch of reeds, near the stream. Taaroa knew the reeds were the favorite place where it would nest. So, here it lived, as a friendly neighbor of a decaying leper. Taaroa recalled the bird was most useful as a prime killer of myriapods, ants, worms, flies and mosquitoes. The bird was a gift to this earth. Therefore it was sacred.

"Who are you, Kon Teke?" the leper murmured with a croaking voice. "Why did you come to me?"

The warbler of the valleys answered with its song. It was horror and repugnance communicating with perfect beauty. Somehow, loud and clear, the voice of Kon Tici Viracocha was present in Taaroa's mind, telling him there was a reason for everything. Now, he knew he would learn the reason for his misfortune.

Kon washed his hands with the black sand of the river, rinsed them and noticed Hina approaching.

"Can we talk?" she asked.

"This man is important for the destiny of your people," he replied, looking at the running river.

"How can you tell?" she asked.

"There is a reason for everything," Kon said. "He is a priest, and it was not by chance that he was chosen. Something will happen soon and Taaroa will merit the glory. Furthermore, it was not by chance that he was named Taaroa, the most sacred name of this land."

Puzzled by his words she shook her head, then took his hands, gently.

"My father wants to talk to you, at his house."

"He wants to blame me because I violated a taboo."

"No, on the contrary, I think you impressed him."

Kon and Hina found Tupua and Vana waiting for them.

"What you did was generous," Tupua said. "But, why did you do such a thing?"

"Who are we, if we cannot cherish the clear souls of others?" Kon replied." Who are we, if we cannot see the smiling brightness of an elder almost ready to go home?"

Tupua glanced at Vana. The king did not understand Kon's words.

"Let me explain," Kon said. "Why do you think this man was named Taaroa? Why did you choose him to be a high priest? Because he had a destiny, and his illness cannot and will not change that."

"It is rather obvious that his illness has changed his destiny," Vana replied, with a mocking smile.

"Not so!" Kon argued. "Do you know what his destiny is? There is a link between Taaroa the great priest and Taaroa the ill one. Soon, you shall learn what that link is. Then, Taaroa will enter the Tahitian legend with force. In due time, you will remember my words."

"How can you tell?" Tupua asked. "Can you predict the future?"

"No, I cannot. But, this world is harmony, and as such something is missing along the journey of that man. Let's make sure you give Taaroa fair consideration, before he leaves at the sunset of his life."

"You are a wise man, Kon Teke," Tupua said. "Your words are profound, and we will build a new home for Taaroa, near the seashore where he will see the sunsets beyond Moorea. These are my words, and so be it."

"I have a request." Kon said, looking at Vana.

"I am listening."

"Could you prepare a mixture of all the vegetable oils you can find on this island? Some of these oils may be beneficial to Taaroa's skin."

"I shall give you such mixture in a few days," Vana said. "Hina will help me; it will be a good lesson for her."

A few days later, the leper was meditating under the banyan tree. It was hot and humid. Taaroa waited for Kon Tici Viracocha. He knew he would come back.

Around midday, he saw the unmistakable silhouette of the man he waited for. He saw his long hair pinned above his head, falling on his shoulders. He saw his beard, the gold rings in his earlobes, and the fascinating gold bracelets reflecting the sun. The man was slender but powerful. The way he walked exuded grace and self-confidence. He saw the red drawings representing suns and birds on his headband and belt. Finally, he saw the smiling deep blue eyes. This man was so different, with an imposing mien. Yet, Taaroa was comfortable with him, with no shame. Taaroa knew there was no possible malice in Kon's intentions. From instinct and experience, Taaroa knew there was no possible mistake: Kon Tici was all honesty and goodwill, but what was he doing on this island?

"I was waiting for you," Taaroa said in his croaking voice.

"I told you I would come."

"I knew, but I did not know when."

Kon sat near the leper, offered him a few fresh fruits, and some warm breadfruit. They both ate in silence.

"You like birds," Taaroa said with his eyes lost in the banyan tree.

"Yes I do," Kon said, surprised. "How did you know?"

"They are on your belt and headband. Besides, you are a good, peaceful man, therefore you must like birds. You also worship light."

"Light is the true, fundamental form of intelligent life," Kon replied, making his bracelets send a beam of sun on the banyan tree.

"So, without light, nothing is possible, not even death," Taaroa said.

"Death is the door beyond which we begin to understand the purpose of light."

"You are many generations ahead of our time," Taaroa murmured. "Come, I want to show you my little companions."

They both walked slowly toward the stream, approached a patch of reeds and stopped. With a mutilated finger, Taaroa pointed at the yellow warbler of the valleys on its nest.

Kon admired the colorful bird, its long, thin beak, and the tiny hairs around its nares. Then, they backed off quietly.

"The male comes to feed her at times," Taaroa said, "at other times he sings for her. They are not afraid of me, and they accept me the way I am."

Kon looked at him with immense sympathy.

"They all like you. They are afraid of your illness, but they care for you. Yet, they don't know what to do."

"Sometimes, I wish there could be a faster way to fade away from this body. There are ways, but I never found the necessary courage."

"Your time has not come yet," Kon said, looking at Mount Orohena.

"I used to go near the summit, to watch the red ducks as you did with Hina. It is an astonishing place."

"Yes, you are right, you do indeed belong in an astonishing place."

"Why did you say this?" Taaroa asked, surprised.

"If your body cannot reach this world around you, your mind can still reach Mount Orohena. You are a great priest, therefore you know: There are no limitations for a well-born soul."

With a smile widening in approval, Taaroa glanced at Kon.

"Are you afraid of death?" the leper asked.

"There is no such thing as death. We are and always will be. This body will return to the earth, while our soul will proceed to the stars. Our soul is pure light traveling in our complex body for a short moment. Light is the form of life we don't understand. Everything we do understand is a transient illusion."

For a moment, the leper weighed Kon's words, until a glint of wonder passed through his eyes.

"Perhaps, we are all part of a wonderful everlasting story," Taaroa said.

"True! When starlight enters my eyes, something happens. I can feel a presence, strong, mysterious and peaceful. I don't know its meaning."

"Maybe she will find out for you one day," Taaroa said, pointing at Hina, who was coming.

"She is very dear to me."

"Who else could suit you better than Hina, on this island?" Taaroa said with a serene smile. "I am sure you noticed that she is different, as you are."

Hina held a bamboo cup filled with thick, oily liquid.

"This is the mixture you asked for," Hina said.

"This is to rub your skin with, after you take a bath in the sea, and rinse in the river, every day."

"This is for women!" Taaroa said with annoyance.

"No, it is a preparation made especially for you," Kon argued.

"Well! What do I have to lose?"

"My father told me that Taaroa's new house is ready."

"What do you mean?" Taaroa asked, irritated.

"This was my idea," Kon said. "I told them to build a new house for you near the sea."

"I don't need a new house. I belong under the banyan tree, and I don't need your help."

"Maybe so, but what if we need yours?" Hina asked in a friendly tone.

"You are nice, young woman, but nobody needs any help from a rotten body like this," Taaroa said, showing his mutilated hands.

"We don't need any help from your body," Hina said, "but we need help from your mind."

"You talk like this stranger. Leave me alone. Everybody hates me at the village."

"This is not true," Hina replied sharply. "Everyone is afraid of your illness, but nobody hates you. Your new place will be more appropriate for a great priest."

"I am not a priest anymore," Taaroa said, humiliated. "Priests are selected because their body is perfect."

"It takes much more than a perfect body to make a priest," Hina said firmly. "Destroy not who you are; tell us where you go, and why."

The leper smiled, but was in no mood to argue.

"You have been in this damp valley for too long," Hina said with unusual authority. "You must come with us, or I will carry you."

The old man was caught off guard by the sudden force of Hina's words. At last, his eyes calmly glittered. He knew he was wrong. For a very long time, he had not felt so much pleasure as being with Kon and Hina. He knew it was a new time for him, a new test. He would watch the sea and the sunsets, again.

"So be it, my friends!" Taaroa said, standing tall.

****

CHAPTER 10

"I was mystified by the blue dotted, powerful moray eel. The frightful predator pulled the arm of the man with astonishing brutality and tenacity. I was helpless and amazed."

Hina of the Valley

It was dawn, far away in the west, on the island of Rarotonga. Barefooted, a giant man walked with ponderous steps on the beach. His name was Tamatoa. For every step he took, someone would follow. For every word he said, someone would carefully listen. Ambitious, intelligent, respected, but also mad, he pointed at the sun rising in the east and harangued the old man by his side.

"These islands in the east are mine. I, Tamatoa, king of Rarotonga and all the surrounding islands, will conquer Maupiti, Pora Pora, Havaiki, Huahine, Moorea, Tahiti-nui..."

"Nothing can stop you," the old man replied. "You have prepared for this for a long time. Your warriors are perfectly trained, and your plan is clever."

"Mato, my friend, friend of my late father, high priest of my people, I want to show you the day when my empire will range from here to these distant islands."

"That day, you will fulfill the wish of your father. His last words told me it was your mission."

The two men smiled at one another. Their eyes glittered at the view of the impressive armada they had built. The sea was covered with war galleys.

"I shall fight my enemy until his last drop of blood," Tamatoa swore.

****

At the same instant, on Papenoo's beach, Taaroa watched Tupua's long outrigger glide on the calm lagoon. The sea was silent, and the tide low. The leper dreamed about the good old days when he used to go fishing. Watching his friends gave him pleasure.

It had been Tupua's idea to take Kon, Hina, Aru, and Fenua on a lobster hunting party, behind the collapsed reef. Even at low tide, the reef was still under the waters. When they reached the inner part of the reef, Taaroa could barely see them as tiny distant dots.

"I know a much better place," Taaroa murmured.

The surface of the water was perfectly still. Kon thought he was paddling in oil, and was fascinated by the transparency of the world under the gliding outrigger. Once, he had been fearful about such beauty, on a faraway atoll. For a moment, the memories of Ra and Ilo came to his mind, but Hina guessed his thoughts. With her paddle she splashed some water on his face, which instantly brought him back to the present. He smiled at how well she knew him. Then, he marveled at the corals, the fish, the urchins and the numerous shell tracks on the white sand between corals. They were all amused by the contradiction between who he was, and his childish attitude in discovering the secrets of the lagoon.

"Look at this shell crawling on the sand!" Kon exclaimed.

Hina removed her clothes, dived and quickly reached the

magnificent harp shell. Swiftly, she came and gave it to Kon, who could not believe his eyes. Silent, he admired the pink, deep, flawless grooves of the shell.

"The regularity of these spiraling furrows is incredible," Kon marveled.

Fenua removed her clothes and joined Hina in the water. Neither Tupua nor Aru paid attention to the beautiful young women, but Kon could not ignore the two sisters. They were beauties among beauty, and like the shell, they were flawless. Fenua came back and gave him a large miter circled with ridges and red dots on a white background. For a moment Kon hesitated, considering if he should admire the shell or the young woman, and wondered if all this was reality or a dream. These people were free with everything, and above all, they were free with themselves in a quiet paradise. To them, yesterday and tomorrow were secondary to the sacred present. He followed the gliding bodies of the two sisters under water. For an instant he thought he had vertigo for the first time in his life.

Tupua splashed the water three times with his paddle. Instantly, Hina and Fenua came back to the outrigger.

"Let's go behind the reef," Tupua said.

The sisters climbed into the canoe, and they all paddled slowly toward the deeper part of the lagoon. Suddenly, the barrier of reefs appeared under them, large, new and mysterious, a living garden from another world. Corals displayed delicate colors like yellows, reds and pinks. From place to place Kon saw huge, yellow brain-like corals. There were deep pools at the bottom of which the sand seemed light blue. At times, dark and fathomless crevasses led to unknown territories.

Then, they reached the limit of the barrier, behind which this mysterious world beyond description fell abruptly into the darkness of abysses.

Deep in the dark blue water, Kon could see the corals shaped like several plates piled above one another. They were so deep that all looked blue. From place to place, some corals looked like trees without leaves.

"This is lobster territory," Tupua said.

"Are you going to dive here?" Kon asked, with concern in his voice.

"It is deep, but it is a good spot," Tupua said. "How deep can you dive?"

"I can dive like the girls did, but not here," Kon said.

"I can dive here," Hina said.

Tupua dropped a heavy stone attached to a long rope to anchor the outrigger. Kon looked at the length of the rope going in the water and gasped. He had vertigo again.

Aru jumped into the water, swam around the canoe, then dived into the blue. They all watched him disappear. Instants later he came back.

"They are here," he said.

Kon noticed something unusual: Aru filled his lungs several times as if he was trying to build up a reserve of air, then expelled the air before diving again. They all waited.

After what seemed a little too long, Kon looked at Tupua with concern.

"He should be back by now."

"Not yet," Tupua said. "He is exploring the reef."

Hina came close to Kon and kissed him.

"Don't worry," she said. "He is almost a fish."

As time went by, Kon became astonished by the man's performance. He had never seen anyone stay under water so long and remain alive, yet nobody except him seemed concerned. He realized he had much more to learn from these islanders.

There was no sign of Aru. Kon shook his head in disbelief.

"Here he comes!" Fenua said.

Aru was coming back slowly to the surface, taking his time. He broke the surface, and placed two lobsters into the outrigger. He started another conditioning cycle, and dived for a second journey into the blue depths.

"I cannot do this anymore," Tupua noted. "Remember, Vana said I was perfect."

"Sure, your body is unsinkable," Hina chuckled.

They all laughed in sheer joy.

"Would Taaroa still dive?" Kon asked.

"No, he cannot," Tupua replied, wondering if Kon was joking. "But, he used to be good at this."

"I think he still can," Kon said.

Tupua glanced at the two women, who shrugged their shoulders.

"I want to bring him here," Kon insisted.

"You want to kill him," Tupua said with a hint of disapproval.

"No, I want him to be born again and enjoy the beauty of these waters."

Aru came back with two more lobsters. Kon saw a long shark gliding under the outrigger, and they all saw the fear on his face.

"Sharks come visiting often," Tupua explained. "Many are curious, but not dangerous. However, never attack them, and if there are two or three of them circling around you, come back to the canoe and go to another place."

"What happens if you don't see them?" Kon asked with mixed emotions.

"If you don't see them, you still feel them." Tupua explained. "You know they are here. Your body hears them. Yes, unexplained fears can be a sign you should go back to the canoe."

"Another thing," Hina said, "do not attach fish near your body or around your belt. The shark may take the fish and wound you severely in the process."

"So, whatever you take, bring it back quickly to the canoe," Kon added.

"Yes," Tupua said and smiled. "If the shark wants your fish, gladly give it to him."

Aru came back with another lobster.

"Father, I want to catch my lobster," Hina said.

"It may be a little deep for you," Tupua replied.

Fenua objected for her sister to dive so deeply. But, Hina had her mind made up, and she jumped into the sea. She followed the same breathing cycle as Aru, expelled a last time, and dived. Anxious, Kon looked at her. Halfway down, she pinched her nose and blew air into her inner ears. Then, she went down and disappeared in the blue.

Kon was not happy about this development, especially as he looked at the concerned face of Hina's sister. Then, Hina came back and asked for a piece of bark-cloth to wrap around her right hand.

"I am going to get one," she said with confidence. Swiftly, she returned to the mysterious depths.

"Aru, keep an eye on that girl!" Tupua ordered with a dissatisfied tone. Aru went down immediately.

They waited and waited. Kon felt perspiration rolling down his burned forehead. Finally, Aru came back to the surface.

"She is all right, and got a big lobster," Aru said.

They saw Hina coming back very slowly to the surface.

"Look at that lobster!" Fenua exclaimed. "She did it."

When the young woman broke the surface, pride was all

evident over her face. She had caught the largest lobster.

"I want to find out how deep I can go here," Kon said, jumping into the water.

"You cannot reach the reef," Hina said.

"Don't push beyond your limits," Tupua recommended.

Kon followed the breathing sequence he had observed, and went down. At first everything was blue and blurry. When he saw the corals shaped like plates, he was only halfway. Already, his ears sent signals that the pressure was too much for him. He continued for a short distance, then was out of breath, his head pounding, and his ears in pain: It was time for him to go back to the surface. When he climbed inside the outrigger, he looked back at the deep corals, frustrated, and astonished by the swimming and diving capabilities of these seafaring people.

Tupua put his hand on Kon's shoulder, showing joy in his eyes.

"In water, Mahois have Mana's power."

Kon looked at him, surprised by his analysis.

"Yes, definitely!"

"Now, I understand your words: Mana is inherent to both practice and cleverness."

"Very good!" Kon said putting his hand on Tupua's shoulder.

"So, Mahois have always known Mana," the King proudly said.

As they came back to shore, they waved at Taaroa, who was swimming in shallow water.

"You see, I told you he could swim," Kon said, amused.

"Would you come fishing with us tomorrow?" Hina asked Taaroa.

"Why not," the leper said, with his croaking voice. "I know a good place."

"Be ready at dawn," Kon said.

Later, Hina and Fenua cut the lobsters in half lengthwise, and removed the intestines. On the fresh meat, they spread a mixture of fermented coconut milk, limejuice, and hot spices. They wrapped each half with banana tree leaves, and cooked them gently on the glowing embers of a fire.

The evening meal was a charming delight, and they all listened to an old legend told in Vana's words.

"On one occasion, a king of this land ruled his people with tyranny. One day, he went with his subjects, determined to explore an underwater cave not far from where you went fishing. A thing of unknown origin dwelt there. He had a long rope, and being the bravest man, attached himself to one end of it. His subjects were told to pull him up quickly when he gave the signal by jerking the rope. Shortly after he entered the cave under water, the king violently jerked the rope. They all smiled and did not pull him up. Long after the jerking ceased, they drew up their king and all his flesh had been devoured from his bones. Ever since, this land has been free from a bad king. To be a king is an honor won by kind wisdom, but never by despotism...."

"Hina, this lobster is wonderful," Kon whispered. "I have never tasted anything as good as this."

She tried to take a small piece of his lobster.

"No!" he objected. "This is mine!"

They all stared at Kon. Then, they laughed at his mimicry, as if he was guarding his share of a valuable treasure.

At dawn, Taaroa met Kon and Hina on the beach. It was cloudy and cool, with no breeze. At Tupua's request, they took his outrigger. Taaroa guided their way, farther north from the Papenoo River. The old priest knew exactly where to go, and alive again, he sang in joy:

"Taaroa is the forefather of all spirits.
Taaroa created what is, before our time.
Taaroa developed his soul, in loneliness.
Taaroa taught himself; he had no parents.
Taaroa was the only source of truth.
Taaroa always fought ill forces.
Taaroa freed his brother from the malediction.
Taaroa was a terror in the kingdom of darkness.
Taaroa cried in the darkness,
Because there was no sun, no moon, and no stars.
In the infinite space, there was no earth,
No land, no sea, no water and no loved ones.
Taaroa swam for a long time in the sea, then in the river.
Afterward, he walked far away, in the valley.
He found the tree and the oil for his skin.
Taaroa found new friends, true friends, the loved ones..."

Kon glanced at Hina: She had tears in her eyes. Taaroa stopped singing, as the words could not find their way through his throat. With tears on his cheeks, he looked at the beautiful sea. Seemingly with respect to the old priest, the surface of the water was still. The sea listened to Taaroa's song, and so did the thing nearby.

Still as the coral, the thing looked through the deep blue water. Fish swam near its powerful jaws, but it was uninterested. The tempting leftover from a shark's prey did not even bother it.

Only the approaching melody of the old priest was of interest. Far back in its memory, it remembered the priest. Once more, it waited for him; it waited for the smell of fresh blood.

"That song was beautiful," Kon said.

"I often meditated here, for long periods," Taaroa replied. "I used to enjoy it."

"Why did you stop?" Kon asked.

"After I became ill, others stopped listening to my words. My words spoke for Taaroa, alone. The Taaroa of my song is not I. He is our God, our Creator. One day I may tell you the reasons why my people gave me that name. I am not sure I deserved it."

"Now, your people will listen to your words again," Kon said.

"They shall not," Taaroa said. "Priests are not ill men. They are the best of us. They should have good posture, good health and they must inspire. I am a physical wreck. I am the result of a failure, and failures belong to the past. Our children shall look forward, so they may succeed."

"Our children shall learn from our failures," Kon argued. "Only then they may not repeat the same mistakes, and may succeed. You have no control over your fate, and there is a reason for it. Search for this reason!"

Taaroa raised his head, looked straight to the north where the sea touched the sky.

"I never thought of myself in those terms. So, I may still have something to share, to give..."

"To leave this life, you have two ways," Kon said. "You fade away, destroyed by your fate. Or, you enter the legend, enlarged by your fate. Make sure you inspire our children by the second choice."

They headed toward a large crown of reefs that almost

reached the surface. They almost forgot they were going fishing. Only the view of the colorful corals brought them back to reality. Kon stopped paddling, glanced around and felt a presence. Somewhere around, there was something very unusual.

"Where do we go?" Hina asked.

"Somewhere, on the other side of this crown of reefs there is an underwater cavern," Taaroa said. "That is where we go. Inside, I used to have good luck finding large lobsters. Keep going, slowly now."

Hina paddled gently, and she noticed an unusual frown on Kon's face.

"You see, where it is deeper," Taaroa said. "The cavern is underneath this table of coral."

Slowly, the canoe circled the huge table. Then they saw the wide opening beyond which everything was black.

"Stop the canoe," Taaroa said.

Kon lowered the large stone attached to a long rope, and they stayed here, doing nothing, searching the magnificent surroundings. Several green parrotfish went in and out the dark entry. Kon had a shiver down his spine at the thought that they would dive inside this dark hole.

"Sometimes, there are sleeping sharks, large groupers or passive moray eels inside," Taaroa said. "Nothing to worry about."

Hina removed her clothes and dived immediately. She entered the cavern for a quick inspection, and they waited for her. A small shark came out and disappeared in the blue depths. Hina pursued deeper, to the point where the visibility was poor, then went back to the surface.

"This is a huge hole," she said. "I cannot see well inside, it is too dark. But, how come I never heard about this hole before?"

"Yes, you did," Taaroa smiled, "last night, in Vana's legend."

Hina glanced at Kon, who was watching the dark hole.

"Is this a sacred place?" Kon asked.

"No, but somehow, a lot of people just don't like to come here," Taaroa replied.

Kon jumped into the water, dived toward the cavern, and entered. He could see the parrotfish dancing around him. He saw the antennae of a lobster coming out of the dark wall. He pulled on them, and found out that it must not have been the way to catch them. Deeper in the wall, he thought he saw a large grouper with blue dots, but he was not sure. Short of breath, he went back to the canoe.

Hina swam around the large table of coral. At one point, she must have disturbed the nap of a large fish. Taaroa and Kon noticed a massive shadow glide under the canoe and enter the cavern.

"Did you see that grouper with blue dots?" Hina asked.

"Yes, I think there is a second one like it in the cavern," Kon replied.

"Those are the best," Taaroa said. "We should try to catch one."

Hina took the harpoon Taaroa had prepared, and dived toward the cavern. She went deeper than the first time, and held herself to the wall until she became accustomed to the dark. She saw one grouper looking at her. His long, sharp, white cuspids waited. She hurled the harpoon toward his back but missed. The large fish circled around her, visibly upset. She swam in his direction, looking at the fish with the corner of her eyes. She knew the fish watched her eyes. When she got close enough, she quickly turned toward the grouper and speared it. The harpoon deeply entered its back. Instantly, a cloud of sand came up from the bottom of the cavern. She felt the power of the fish pull on the string attached to the harpoon and to her wrist. She tried to push the harpoon deeper inside its flesh. Instead, she tore its wound and the grouper swam away. A large flow of blood mixed with the settling white sand. Out of breath, she went back to the canoe.

"I saw the grouper go away," Kon said. "But, I think there is another one in here."

"Give me the harpoon," Taaroa said.

Kon looked at Hina, and Hina glanced at Kon. They could not believe what they just heard and saw. Taaroa was agitated and completely forgot his condition.

Suddenly, he appeared taller and younger.

"Give me that thing!" Taaroa said.

"You cannot do that," Hina objected.

"Yes, I can." Taaroa smiled. "I was a good diver; I must have something left."

"Let Taaroa challenge his fate." Kon said.

Taaroa took the harpoon, dived and entered the cavern. He saw blood floating everywhere, and studied the friendly surroundings. He vaguely saw something moving, something with blue dots, but it was too deep for him, and he went back to the surface. Taaroa did not recognized the thing, powerful and crawling, smelling the odor of fresh blood.

"Let me try again," Hina said.

"No, Hina, leave it to me." Taaroa said. "It is deep, but this time, this grouper is ours."

She could not stop the old priest, and he was already gone. Taaroa dived directly to the spot where he saw the dark mass of a grouper with blue dots. He slowly became accustomed to the dark, but suspended fine sand limited his visibility. At last, he saw the blue dots.

Kon felt a premonition, a sort of signal he had experienced many times before.

"There is something wrong around here."

"I can see that in your face," Hina said.

With all his energy, Taaroa pushed the harpoon inside the flesh of the fish. He pushed as deeply as he could, expecting a strong reaction from the massive grouper, but the grouper did not move. He knew the grouper should have started spinning, shaking and struggling in all directions. Maybe it was the one Hina had wounded. He waited, shook the harpoon a little, but nothing happened. Then, he felt a slow, constant, powerful pull on the harpoon. The fish was alive, but something was odd. Something told Taaroa that the grouper was long gone. The leper felt a shiver down his spine, and realized he had made a terrible mistake. What was ahead of him was also hunting the wounded grouper; it came to find out where the fresh blood was coming from. Taaroa tried to remove the rope from around his wrist. It was too late. The pull was stronger, and nothing could stop this monster of the lagoon. The old man knew it was his last day, and he was frightened. Then, he remembered his condition, and in a way Taaroa was glad. Kon had been right; he could go at a climax of his life. He could die proudly as a hunter, and not as a leper.

Kon and Hina waited long minutes.

"I don't like it," she murmured, her eyes looking at the cavern.

She dived and went straight to Taaroa. At the same instant, she saw the grouper still bleeding. The fish left the cavern for the blue depths. Then, she saw Taaroa struggle with something. She came closer, and realized he was in trouble. She tried to remove the rope from around his wrist, but when she touched the rope she noticed the stretch on his arm was incredible. She looked above and saw the source of the problem. The head of the giant moray eel was coming out from another hole, and hung above them, looking at them with the cold eyes of a killer. The long, needle-sharp teeth seemed to laugh at them. Farther down, inside the hole, the other end of the formidable predator pulled with astonishing tenacity. Hina was fascinated by the moray. Never before had she seen so large a moray. Its body was covered with blue dots that Taaroa had mistaken for the grouper. She was helpless and upset. She quickly went back to the canoe.

By the way she swam, Kon knew there was a problem.

"Kon, it is terrible. The moray is going to kill him. His arm is... We must cut the rope around his wrist."

Kon immediately understood, took his obsidian knife, dived, and Hina followed him. She knew at one point he would be short of breath and she would have to take his knife.

Kon found Taaroa, and saw his stretched shoulder. He followed his wounded arm deep inside a narrow hole. Above them, the moray watched, fearless, cold and in control. The animal, as large as Kon's body and much longer, was all muscle.

Kon felt out of breath, but would not turn back. He knew he was Taaroa's only chance. At any time, the moray could tear out Taaroa's arm. He found the rope, tried pulling on it, but found that the moray could tug even stronger. The moray was definitely in the process of pulling Taaroa's arm. With his knife, Kon sawed the rope as quickly as he could. Suddenly, the rope broke, the pressure was released and the moray swam out of the hole with the harpoon through its body. The incredible animal went directly toward Hina, who backed off and panicked when she felt the powerful slimy animal crawling between her legs.

Kon struggled to drag Taaroa's body to the surface, and

swallowed too much water. With the little energy he had left, he pushed Taaroa above the outrigger, climbed in the canoe and pulled Taaroa until he could lie down comfortably. Taaroa was still breathing, but where was Hina? The last time he had seen her was when the moray went away from its hole. Hina should have been in the canoe with him, unless... The frightening thought did not have time to cross his mind. Hina came to the surface.

When she broke the surface, she was terrified, and sobbing. Kon helped her climb into the canoe, and she grabbed and scratched his arm. Her eyes were dilated, and he did not recognize her. He took her in his arms to comfort her, while Taaroa slowly came back to life.

"Oh! My shoulder hurts," the leper said, "and my arm is numb."

With no further words, the three companions rested, still in shock. The low-pitched calls of a brown noddy brought them back to reality. They had gone through a nightmare none of them would forget.

"You are going to have a sore arm for a long time," Kon said.

Taaroa coughed several times, vomited water and food, and smiled to his friends.

"This is what I call fishing!" Taaroa joked, with shiny eyes.

The old priest had been perfectly aware of what Kon and Hina endured to save his life. They laughed, happy.

"Kon, a little farther from here," Taaroa said with a glint of humor in his eyes, "there is a spot you and Hina should check for lobsters."

"You know what you can do with your spot!" Hina said with fire in her eyes. "Do you really want me to tell you?"

"Well! I guess... I did not mean..."

Hina swiftly pushed the old man overboard, to Kon's

surprise. Then, she helped him to climb back in the canoe.

"Let's get out of here, before she really gets mad," Kon said, as he lifted the anchor.

"Let's go!" Taaroa exclaimed. "Let's go, yah! yah!..."

Then, the old priest started another song.

"Hina of the Valley, look at the depth of the river!
Look at the freshness of its running water.
Admire the small shrimps of the river.
Then, marvel at the large shrimps of the deep ponds.
Hina of the Valley, protect the fullness of the purest water!
It is the water of our life, flowing just for us.
Hina of the Valley, contemplate the heights of the mountains,
Origins of this clear water, and rejoice in the sight.
Hina of the Valley, look at the sea, as far as you can.
Remember, those who possess this earth, and also the sea,
Also possess the entire universe.
But, aware of this they are not.
Hina of the Valley, look at the foamy waves beyond the reef.
Listen to the ocean singing for you.
Listen to the ocean pounding on the barrier.
Listen to the ocean speaking to your heart.
Listen! The waves assault the beach, just for you!
Listen! The waves regress, rolling stones.
Hina of the Valley, listen! The Earth calls a priestess.
The slimy giant touched your legs, but you are fine.
The friendly creature went to you, but did not hurt you.
The moray is not mean. It was my mistake.
In all this, I see a sign.
Hina of the Valley, the king of the lagoon honored you."

Taaroa stopped singing when he felt the hand of the young woman on his shoulder. He turned around. Hina went to him and hugged him. With tears in her eyes, she looked at him.

"I am sorry, Taaroa. I am sorry I betrayed you for so long. Never again will we leave you alone in the dark valley."

Taaroa looked at Kon, who also was deeply moved.

"My two friends, this is the happiest day of my life," Taaroa said, with his usual croaking voice.

Late in the afternoon, they came back to the beach empty-handed. However, they came back with a lot to tell. They had indeed found one another's soul. They were richer, happier and changed: They had created a lasting bond.

Vana saw them come back. His mouth dropped open when he saw Hina hugging the leper. As she jumped out of the canoe, he went to her.

"Hina, you cannot do that, you know better. It is dangerous for you."

The beautiful woman turned around, and looked at him. The priest felt a warning. What he saw was not annoyance in the eyes of a woman. What he saw was compassion in the eyes of a priestess.

"Vana," she said, "the only thing that is dangerous for me is the poor sight of people with cold hearts. From now on, Taaroa is a great priest I shall love and respect. His heart is noble; his mind is clear as Orohena's water. His soul reaches the earth and the sea. This man, with a legendary name, needs us. Therefore, we need him as well. With him I shall be."

Vana did not know what to reply. Behind him, Tupua heard his daughter's words.

"What do you think, old friend?" Tupua asked.

"I don't know," Vana replied. "All this is the work of Kon Teke. This I know."

****

CHAPTER 11

"A dream is not always only a dream. It could be so clear and real that you may wonder. Don't be foolish enough to be matter-of-fact. Instead, honor your mind, and dream about your dream."

Kon Tici Viracocha

On Rarotonga Island, the day was vanishing. Dawn would come again, then another one. The tattooed face of Tamatoa was still, cold and lost in a dream. The feared monarch watched his warriors perform the dance of fire. They danced for him, yet he did not see them. Tamatoa's mind was far away on the sea, already crushing the people of the distant eastern islands.

"At the Havaiki gathering, you will have the dignitaries of all islands at your feet," Mato, the old priest, said.

Tamatoa's face did not move. Only a sarcastic grin showed his amusement.

"What are you going to do with the people already on Havaiki, Pora Pora and Tahiti-nui?" Mato asked with some uneasiness.

Tamatoa looked at him with savage fire in his eyes, took a piece of dead coral and crushed it into sand between his powerful fingers.

"When we will come to shore," Tamatoa said, "they will have two days to leave toward the south where there are no other islands. Those who dare pass the deadline will be fed to the sharks."

"With all due respect, do you think it is right to kill so many brothers of blood?" Mato asked.

"Those who killed my father were also brothers of blood," Tamatoa said with a mocking smile. "I will have compassion only for those who proved their fidelity to my authority for a long time. Emotions shall not affect you. The strongest shall prevail, which is the law that shall remain true until the end of time."

****

Kon bathed in the fresh water of the Papenoo River with Hina, Aru, and Fenua. At the end of a hot day, it was wonderfully relaxing.

"Hina told us you were an outstanding climber," Aru began.

"I think I am good at that," Kon replied.

"Nobody can challenge Kon's skills at climbing," Hina proudly said.

"You know nothing about climbing," Aru said, irritated by Hina's remark. "I am the best climber of Tahiti-nui, until proven otherwise by facts."

"If you want facts, I know a place where we can get them," Hina retorted with defiance.

"And where this could be?" Aru asked.

"Very high in the valley," Kon said, "at the great falls where the tropicbirds like to nest."

"I know the place," Aru said. "We could do two races: one for the fastest man who will reach the first tropicbird nest, and the other for the most skilled man who will be capable of climbing the farthest above that nest."

"Why would you be a better climber than Aru?" Fenua asked.

"As water is your element, the mountain is mine," Kon replied. "I was born in high, steep mountains where I excel."

There was no turning back: With shining eyes, the two men agreed to compete.

"You may know your mountains well, but I know mine better," Aru said.

"Of this, I am not sure," Hina chuckled, going under water, bubbling.

As she broke the surface of the water, she had a radiant smile of contentment.

"Shall we go, the four of us, tomorrow morning?" Fenua asked.

"Oh no!" Hina objected. "The entire village is going. Even Taaroa will come."

At Hina's words, Aru had a disgusted look. Kon immediately saw Hina's anger, and calmed her down.

"A few days ago," Kon said, "you would have reacted exactly as Aru. So, be tolerant."

However, Kon's words did not convince Aru he had to spend part of the day around the leper, but Fenua came to the rescue.

"Would you accept Taaroa's presence," she said, "if I told you it would please me?"

"If you say so," Aru replied, conciliatory.

"Yes, give this poor man the joy of seeing a formidable race," Fenua added with determination.

Silent, Hina glanced at Kon with a smile: There was no need for words.

Fenua and Aru left, spread the word around the village and awakened everyone from a long lethargy.

Kon and Hina took their time, and walked in the shade, along the river. Suddenly, Kon stopped.

"What is it?" Hina asked.

"Look, just ahead of us, on the branch touching the running water."

Hina searched, but did not see anything. Then, she saw a dry little branch coming out of the main one. It was not a branch. It was a bird, perfectly mimicking its environment.

"It is the little bittern," Hina said, "the favorite bird of my father. We often hear its sharp call in valleys, but we rarely see it."

"Why does your father like that bird most?"

"My father is pragmatic, so he does not like a bird for its beauty. He likes the little bittern because it is always perched in these "purau" trees, whose flowers mollify his rough skin. If he is not familiar with a place, he would listen at the valley, hear the little bittern call, and immediately he would find the "purau" tree."

The contorted tree was covered with pink flowers whose center was dark red.

"These flowers open at sunrise," Hina said as she played with one heart-shaped leaf from the "purau" tree. "They stay yellow until noon, then they turn pink and fall at dusk."

The bird and the tree fascinated Kon. On one branch, tiny yellow orchids grew on a carpet of green moss and a few tiny ferns. Everything was beauty and delicateness.

They did not see Tupua approaching.

"This is a daring bird," the king said. "There is not much you can do to scare him."

"If you throw a stick of wood at it, it will not even move." Hina giggled, and so she did several times. The first time, the bird protested with a strident call. The second time, it bent its neck just enough for the stick to miss it. The bittern looked at Hina straight in the eyes, remained still, calm, unchallenged, and mad enough for its long beak to spear her face. She was so close that she could have caressed it.

"Can you touch it?" Kon asked.

"No, that it would not tolerate," Tupua said, "and would fly to another branch screaming at you."

"If you fish or rest near the river," Hina said, "it may come to inspect what you are doing. He obviously watched us bathing in the river."

"It eats many of these little blue, green and orange fish which lay between stones where the water is shallow," Tupua said.

"Where does it nest?" Kon asked.

"In the reeds," Tupua replied. "That little warrior would die defending its nest against anything."

The little bittern tried to hide by freezing its head pointed straight upward. Its green back was like moss, its brown belly like wood, and the yellow dots on its belly like orchids. Only two narrow, white bands starting under its throat and ending on its breast revealed the presence of an unknown flower.

"Amazing bird!" Kon said.

They left the aquatic creature in peace.

"I heard about your race with Aru," Tupua said. "I approved it. I have wanted to see you climb for some time. But, I warn you, Aru is a tough climber."

"Perhaps," Hina said, "but there is a difference between a climber fighting the mountain, and a climber in harmony with it. In due time, you will understand my words, father."

A crowd went to the deep valley, before dawn. When Kon and Hina reached the falls, half the village waited for them. Tupua was joking with Vana and Taaroa. Atea was combing Fenua's long black hair. Aru was already testing the mountain above the pond where the falls misted the meadow.

Tupua called Kon and Aru, and explained the rules.

"First, you race to the first tropicbird's nest, and the fastest man will be considered the strongest climber. Then, you will continue above the nest, and whoever reaches the highest point on Orohena's forbidden cliff will be the best and most daring climber."

Hina and Fenua hugged one another. At the breathtaking sight of the grandiose Orohena, the two sisters were suddenly apprehensive. They knew the dangers. One mistake could be fatal.

"You start now!" Tupua roared.

The mountain echoed his signal: "Now,...now,...now,..."

Vana comforted the two trembling sisters.

"Hina, I thought it was your idea," Vana said.

"Yes it was," Hina whispered, "and I am not proud of this."

"They would have done it anyway, soon or later," Fenua said gently.

"Kon and Aru will nourish our memories," Vana explained. "For many evenings, we will all share the vision of their courage. Sometime, bravery seems futile, yet it is a necessity to our values. So, let's watch these brave men."

The two climbers assaulted the gigantic mountain, and everyone clapped their hands, on their clothes, on dead wood, on trees, in the water, on anything. Then, the melancholic notes of conch shells rang out across the valley.

"Go, my boys!" Tupua mumbled, with his arms crossed on his broad chest.

"May I ask what is the purpose of this race?" Taaroa asked with his croaking voice.

Tupua looked at him, annoyed by what he thought a trivial question. Then he looked at Vana.

"Do you know what is the purpose of this race?" the king asked, a bit confused.

"I may answer, father." Hina said. "The purpose is not to find out who will win, or how high they may climb, or to give us the pleasure of seeing them daring death. The real purpose is for them to find their limits, and come back content. That would be enough."

"Men like them are never content," Taaroa said.

"Maybe not," Hina replied. "But, what is important is for them to be content, one day at a time."

"I like your answer," Taaroa said. "For now, I am content."

"Am I content?" Tupua asked, looking at Vana. "Are you content?"

"I don't have a clue!" Vana replied, bursting into laughter.

Kon slid once on the wet rocks surrounding the pond. The crowd gasped. Then he slid a second time, and the crowd laughed.

"Did he do that on purpose?" Vana asked.

Hina glanced at the priest, smiled, but did not answer.

Kon and Aru were side by side, often in the way of one another, but they never showed aggressiveness. They even giggled at one another. They knew the steep cliff would separate them soon.

A white-tailed tropicbird flew a reconnaissance mission, disturbed by the unusual crowd and the climbing men. Kon looked at it and smiled, recalling the storm and the night he spent with a similar bird on the raft.

Soon, the mountain became much steeper, and Aru was ahead. The young islander was jumping from rock to rock with extreme precision and will. Kon suddenly thought he better get serious about the race. Aru immediately sensed the change of his adversary's attitude, and accelerated his pace. Kon wondered if he had underestimated Aru's climbing capabilities.

The cliff became more difficult, the vegetation scarce and places to safely step and hang few. Now, it was the mountain, it was Mount Orohena. Instantly, it became an entirely different race. Aru stopped, and looked up planning his path. Then, he looked down and saw Kon closing on him rapidly. As a matter of honor, he could not let Kon win, especially with the entire village watching. Moved by fear and despair he took larger steps, and ignored all danger. As Kon's hands almost reached Aru's feet, something inconceivable happened.

Aru saw a sharp rock to his left. Instinctively, he jumped like a wild animal against the steep wall in front of him, where there was no place for him to safely land. His foot smashed on the slick mountain. He bounced toward the sharp peak, literally flying in the air, managed to land his other foot on the apex of the sharp rock, which immediately crumbled. Stillt, it was enough for Aru to rebound toward the cliff and grab some ferns on a tiny ledge. Kon looked at the man, astonished by his resolve to win, and wondered if he could rate his act as bravery or recklessness. Because of this remarkable display of strength, and gambling capabilities, Aru had won the first part of the race. He reached the tropicbird nest, and like a wave pounding on the barrier reef, a loud and continuous roar came from the crowd. They were proud of what Aru had done.

Kon congratulated his adversary, and both men, covered with perspiration, recovered their breath.

"Your jump was a brave deed, and your victory deserved," Kon said. "But, you were also lucky."

"I know, but I won. So, falling here was not my fate."

"Considering what is ahead of us," Kon said, "I suggest you don't try that again."

"From here, we cannot go very far," Aru said looking up. "You see this second tropicbird nest above. Nobody ever climbed above this point. It is just impossible."

"We shall see," Kon said, calmly.

Blown by powerful men, conch shells signaled for the second race to start. Rasping screams from a white-tailed tropicbird sitting on its nest mixed with the sound of the conchs. When the drums rumbled across the valley, a loud, rattling cry came from above the two men. It was a flying tropicbird expressing its extreme discontent to the two intruders.

"We are getting a lot of attention," Kon joked.

"They all want us to keep moving."

"Are you ready?"

"Yes, I am. Show me who you are, Kon Teke."

Aru looked at a smiling Kon Tici. The mysterious alien had his dark blue eyes fixed on Mount Orohena. His long black hair flowed in the light breeze. His blue dress supported the life of many red suns. His belt and his headband displayed strange, soaring birds he called condors. His golden bracelets and earlobe plugs reflected sunlight that could be seen from all across the valley. Aru had the feeling that his victory had been too easy. This man of peace, whose kindness was taken for granted, was as mysterious as the first day he had met him. This man, who seemed childish and clumsy in the lagoon, was now in command and inhabited by a strong force. Even before they started, Aru knew a sleeping giant had awakened.

Aru started climbing, skillfully. Kon observed him, looked at the cliff, and decided on a different path. Kon had a more relaxed style, more fluid, and more confident. He progressed rapidly from one crack to one edge, from one edge to one fern, from one fern to another crack. He passed Aru without even noticing him, and knew that the young Maohi did not have a chance in this ultimate test of climbing.

When they reached the level of the second tropicbird's nest, Aru was at his limit. He stopped and looked at Kon above him, already far away, beyond the point where no man had ventured before. The more difficult the cliff was, the more Kon showed skill, effectiveness and daring confidence. The young islander searched for an edge, found one, and sat on it. From now on, he was only interested in watching Kon Tici.

Down in the valley, near the falls, everyone was startled and mouths dropped open. Now, Hina was more confident and giggled with pleasure. From now on, nobody would ever dare question her words. She had spoken the truth, and her eyes seemed to roar "I told you so."

"This man is incredible," Tupua said.

"This man shows us something I would have never believed," Vana said.

"He shows us the way to the sacred limit beyond which death becomes life." Taaroa murmured. "We shall all remember his path."

Hina came closer to the king.

"Father, you have not seen anything yet."

"What more can I see?" Tupua asked with surprise.

"It takes much more than skill and courage to do what you are going to witness," Hina replied. "It takes the power of that mysterious force that is living in him. You are going to see Mana at its best."

Kon reached a narrow ledge and sat on it, and waved at Aru, who observed him.

"This is as far as you will ever go," Aru said.

"This is just the beginning," Kon answered.

Aru looked up at the giant wall going straight to the summit of Mount Orohena, lost inside the clouds, and felt a shiver down his spine.

"You cannot climb this; nobody can," Aru said.

Kon stood up, turned his face toward the mountain, found a few cracks in which to wedge his toes and fingers, and was on his way up again, but this time climbing was no longer the appropriate word. To everyone in the valley, the word was "Mana."

As if his hands had claws, Kon progressed along the smooth cliff, clutching at invisible cracks. Only the tips of his fingers and toes were of any use. Yet the rock, continuously weathered by rain, was unreliable. Amazingly, Kon seemed sure of every move he made, and there was never any indecision. There was no more looking back. As soon as his fingers and toes were secured, his eyes searched ahead for possible paths.

"It gives me vertigo to watch him," Tupua said. "This is incredible."

"And it seems so easy for him," Vana added.

"It does not mean he is safe," Taaroa remarked. "He takes considerable risk."

Hina's chest was pounding. She was proud, but her cheeks were flushed with great fear. Once more, she regretted it had been her idea. Once more, she remembered that Kon could not be challenged by the mountain, or by anything. Whatever it would take to baffle the unknown, he would do.

It drizzled, but nobody cared. The view was good, and Kon still had a long way to climb before he would reach the clouds circling Orohena. Aru climbed to a more comfortable place, and paused to admire a supremely skilled man filled with uncommon courage.

Kon communicated with the mountain, his mountain. What

he did was no foolish act, but a matter of precision and good judgment. Each move was well planned, and was an adventure through necessity. Tiny details of the giant wall were, observed touched, tested and explored by his fingers and his toes. Every step was completed so fast that he never seemed to stop. Kon Tici gave his best, and inside himself was happiness. He forgot the crowd, but not Hina. He was all action mixed with contemplation, somewhere between the earth and the sky. Mana lived in him.

A noble red-tailed tropicbird soared toward Kon. The magnificent bird looked at him, but did not make its harsh, rasping scream as usual. The bird passed once above him, once under him, then hovered near him. The gliding tropicbird showed its grace, and Kon Tici showed his mastery. For an instant, both had something in common: Both could do what no man could do, and both communicated through the secret paths of Mana's garden. Silent, fearless and in an ecstasy of joy, they were the mountain.

"What I find most remarkable is the very little crumbling of rocks under his feet and fingers," Tupua said. "Long ago I tried to climb where Aru is, and everything crumbled under me."

"Of course, as you were climbing, your tummy was plowing the mountain," Vana replied.

Kon heard the remark, heard the roaring laughter of everyone. He stopped, bit his arm and laughed.

"Do you see the large ledge some distance above him?" Hina asked.

"Yes," Taaroa answered.

"This is where he is going," Hina said. "It is just under the clouds, and he will not pursue higher. I know why he wants to go there."

"Why is that?" Tupua asked.

"Long ago, he climbed to the same level, but much more to

the left, and saw a cave in the cliff that nobody can see from any other angle. This is where he is going."

"Did you know about this cave?" Tupua asked.

"No," Vana replied.

"I did," Taaroa replied. "It is the legendary Orohena's jaw, and nobody has ever found it."

"This place is therefore taboo," Tupua said.

"There are no taboos for Kon Teke," Taaroa replied.

The old leper was suddenly surrounded by swirling dust, as he was looking up at Kon Tici. A vortex seemed to emerge from his body, then hesitated along the edge of the pond, then crossed the pond and climbed toward the mountain. Everyone was astonished and silent.

"There are no taboos for the gods," Taaroa said.

The vortex disappeared on the ledge where Kon was going.

"My friends, I feel uneasy about all this," Tupua said.

"In that place, Kon Teke will find some answers," Taaroa said. "I trust he will come out of it."

"And, he will triumph with his usual modesty," Hina said.

"Modesty is a great force," the leper replied.

Clouds were all around Kon, almost obscuring the view of the valley. It was the last effort, the last fern and the last step. He reached the ledge where he had seen the cave, long ago. His surprise was great to see a cover of tiny, creeping, feathery and undisturbed green ferns. It was a kind he had never seen before, and they grew deep inside the dark, damp cave. He slowly entered inside Mount Orohena, almost ashamed of walking on the ferns. He had to bend over to enter. Kon Tici was inside the jaw of the legendary shark.

Only his feet received light from outside, and for an instant he was apprehensive. The reason was still unclear. Slowly, apprehension turned into peace and comfort when he touched the walls of the dark cave. As his fingers traveled along the details of the walls, something became obvious. The walls were too smooth to be natural. Someone had been here before. Slowly, he circled the room.

At the farthest point from the entry, he found a narrow opening in the wall. With both hands he measured the passage. It was large enough for his body. He sat on the ground, and waited for his eyes to become accustomed to the darkness. He listened to the silence, and heard the wind far inside the mountain. Exhausted by the arduous climb, he slowly drifted into a peaceful sleep. He heard dripping water falling in a pond. Then, he heard the rain, cold and pelting, and the swirling wind. A rumble came, with thundering power. It was the waves of the cold sea, smashing against a giant cliff. On ledges along the cliff, long, dry grass waved in the Antarctic wind. It was another place, where he had never been before. Yet, he knew the place. Something in his mind told him it was a familiar place. He climbed the cliff to stay away from the splashing waves. In the howling wind, he heard voices coming from far above. He decided to climb all the way to the top of the cliff.

Now, the voices became stronger, and he knew it was not the wind, or his imagination. They were women's voices, and he knew them well. He walked in their direction, and found them. Both women were near a block of grey lava, on the edge of an ancient caldera. The panorama was of astonishing grandeur, and the bottom of the caldera was covered with blue ponds and green reeds.

One woman sat on the lava block, and he saw only her back, but he unmistakably recognized her long, wavy black hair, her shoulders and her back. She was Hina of the Valley.

The other woman combed Hina's hair. She stood up by Hina's side. He also knew her well. She was tall and of remarkable beauty. Her long, straight black hair flowed in the wind. Her skin was not as dark as Hina's. She turned around and looked at Kon, but she did not seem to see him. He knew those friendly dark blue eyes. He knew this gentle and contemplative woman, and saw a touch of sadness in her eyes. She was Kama Tici Viracocha, his brother's wife.

Kon waved, and called them, but they ignored him. They were alone. He walked to them, but they were always the same distance away. Discouraged, he sat on the dry grass and listened to their conversation.

"Why did you called this island Mata-Kite-Rani? Hina asked.

"This is our new land," Kama replied. "The navel of the world was our great city of Tiahuanacu. Now the navel of the world is Mata-Kite-Rani. It means, the eyes looking at the stars."

"Why are you always looking at the stars?" Hina asked.

"Because it is where we are from, and they hold the ultimate truth, the ultimate peace and the powerful light feeding each of us," Kama said, with a smooth tone, barely opening her thin lips.

Kon stood up and ran to them. Kama smiled at him, but her image became blurred. When he reached her, she instantly vanished in a swirling cloud of dust. Hina also turned into a dust whirl and vanished across the caldera. Kon woke up, and found himself lying on the damp ground of a cool, dark cave: It had been only a dream, but he was astonished by the quality of the details. Where was this island Kama named Mata-Kite-Rani? What was Hina doing there? Was it really a dream? Or, was it a preview of events to come?

"This was a vision," he murmured to himself.

He stayed silent for a moment, trying to memorize the place

of his dream. It was a cool place, far more south. Could his brother have drifted that far south? The thought sparked new possibilities in his mind.

"If Mata-Kite-Rani exists, I will find it."

Slowly, he came back to reality, and listened. He could see the narrow opening in the wall, above him. Wind came from the opening, and he heard the distant sound of dripping water. He heard the rain and the rumble: It was the storm outside. Kon shook his head, forcing himself to remain realistic. With difficulty, he went through the hole, head first, managed to pass his shoulders, then stepped in another room, in total darkness. Behind him, he could see a tiny halo of light coming through the narrow passage. At least, it was enough to find his way back. Cautiously, he inspected the room with his arms, and feet. He bumped into some objects on the ground. Then, he felt wind swirling around him, and heard something moving. His heartbeat instantly accelerated, as he was defenseless in absolute darkness. He reached in all directions with his arms, trying to find something. There was nothing. So, silently, he listened, and wished his heart was not so noisy. Suddenly, something touched his neck, and he instantly realized he had disturbed a few bats. He crouched and felt familiar contours with his fingers. The objects on the ground were bones, human bones.

Puzzled, Kon sat on the damp ground, and carefully studied the skull with his fingers, but could not tell if it belonged to an islander or not. It seemed that the skeleton was smaller than the average Maohi. They probably were bones of a child. Then, his fingers found an unusual object. It was a polished, heavy, flat stone. He inspected both sides with the tip of his fingers, found some grooves and followed them several times, until a picture took place in his mind. Suddenly, he felt his blood flush to his face. He felt the stone was decorated with glyphs, and they were birds. He placed the stone near the exit, and he would take it outside and look at it in more detail later, but now, he had to explore more.

This place must have been a sacred burial place, but how did they bring someone here, and who could have done it? Before he could answer, he heard water dripping again, went in its direction and bumped into a wall. He felt a draft of air on his face. He explored with his hands and found another hole, too small for him to pass through it. Obviously, behind was another room, with a pond. What secret did Orohena guard? He might never know.

Reluctantly, he went back to the flat stone he had found, exited and sat on the carpet of green ferns. He looked at the stone. He had been right; the glyphs were birds. Then, looking at them closer he found that they were birdmen. Most striking to him, they were like some of the drawings his forefathers had drawn on a giant scale on the Nazca land. Was it possible? Or, was it only a coincidence? Assaulted by too many questions, he felt helpless. Then, along the ledge, he witnessed a most interesting phenomenon.

The whirl of dust was slowly coming to him. He felt obliged to lay the flat stone on the ground. The vortex became still above the stone, and he could feel the warm tranquillity of an immense force. Kon Tici knew there was life in the vortex, a kind of life unknown to him. The whirling air pushed the stone inside the cavern, until both disappeared. He understood he had violated a taboo; his visit had been tolerated, but he should not push his luck too far.

So, many questions would remain unanswered, but was it important? Perhaps, his dream was most important, and there was an unmistakable sign in it: Hina and Kama took the form of a tornado as they vanished. This vortex was only a sign that he should listen to his soul. He looked at the valley, and the sun was shining. He had to go back to his friends, but he was a different man. Kon Tici had been touched by something he would never forget. He had been touched by another form of intelligence, well known by some of his Viracocha ancestors. Now, there was a bond between Hina and Kama, somewhere on a distant place called Mata-Kite-Rani.

When Kon reached the valley, drums rumbled for everyone to honor and respect his victory. The king walked to him and put his hands on his shoulders.

"Incredible!" Tupau said. "From now on, I shall call you son."

"From now on, everyone will be proud to be your friend," Hina said.

"What did you find in the cave?" Taaroa asked.

"A vortex of wind," Kon replied.

Everyone stayed silent, remembering the vortex they had seen taking form close to Taaroa when Kon was in the cave.

"Did you talk to him?" Taaroa asked.

"No, but I understood his message," Kon replied.

"And, what was that message?" Taaroa asked.

"The vortex is intelligent energy," Kon said. "You should not listen to him, but meditate on his behavior." "Therefore, it is a spirit," Vana said.

"Perhaps," Kon said, "the mental state close to ecstasy of one of us, invited his presence."

Kon noticed that everyone was starring at Taaroa.

"Well!" Taaroa smiled. "The true Taaroa is the Creator of everything, isn't he?"

Much later, at the king's place, Kon explained what he saw, what he did and told about his vision of Hina and Kama on a distant, colder island. Then the question came, the question nobody expected.

"When your forefathers came the first time to Tahiti-nui," Kon asked, "did they find another race?"

The silence that followed awoke Tupua from his short nap. Vana and Taaroa glanced at the king. Kon repeated his question, and felt some embarrassment from the three men: They were hiding something.

"There was indeed another race living on these islands before us, with much darker skin." Tupua said. "Terrorized, they went into the mountains in inaccessible places. They traveled to the valleys only at night, searching for food. Nobody saw any of them for several generations."

"What did you do to terrorize them?" Kon asked.

"They were terrorized by human sacrifices," Tupua said, his face clouded with gilt.

Hina saw Kon's distress, and she came close to him.

"Tupua has fought this custom very hard," Vana said, "and prohibited it the day he became the king. But, the custom is still in effect on some other islands."

"Kon Teke, if you have something to say, say it," Tupua ordered.

"Indeed, I have something to say: There are times when I am convinced that most men and women in this world are nothing else but manure machines."

Kon stood up, glanced at everyone and vanished through the night.

****

CHAPTER 12

Hina of the Valley

Eight moon-cycles before the Havaiki gathering, every Maohi priest prepared for the long-awaited event some would see only once in their lifetime. Havaiki was much more than a religious center, it was the center of the Maohi's world. Pilgrims would come from everywhere, across the awesome sea. Some fearless voyagers would stay more than two moon-cycles at sea, fighting the waves, the wind, their suffering body and distressed mind. What they would endure was appalling and beyond imagination, but at sea, the Maohi's will was unshakable. By the trajectory of stars, the shape of waves, the position of clouds, the direction of currents, their encounters with seabirds and migrating fish, they always knew exactly where they were and where the islands were.

Their behavior at sea was not an act of courage, but an act of necessity. For a thousand years they had centered their life on the sea, and for a thousand years they had been an intrinsic part of the awesome sea. In their mind, there never was the sea, the islands, and the Maohis. In their mind, the sea, the islands, and the Maohis were the awesome sea. Some of them would start their fantastic journey and never finish it, but it was irrelevant to their belief, as dying for what needed to be done was accepted. At all costs, they were seafaring people.

They would come to Havaiki in great numbers. They would meet, share feelings, beliefs, discoveries, ambitions and moral principles. They would have grievances, disputes, wars, but in the end they would be one people, one family. They would be the Maohis, voyagers by choice and necessity.

After many days on Havaiki, they would leave, and sail back to their respective islands. They would be different, richer, and confident, after all they would have learned from their blood brothers and sisters. From all their distant neighbors and their respective tales at sea, they would accurately map in their mind the awesome sea as their home. At home, they had no secret.

The Havaiki gathering was a sacred reunion, planned long in advance, the purpose of which was to enrich the Maohi's knowledge of the world. At the gathering, every Maohi had the freedom to speak his words, and someone would listen, and answer. However, not everyone was allowed to make the sacred trip. Pilgrims were carefully selected among priests, chiefs, children of kings or kings themselves. They were all the best educated and finest type of the Maohi aristocracy.

At Papenoo, preparation for the gathering became a daily way of life. Tahiti-nui was a sister island of Havaiki, and as such its priests were highly respected, but there was something new: Tupua and Vana would present Kon Tici, and they knew he would be the focus of endless interest. Accordingly, Tupua and Vana would receive immense respect for hosting such a knowledgeable man, but the two Maohi dignitaries also feared that some of Kon's people would come from other islands. In that case, Kon's presence would be essential, otherwise nobody would pay attention to Tupua and Vana, an insult to their egos.

Vana came with a winning idea that pleased the king: Somehow, Hina would be part of the show. They wanted to demonstrate that she could be the youngest and most promising priestess among the Maohis. Kon Tici and Hina of the Valley were one body, inseparable, and an outstanding combination.

However, they had one problem: Hina would soon be only fifteen years old, and was no priestess yet. Time was short, and something had to be done. Hina had to become a priestess before the gathering. It was easier said than done, as a priest had to show great knowledge and skill in one particular field. Because Hina was a woman, only one field was open to her. She would have to become a medicine woman, one of the most difficult fields.

"She is too young, and time is too short," Tupua said.

"Maybe we should concentrate on her assets," Vana suggested.

"She has a good memory," Tupua said. "She is detailed, clean, and extremely observant."

"And much more!" Vana said. "As a young child, she knew plants, animals, and loved to challenge me."

"She is devoted to those in need, and kind to everyone," Tupua said.

"And, she already learned many things from Kon Tici, and from Taaroa."

Their minds were set. They would make her a priestess, a medicine woman, right now, and worry about completing her formal education later. Vana also convinced the king that the idea would be a tremendous incentive to the young woman to learn quickly.

"The sooner she will be a priestess," Vana said, "the faster she will learn before the gathering."

To become a priestess, Hina had to pass a difficult test in front of a committee of priests coming from many villages around the island, but they all knew her well, and they all liked her. Besides, her name was Hina of the Valley, a legendary name, and she was the daughter of the king.

A few days later, after bending the rules for the required formalities, Vana held a ceremony for the start of Hina's priesthood. Such a ceremony was not taken lightly, because as a priestess, it became possible that one day Hina could become a great priestess or a queen. Therefore, they all felt responsible for their actions, but from past experience, good or bad, they knew she was clever, with clear, logical, and swift ability for judgment. They were convinced she would rapidly acquire considerable political prestige and credibility: In a way, she was the darling of kings and priests.

Hina wore a long, white robe made of the softest and finest bark-cloth. The sacred bark of a rare kind of breadfruit tree had been used. The robe had been specially designed and made for her by her mother and sister. Skilled craftswomen from the village had helped them in their project. The robe nearly touched the ground. A wide belt heavily decorated with shiny, brown cowries tied the robe around her waist. The belt was a gift to her from the priests of the Haapape village, where she had many friends. Around her forehead, a beautiful wreath made of two solid lines of white, fragrant tiares gave her the charm of living flowers. The wreath would never be given away, or disposed of. It was sacred. She would keep it all her life. The tiares would dry and fade. Nevertheless it would be her token for good luck as a priestess.

On her head, she wore a tall, majestic hat crested with the feathers of the green pigeon of the valley. Around her neck, she wore the golden rising sun and the flying condor. These items from another world made her unique. Her bronzed face showed an enigmatic smile. Her up-turned chin showed her inner confidence and serene peace. She was proud of herself, proud to be an islander, proud to be a Maohi.

The first part of the ceremony took place in Vana's dwelling house. All the aristocracy of Tahiti-nui circled Hina and the great priest. Kon was on the king's side with Atea and Fenua, who had tears blinding her eyes.

"What is the matter?" Kon whispered, putting his hand on Fenua's shoulder. "You should be happy."

"Do you see what you did to my sister?" Fenua sobbed, laying her head on Kon's chest.

"Hina is very happy," Kon said.

"Perhaps, but she is losing her freedom," Fenua replied. "From now on, she will be observed, wanted and giving always. The wild little girl walking on the black sand beach is dead. I loved her the way she was. As time will pass, I will understand her less and less."

Moved by her words, Kon hugged her strongly.

"Do you really love my sister?" Fenua asked.

"Of course I do, why do you ask?"

"Because she loves you immensely, and I care for her. Without you, she would be devastated and I don't want her to be miserable. Wherever you go, she needs you forever."

Fenua's words went straight to his heart, like a powerful spear. He knew perfectly well what she meant. In her simple way, the young woman saw the drama into which Kon and Hina were stepping. She had that deep feeling that something would go wrong. On one hand Hina was sinking deep roots in Tahiti-nui. On the other hand Kon would travel the sea searching for phantoms of the past. Fenua had the unexplainable fear that her sister would suffer. Her tears were the early signals of coming events nobody suspected.

"Hina is the same person you have always known, with a little more perhaps," Kon said, gently. "But, this little more would have never gone that far if she had not been who she is. Your little sister is alive and well, and she still walks, wild, on the black sand beach. She always will."

With his elbow, Tupua quietly gestured for Kon and Fenua to become silent: Vana spoke.

"Young Hina, young priestess, your home is the valley, where you shall find all the plants there are to know. In the valley, you shall find all the secrets of the medicine woman. Very young, on your own, you went to the valley. On your own, you chose to learn the priestess knowledge. On your own, you decided upon your destiny. Few are the ones who are gifted as you are. Therefore, we all agreed our great God Taaroa, selected you. Today, we honor you by giving the prestigious title of priestess to you. But, priestess you were from the very first day your parents conceived you, which is the reason why they called you Hina."

Vana turned around, looked at the crowd, and at a wandering vortex of wind.

"Now, my friends, we must go to the Marae of our ancestors."

Slowly and respectfully, they went to the Marae, some distance along the Papenoo River. They grouped orderly around the main temple called Ahu. It was a four-sided and crude pyramid, about three times the height of a man, built with the stones from the river. Walls made of flat, upright coral slabs surrounded the court where they gathered. Thick tiare bushes, those fragrant flowers, were a delight to smell, hidden behind the walls. On one side, there was a dwelling house where priests could gather. The entire complex, built in the center of a remote and sunny meadow, was called the Marae.

"Hina, this is the Marae of medicine priests," Vana said on a gentle tone. "They all come here to start their priesthood. You will stay here for an entire moon-cycle. You shall not leave under any circumstance. You will be fed and taken care of. Other priests will transmit their knowledge to you. Do you understand?"

"Yes, I do."

"You are given great responsibility, as you will protect the health of our people. You will heal their wounds, their illness, and their mind. They will trust you, therefore a trustee you shall be. Do you agree to be of service to them, regardless of their condition?"

This was the word she did not expect, and the word Vana instantly regretted. Hina glanced at him, then at Taaroa, aside from the crowd. The great priest knew her thought. Hina's swift mind was at work, and she judged her master. How could she dare test the great priest? But, Hina of the Valley was kind enough to look back at the ground, and not embarrass Vana.

"Yes, I do."

Vana put his hands on Hina's shoulders, and gave her a bad look she understood well. Then, he proceeded with the ceremony. Tupua noticed something was wrong, and instantly developed a skin rash.

"Hina," Vana said, "one moon-cycle from now, after your formal education is complete, you will build your own Marae. You alone shall select the location. It must be isolated from the village, and suit you. Remember, on the Ahu of your Marae you will often meditate, and communicate with our gods and spirits. Therefore, your Marae must inspire you. Do you understand?"

"Yes, I do."

"In your Marae, you will build your Fare, which will be your house with your tools, plants, oils, preparations, and belongings. Nobody shall profane your place, and live. In this place, you shall have total privacy as you wish. You shall bring inside your place only those who need you, or those who are dear to you. Do you have questions?"

"After my formal education is completed, for how long shall I continue learning medicine?"

"Very good question!" Vana said, with a broad smile.

Tupua's rash went away instantly.

"Starting today," Vana said, "you enter an everlasting process, the learning process. You will like your priesthood, and you will become good at it. With no obligation from anyone, you will learn until your last day. You shall never let a single day go by, without improving your skills. This is why priests are unique. They never stop learning. Your formal education is only a test, to give you the starting will. That is all."

Vana removed his hands from Hina's shoulders, took her hand, and talked to her in a more casual way.

"As a priestess in medicine, you carry other responsibilities. You shall support our people morally, as minds are often the ill part of a society. This is a difficult task, frustrating and dangerous. There are no special rules to follow, and every case requires special treatment. The key is patience, understanding, creativity and willingness to give. At that, I know you will excel."

The ceremony went on, all day. For a full moon-cycle, Hina listened to Vana, and to medicine priests. She was the only woman. Again and again, she had to listen, and recite word for word everything she had been told. She thought some of that knowledge was interesting, some was fun and some was useless. Determined to satisfy everyone, she forced herself to listen, accept and comply. Later, she knew she would do things her way. At times, she wanted to laugh and argue, but she was a woman with principles. She would respect the tradition transmitted by her forefathers: The sacred word of mouth was the only way to learn from the past.

After the long and tedious memorizing phase was at last completed, she searched for the site where she would build her Marae. First, for several days, she searched alone. Then, one afternoon, she insisted that Kon choose her site with her. She already had an idea, but she wanted his opinion. Vana granted his permission.

Kon and Hina left the village, crossed the Papenoo River, and followed the narrow beach of black sand, until they reached a point where they had a spectacular view of the northern rocky coast. At some distance from the point, they found a terrace covered with tiare bushes. It was small, but large enough for Hina's settlement. It was not far from the village, yet isolated enough on the side of the river that was rarely visited.

At the point, there was no beach, but only a steep cliff, pounded by booming waves. Little by little, the awesome sea was busy destroying the island. With force, the waves found their way into caves, cracks, coves and crevices. The shore was indeed an inspiring place to watch.

"It is a windy place," Kon said.

"This is why nobody comes here, and the reason why we call it Toerau," Hina replied, looking at the horizon.

He looked at her with a smile, knowing she had already made up her mind. She did not need his opinion, and she showed him the place she had chosen.

"What does Toerau mean?" Kon asked.

"It is the name of the northwestern wind, the wind that blows right now. Toerau brings rain and the green life to the valley. Toerau gives birth to the rain forest. Toerau is the father of the ferns you like. Toerau brings food to my people, therefore it brings peace."

As she spoke, Kon glanced at her face and thought she was superb.

"Let it be so," he said, raising his arms toward the sea. "This place shall be the Marae of Toerau."

"Would you help me build my Marae?" she asked, gently.

He put his arms around her naked shoulders.

"I already talked to your father about this, and yes, we all are going to help you."

She did not reply. She did not show excitement. Only a tear slowly found its way down on her cheek, showing how thankful she was. For the time being, she was blissfully happy.

They both studied the place until sunset. Then, Kon started a fire by rubbing two sticks together. The flames rapidly spread into a pile of dry grass, then to the old fronds they had collected under coconut trees. They sat near the fire, and made plans for Hina's Marae.

"I want you to decide about the shape of the Ahu," Hina said.

"I may, but it should also please Vana, and your father."

"No, it should please me first; Vana said so." Hina replied. "How would you do it?"

"Maybe with three steps," Kon answered.

"How is that?"

With a piece of wood, he drew the platform she called Ahu. She watched the drawing progressing on the black sand. First she frowned, confused by a structure she had never seen.

"This is the base," Kon explained, "what you call Ahu. On

the top, you build another Ahu, smaller. Then, you build a third Ahu on the top of the second one, even smaller. So, when it is completed, you have three levels."

"I like this," she said, staring at Kon with astonishment. "I never saw anything like it. I am sure Vana and my father will like the idea."

Content, they stayed silent for awhile. He put his hand around her waist, and she laid her head on his lap. He looked at the stars, and so did she. Kon remembered, long ago he had held Nina in the same position, but this time it was immensely different. The contact of Hina's skin sent a shock wave through his entire body, something he had never experienced before. Suddenly, their eyes met, questioning and glowing with tenderness. Their eyes showed much more than love, they showed passion. She closed her eyes, felt his hand on her breast, and his lips on hers.

Not far from the village, Vana and Taaroa walked together on the beach, for the first time in many sun-cycles. At first, they did not say anything. The tide was high, and the waves rolled on the black sand, at regular intervals, with a roaring sound, the only sound in the silent night. The full moon reflected its light into a golden stripe from the shore to the horizon. Vana, the great priest, climbed on a large boulder and sat. Taaroa, the leper, did the same on a smaller boulder nearby. They listened to the sounds of their environment. The northwestern wind blew in the trees, and the shadow of the two men extended behind them on the sand. The entire earth seemed a living spirit where light could play many games.

At some distance to the east, they saw a fire, an unmistakable signal.

"Hina chose her place," Vana whispered. "Her selection is most unusual."

"Unusual she is, unusual her place will be," Taaroa replied.

Dressed in white, both men listened to the subtleties of the clear night, between each rolling wave. They were like two phantoms, petrified on a rock into an everlasting meditation, a meditation of their priesthood.

"I have been foolish to leave you to rot under the banyan tree," Vana said in a sad tone.

"I understood, and did not blame you," Taaroa replied.

"It was hard for me to take your place as the great priest." Vana said, apologetic.

"Kon Teke told me there was a reason for my condition," Taaroa said. "He told me to be ready for the most important part of my priesthood, yet to come."

Disoriented, stunned and annoyed, Vana felt his blood flowing through his brain.

"What does he know about all this?" Vana said. "Is he a god? Is he a living spirit?"

"No, he is a man," Taaroa answered. "But, he knows much more than we do. I take his word very seriously."

"Most of Hina's knowledge comes from him," Vana said.

"This is my point," Taaroa replied. "The few he will select may become our leaders of tomorrow."

"Why would he do such a thing?"

"Because he is the last survivor of a lost race."

It took a full moon-cycle for Kon, Hina and people from the village to clean the area of Hina's settlement, and build a long court walled with stones from the Papenoo River. The entire court, except the center, was paved with several layers of volcanic gravel. At the center of the court, another wall, about the height of a child, circled the original tiare bushes, whose majestic flowers were dear to Hina. She loved the fragrant, white flower made of seven spiraling petals. The bush was elegant, and covered with many lustrous, oval, green leaves.

It took another moon-cycle to build the Ahu at one end of the court, and the house at the other end. The unusual stepped Ahu pleased the king and became a curiosity for all travelers. For Tupua, it was something more he would be proud to talk about during the gathering. Hina's Marae was small, but in perfect harmony with its surroundings.

The evening before the completion of the work, Hina made an unusual request of her father.

"Father, tonight I would like to stay alone here, with Kon."

Tupua looked at her with a grin of amusement.

"I declare this place taboo until dawn." he roared, and everybody complied in total confusion. All night, they would wonder.

Kon and Hina walked around the house, went to the tiare bushes, and climbed to the top of the stepped Ahu.

"The stone work is well done," Kon said with satisfaction.

"My father is a perfectionist," Hina replied. "Everything he builds must be perfect in size, shape, and strength, or he would be obsessed for many moon-cycles and constantly grumble about it."

They went back to the oval house, partly surrounded by a well-made wall of giant bamboo. Strong coconut tree pillars supported the frame of a thick vegetal roof made of woven pandanus leaves. Kon bent a little to enter the house. A large room was Hina's working area and storage for tools, plants and preparations of all kinds. Another small room, slightly raised, was her sleeping area with the floor covered with several layers of vegetal rugs and soft bark-cloth. It was shady, cool and comfortable. Hina inspected her house with excitement.

"Tonight, I wanted us to be alone," she said, with fire in her black eyes.

Kon came behind her, put his hands around her shoulders, and kissed her neck. She felt a shiver in her spine, and laid the back of her head on his chest.

"I have dreamed of this moment, lately," she whispered.

Kon did not say anything, and caressed her long black hair. Then, they walked to the rocky point, some distance away from the Marae, and sat on the cliff. Once more, the full moon rose in the east, while the western horizon was unusually flamboyant.

"When the sky is red like this, the people of Havaiki and Huahine believe they will be attacked by invaders," Hina said. "I don't believe in this omen: I think it is silly."

"Unusual coincidences are often the origin of such convictions," Kon said.

"Do you believe in omens?" Hina asked. "Our priests see signs in almost everything."

"We should respect these beliefs," Kon said.

"Why? You don't believe in them. Why should a nice moment like this be spoiled because the western sky is bloody red?"

"Silly perhaps, but it is among the order of things in your society. If you disagree with these beliefs, you have to prove them wrong first. If you disagree with something, don't say it is wrong, and never leave. You shall stay, be an active part of the social body, and little by little prove your point, with all the facts, and with distinction. If you do this, you will be remembered as a great achiever."

"I have been learning ever since you came," Hina said with an exasperated smile. "Yet, today I am empty, and I have the impression of knowing nothing."

"Never doubt yourself," Kon said, "or regret anything. Keep

learning more and more. As you progress, yes, you will find out that you know nothing. This is a good sign, because the more you know, the more you want to know. Now, learning is a part of you, a necessity, a must, and there is nothing you should do to stop it."

"I am going to learn so much at the gathering," she said.

"How long before the gathering are people arriving from the other islands?" Kon asked, looking at the horizon.

"The gathering starts in about five moon-cycles. The first travelers should arrive two moon-cycles from now, and many of them will stop here in Tahiti-nui."

Kon seemed far away, and was silent.

"You wonder if some of your people will come," Hina inquired.

"It is my only chance to find them," Kon replied in a low voice.

"Your best chances are with the people coming from Hiva in the northeast, the Tuamotu atolls in the east, and Rapa in the southeast." she said.

"Do you know these people?"

"My father is a lifetime friend of Hotu Matua, Hiva's king," Hina said.

"What kind of man is this Hotu Matua?"

"He is very much like my father, but he is also a great explorer. He would have treated your people well."

Suddenly, anxiety filled her mind. Accustomed to Kon's presence, she took him for granted, but what would happen, after he found his people? Would he leave forever, searching for the missing ones?

Kon observed her conflicting emotion, and knew her thoughts exactly. He also had the same problem, because he knew

Hina would never leave her island, unless she would have the assurance it would be only for a short time. He was determined to find his brother Illa, even if it meant traveling on the empty sea for the rest of his life. Would he be strong enough to leave Hina? Desperately, he found refuge in the dream he had in the cave, recalling Hina with Kama. The vision gave him courage, gave him the strength to ask no more questions. There was something missing, and time alone would tell what it was.

Both, standing up on the windy cliff, forgot the future for a moment. He looked at the beautiful priestess, and caressed her full lips with his long fingers. Her skin was soft, warm, and her mouth demanding. His nose touched hers, and she slowly kissed him, savoring every instant. They knew their love would be a powerful drama, and with passion, they began a formidable saga in which they would be trapped. Their life would be a hurricane sweeping the awesome sea.

****

CHAPTER 13

"My master trusts that violence and oppression are the only ways to unify and pacify the Maohi people. I used to lose my temper with this opinion. But, I am too old. I no longer flap my wings. I only ruffle my feathers."

Mato the great priest

Somewhere, southwest of Havaiki, an armada of war galleys was ready for a mass slaughter. Many did not agree with what they had to do, but they had been well trained to obey, and obey they would. Right or wrong, they thought Tamatoa the Great was invincible. Right or wrong, they thought he would ultimately bring stability and peace to the Maohi people.

In Pora Pora, when Tamatoa was a child, his father, at the time king of Tahaa, lost a battle against his powerful neighbor. To crush the young Tamatoa, the king of Pora Pora let him witness the sacrifice of his father. Crushed he was, but revenge became his only goal. With an amazing resolve, the peaceful Tamatoa became the king of his father's people. Well organized and self-disciplined, he started his long march and wandered from island to island for many years. One day, Tamatoa knew he would go back to Tahaa. When he was twenty, he became the king of the Rarotonga archipelago. Far away, this was the perfect place for him to prepare for war, to prepare for revenge. Now, Tamatoa was back. For thirty years, he had been waiting in silence. It was only a few moon-cycles ago that the great priest Mato learned about Tamatoa's plans.

Three days from now, his fleet would reach Maupiti, Pora Pora, Tahaa, Havaiki and Huahine. A few days later, he would invade Moorea and Tahiti-nui. He had chosen the time of the Maohi gathering to show his madness and his power. In the process, he would become the uncontested ruler of the entire archipelago.

Tamatoa had more than two hundred giant war galleys. Each of them, with double hulls, could transport one hundred warriors and their supplies. Many smaller galleys followed with families, animals and food. They came to stay. Then, a multitude of double canoes, built for high speed and short trips, capable of carrying ten warriors inside shallow lagoons, would give Tamatoa the advantage of surprise. His deadly war machine headed to the islands of his forefathers, where islanders would have to be fought, pushed away and killed without contest.

Standing up at the front of his powerful galley, Tamatoa watched the waves, waiting for the first sight of crosscurrents and cross patterns among sea swells. From the position of the stars before dawn, he knew the islands were near, and they came, right on time, in the middle of the afternoon. Cloud formations showed the exact position of each island. Then, at last, the first seabirds flew around the galleys.

Mato, the old priest, shook his head and spat in the sea.

"What are you frustrated about, old man?" Tamatoa said with a smile.

"I spit on the sea, before it turns red," Mato replied, in cold sarcasm.

"I know you don't agree with me," Tamatoa said.

"The closer we come to our target, the more I am convinced I was a fool to approve this endeavor: It just makes me sick!"

"You know they killed my father in front of my eyes," Tamatoa said. "However, I never told you how they did it."

Mato looked at his master with surprise and cloudy eyes, waiting for details.

"What they did to my father was intended to crush me," Tamatoa said. "They attached me to a post, and they made sure I would see and hear everything. They made sure my father would die slowly and suffer. What they did horrified me, and to my last day I will have the vision of him cut up, piece by piece. When he died, he had no eyes, no legs and no arms. I see him when I close my eyes, and when I sleep. I hear him all the time. They crushed me all right, but in the process, they changed the little boy into a monster. Yes, I know I am a madman."

"These people you are mad about are probably dead," Mato said. "I doubt you will find any of them."

"I don't need to find them. The Pora Pora people rule three islands on which there will be no mercy, and no survivors. That, I swear."

"But, the Tahiti-nui people did not do anything to you. Why should you treat them the same way?"

"They are all the same," Tamatoa said with bitterness. "For the people of other islands, except Pora Pora, Tahaa, and Maupiti, I will give them a chance: They must leave by sea within two days, or face extermination. I want no prisoners."

Mato knew it was useless to argue. It was much too late.

"As you please, Tamatoa. My wisdom has no effect on you anymore. I hope you will never regret what you are going to do. You already wasted the life of your two youngest sons, Mehao and Tera."

Humiliated by the comment, Tamatoa glared at Mato with burning eyes.

"My two sons are skilled, brave warriors, and respected fleet commanders. How can you say such a thing?"

"They could have become priests of great knowledge."

"I have you as a priest, and it is more than enough," Tamatoa replied. "If you want one of my children in priesthood, why don't you look at my daughter?"

"I did not want to upset you, and I apologize if I did," Mato said, bending in front of the king.

Mato went to the other end of the galley, and looked at the clouds. In his anger, his master had given him an idea, and he wondered why he had never thought about Mahine, Tamatoa's daughter: perhaps because she was a woman. The thought that he had been prejudiced disturbed him. In the history of Maohis there had been great women who became respected priestesses and queens. Why was it that he had never thought about Mahine? Then, he thought about Tehani, Tamatoa's wife. Would it be possible to use feminine influence against Tamatoa's madness? The idea seemed of no interest, but he was desperate, and Mahine and Tehani were his last chance. He looked at his long arthritic fingers: They trembled.

"I am old," he murmured to himself. "Soon, I will start the afterlife, so what do I have to lose?"

Tamatoa watched Mato leave with two warriors in a small outrigger, toward the back of the fleet. He smiled at the thought that Mato would go as far as to try the influence of his daughter and wife to change his mind. He knew the old priest too well, and he knew exactly what he was up to. Tamatoa never blamed Mato for being in disagreement with him. He had deep respect for Mato, who had been a good friend of his father's. In some ways,

Mato had been a father to him. Perhaps, the spirit of his father lived in Mato's soul. Never would the thought have occurred to Tamatoa to cause harm to the old companion because of a difference in opinion. Tamatoa was a madman. Nevertheless, he was not born that way. It was the unfathomable cruelty of man that made him who he was. The giant was also human, dedicated to his people, and with strong sentiments toward his family. Above all, Tamatoa had an unshakable sense of honor with others and with himself.

Tehani watched Mato approaching in the outrigger. From far away she could recognize him in his long white robe, and she wondered what his motive could be. It was most unusual for the priest to come alone, without Tamatoa. She helped him board her ship.

"What brings you alone like this?" Tehani asked.

"I am not alone. I could not have come without these two strong boys," Mato said. "Arguments! Tamatoa and I quarreled about the coming battle. I have to admit that I am frustrated, and I can use your friendship."

Mato told the two warriors to come back to get him in the morning.

"You know Tamatoa as well as I do," Tehani said. "You talk to him, and he may or may not listen. If he has made up his mind, nobody can change his course. He thinks about strategies for a long time before he makes irreversible decisions."

Tehani was a tall and strong woman, well built, and looked younger than her thirty-eight years. In her talk, she was direct and a no-nonsense woman. She had the good manners of the Maohi high aristocracy inborn in her blood. She was from a powerful family in Rarotonga.

"I need to talk to you and Mahine," Mato said, "it would cure my bad mood. I am becoming very negative. I guess my old age does not help."

"Come my friend, let's go to my cabin," Tehani said. "Mahine will be happy to see you."

Inside the cabin, Mato sat on floor mats, and felt his aching joints crack. An instant later, Mahine entered the cabin, and went directly to Mato and hugged the old man. The young woman was tall and strongly built like her parents, but she was graceful with her long, straight, black hair falling to her waist. Mato was convinced her body had been carved by the great god Taaroa, so he would have the pleasure to watch what he had done.

"What is bothering you, Mato?" Tehani asked.

"As you know, Tamatoa is going to crush the Pora Pora people."

"So, what is the problem?" Tehani said.

"Tamatoa wants to proceed with the same slaughter on Havaiki, Huahine, Moorea and Tahiti-nui, for which I disagree. Revenge is one thing; to exterminate innocent people is another thing."

Mahine gave some warm breadfruit and water to Mato.

"Tamatoa is the king," Tehani said with authority. "He knows what he is doing."

"I am only his counselor," Mato replied, "But I don't want an unnecessary genocide among the Maohi people, especially at the gathering time."

"I suppose you would like for me to do something about this," Tehani said with annoyance.

"I have nobody else to talk to," Mato confessed, with fatigue showing in the deep pockets under his eyes.

"I have been too harsh to you, Tehani said, taking Mato's trembling hands.

"It is all right," Mato said.

"I have never been agreeable to anyone who does not agree with Tamatoa," Tehani said. "But, I am grateful he has you as a counselor. He may not always listen to what you say, but he needs you, and now more than ever."

"Would you talk to him?" Mato asked.

"No, I will not!" Tehani answered. "It would only make him angry, and produce the opposite effect from what you expect. Do you imagine Tamatoa to be told by a woman what he should do?"

"Yes, I do," Mato said and smiled. "Perhaps, it would be better if you don't say anything to him. It was not clever on my part."

"I am also tired of this endless wandering on the sea," Tehani said, caressing the priest's old hands. "On Tahaa my man was born, on Tahaa we would like to live, on Tahaa we would like to die. Mato, my friend, trust Tamatoa, and let him do it his way."

"Maybe you are right," Mato said. "He is a formidable strategist; I am only a wise priest, and wisdom alone could not have saved our people."

"Can Mahine do anything for you?" Tehani asked after an instant of silence.

"Yes," Mato replied, "I would like to talk to that girl about her future"

"Sure!" Tehani said, leaving. "You are a grandfather to her. Every time she is with you, she feels at peace."

Mahine looked at the old man for whom little time was left. A world without Mato was an unbearable thought to her: He was much more than a wise man; he was lovable, and in her heart this was enough.

"We have too few priests," Mato said. "All men who could have a good future in priesthood have been taken by your father to become warmongers. Who will spread the words of wisdom for the next generation? Would you?"

Mahine looked at Mato with surprise, unable to articulate a single word, but her wide black eyes glowed, as it had never occurred to her that Mato would one day ask her such a question. She felt a strange combination of pride, joy, and fear.

"Me, a priestess! How can I?"

"Why not, you are beautiful, smart, well educated, you have royal blood, and I like the idea. I will teach you everything before I die."

"You still have a long time to live."

"I am not so sure about this, Mahine. The spirits of the other life spiral around me, and are ready to take me home. Would you be my heir?"

"Yes grandfather, I will, but..." Mahine said.

"Is something bothering you?"

"This is your home. Why did you called the world of spirits your home?"

"We come from eternity, in a vortex of wind we shall return to eternity. You are too young to understand this, my child. We are a spark of light welding the future with the past. Our life is so short that we are only an illusion, and yet, we manage to make the worse of it."

Mahine was silent, repeating and weighing Mato's words.

"I never looked at my life in such a way," she finally said, with dismay.

"Don't be sad, Mahine. Along the great illusion, you have a mission to fulfill, as a priestess."

"But, what about my relationship with Taatamao?"

Mato knew for some time that Mahine and Taatamao were deeply in love, and he liked the young warrior. He was intelligent, strong and, above all, naturally peaceful, which was the opposite of Tamatoa's arrogant sons. Tamatoa himself liked Taatamao enough to make him one of his key commanders.

"You will still be his mate," Mato replied. "You will have his children. But, because of your knowledge you will behave differently, and in many ways you will have more freedom than he."

Mato wished Taatamao was Tamatoa's son. Yet, only Tera or Mehao could become Tamatoa's successor, but if Mahine could become a priestess, maybe Taatamao would one day become more powerful: Tamatoa being a family man, he would give more power to the mate of a respected daughter.

"I want to start your education right now," Mato said. "I dread the next few days. With you as my heir, my heart will not bleed as much."

She hugged the old priest with tender affection.

The next morning, after Mato left, Mahine looked at the shearwaters flying around the galleys. They were free, and their graceful soaring flight amused her. She thought about her father, and deeply wished he was right. She found it ironic that a massive killing of humans would not in any way affect the life of the peaceful shearwater. Why was it that humans were so implacable with one another? The bird had its fights, but was always in harmony with its environment. At worst, it was a quarrel for sharing food, a mate, a nesting place or a tiny territory. Never, would the animal have gathered in great numbers to proceed with massive killing of its own kind: Why was it that man could premeditate such a thing with such alacrity?

"What kind of blockhead monsters are we?" she murmured.

A brown noddy flew to her, very tired. She held her hand above her head, and immediately the bird landed on her finger.

She admired its long, slender wings and dark wedge-shaped tail. Its forehead and crown were beautiful smoky gray. A tiny white circle circled its black eyes. Its dark beak was long and sharp.

What can I do for you?" she said gently.

She tried to caress the noddy, which instantly pinched her familiar hand, and flew away to the top of a carved stern at the fore end of the galley.

"What do you think of Mato's visit?" Tehani asked.

"I don't know. I trust my father, but Mato may be right. I am confused."

"Maybe you could talk to Taatamao, who is influential with your father."

"Mother, you don't know Taatamao. He is too loyal to my father to attempt anything against his will. Besides, they are all prepared for this battle, and nobody will ever change their minds. It is much too late."

"Then, let's wait and see," Tehani said.

At some distance from Pora Pora, the evening before the day of ignominy, Tamatoa gave his last instructions:

"Surprise is essential. Taatamao's battle group will take Havaiki, and Mehao's will take Huahine. These two islands are not inhabited by the Pora Pora people, therefore you give them two days' warning to leave by sea. If they don't leave, they shall be exterminated. Now, for the Pora Pora people, I have a special treatment. Tera's battle group will take Tahaa, Teahu's will take Maupiti and mine will take Pora Pora. For these three islands there will be no warning, and no mercy. We shall circle the islands and infiltrate their lagoons during the night. The sea is calm, which should make things easy for us. Four days from now, we shall regroup at Havaiki. Good luck to all of you."

A the same instant, on Pora Pora, the old king who ruled

for thirty years, looked at the unusually red sunset. It was a bad omen. His priests told him to prepare for war, but after so many years of peace he did not take their advice seriously. Besides, the people from the surrounding islands were all friendly with him, but he had forgotten the young boy he had crushed once. It never occurred to him that the young Tamatoa, now a powerful man, would come back. It never occurred to him that it was the last sunset he and his people would ever see.

Four days later, exactly as planned, Tamatoa's armada regrouped in Havaiki. At little human cost, his dream came true, his father had been avenged and his people could at last live in the islands of his forefathers. Tamatoa crushed the Pora Pora people in a horrible river of blood, and the days of the rare survivors were counted. On Havaiki and Huahine, the inhabitants took the two-day warning seriously and vanished by sea. Mehao and Taatamao could take the islands without a fight, but all these people had only one place to go. They all went to Tahiti-nui. They hoped that in the deep valleys and high mountains of the largest island of the archipelago, they could better fight against Tamatoa. They had an advantage: They would reach Tahiti-nui at least two or three days before him, which could make a huge difference. Tamatoa might indeed have his victory, but he most certainly would have to pay a dear price for it. The great warrior was not naive, and had accepted the price.

"It is my view that you should give up Tahiti-nui," Mato said.

"It is my view that you should take a walk on the beach," Tamatoa roared. "Your suggestion is the perfect way to have endless wars with these frustrated neighbors. I want to take care of the problem now. I am aware of the cost. Yet, there will be no contest."

"Maybe," Mato said, shrugging his shoulders. "In that case, I would suggest you don't wait too long, otherwise you may face a powerful force."

"We shall leave after tomorrow, at dawn," Tamatoa said. "Elders, women, and children will stay on these islands with a few warriors: There is a lot of cleaning to do and it is time for them to settle. I want the royal family to stay with Mehao's fleet, in reserve in Moorea. I, Tera, Teahu and Taatamao will take care of Tahiti-nui."

"How are you going to approach these people?" Mato asked. "Are you going to tell them to leave the island within two days?"

"Yes, it is exactly what I am going to tell them."

"This will give them more time to prepare."

"No, my dear Mato, I know human nature too well. This will divide them, as they struggle to find out who shall take command."

"May the spirits inspire you, Tamatoa," Mato said. "We are all tired of this life. Do what you have to do. Let's conquer the most beautiful island in the world."

Following his master's recommendations, Mato left the headquarters, went to the beach and walked toward the south. The warm, white sand was agreeable between his toes. There was no wind, and the sun was hot. A few clouds covered the nearby summits. He thought the place of the great gathering was indeed a magnificent place. He went to the great Marae of the Maohis, the Marae of Taputapu-atea. He could have taken an outrigger to go faster, but he was tired of boats and he had plenty of time. He wanted to see the place where he had been only once, many years ago. The Marae was a huge complex, with many temples, living houses, round-ended dwelling houses and courts paved with superb coral slabs. It took many generations to build the place, improve it and maintain it. The entire complex was on a large point on the east side of the island.

When Mato saw the main temple, he felt a deep sentiment of respect. At its center was the famous white monolith. Carefully, he caressed the legendary giant stone. Its contact sent shivers up his spine. Spirits from another world inhabited the stone, and the legend said that a living man was buried under each corner. So, the monolith would be guarded by four living souls. Kings and queens were placed on its sacred top, the day of their coronation. Five moon-cycles from now, if everything went well, at this place, he would meet all the great priests, kings, and queens of the Maohi world. He wished very hard that Tamatoa would handle the last phase of his conquest with wisdom. He knew it was wishful thinking. Yet, he had faith, and caressed the white monolith once more.

"Great Spirit, make something different happen, bring us a surprise, protect our children."

Mato looked at the stone. It was still, silent and bore no life. He felt empty, discouraged and baffled by fate. He walked toward the beach, going south. In the east, across the lagoon, he could see the sacred pass through which all the pilgrims would enter, leaving their grief, disputes and corruption behind.

Taatamao's fleet was anchored in the lagoon, near shore. At some distance, Mato saw Mahine sitting on the beach. She waited for Taatamao, but he was busy with other matters, at her father's headquarters. As he got closer, Mato realized she was sobbing, and never before had he seen her in such anguish. Moved, he sat close to her and hugged his young treasure. He himself felt a few tears blinding his old, cloudy eyes.

"Mato, I am so glad to see you. Why Tahiti-nui?"

"I guess your father does not know when to stop."

"I am so afraid of losing Taatamao."

"You shall not. Taatamao is the most brilliant man of your father's army, and he will not step into unnecessary danger."

"But,..." She started sobbing again.

"But what, little girl?"

"I saw Taatamao falling from the mountain in my dreams."

Mato's brow pulled into a frown.

"Did I hear you say dreams?"

"Yes, I dreamed this at least three times."

Every word she said hammered in his head. She had been touched by a vision: She was gifted.

"Did you dream about things that indeed happened later?"

She thought for awhile, looking at the sand.

"A long time ago, I dreamed about a place with a large white stone. It was well cut. I dreamed about it many times, then it faded away. Last night, I dreamed about it again, but I never saw it in real life."

Mato was completely caught off guard by her startling revelation. She saw his dilated eyes, looking at her. He had never looked at her in such a way. She was afraid, but did not know the reason.

"How long ago did you come here?"

"I just arrived with this canoe. I have never been here before."

"Come with me, I want to show you something."

They walked across a green valley, went to a point covered by many ironwood trees. The exceptionally hard wood was sacred and a symbol of the brave warrior. It was Oro's tree. Oro was the god of war, and his son was Taaroa. After they crossed the forest, Mahine saw the great Marae. They went to the main temple.

"Are you sure you did not come here before?"

"Never," Mahine replied. "This place is amazing."

"Come near me, and look atop the main temple."

A soft gasp escaped her mouth. She was stunned, unable to say anything. She walked slowly toward the white monolith. Before she could touch it, she stopped and admired it. Then, she came closer, caressed it and instantly retrieved her hand. She tried again, with both hands flat on the stone. Horrified, she turned around, looked at Mato with dilated eyes.

"Then, Taatamao is going to die," se said. "I saw this stone in my dreams. I saw Taatamao falling from the mountain. Some of my dreams are not dreams, they are omens."

"Calm down, little princess. Don't jump to conclusions too soon. Understanding visions is a complex matter. You are gifted with a rare talent. Of that, I was not aware, and it pleases me immensely."

"But, what is going to happen to Taatamao?"

"Something will happen. But, Taatamao will not necessarily die. What you saw is only a signal for awareness. What will really happen, we will not know until then."

At last, Mato had found the person for whom he had been searching for many years. With patience, tenacity and hope he had been studying every man he knew. He was stunned that the person he had been searching for so long had been so close to him all that time.

"Climb with me on that stone," Mato said. "Sit, cross-legged, facing the southeast. Close your eyes, and concentrate hard. Tell me if you see anything."

Confused, Mahine complied.

"I don't see anything."

"You did not try properly. Don't pay attention to me. You are alone. You are looking in space in the darkness of your mind. You must see something."

After a short time, Mahine seemed agitated. She opened her eyes and looked at the horizon.

"It is strange. I saw the dorsal fin of a shark."

"Are you sure it was a shark?"

"No, it was fuzzy, it could have been a mountain, a very sharp mountain."

Mato's mouth dropped open.

"You saw Mount Orohena," he said, emphasizing every word.

"What is Mount Orohena?"

"It is the sacred mountain of Tahiti-nui. It is the highest mountain of the Maohi's world."

"Then what?"

"Then, from now on, you are going to stay with me. I, the great priest, say so. You and I have a war to win."

****

CHAPTER 14

"Hina and I became one body. She was the foundation of whom I should become. She was under my arm to be protected, and near my heart to be loved. I was the head, and she was the crown."

Kon Tici Viracocha

Hina swam near the beach, in the cool water of the early morning. The sun was barely above the horizon. Kon felt his heart jolt and his pulse pound at the sight of her magnificent gliding body. Like her mind, and the pure water of the blue lagoon, her shape was perfect. Hina noticed he was watching her intently. She knew he was unaware of what she had planned for the day, and the idea amused her. Yet, she hoped it would please him. She ran out of the sea, superb, and nude. She lay down on the black sand, studied his lean face and caressed his short beard. His deep blue eyes were more appealing and devastating than ever before. She wanted him. Her eyes turned around toward the mountain.

"Do you remember there is a place up there," she whispered, "where I told you long ago we would share our most intimate secrets?"

"Yes, I often think about this."

"If we start now, we could make it before dark."

He thought she was more attractive than ever. She was ready, and she waited for him. A delightful frisson of desire ran through his entire body. He felt the tide of his own desire rising with force. It was strong and almost unbearable.

"We are not prepared for the two-day trip," he smiled with obvious regret.

"Yes, we are," she replied. "Come, and I will show you."

They walked to the king's house. They crossed the living room, and went to the garden full of fragrant flowers. Tupua and Atea were waiting for them. For an instant Kon became confused, until Tupua came to him.

"My son from another world, take this food for your trip."

Atea came to him, with tears in her eyes.

"Kon, take these soft bark-cloth robes and blankets. You are going to need them. In the basket Tupua gave you, there are a few other things you may use in due time."

She kissed him on his lips.

"Take good care of our little girl," she added with a beautiful smile.

Unable to express their happiness with words, Tupua and Atea were only capable of showing tears of joy. Moved by their love, their approval and trust, Kon hugged both of them. Their gesture was very special to him.

"Do not tell anyone where we are going," Kon said.

"You have my word on that," Tupua said. "Besides, you will be on taboo territory. Go, my children, to Orohena's sacred land, which is yours. The Great Spirit is with you."

This time, Hina was a stronger and more experienced climber. The weather was clear and they progressed much faster. Far away, the horizon was a clear cut between the dark blue sea and the clear blue sky. Around midday, before they challenged the formidable ridge of Mount Pitohiti, Kon sat among tiny ferns and waited for Hina a short distance behind.

"You are doing well," he said. "You may finish this trip without a scratch."

"I doubt it," she replied. "This afternoon, I know I am going to have vertigo again."

"When it happens, do not look below, and concentrate only on where you put your feet and your hands."

"I cannot believe I climbed this before," she said, looking ahead. "Yet, to you it is nothing. For me, the tropicbird cliff will remain a forbidden territory forever...."

Suddenly, Hina saw Kon was preoccupied by something. At first, she asked no question, but when he did not even listen to what she was saying, she knew something was wrong.

"Kon!"

He did not answer.

"Do you want to talk about it?" she asked, shaking his shoulder.

"I don't know. I had a strange sensation, like a signal I experienced only once before, on the eve of the day of shame, on the continent."

His words troubled her. She knew his feelings were to be taken seriously, always.

"Could it be your imagination?"

"No, I have been trained to communicate with other minds far away. It is a strange world, cold and lonely, where you may see things you wish you would never see."

"Do you want to go back?"

"No!" he replied. "Let's not spoil this day. Let Tupua and Vana handle the island for now."

All afternoon, they edged their way along the dangerous

ridge. Once more, just before she reached the top of Mount Pitohiti, she rested her face against the wet rootstocks of ferns. Her nose lost between young fiddleheads, she bit her lips and giggled with pleasure. It was her second victory over the mountain. Once more, through physical agony, she found that joy was a concept without limits.

They passed the cave, and went to the small lake where they disturbed a flock of sacred, red ducks. Kon kissed the tip of Hina's nose, and started to undress her. Then, he wrapped his arms around her midriff. She turned around and slowly undressed him. They were covered with mud mixed with perspiration. With pleasure, they dived into the cold water. She jumped on his shoulders and drove him deep underwater. On their way back to the surface, they looked at one another. She parted her lips, and the way he kissed her was surprisingly gentle. They came out of the cold lake, trembling. They quickly wrapped themselves inside the fresh, clean bark-cloth robes, took their dirty clothes, the blankets, the basket, and went to the cave.

They reached the secret place as the sun disappeared behind Moorea. They entered the cave and removed all the spider webs. They spread the largest blanket on the cushion of tiny ferns, went outside, sat at the edge of the cliff, and watched the burning sky.

She collected a few dry ferns and started a fire, but there was little fuel around to burn. Before the last flames died, Hina took a short stick from the basket, and strung five small oily nuts on it. Atea had collected the nuts from the tutui tree, knowing they would enjoy the light they can provide.

"My mother thought of everything," Hina said.

Kon lighted the first nut: Its burning oil would last some time, then the fire would spread to the second nut, and so on. His eyes could not turn away from the burning sky. She laid her head on his shoulder and waited for him.

"Far away on other islands, there are people killing other people," he said with a sad voice.

"On this island, Hina waits for you," she whispered.

He turned around, and looked at her flashing eyes.

"I am deeply touched you wanted to come back here for us to love one another," he said, "and you knew the mountain was important to me. You knew it was the place where I wished to honor you."

"Tonight is our night, Kon Teke. Tomorrow, we will have time to worry about the world," she whispered in his ear.

He took her in his arms, and gently eased her down onto the bark-cloth blanket. The small flames on the tutui nut danced in the evening breeze, at the entrance. The phantoms of their shadows hovered on the walls of the cave. A man and a woman, from two different worlds, rediscovered the subtleties of creation. They discovered the beauty of one another.

With respect and dignity, they undressed one another, and put their robes aside, on the ferns. With religious care, they oiled each other's body with Atea's sacred oil. Fragrant tiare flowers mixed with precious sandalwood had been macerated in the oil for several moon-cycles. Its scent rapidly invaded the entire cave, and became the only thing they could smell.

When the oily ritual was completed, Kon took the other bark-cloth blanket and spread it above them. He came close to Hina, slipped one hand under her head, and caressed her face with his other hand. She felt wrapped in comfortable warmth, and buried her face against the hair of his chest. He encircled her with his arms, and felt her warm breast press against his chest: The feeling was so strong, so new, that they both closed their eyes.

Kon traced his fingertip across her parted lips. Then, he

gently outlined the circle of her breast, sending a wave of pleasure within her body. When his hand searched for a path down, all the way to her soft thigh, she grabbed him with both arms and pressed her nails into his back. Long before they found one another's ultimate intimacy, their sense of reality was annihilated among an infinity of glowing stars.

The last tutui nut started burning. Contentment and peace flowed between them. They found their bodies were in perfect harmony. For them, there was no light, no wind, no cave, no mountain. There was only a glowing wave of passion. Hina had never dreamed Kon's body would feel so warm, so familiar, so complementary and so gentle. She was transported beyond the point of return. She wanted more. She wanted him, now.

With her arms, she rotated his body atop hers. His lips pressed against hers, and covered her mouth with passion. Her arms stretched slowly across the blanket. Her eyes were fixed on the ceiling. She slowly parted her legs, and she offered herself to the man she loved, completely, unconditionally.

He slowly raised himself on his elbows and looked at her superb black eyes. They reflected intense, powerful love. She looked at him with a widening smile of approval. Her thick, black hair framed her lovely face. The golden condor shined between her hardening nipples. She was beautiful.

When the Son of the Sun entered Hina of the Valley's temple, her eyes grew wider in ecstasy. With her, the breeze, the cave and the mountain moaned.

When the small flame on the last tutui nut died, they did not even notice. In their soul, spiraling stars showed them the way to creation. The priestess and Kon Tici Viracocha reached a climax they had never known possible. At this very moment, they entered a new territory where they alone could dare to travel. Even the spirits of the night left the cave, left the mountain. Even the night breeze calmed down and died. Orohena's children were at peace. Nobody and nothing would invade their privacy, but during the silent night, they would discover the many treasures that would give them infinite wealth.

At dawn, Hina woke up first. It was most unusual for Kon to sleep so deeply at this time of the day. She kneeled above the blanket, and looked at him, amused. She looked at her body, slowly massaged her breast, and smiled at her wonderful experience. She stood up, took a bark-cloth robe and went outside.

The sun was rising, but being on the northwestern side of the mountain, she could only see its reflection on Moorea. She looked at the valley, the river, the beach and then the lagoon where a startling vision froze her where she stood.

The lagoon was covered with canoes, outriggers and galleys. She had never seen so many. She immediately recalled Kon's vision. Once more, he had been right to be concerned. Shocked and angry, she ran inside the cave, where she found Kon breathing rapidly. His hands and eyebrows were agitated by a nightmare. She gently shook his shoulder. When he opened his eyes, he looked disoriented, then sat on the blanket.

"You had a bad dream," she said. "Come outside, I want to show you reality."

But, she did not have the time to show him. She stopped, listened and looked at him with terrified eyes."

"What is it?... Hina!"

"Listen! Do you hear the drums?"

"Do they mean something?"

"Yes, they are drums of war, calling every one of us to prepare for the sacred fight.... An invader will arrive in a few days.... Kon, this is terrible."

She collapsed on his chest, sobbing in anger, protest and misery.

"Let's go," Kon said. "These boats in the lagoon are not the enemy."

"How do you know that?" she said, looking at him with trust.

"You just told me the invader will arrive in a few days."

"You, and your logic!" she frowned.

"In the next few days, I will need you and your complete trust," he said. "You still don't know Kon Tici."

She managed a smile, and a little joke.

"I know I learned a lot about him last night."

He cupped her head in his hands.

"As long as I live, I will never forget last night," he said.

With regret, they left their secret cave. The spiders would come back, and close the entrance. The place was taboo, reserved for very special occasions. It never occurred to Hina that she would be back soon.

"What are we going to find, on our way back?" she asked.

"Total confusion!" he replied. "But, don't panic, and remain the priestess at her best."

"What am I going to do?"

"I don't know yet, and we have little time to prepare. All those people who came from other islands are terrified. The invader is tough."

"How do you know this?"

"It fits my vision!"

She listened to his words, and could not refrain uneasiness about the man she loved. In many ways he was so human, so young and so gentle. Yet, in many ways, he was so different, so mature, so mysterious and so far away. However, Hina was a woman of many resources, and she would never let her strange feeling affect her love for him. On the contrary, he filled her with will power. A priestess he wanted her to be, so priestess she would be. With unconditional trust, she would give him her best.

It was early in the afternoon when they entered the village, where people screamed, yelled and ran everywhere. Many were strangers from other islands, confused, erratic and wandering. It was total chaos. Kon and Hina ran to Tupua's house. It was empty. On their way to the beach, they saw Taaroa sitting on a coral slab.

"Where is my father?" Hina asked.

"He is at the Teauroa point, where most of the refugees came."

"Who are they?" she asked.

"They are from Havaiki and Huahine. There are no survivors in Pora Pora, Tahaa and Maupiti."

"Who is the invader?" Kon asked.

"Tamatoa, a brutal giant, they say," Taaroa said. "His father was king of Tahaa many years ago, and I knew him well. When Tamatoa was a young boy, the Pora Pora people killed his father. Since then, Tamatoa and his people vanished at sea. Now, he is back for revenge."

"At least, he has a motive," Kon said.

"Is he coming here?" Hina asked.

"Yes, he wants to conquer the entire archipelago before the great gathering. His war fleet is huge, and disciplined, and he is a man of no concession."

Kon felt Hina's nails penetrate his skin. He did not flinch, and fully measured the devastating seriousness of a new era. They quickly went to the Teauroa point, where they found Tupua and Vana among high dignitaries from Havaiki and Huahine in the shade of an ironwood tree. They all yelled at one another.

Tupua and Vana did not notice Kon and Hina, until the other leaders became silent.

"Finally, you are here," Tupua said. "I want to..."

Ignoring Tupua, all the leaders encircled Kon, surprised to see the tall man with fair skin. Their surprise turned to a collective murmur when they saw his blue eyes. They touched his beard, admired his long black hair tied on the top of his head and falling around his shoulders. Their surprise turned to euphoria and confusion when they saw the gold plugs in his earlobes, and the gold bracelets shining around his wrists. Now, scared, they backed away from him, and looked at Tupua for answers, who was most obliged.

Slowly, they became accustomed to Kon's presence, and started to talk about their fate. Soon, they argued and yelled again, listening to their own words. Nobody was willing to listen to anyone else. Kon glanced at Hina, who grinned with amusement. They walked away from the group, went to the beach and sat on the black sand.

"What is your opinion of all these fools?" she asked.

"For those not prepared to see me, the shock is considerable: In due time, I may turn this to our advantage."

"It is impossible to control them," she murmured.

"Tamatoa is a clever man." Kon said. "He did not have to fight to take Havaiki and Huahine. Furthermore, he knows perfectly well that there would be so many leaders arguing and yelling on Tahiti-nui that nobody would be capable of regrouping forces and preparing for a fight."

Hina's eyes were fixed on the shiny black sand. She felt helpless, and overwhelmed.

"What could we do?" she asked.

"I need to talk to your father."

"If you need me, I am here," Tupua said.

They turned around, surprised that he had noticed their departure.

"How did you succeed to escape that crowd?" Kon asked.

"Simple, nobody saw me!" Tupua said, shrugging his shoulders.

"What are we going to do?" Hina asked.

"I don't know. It is bad, and nobody was prepared for this. Our warriors are not well trained and no match for Tamatoa's large fleet. I have work for you both."

"You are my king," Hina said.

"You are a medicine woman," Tupua said. "There are many ill people, children and elderly from the other islands who need your help. Use your judgment, little girl."

"How can I serve you?" Kon asked.

"You stay with me, and figh," Tupua roared.

"You know I will not fight," Kon replied.

"Oh no! You misunderstood me, my son," Tupua said. "You will not fight with your arms, but you most certainly will with your brain. I count on you to come up with a plan of action, with anything, and quickly. We have only three days to shape up, four at most."

As a Viracocha, Kon Tici was well prepared to face such conflict. He had felt the danger coming before anyone else did, so he was ready. Once, he and his blood brothers had failed to reverse human madness; nevertheless, they had succeeded to do so many times in the past. Those skills had helped the small Viracocha colony to survive for thousands of years.

"I shall find a peaceful settlement," Kon said. "But, I will need your total support, and in due time you shall do exactly what I say. In the meantime, you must control all these people."

Tupua felt awestruck by the sudden imposing mien of Kon Tici. Within instants, the Son of the Sun proceeded with a striking metamorphosis, and more than ever he became a total mystery to his friends. Tupua had never imagined that this man from another world could talk to him with such authority. It had never occurred to him that Kon would order him about, on his own island, in his own kingdom. Yet, Tupua did not feel angry. Kon's words were not aggressive. Yet, they had the unmistakable touch of certitude. Tupua looked at his charismatic son, immediately trusted him immensely, and put a friendly arm on Kon's shoulder.

"How much time do you need, my son?"

"I will meditate at the top of Hina's Marae," Kon replied. "I will leave this physical life and travel through my mind. You shall not feed me, or talk to me. Tomorrow night, my meditation will be completed, and I will tell you about the first phase of my plan."

Kon turned around and went to the Marae of Toerau. Hina understood, and went among the people, trying to relieve their suffering from dehydration: They had not prepared for their long trip at sea.

Kon walked slowly on the warm, black sand. His mind entered a state where no one could disturb him. He passed many friends, never saw anyone and was already assembling an intricate puzzle.

He climbed to the top of the small pyramid, sat cross-legged and faced the northwestern sea. Instantly, the Toreau wind started blowing. He closed his eyes and slowly drifted into a state of profound absorption, while a whirl of dust was dancing around him. From now on, there were only two sides in his mind: his side, and Tamatoa's side.

For a long time, he thought about Tamatoa's motives. The

young Tamatoa had been traumatized when he saw his father tortured and slaughtered by the Pora Pora people. He not only suffered from his own fate, but also from seeing his people outcast from their island. Over the years, Tamatoa rapidly became a giant, physically and mentally. Then, with courage and patience, he had built his empire. With faith and discipline, he became demanding and built an authoritarian social structure. Now, Tamatoa was a powerful madman. What could a fragile Kon Tici do? What was left from Tamatoa's humanity? Did he have a wife? Did he have children? If so, who were they? Kon Tici analyzed Tamatoa's personality so deeply that he dreamed he was on the deck of a giant galley. He looked at the clouds above Pora Pora, and gave orders to his commanders. He became Tamatoa himself. He had his revenge. Now, he was looking forward to the other islands. He found himself arguing with an old priest about the necessity to pursue farther than the Pora Pora people. Was ambition his only motive, or was it something else? Was it simply a pursuit for elusive stability, to protect the future of his people?

Tamatoa was a great leader. Waiting thirty years for revenge showed a remarkable will power. His preparation showed good organization, and logic. Every move was well planned, and always justified. Kon Tici found the key words: Tamatoa's actions were always justified. Tamatoa was not seeking Havaiki, Huahine, Moorea and Tahiti-nui out of personal ambition. His main goal was much more farsighted, as he placed his people far above himself, and they all knew it. The conclusion was unmistakable: After the Pora Pora slaughter, Tamatoa's only motive was to establish the security of his people, once for all, by dominating the entire archipelago. He would not do it for the fun of it, but he would do it by necessity. Kon Tici was content: He knew that he now understood the man.

It was dawn when Kon opened his eyes for the first time. He could hear voices coming from the village. At some distance, seated on an old coconut tree trunk, Taaroa observed him. Hina came, and placed an opened coconut full of milk in front of Kon. She put her hand on his shoulder. The slight pressure of her fingers told him she loved him, but she did not say one word, and went away. She went to Taaroa, who gave her a signal with his hand.

"You should tell your father to keep three guards around here," Taaroa said. "Sightseers are too numerous, and this man must be undisturbed."

"Good idea," she said, giving him a fresh coconut to drink.

"How did you know it was the right time to come and give him a drink?" Taaroa asked.

"Mana told me!" she replied, as she went away.

Taaroa smiled, and shook his head in dismay.

Kon drank his beverage and immediately closed his eyes. Once more, the physical world was gone, and time stopped. He traveled without bonds to all the places he knew on the island, searching for something that could help him. He was on the giant cliff with the tropicbirds. He was on Mount Orohena, and saw Hina claim her victory. Then, the two names echoed in his mind: Orohena, Hina, Orohena,... Unaware of the reasons yet, he knew they were his best assets. Somehow, he had to make them fit together, but what about himself, Kon Tici? What should he do? Of course, this was the key: Kon Tici, Hina and Orohena. They were his three assets. Then, for a long time, his mind wandered between Tamatoa and his three assets. He was far away from the unreliability of touch, from the notorious sense of taste or smell, from the disturbance of sounds and from the great illusion of sight. With simplicity, his mind explored the unthinkable for common man. With effectiveness, he built on his three assets, and sought an answer.

He was sure of something: The greater the simplicity of the premise of his answer, the more impressive his answer would be, the more the people would relate to it and the more their fate would be shaped by the goodness of what they cherished most.

Kon's power of analysis gained momentum, and a tiny idea germinated in his mind. He thought about a race. Now, he had four assets: himself, Hina, Orohena and a race. However, it was not that simple; Tamatoa was not naive. Furthermore, Kon did not want any loser, but two winners, which was easier said than done.

All afternoon, under the rain brought by the Toerau wind, he struggled with how to deploy his four assets, and thought he was going nowhere. He became discouraged, and Taaroa could see his fatigue in his slump shoulders. Indeed, Kon became desperate, his thoughts fuzzy and his mind gloomy. Slowly, his self-confidence disappeared. He was finished. He had failed in his search for an answer.

He opened his eyes, and looked far away, toward the village. He saw four children racing on the beach; one fell, and they all stopped to look at their companion. Kon immediately felt a tidal wave crossing his mind, and closed his eyes. It was only then that he measured how far he had gone. It was only then that he realized he had found a wonderful answer. Suddenly, everything was clear.

Kon Tici had his place, Hina had her place and Mount Orohena was indeed the key. What he had to do was entirely revealed in the form of a daring vision. Then, peace invaded him. He opened his eyes and smiled at Taaroa. He had the absolute conviction that he was right. For the next few days, he knew his strategy would remain unshakable. He had found the very essence of a formidable premise.

"Give them action!" Kon exclaimed.

"What kind of action?" Taaroa asked, with excitement.

"Action that will develop emotional ties, ties so strong that many unexpected events will result, events that none of us or Tamatoa will ever forget."

"How do you suggest we accomplish this?" Taaroa asked, puzzled.

"Dear companion," Kon said, pressing a friendly hand on the shoulder of the old man, "there are still weaknesses in my plan. But, for the time being I am content. Only remember my premise: At all cost, create emotional ties between Tamatoa and us."

Right at this moment, Kon Tici's idea was like a tiny fish swimming freely in the clear lagoon. Within one moon-cycle, the tiny fish would become a whale.

****

CHAPTER 15

"A powerful force touched me, whose premise is simple: Man's ethical behavior should be based on sympathy, knowledge and ties. Therefore, my father's army is a remnant part of perfect absurdity."

Mahine, Tamatoa's daughter

Mato and Mahine spent the night and the next day among the temples and dwelling houses of the Marae of Taputapu-atea. Mahine was fascinated by the place where the great gathering of Maohis would take place, and she wished she had more time to spend on the immense site with her teacher, but at dawn they would be back on the galleys, and they would sail to Moorea, then to Tahiti-nui.

Exhausted by her desire to learn and her buoyancy, Mato lay in the shade of an ironwood tree and went to sleep. The afternoon was half gone, and he thought it would be good for Mahine to be alone. His mind drifted among the familiar world of spirits. Floating in the haze of heat, a vortex of dust followed Mahine around the temples.

Her curiosity was insatiable, as she was scrutinizing each house, each wall and each stone with the thirst of discovery. Mato had never realized that Tamatoa's daughter could be deeply enchanted by the legends of her forefathers. Yes, she was worried about Taatamao and about the terrible endeavor of her father, but today she was transported in a thrilling contact with the mysteries of her distant past, looking at life with different eyes. Suddenly, she was fully aware of the precariousness of the present. Many generations had walked within these walls. Like her, they had a good time, and did not worry about how short life would be. Like them, she would pass, die, and be forgotten, but the stones would remain, and inspire other generations, maybe her children. She laid her hands on many stones: They felt warm, alive and filled with legends, some transmitted from mouth to ear so many times that only a small part of them was true. It did not matter. They had their beauty, their depth and their message.

"Who am I, and who should I be?" she murmured.

The remarkable site was empty. Only Mato slept some distance away. She was alone, perfectly aware that on a normal day the place was occupied by a large number of priests and their families. She thought this moment of solitude was priceless. Probably never again would she see this place under the same light. It was as if all humans had vanished.

Because of her solitude, and the stationary presence of the stones, she thought time had stopped. She sat on a coral slab, listened to the silence and watched some dust slowly cover her feet. In the sky, white terns grunted. She followed their erratic flight, until one of them hovered in the gentle breeze. The birds, the trees and the flowers were the only life: Man was gone. She thought that life would not stop if man exterminated himself. The beauty of the islands would remain forever, like the stones. Some other life would take place, and perhaps would evolve higher. At this moment, Mahine saw the roots of her problem. She looked at her soft, shapely brown legs, and wondered what she should do with her life. She was from royal blood, well educated, beautiful, young and in love: She had everything. Yet, something was missing. She was not happy.

Life comprises only two things: a long march and some stops. Mahine was stopped, and she felt abysmal emptiness, unable to control her destiny. Her life presented no challenge. With her immense wealth, she felt she had nothing. The walls of the city laughed at her. She was there, sitting, useless. She was nobody. Yet, she was full of energy, but did not have a clue what to do with it.

Mato himself did not know what her skills would be. He wanted her to become a priestess, but in what? He vaguely saw that she was gifted with her mind, she had remarkable visions, and she saw omens.

"Then what?" she murmured, discouraged, but feeling a mysterious presence around her.

She was enthused by many things, but always superficial because of poor will power. Mato thought she was exuberant, but he did not know anything about the inner drama that could shatter her soul. Indeed, deep inside, she did not have self-esteem. Furthermore, she did not have esteem for the human race. She had grown up in a military environment where everyone was told what to do. She had no choice, but to become superficial. Her world lacked feelings, including sympathy, compassion, and emotional ties. Nothing was worth living for. Once more she shuddered inwardly, felt torment and misery choking her throat. Her worst enemy defeated her: herself!

She held back tears, but could not control compulsive sobs. Angry at herself, she stood up and walked among the temples. Moments ago she was happy to discover this remarkable place; moments later she was in the darkness of depression. Confused, she wandered restlessly until the night wrapped the island in a cocoon of peace, until she found herself near the white monolith. She inspected it, touched it and climbed on it, but she backed off, afraid she would sink once more into depression. At this moment, once more, she felt a presence. She looked around, but she was alone. A current of energy invaded her, like someone entering inside her. Then, she suddenly wanted to sit on the stone of the four souls where she distinctly saw a dust whirl for a short instant. Puzzled by something she did not understand, she climbed the giant stone, and sat cross-legged facing the southeast, facing Tahiti-nui. The night was very dark, and thick clouds masked the stars. The Toerau wind blew while she listened to some wandering land crabs and the cheerful chirp of crickets. She heard distant voices, but it was only the ululating wind. She closed her eyes, and explored the darkness of her mind as Mato had told her.

Slowly, her mind left her physical body, and an alien man was holding her hand. She could not see him very well, or touch him, but he was most certainly in control of her. She felt again an incredible current of energy enter her body. It was a continuous flow. At first she was afraid, then it became agreeable, and she felt the power of tranquillity. The alien ghost vanished, and so did all the sounds around her. Then, she saw the tall alien man coming back to her. This time she saw his face, and she was astonished at his blue eyes. He suddenly walked through her and vanished inside her body. She felt possessed by an unknown force, but she was not afraid. She smiled with candor, and traveled where time was meaningless.

Transported to another place, she found herself on the deck of her father's galley. She looked at the red clouds above the Pora Pora Island. She was within her own father, who gave orders to his commanders. Instants later, she was with him on a fast double canoe, paddled by twelve gourd-helmeted warriors. On the top of their helmets they had long red feathers, the feather of Oro, the god of war. They rapidly crossed the lagoon. Many similar double canoes touched the beaches at the same time. Then, as planned for years, with no mercy, they began the killing,....

Mato saw her head spinning, and her hands agitated by erratic pulses. When Mahine opened her eyes, they were filled with horror.

"No! My father is a murderer!" she screamed.

Her words echoed several times within the temples. Mato climbed the monolith and wrapped her in his arms.

"Calm down, it was only a bad dream."

She pushed him aside.

"A bad dream!" she exclaimed with anger in her eyes. "Oh no, Mato, it was not a bad dream. It was exactly what happened a few days ago on Pora Pora. He is a murderer. We are all murderers. Man is insane, worse than animals. Man is a doomed manure machine. This world would have more beauty without man."

Mato was startled by her choice of words: They were not hers.

"What are you talking about?" Mato said, a little worried.

She recovered her calm, then sat on the edge of the monolith, beside the old priest.

"Before my Pora Pora experience, something wonderful happened to me," she said. "I was touched by the force of truth. It was as if an alien entered my body and reached my soul. It was a charismatic man with blue eyes who took my hand, traveled in time and space with me, and showed me the truth of innocent men, women and children killed out of cruelty. Never again will I be capable of looking at my father with the same eyes."

Astonished by Mahine's vision, Mato immediately thought it

was a bad omen. He was afraid he had turned the young woman against her own father.

"You are not aware of what the Pora Pora people did to your grandfather, my child," Mato tried to explain.

"This is irrelevant," she argued. "If he had found the guilty men, I would understand. But, to exterminate the people as he did, I will never forget. To my grave, I will take that vision. Yes, Mato, I will be a priestess!"

"Mahine, don't let anger invade your heart."

She jumped to the ground, and walked some distance away from the monolith.

"I am not angry. I told you something wonderful happened to me. I simply found the premise of my priesthood."

"And, what could that be?" Mato asked, surprised by her sudden confidence.

"Teaching our children sympathy, caring and how to build emotional ties," she said, emphasizing every word.

The choice of words hit him full force a second time: They were not hers.

"How did you learn to use such words?"

"They just came to me during my meditation on the stone of the four souls, after the alien entered inside me. Don't you think they make sense?"

"Yes indeed, they certainly do," Mato replied. "There is more power in that monolith than I thought."

"I will always remember that place," she said. "When you were asleep, I was depressed, as many times before. I never knew the reasons. Then, I was invaded by this flow of energy. The spirit was with me, talking to me. Words I never heard before came to my mind. Everything was clear, simple and beautiful. Then, I had that vision, which I hated. But, I realize it was necessary for me to see it. Now, I am at peace with myself, I regained self-esteem, and I don't know what is happening to me."

"I don't know either," Mato said. "But, you have everything that is needed to promote self-esteem, and gain esteem from others. I have great esteem for you, and I guess it was a good idea for you and me to come here."

With regret they left the majestic Marae of Taputapu-atea. The stone of the four souls had spoken to them. In the crowd of the great gathering they had thought they would find some answers, and yet in the silent solitude of the empty place they found them.

"There is a purpose for everything," Mahine murmured.

When the sun rose, they found Tamatoa on the beach.

"Where were you both?" Tamatoa asked in bad mood.

"Well, you told me to go take a walk on the beach," Mato replied.

"Father, I don't like what you are doing," Mahine said, taking both men by surprise.

"What did you anchor in the mind of my daughter?" Tamatoa asked with vehemence.

"Mato has nothing to do with my thinking. Don't blame him, blame me, blame yourself."

"I don't need your opinion, young girl," Tamatoa said, aggravated.

"I am aware of that," she grinned. "Nevertheless, your war is dirty. You killed innocent Maohis who were brothers and sisters of blood. You will have no rest, no victory."

Her last words had a devastating effect on Tamatoa, who slapped her face with anger.

"This, you shall not do," Mato protested. "Even if you don't agree with her, you shall love and respect her. Or, she will destroy you."

Mahine did not flinch, and looked at her father with a cynical smile.

"Go on your respective galleys," Tamatoa roared. " Now, I have other things to do than to listen to your nonsense. But, the three of us, shall have another talk, soon."

****

CHAPTER 16

"Often, there are dangers bound to the actions of our leaders, so wise men and women are the prey of ills generated by the imperfection of human nature. Therefore, wise men and women have the duty to look upon these faults and prevent the adventurer, tyrant, fanatic or opportunist from ruling this world."

Kon Tici Viracocha

After three days of confusion and anguish, the people of Tahiti-nui and their friends from Havaiki and Huahine slowly realized that unity was their only chance to face Tamatoa with hope and pride. The kings officially elected Tupua as the supreme chief. Drums pounded their message of apocalypse around the island and ordered everyone to prepare for the invasion. The message was clear: Do not fight Tamatoa on the sea, or in the lagoon. Let him come inside the valleys and in the mountains. Let him fight the deadly ghosts of the dark rain forest.

At Tupua's request, a meeting was called at Vana's dwelling house. All high dignitaries were invited, and everyone was told that only one person at a time would be allowed to speak. Anyone who would fail to obey this rule would be excused from the group. They all agreed with no resistance, but right at the beginning, Tupua surprised everyone with an unexpected move.

"The fight as we know it," the king said, "the physical fight, will be our last resort, after we have exhausted all the possible solutions that would lead to a peaceful settlement."

Instantly, the entire house was in total chaos, but this time Tupua was prepared. With anger, he slapped a drum near him: Everyone became silent and listened.

"If we fight Tamatoa on the sea, we will be finished in less than one day," Tupua said. "If we fight him inland, we will be finished after one moon-cycle. So, either way, we lose. But, if you listen to me, we may win; everybody may win, us and Tamatoa as well."

This time Tupua had gone too far. The most aggressive leaders from other districts and from Huahine in particular roared their opposition. Tupua was publicly accused of unacceptable weakness, and of being an incompetent military leader.

"You are acting as if you were afraid of Tamatoa," the Huahine king said. "Your proposition is humiliating."

"Yes, I am afraid," Tupua said. "But, I am not afraid for myself. I am afraid for our children, wives and elders."

With no more argument, some leaders left the dwelling house. Then, two men stood up, and with a powerful voice stopped the defectors. They were the king and the great priest of Havaiki, the supreme dignitaries from the famous Marae of Taputapu-atea.

"I, king of Havaiki, thank my friend Tupua, for his words of wisdom. All of you should remember that some time from now we will proceed with the great gathering of the Maohis. Many brothers and sisters of blood are already on their long and daring journey to Havaiki, paddling and fighting the awesome sea with courage. We shall not disappoint them. It is our duty to look for a peaceful settlement, one acceptable to all of us. And, if such a thing is possible, I want to know about it. So, come back, and listen to Tupua's proposal."

Everyone went back into the dwelling house, and Tupua looked at everyone with a wide smile on his face.

"I guess we should bend the rules of this meeting, or soon I will be the only one left to talk to myself."

They all burst out laughing. Tupua's joke relaxed the tension. Now, they were ready to listen.

"In due time, I will talk to Tamatoa," Tupua said. "If he throws me overboard, I guess it will be a sign that we are at war."

They all threw their heads back and roared with laughter. The drums rumbled. It was a sign that a crucial moment had come. Tupua's face became solemn, and he assumed a posture of commanding self-confidence.

"Before I give you my last words, I want you to listen to Kon Teke, Tupua said.

A spreading murmur crossed the dwelling house. The drums rumbled, warning everyone to remain silent.

"You don't know who Kon Teke is," Tupua said. "Even if you had been here for many moon-cycles, you still would not know who Kon Teke is. I have been with him for a long time, and I still don't know who Kon Teke is. My daughter knows, but of course, she has an advantage over me."

They all laughed in sheer joy. With his simple style, Tupua had a way with words.

"Anyway, I have immense confidence in this man. He is the mate of my daughter, Hina of the valley, priestess in medicine. Therefore, Kon Teke is my own son. Listen to his words."

For the occasion Kon wore his best garments. Most people wore white bark-cloths, which made his appearance seem most peculiar in contrast. The blue robe, white belt and headband decorated with red suns and condors were bizarre. The gold earlobe plugs, hairpin and bracelets were extraordinary. They intuitively knew his words should be the measure of his mien: They expected nothing less.

Kon walked around, staring everyone straight in the eyes. They were all compelled, magnetized and wondering.

"My name is Kon Tici Viracocha; I am the Son of the Sun!"

The statement had power, and everyone felt a current of fear hovering inside the dwelling house. Something was unreal in this man, and they wondered if he was a living spirit.

"Don't be afraid," Kon said, "for me, your life is sacred, and I am here only to help you. I come from another world, far away where the sun rises. My forefathers taught us a key principle for man's survival, for your survival: I shall not go to war with my adversary; my adversary shall not become my enemy. War is never the result of wisdom,... Never!... It is the result of failure alone. The wise man or woman shall prevail; he or she alone has the imperative duty of looking upon the faults created by the imperfection of human nature. When your quest for peace fails, you fail, we all fail, and the man of poor ethics triumphs. He triumphs because he is the only one to propose a solution. He triumphs because you failed to explore the unlimited resources of wisdom. He triumphs because you are shy to stand up for your convictions. Don't let him stand in your way, and give him what he deserves. Give him isolation! Send him back where you cannot see him, or hear him. Your quest for peace shall not fail, ever!"

The king of Havaiki stood up, giving the signal that he wanted to speak. Kon went to him, and politely gave him permission.

"I like your words," the king said. "But, how do you apply them in Tamatoa's case?"

"You, I and all of us, are going to solve that problem," Kon said. "But first let me continue with a fundamental question: Did it ever occur in your life, that one day an enemy became a good friend? Yes, it happens to all of us. You could have gone to war. You could have lost a good friendship. We go to war because we fail to understand our adversary, because we obey our first impulse, because we are too selfish to even consider our adversary's ethics, concerns and what he stands for. We go to war because we never received the appropriate education that would help us to build emotional ties. Whoever receives such an education necessarily becomes a pacifist."

The great priest of Havaiki stood up, asking permission to speak.

"We left our island. Would you think this was an act of cowardice?"

"Absolutely not!" Kon replied. "You did the only thing that was wise. You did not have time to think of an alternative. If you had stayed, you would have condemned your people to death in vain. However, now you have time; you shall think, and you cannot go wrong. We have to learn about our adversary, about Tamatoa. Who is he? What are his motives?"

Kon walked around, silent, looking at everyone.

"Close your eyes," he said, "concentrate hard, and become Tamatoa himself. Who is he? What are his motives?"

Everyone glanced at one another, and a long murmur invaded the dwelling house. Drums rumbled, commanding everyone to remain silent.

"Each of you is a ten-year-old boy," Kon said. "Each of you is on the Tahaa Island, long ago. You have a father, and you love him. He is the king. One day, you witness the sacrifice of your father by the Pora Pora people. Then for many years, you wander on the awesome sea, and wait for revenge. You have your revenge. But, you go one step further, and you give a warning to the surrounding neighbors. Now, what is your new motive?"

Everyone stayed silent, but Kon would not give the answer.

"If exterminating your neighbors is your motive, would you give them a warning? Would you give them a chance to regroup here in Tahiti-nui and become a frightening force? Let's not be naive, your motive is something else."

The silence was total: no comments, and no murmur.

"If ambition and power over the entire archipelago were Tamatoa's motives, do you really think you would be here today listening to me? No, his motive is something else."

Finally, the great priest of the Marae of Taputapu-atea stood up.

"His motive is to protect his people."

"Exactly!" Kon exclaimed. "Now, what would be the most logical sign for us to give him?"

"To give him the proof that his fears have no foundation," the priest replied.

Kon went to him, and put his hands on his shoulders.

"You are a wise man. When the day will come, I will help you. I will go with Tupua on Tamatoa's ship, and I will give him the proof that his fears have no foundation. He will not believe my words, and it will take several days before he will change his mind. So, what will happen in the meantime? I will give him action, in a way you will never forget. Ask me not what I will do; ask yourself if you are willing to build a legend."

The restless king of Huahine stood up, and went to Kon.

"As Tupua said, the more you speak, the less I know you. But, the spirits may inspire you. Yes, I do trust you, and I present my apologies to Tupua for my earlier impatience."

"When the day will come," Kon said, "take your people to the valleys and the mountains. Conchs and drums will keep you informed. Make sure no one starts a fight with Tamatoa at a crucial time. It takes patience and hard work to promote peace; it takes only the blink of an eye for the folly of war to spread."

Kon left the dwelling house, and went to the beach. Tupua would continue the meeting. Then, a long wait would take place, exhausting, nerve-racking, and frightful.

Later, the same day, Tupua, Vana and Taaroa went to the Toerau Marae to visit Hina and Kon. It was the best place for privacy, and for their friendship to give them ideas. They all sat near a fragrant tiare bush.

"Mount Orohena is the key," Kon said, looking at the majestic mountain.

"What are your intentions?" Tupua asked.

"I shall not tell anyone before the day will come," Kon replied. "But, remember, the mountain is in me, the mountain inspires me, and I am the mountain.

When the day will come, the higher I will be, the greater our victory will be."

Hina gave some warm breadfruit to everyone. Tupua went away for a short time, and came back with fresh, green coconuts. Vana opened them and gave one to each of his companions.

"This is a wonderful place," Taaroa said, looking at the lagoon.

As she drank the milk of her coconut, Hina glanced at a couple of sandpipers racing quietly, as they were feeding near waves pounding the beach.

"Yes indeed," she said, "this place is the heart of my island, and my island shall be the heart of peace. On my island, something special shall take place. Tahiti-nui shall be the unique place where people can learn how to build emotional ties."

They saw sadness on her face, and her eyes brimming with tears because of inward pain she needed to release. They listened to their young and dear priestess. Hina of the Valley was torn apart by two opposite forces: sorrow and will. She stood up, looked at the sunset and offered her soul to the ones she loved.

"What is wrong with us, and with our killing? You were right, Kon Teke, when you said there are no bad spirits, but only bad thoughts in the minds of bad people. Why is it that conflict is always our primary choice, when kissing is so beautiful and simple?

She stopped for a moment, her face covered with tears. They all turned their eyes on her. They were moved by the young woman they cherished and admired. Kon went to her, and put his arms around her shoulders. She turned around, and laid her head on his chest, sobbing. He knew her tears were not the tears of pain. They were the tears of someone who wants to live, of someone who wants to drink at the well of light. Her tears were the reflection of life's triumph.

With a stick, Vana drew signs on the dusty ground, trying to find answers to Hina's questions, but he did not find any. He breathed deeply, as if he was hurting, closed his eyes and explored the darkness of his mind. For the first time as the great priest, Vana was challenged by questions with no answers, but Taaroa the ill would answer some of Hina's questions.

"Hina, my child," he said with a croaking voice, "you are logical, but human behavior is not. Leaders like your father should be carefully selected. Tupua is a good king, but too often this happens by luck because his goodness is not necessarily the reason for his status. Having a good leader rarely happens by design, but because of the rank of his parents. Or, sometime, a powerful and courageous commander may become a king. Unfortunately, it takes much more than power and courage to be a good king. It requires compassion, forgiveness, tolerance, goodwill, self-discipline and above all, magnanimity. How can we expect these qualities from our leaders if we don't teach them to our children, to our leaders of tomorrow? This is what Kon Teke is trying so hard to teach. They are simple qualities, and they are not new. We simply forgot them."

Kon listened to the poor leper: His body was decimated, but his soul was intact.

"A good leader is not a solitary leader," Tupua said. "In order to do my job, I need each of you who is one facet of my wealth. A good leader is a listener, a coordinator, and a facilitator, nothing else. Because of our selfishness, we may often forget who we should be and what we should do."

"The key word is selfishness," Kon said. "If the five sun-cycles-old child is not already aware of what selfishness is, and how to control it, he or she becomes self-centered, inconsiderate, incapable of using compassion, forgiveness, goodwill and magnanimity. Our priority should not be to find out who we are, but who we want to be, and go from here with unshakable ethics."

"This is what our great gathering at the Marae of Taputapu-atea is all about," Vana said.

"But, this applies to our families as well." Tupua said. "The family is a group where each member has a duty to find out who he or she should be, and what he or she should do, with respect to all others."

"The resources of the human mind are infinite," Kon said. "Yet, we don't tap these resources. We frame ourselves inside structures and systems, and become prisoners of them. We need them, but often the cost is great as they slowly erase our creativity. Inside the shell of a system, we mellow, wait and fade away. Our life becomes a shooting star with no energy, no light, no target."

"This goes a long way from Tamatoa," Tupua murmured.

"No!" Kon replied. "If we underestimate ourselves, we no longer look at our inner universe. We become disciplined animals, prisoner of the material universe and its limitations. Instead, we should be the self-disciplined marvel, able to create a nobler universe. Close your eyes, and take a look inside yourself, and for the time being, let's find a way inside the place of torment we have created."

Hina stared at the four men. Her tears had dried. Then, she isolated herself behind the tiare bushes.

"I will not accept that my island may become a place of torment," she murmured to herself. "I will fight you, Tamatoa, with weapons unknown to you, with weapons you cannot see."

She came back with five tiare flowers, her favorite, sacred flowers. She delicately put one flower in her hair above her ear.

"Do you see these flowers?" she asked. "Someone with infinite goodwill put them here, just for us, just for the team."

She put one tiare above Taaroa's ear.

"Brave, old explorer of the human mind," she said, "may you have many more sun-cycles with us. You still have much to give, and we still need you. The shooting star still bears energy and light."

Then, she went to Vana, and put a tiare above his ear.

"Dear great priest, I misunderstood you when I was a young girl. You have your own ways, very special ways, and you are a good man. My father will always need your wisdom, your humor and your friendship."

She went to her father, and put a tiare above his ear.

"You are my father, and also my king. The next few days, with Kon's help, I shall serve you with all my strength, and all my soul. Tahiti-nui will never be a place of torment, but only a shining star, showing to all of us that a paradise is not and will not be an illusion."

She went to Kon, and put a tiare above his ear.

"Kon Teke, what would my world be without you? What would be our fate if you had not come to this island? Your fight does not smell like blood, but smells like these flowers. Your fight does not build empires, but builds explorers. You are a shooting star with blazing energy, and your target is to promote harmony. In the end, your triumph will be total."

****

CHAPTER 17

"The overwhelming beauty of Moorea gave my soul a sense of soaring. The jagged mountains of the island were unconquerable treasures, and its deep bays an invitation to settle for a lifetime."

Mahine, Tamatoa's daughter

Standing on the deck of his warship, Tamatoa was fascinated by the incredible beauty of Moorea. The island offered a breathtaking display of nature at its best. For a moment, the powerful leader became humble and forgot his war. It had never occurred to him that the small neighboring island of Tahiti-nui would offer the most extraordinary vision of his life. No one who watched its forbidden mountains, its blue lagoon, and its deep bays, would be disposed to question Moorea's right to be the pearl of the awesome sea.

Mato had seen the island before, but it was distant in his memory. Once more, his mouth dropped open and he gasped in amazement at the unimaginable scenery.

"My dear Tamatoa, if I were in your place, I would stay right here on this island," Mato said. "It is the kind of beauty that your mind is incapable of memorizing. Every time you see it again, you fully measure how much you have forgotten, and the beautiful image you remembered was a mockery."

"I agree," Tamatoa said. "Let's stop inside its bays for three days. My men need the rest."

They followed the north side of the island, which had the two most beautiful, natural harbors they had seen. Tamatoa hesitated about which bay he would enter first. Then, he decided on the northeastern bay because of its easier access. Its waters were clear and calm, and he would be closer to the extremity of the island facing Tahiti-nui.

As they entered the pass, they overcame a gentle current.

"I don't see anybody on the beaches," Tamatoa said. "I am sure most people have already left."

"I most certainly would have!" Mato said sarcastically.

Then, they saw three men board a small outrigger and paddle in their direction. They were from a village whose houses were visible between the many coconut trees.

"Mato, you talk to them first," Tamatoa ordered. "It will give me time to study them."

When the outrigger reached the side of the galley, one of the men requested permission to come aboard. Mato went to him.

"My name is Mato, and I am the great priest. This is our king, Tamatoa. We intend to occupy this island."

"My name is Tetuma. I am the chief of this village. Many of our people have already left. They were afraid of you after what you did to the Pora Pora people. What are your intentions?"

"Mato already told you our intentions," Tamatoa roared, "you were not listening. How many people are still on the island?"

"Very few," Tetuma answered, visibly afraid of the tattooed giant.

"Who are those who are still here?" Tamatoa asked.

"Most of them were rejected from Tahiti-nui. They could be criminals, robbers or social misfits," Tetuma said with a timid voice.

"Then it is simple," Tamatoa said with sarcasm. "I shall clean this paradise. By tomorrow at dawn, anyone left on the island, including you, will be exterminated. Go away!"

Shocked and scared, the trembling Tetuma went back to his canoe and left with the other men. On the beach, a few people were waiting for them. Immediately, the sound of drums and conchs spread all around the island. The message was clear: Leave the island before dawn.

Tamatoa smiled. He was satisfied that one more island would be occupied without a fight. Furthermore, all these misfits would add to the confusion on Tahiti-nui: They had nowhere else to go.

Early in the morning, Tamatoa and Mato went to the beach with a double canoe and a group of warriors. All houses were empty.

"I saw many canoes leave last night, under the moonlight," Mato said.

"I saw a few leave at dawn," Tamatoa said. "If there are some specimens who went to the mountains, they are not dangerous."

"How would you name such a beautiful bay?" Mato asked.

"The Paopao Bay," Tamatoa replied, "in remembrance of my grandfather's name. He was a great navigator and always said that if we find an island with deep, protected bays, surrounded by high mountains, it would be a good place to settle."

The next day, Tamatoa went to the other bay and named it the Opunohu Bay, in remembrance of a poisonous fish common in this bay. Then, Tamatoa, Mato, Mahine and Taatamao went to explore the eastern end of the island, where they could have a good view of Tahiti-nui. In a fast, double canoe, paddled by ten gourd-helmeted warriors, they followed the northern coast, inside the lagoon, going eastward to the extremity of the island.

A short distance before the point, they saw a small river, and across the lagoon was a narrow pass where the dark blue water indicated it was a deep passage leading to the open sea. On the east side of the pass were two islets bearing no vegetation, but surrounded by attractive white beaches.

"Father, may I go with Taatamao to these islets?" Mahine asked. "You go explore the extremity of the island, and pick us up on your way back."

After a brief hesitation, Tamatoa agreed. The double canoe went near the islets. Taatamao and Mahine jumped in the clear, shallow water barely covering their knees.

"Be careful," Mahine said to her father.

"We won't be long," Tamatoa said. "You both have a good time."

Mato smiled and waved at the young couple.

Taatamao held Mahine's hand, and they walked to the islets. The water was so clear that it was almost impossible to see where the surface was. Shell tracks on the white sand were everywhere. Yellow brain corals were encircled by colonies of black urchins. Their long spines attached to a shell striated with bright purple cavities, searched for any intruder. Starfish crawled among violet elkhorn corals. Convoluted giant clams displayed their powerful, emerald muscle inside their parted valves. When they reached the first islet, they disturbed a small shark lurking in the shallow water. Its entire dorsal and caudal fins were above the surface, and its belly lay on the white sand. Terrorized, the animal wriggled its way back to deeper water in a tumultuous bubbling, making Taatamao and Mahine laugh in sheer joy.

On the tiny beach, they lay on the hot white sand, and looked at each other with deep love. Taatamao whispered in her hair. His nose touched hers, and his lips pressed against hers. He wrapped one arm around her waist. She moved toward him, impelled by her own passion, but she suddenly recalled her vision on the white monolith, pushed Taatamao aside and looked at him with distress. He saw tears trembling on her eyelids.

"Mahine, what is wrong?" he asked, confused.

"Do you like what you are doing for my father?"

"Of course I do."

"I don't like it, and I don't like what he is doing. We are all murderers."

Astonished by her words, Taatamao stood up and walked to the top of the rocky islet.

"Is it Mato who stirred up your mind?"

"No, it is not Mato's fault. Don't blame him. It is my own judgment."

"I have complete trust in your father. Furthermore, I am totally devoted to him and I admire him."

"True, your devotion to him makes it impossible for you to see his mistakes."

"I don't see any mistake in his actions."

"Maybe you don't, but I do, and Mato does. Maybe we don't belong to one another. I certainly do not belong to this world of killing. Go to my father, be his servant, kill Maohis, kill women and children, kill everything. Kill me if you wish, because it is what you are doing."

Humiliated by her words, Taatamao went to the other end of the islet where the current was strong, dived, and swam toward the deep blue pass. Mahine dropped on her knees, and sobbed in her hands. She regretted her harsh words. He was the last person she wanted to hurt.

The cool water helped Taatamao to better understand Mahine's words, and he suddenly became aware of her inner conflict, which he had never suspected. He dived to check the depth of the lagoon, and felt the current pulling toward the pass. Aware of the danger, he swam toward the barrier where the water was more shallow, and finally found himself in a field of table corals looking like giant funnels: It was the perfect habitat for lobsters. He dived to explore the dark world under the tables.

At that moment, Taatamao had a premonition. He stopped swimming and turned around. Far away, he saw a massive shadow gliding toward the pass, but could not tell if it was a large shark or one of those immense rays common in the lagoon. He did not worry about it, and went back to the coral tables. Within a short time, he found two lobsters and took them back to the islet.

Mahine was sitting at the end of the islet, watching Taatamao coming back.

"They are beautiful!" she said.

Without a smile, he gave the lobsters to Mahine.

"I did not mean to hurt you," she said with sadness.

"I know. But, the last thing your father needs now, is some indecision from us. You shall not interfere with his judgment."

Taatamao did not wait for her answer, and swam back to the field of coral tables. She watched him swim away, and noticed something following him, deep in the clear water. She immediately recognized the profile of a formidable killer, silent, confident, trailing its prey. It was the great blue shark: The dark stripes on its sides were unmistakable. She screamed to alert Taatamao, but the waves pounding the reef drowned her voice.

Taatamao circled the first coral table, went to the second one and dived for a quick inspection of the lobster world. He saw a pair of long antennae. With no difficulty, he caught the largest lobster of the day. Suddenly, he had that premonition again. He turned around, but saw nothing. He was an experienced diver, and he knew his mind was receiving sounds he could not hear.

He knew there was a large predator in the area scaring many fish. He went to the table, stood on the top of it, and looked around.

He immediately saw Mahine waving at him, trying to say something. Then, from his left he spotted a pair of large fins coming in his direction. He knew the two fins belonged to the same shark. One was the dorsal fin, the other fin way behind, too far behind, was its tail. It was the great blue shark, the most deadly of all. He let the animal approach, then violently slapped on the water to scare it. The shark turned around, and left, but it was a patient predator. Taatamao was alone, and a vulnerable prey. He knew the shark would be back, and each time it would come closer and closer.

Taatamao looked around, and saw two giant, convoluted bivalves. He took his knife, dived to the massive shells, and plunged the long blade between the valves, which instantly closed. Taatamao was quicker, and the blade cut the powerful muscle of the shell that became defenseless. He opened the valves, cut the meat deeply in several directions and repeated the same scenario with the second shell. The shark came back. Once more, Taatamao scared it away. This time the shark was more reluctant to leave. It was time for Taatamao to leave. He swam back to the islet making as much noise as he could, knowing the shark would not turn away from an easy prey. By the time it would be finished devoring the meat of the shells, he would be far away.

"Here is a third lobster," Taatamao said, with a smile.

"You better stay here," Mahine said. "You could have been in trouble."

"I was in trouble."

"It was my fault; I have been hard on you."

"No Mahine, you have been straightforward, and you trusted me with your words. You did well."

Instants later, Tamatoa and Mato came back on the fast double canoe.

"At the end of this river, not far away, there is a clear lake," Tamatoa said.

"Tonight, we shall stay near it," Mato said. "It would be a good place to observe Tahiti-nui at dusk."

"You caught three remarkable lobsters," Tamatoa said.

"Do you remember your mother recipe?" Mato asked.

"Yes, I will use mother's recipe." Mahine replied.

"If you prepare them well I may forgive what you said to me the other day," Tamatoa said.

Mahine glanced at her father, and managed a sad smile.

They went to the beach bordered by coconut and ironwood trees, reached the outlet of the river and followed its swampy course on foot. The ground was covered with tiny burrows, whose openings were protected by a blue and red flower. The flower was a small, blue land crab, whose large, red claw defended the entry against intruders. Shortly afterward, they reached the lake, whose clear water fell directly from the mountain. Many ducks swam peacefully there, to Mahine's delight. Near shore, under coconut trees, they selected a place where they would spend the night. The men prepared the campsite, and Mahine went to the nearby mountain, looking for spicy plants she would use to cook the lobsters. Mato followed her, with no special thought in mind.

They reached a cliff from which they had a dramatic overview of the eastern end of the island. Below, they could see the lake and the ducks, completely surrounded by a forest of coconut trees, beyond which was a long beach of white sand assaulted by the pounding waves of the open sea. Farther to the south, was an immense blue lagoon. Far away on the horizon, they saw the imposing outline of Tahiti-nui. For an instant, Mahine looked at Mount Orohena. Mato had been right; it was a formidable mountain.

"I thought the Paopao Bay was beautiful," Mato said, "but if I had to choose, I would live right here, near the lake."

"It is breathtaking," Mahine replied. "Everything is here: the coconuts, the lagoon, a white sand beach, the sea, the river, the lake, the falls, the ducks, the cliff and plenty of good land."

Sitting on a large stone, Mahine could not turn her eyes away from the peaceful beauty of the island. Never had she dreamed that so magnificent a land could exist. Her soul became possessed by unknown splendor, and she felt a sense of soaring. Once more, she looked at Mount Orohena on the horizon, and felt a flow of images enter her mind. For some unknown reason, she knew this high mountain was important.

"I found what you are looking for," Mato said.

Mato had to repeat what he had said to bring her back to reality.

"The spicy plants!"

She went to the priest, who showed her a reamaohi plant: It was exactly what she was looking for.

"I did not know you knew my mother's recipe," Mahine said, surprised.

"I don't know the recipe, but I remember what the lobsters tasted like."

Mahine would grind the roots of the plant and prepare a spicy kari powder, the aroma of which was most agreeable.

Back at the camp, she went to look for two coconuts with small roots and at least two leaves. This was the easy part, there were so many of them. So, she selected the two largest nuts she could find. She opened them on a sharp rock, and extracted the fatty part.

Taatamao started a fire, and had already prepared a thick layer of glowing embers. There was plenty of dead wood, with the dry coconut fronds covering the ground everywhere.

Mahine sat near the fire. She placed each lobster on a flat stone, and with a shark tooth split the animals lengthwise into halves. She removed the intestine, and placed each half on a large banana leaf. Inside half coconut shells, she mixed the milk of a green coconut, the fatty part of the germinated coconuts, and the kari powder she had prepared earlier. She slashed the meat and poured the mixture inside the deep cuts, until they were full. She spread more of the mixture on the top of the meat. She cut thin banana slices and placed them on each lobster until the meat was completely covered, which would prevent it from burning and also would add a delicious taste. Mato gave her two lime-fruits. She cut them and pressed the juice above each lobster. Then, carefully, without turning the lobsters, she wrapped a banana leaf several times around them. She placed the well-protected lobsters above the embers of the fire. Gently, she covered the lobsters with embers.

"They will be ready in a short time," Mahine said.

"Your father is coming," Mato said with a grin on his face. "His sense of smell has total control of him."

"If this were true, how wonderful it would be," Mahine said, with a cold-eyed smile.

Mato and Taatamao glanced at each other without saying anything.

Mahine removed the banana-tree leaves, and a warm and appetizing scent invaded the campsite. Silently, everyone savored a treat they had dreamed about for a long time. For a moment, it let them forget the sordid endeavor they had commenced.

At dusk, they climbed the cliff, and took a good look at Tahiti-nui. They could not see the island, but they saw the many fires around it.

"You went to Tahiti-nui many years ago," Tamatoa said to Mato. "Where does the most powerful king live?"

"Near the Teauroa Point," Mato replied.

"Can we see fires near it?" Tamatoa asked.

"They are the farthest to the left, where you see many."

"Then, this is the direction we shall sail tomorrow night," Tamatoa said. "I want to reach that place just before dawn."

"Can I stay here for a while?" Mahine asked.

"Yes," Tamatoa replied, "but don't be too long."

"I won't be long. Keep the fire burning until I come back."

Mahine was alone. She sat among tiny ferns, and listened to the sounds of night. She heard the distant waves pounding the beach, and a monotonous, high-pitched treat-treat-treat from a cricket. At times, she heard the distant voice of her companions, but she was not interested in them. She was interested in the distant lights on Tahiti-nui, at the Teauroa Point. She looked at them for a long time. Would it be possible that she would have an important role to play in this war? Intuitively, she thought it would be a good idea for her to stay with Mato, who would obviously stay on her father's ship for such a critical moment. She had a strong premonition that it would be the place where something important would happen soon.

For a moment, Mahine dismissed her thoughts and covered her eyes with her hands, but her soul spoke, and she immediately knew she was on the right track. She knew she had to wait for the right opportunity, and in due time a mysterious force would tell her what to do. She opened her eyes, vaguely saw a whirl of dust pass nearby, and heard the wind call her name: She instantly recalled the voice of the man with blue eyes.

****

CHAPTER 18

"Sometimes, everything is against you, and you may see the end of the trail. Walk to an isolated panorama, talk to the Earth, and rediscover who you want to be. Open your soul, and explore your inner universe, where you may find unexpected resources. Nobody else can reach those awaiting forces for you: You are in charge."

Kon Tici Viracocha

Near Papenoo, on the black sand beach, an aging leader desperately sought impossible solutions. Responsible to his people, he had not slept for several days. He wanted to be perfect. Yet, Tupua was far from perfect. In fact, at this sad moment, he was empty and his creativity had vanished. He was just a good human being, waiting for the unavoidable fate. Stressed and controlled by his emotions, he was unaware of his own inner forces: He had never been told. Like a wandering phantom, he walked to the Marae of Toreau. At dusk, he found Kon and Hina sitting close to a fire, and nearly collapsed near his children.

"Kon, I need to know about your plans," Tupua said. "You don't want to reveal them, but I shall prepare myself."

Kon understood his distress, and put a friendly hand on the king's shoulder. Tupua felt a warm current entering his body, something he had not experienced before. Two dark blue eyes looked at him.

"Tomorrow I will go to the valley, alone," Kon said, with a calm voice. "Like you, I shall prepare. The next day, at dawn, we shall go to the Teauroa Point where Tamatoa will be waiting for us on his ship. Make sure we keep our men and women under control, and everything will be fine. Do not fear, and trust me. And, trust yourself."

Hina gave some food to her father, who ate with little appetite.

"Do you really think you can manipulate Tamatoa?" Tupua asked.

"Yes, we will, and Tamatoa will manipulate himself in the process," Kon replied with confidence.

"What should I do for you?" Tupua asked.

"Introduce yourself to Tamatoa, start negotiating with him and show no aggressiveness, but remain charismatic. If he puts too much pressure on you, I will take over. Then you shall listen very carefully, support me in the best way you can, and do not be surprised by anything I say."

Tupua managed a small smile, and left.

"I worry about my father," Hina said. "I never saw him depressed like this. He cannot perform."

"This is what you may think," Kon said. "The day after tomorrow at dawn, you will find your father at his best."

"And, what should I do for you?" Hina asked.

"You will come with us on Tamatoa's ship, where you will quickly find out what you should do. You will be alone in your fight. At the beginning it will be frightful, but don't lose faith. You shall be patient, observant and creative. In what is coming, your role is immense."

"That is all!"

She looked him straight in the eyes, but he would not tell

her anything else. He had a well-craft plan. She knew she had to trust him, and she would, but once more she wondered who Kon Tici Viracocha was. He pulled her gently, and covered her mouth with his lips, but she slowly backed away, to Kon's surprise.

"What is wrong, Hina?"

"Nothing!" she said with a little smile. "I just want to be comfortable at my house. Let's go to my house."

They left the terrace, laughing as they often did in the past. For a moment, they seemed to forget the future, ignore the past and suddenly wanted to live in the present.

Early at dawn, Kon left Hina's house, followed the Papenoo River and went deep inside the valley. This was a critical moment of his life, and he needed to explore the most secret creation of the entire universe: himself.

On each side of the river, the formidable walls of the mountain rose up, and up, covered with luxuriant ferns. Kon heard the strident call of the small bittern. He saw the bird on a branch, hiding in a frozen position with its head pointed upward. The bird observed him, curious as usual. Kon smiled, sat on a rock on the bank, put his head in his hands, looked at the running water and listened to the rejuvenating sounds of many waterfalls.

A kingfisher landed near him, and drank the clear water of the running stream. Kon went to the waterfall where Hina had taken him when they first met. When he reached the meadow, he looked up at the tropicbird nests. He recalled the race with Aru, and the mysterious cave. He suddenly felt attracted by the place where he had a vision of Kama and Hina living in another land called Mata-Kite-Rani: eyes looking at the stars. He recalled the whirl of dust, and its powerful tranquillity. Determined, he climbed to the cave, sat on the ledge, and looked at the valley. More than ever, he found the panorama astonishing. He could see the ocean above the range of mountains, on the other side of the valley. He could hear the valley. Life was on its incredible course, everywhere. He could hear the birds, the rumbling waterfalls, and the voice of humans far away.

Kon went inside the silent cave. He entered the narrow passage leading to the second room, and felt a small bat flying around him. Then, with his foot he felt the flat stone he had taken outside; it was exactly at the place where he had found it the first time. This time, he was not exploring, and would not disturb anything. He was only seeking total isolation from the real world. He was seeking absolute silence. He sat, cross-legged. He saw the dim light coming from outside through the narrow passage. He closed his eyes, held his breath, and heard his heart pounding and some water dripping in a pond, in another secret room, somewhere. He listened to the secret melody between his heart and the dripping water. Slowly, his mind drifted away. He thought about the race. At this particular moment, a startling scenario entered his mind. It was like a voice coming from beyond, coming from the awesome ocean of his soul: "When the man will scream, give him a friendly hand."

The words echoed several times in his mind,...in the room! Then, he heard his blood flow in his temples, and the dripping water far away. He went outside and looked up at Mount Orohena. He knew he would not get anything more from that place, and it was time for him to leave.

"As events will unravel, we shall be observant," Kon murmured. "The time has come when Hina and I shall find and honor the guidance offered by the mysterious force. There is indeed an astonishing, secret melody in our lives. It is up to us to assemble the few notes we are given. And, one day, we shall unravel the intricacy of being."

****

CHAPTER 19

"To challenge your adversary, be prepared to go far beyond your limits: Have a vision and be kind. Then, when at work, remain optimistic to the end. Your victory may inspire many people. If you fail, you will still earn their respect."

Kon Tici Viracocha

At dawn, Hina awoke to the sound of chirping birds. Their song was different. Something was different, and she did not know what it was. She turned over on her elbows and looked at the unusual daylight under the vegetal roof. Everything seemed different. Or, was it her mind that was sending the signal she had waited for the last few days? Was it the fury of man coming?

She went outside and saw Kon sitting on a slab of coral. He seemed preoccupied, looking at the sea. He did not hear her coming, but he knew she was there.

"Today is the day," Kon said. "Today, you shall perform at your best."

"How do you know these things?" Hina asked.

"My mind told me, and everything is different. You noticed the same thing when you woke up."

She was astonished by his words.

"Sometimes, I wonder if the man I love is real or only a living spirit. Your visions are so accurate that I fear your words. No one can hide anything from you."

"You have many other talents," Kon replied. "I am a dreamer. I may have great powers in my mind. But, in your own ways, you have more logic, and you are closer to reality. Because of you, I can channel my dreams to our daily necessities. You are the light guiding the lost man."

"You are no lost man," Hina argued. "Do not let Kon Teke Viracocha be the victim of his own modesty."

Suddenly, the melancholic call of conchs was everywhere, sending their message across valleys and mountains. War drums soon followed. At this moment, the world took on a new dimension in the mind of Hina of the Valley. She jumped to her feet, and felt her heart pound in her chest. Her heart was part of the drums. Her heart was at war.

"Don't be afraid," Kon said, encircling his arms around her shoulders, "the Great Force is living in you: Mana is with you."

They both wore their best garments, and left the Marae of Toreau. On their way, they could see Tupua's galley waiting at some distance from the beach. Numerous outriggers around it were an indication that Tupua was ready to leave, and they met him on the beach.

"Tamatoa's fleet is outside the lagoon, at the Teauroa Point," Tupua said. "He is going to enter the Matavai Bay, and this is where we shall meet him. Are you ready?"

"Are you sending the people inside the valleys?" Kon asked.

"Yes," Tupua replied. "Nobody can challenge Tamatoa at sea. He brought three battle groups: one with him at the Teauroa Point, one on the east side of the island, and another one on the south side. His fleet is awesome."

Vana came with a folded robe.

"Kon, this is what you asked for," the great priest said.

"What is this?" Tupua asked.

"As we approach Tamatoa's ship, I will wear this above my clothes and over my face," Kon replied.

"You really want to attract attention," Tupua said, shrugging his shoulders.

Then, Tupua saw Hina dressed as a priestess, waiting near his outrigger.

"Where do you think you are going?" the king asked.

"Hina comes with us," Kon replied. "She has an important role to carry out."

"This is dangerous for her," Tupua argued.

"It would be far more dangerous, if she could not complete her mission." Kon said.

Tupua shrugged his shoulders.

They embarked on the outrigger, and went to the galley. From the beach, Vana waved to his companions: He would guide the people to the deep valleys, in sacred places, taboo in ordinary times. The spirit of their forefathers would protect them. There, they would wait. It was the beginning of a long journey.

It was a sunny morning, with a calm sea. Ten warriors paddled the huge war galley, and Aru was their leader. They first followed the sunken barrier of coral. Far away, at the Teauroa Point, they could see the tops of a large number of ships. Some were larger than anything they had ever seen. The largest, with higher structures, must have been Tamatoa's ship. Hina's stomach was clenched tight, and she firmly held Kon's arm.

"Are you going to wear that bark-cloth Vana gave you?" Tupua asked.

"Yes," Kon replied, "I don't want them to know who I am before the time is right. If they ask who is that man covering his body and his face, tell them I am your counselor."

"At what specific time do you want to be introduced?" Tupua asked.

"When you can no longer handle Tamatoa," Kon replied. "Do your best, my friend."

Tupua managed a smile, in which Kon saw concern and despair.

As they approached the Teauroa Point, Tamatoa's ships grew in size, and in number. Silence pervaded Tupua's ship. Only the lapping of the paddles could be heard. An uncomfortable tension could be felt. For everyone, the beauty of the island had vanished. Only man-made emotions filled the entire universe: They included fear, courage and hope.

Tamatoa's ship stopped, and waited for the intruder to come closer. Kon was surprised by the size of the giant galley, and its maneuverability within the current of the pass.

"Whoever you are," Kon murmured, "one thing is sure, you are an outstanding navigator."

Tamatoa's ship came to them, fast. An extraordinary stern, beautifully carved with depictions of warriors and birds, extended the front of the superb galley. Fascinated by the carving, Kon forgot the adversary for an instant. They were on a collision course, until Tamatoa 's ship turned around. Then, both ships traveled side by side, to the pass. Tamatoa made sure he would enter the pass first. Finally, they reached the calm waters of the Matavai Bay, where a massive armada waited. Tamatoa anchored his galley and it came to a complete stop. Tupua brought his galley, about half the size, on the side of Tamatoa's ship. A short distance was kept between the two ships with long paddles held on both ends by adversaries.

Without a word, without a sound, both kings glanced at each other: They were not amused. Bored by the contest, Kon looked at the magnificent ship once more. Warriors wearing gourd helmets decorated with long black feathers on the top, stood at the sides of the ship. The paddling men wore the same helmets but without feathers. Both crews looked at each other with cold eyes. Kon immediately noticed the many details showing that Tamatoa's men were well trained for war, which in many ways reminded him of the highly disciplined Incas: They were ready, and appeared deadly.

Completely covered by the large bark-cloth, Kon could not be differentiated from another Maohi. Slowly, his eyes drifted toward the tall, muscular, charismatic leader. Never before had he seen a man of such strength, but he looked familiar. The man who helped Illa pull the giant statue, in his dream, was Tamatoa. The face of the giant was completely tattooed. He had a flowing red robe attached around his neck, and opened wide in the front. He was dressed from the waist down, and wore a helmet on which long red feathers waved in the morning breeze. Simply dressed, if compared to Tupua, Tamatoa was nevertheless far more impressive. He must have been in his late thirties. His posture was very athletic. It looked as if Tupua did not stand a chance against this superb warrior, who was all self-confidence. Kon was a good psychologist, and an idea came to his mind.

Tamatoa is a proud man, Kon thought. Could he also be a man of honor?

It was not the first time that the thought came to his mind, but now he was convinced Tamatoa was indeed a man of honor.

From their respective ships, the two kings still looked at each other, silently, but the silence was long, too long, and became arrogant. Always resourceful at the right time, Hina broke the silence by unwrapping a wet cloth from which she took some tiare flowers, and offered them to each of her companions.

"These flowers will give you good luck," she said loudly. She wanted Tamatoa to hear what she said, but the great warrior expressed only a faint, sarcastic smile, and roared orders to four of his warriors to set a footbridge between the two ships.

"Come on board!" Tamatoa said with a thundering voice. "I presume you are the king of Tahiti-nui."

Tupua went first, followed by Hina. Kon remained on Tupua's ship, close to the footbridge.

"My name is Tupua; this is my daughter Hina of the Valley. She is a priestess."

"Very young for a priestess!" Tamatoa remarked. "Who is the man afraid to show his face?"

"He is not afraid," Tupua replied. "He is my counselor. What are your intentions?"

Kon noticed the clarity of Tupua's words. In action, his apprehension had vanished. Three warriors crossed the bridge and circled Kon, who was suspected of hiding some dangerous weapon to be used against Tamatoa. They did not touch him but remained very close.

"I conquered the land of my forefathers," Tamatoa replied, "and I avenged my father for all the insults and suffering the Pora Pora people inflicted on him."

"I accept that," Tupua said. "But, what is the driving force to conquer the entire string of islands?"

"Simple!" Tamatoa replied. "I trust nobody, and I don't want past mistakes to be repeated, or for my people to endure more devastating torment. When I die, my sons shall have no enemies."

"And, how do you intend to reach this goal?" Tupua asked, a little restless.

"I am asking you to leave this island within two days," Tamatoa said with impatience. "On the second day, at dawn, everyone left on this island shall be exterminated."

"There are many more people here than what you may think," Tupua retorted in cold sarcasm, raising his head, and staring at the giant. "My people shall stay in the valleys, in the mountains, in places unapproachable for your warriors."

"Yes, they will stay in places of shame, I suppose," Tamatoa said.

"There is no shame for my people," Tupua replied. "We will fight you by slow attrition. The conquest of this island will cost you an astonishing amount of blood. This place will be a nightmare for you."

Tamatoa roared in laughter, clenched his teeth, and glowing hate came to his eyes.

"What is your name again?" Tamatoa asked. "Oh yes, Tupua! Do you have any idea how insignificant you are? I am accustomed to costly ventures, and I have no fear of you in these valleys and mountains. If this place shall be torment to us, greater torment it will be for you."

Tupua realized he had been too sarcastic, and tried to temper his adversary.

"You are a Maohi," Tupua said. "We are all Maohis. What do you have against yours brothers of blood?"

"My dear Tupua!" Tamatoa replied with a mocking tone. "There are too many Maohis on these islands. Maohis multiply; islands don't. The strong shall survive; the weak shall fade away."

Hina attempted a word, but Tamatoa stopped her immediately.

"Young woman," he said, "you cannot talk to the great Tamatoa. You belong with women. Go talk to my daughter Mahine, if you wish."

The two women glanced at each other. Mahine went to Hina,

and took her hand.

"Come Hina, don't stay between these men."

Hina complied, but Mahine's comment echoed in her mind. Something told her she should not fear Tamatoa's daughter: She was obviously friendly.

Tupua was at a dead end, and he knew it. He knew the only thing he could do now was to annoy Tamatoa and make Kon's work more difficult. He hesitated a little, then turned around. Kon knew it was the signal for him to come, and he felt warmth spreading throughout his entire body. He quickly recalled his brother Illa daring the old Inca. He remembered him in perfect control. He remembered his words and their amazing force: They were Mana's words.

When Kon attempted to remove his bark-cloth, three spearheads instantly rested on his chest. The three warriors were taking no chances, until Tamatoa told them otherwise.

"Let this man show his face," Tamatoa said. "Let him help his friend. Perhaps, he will be more skilled with his words."

At once, Kon removed his bark-cloth, revealing to everyone who he was. He was not like the others. He was an alien. The three warriors backed up in fear. Kon walked across the bridge, and a rumbling murmur crossed Tamatoa's ship. For an instant everyone was confused, but Tamatoa was cold as ice, in perfect control, unshakable as a rock. He looked at the tall man coming to him, at his most unusual black hair pinned on the top of his head and flowing in the breeze all the way down to his shoulders. Then, he noticed his dark blue garments, the woven red suns and the birds he had never seen.

Kon stopped just in front of Tamatoa, who saw with fascination the golden earplugs and bracelets. For the first time in his life, Tamatoa felt the power of something unknown falling on his shoulders. He stared at these fantastic, deep blue eyes, and saw something in them he could not describe. This man was so different. There was no doubt in Tamatoa's mind: He must have come from another world.

"Who are you, stranger?" Tamatoa asked. "And, where do you come from?"

"My name is Kon Tici Viracocha; I am the Son of the Sun. I come from a large land, far away in the east, where the sun rises. These people are my friends, and I have been with them for many moon-cycles. They are good, peaceful people."

Some distance away, Mahine was fascinated.

"I saw that man in a dream."

"How long ago?" Hina asked

"Four days ago."

"Then, the unknown force touched you," Hina said.

"Where are the others, like you?" Tamatoa asked.

"I am alone," Kon replied, "I lost my companions during a storm on the awesome sea."

"I see," Tamatoa said. "How can you help your friends?"

The question was expected, and came right on time. Kon was ready.

"I want to challenge you to something you may win, or may lose." Kon said with a defiant smile.

"Challenge me!" Tamatoa fulminated. "Do you want to show your fighting skills?"

"No, I never fight. My people never fight. Combat is for those with degenerated souls who worship a world with no spirits. I have no enemies."

"You never fight! You have no enemies!" Tamatoa shouted, coming very close to Kon.

The giant was mad, and slapped Kon's face. Tupua protested

vehemently, and Hina called Tamatoa a "bloodthirsty killer," but Kon did not flinch, and merely smiled to his adversary: It was an insult to Tamatoa.

"Do you still think you have no enemies, young sorcerer?" Tamatoa said. "I have no respect for sorcerers; they are troublemakers, and I hate them."

"I have no enemies, and I am not a sorcerer," Kon said. "I want to challenge you to a contest. I want three of your best warriors to race with me. If you win, we must obey your words. If you lose, you must leave the people of Tahiti-nui in peace. But, if you reject the contest, you will lose your honor in the eyes of all these men and women."

Tamatoa walked around Kon, looked away at the sea, then looked at Mato, his high priest.

"I am not sure I heard well," Tamatoa said with a low voice, poking his finger on Kon's chest. "You, an alien, are trying to tell me what I should do. You, an alien, are trying to manipulate the great Tamatoa. You, an alien, have the insolence of questioning my honor. Do you know I could crush your head with my hands, right now?

"Yes," Kon replied, "and crush your honor in the process. You cannot reject the contest."

Just as Tamatoa raised his hands toward Kon, Mato stopped his master.

"No, don't do this, Tamatoa," Mato said. "Let him speak, and explain what kind of race he has in mind."

Tamatoa looked at the old man, and saw his demanding eyes. Perhaps this once, he should listen to his father's old friend. Slowly, everybody circled around Kon and Tamatoa.

"Explain what the race would consist of," Tamatoa said.

Still in pain from Tamatoa's tremendous blow, and with

a bleeding cheek, Kon turned around and pointed at Mount Orohena.

"That is the sacred mountain where no man shall venture," Kon said, "except under extraordinary circumstances. I, Kon Tici Viracocha, challenge your three best men to race against me, from this beach all the way up to the summit."

Tamatoa looked at the mountain, then looked at Kon, and started laughing.

"You, so weak, against my three best warriors in a race to the top of this mountain!" Tamatoa said, still laughing. "Is this for real?"

Tamatoa took a dazzling look at Kon, and slapped his face a second time.

"Nobody can challenge my honor," Tamatoa roared. "Nobody can manipulate me with a stupid race. Nobody shall distract me from destroying the people of this island."

Once more, Kon did not flinch, though the blow made him dizzy. Kon waited for the unexpected, and the unexpected came.

"Father, let Taatamao race against this man," Mahine said with a gentle voice.

"Taatamao will not race with this man; nobody will." Tamatoa said.

However, Taatamao came, and bent low in front of his master.

"Tamatoa, my king, let me race against this man. I will carry your honor until death, if necessary."

It was obvious that Taatamao's words had a strong impact on Tamatoa. Mato saw that immediately, and tried to expand on it.

"Taatamao is right. Let's accept the challenge in style, and let him give a lesson to this man. Let's give all of them a lesson they shall never forget."

"Why should we satisfy the desire of this man, when he

cannot even defend himself? He is a coward!"

"He is not a coward," Hina objected with dignity. "In fact, it takes a lot of courage to remain impassive under the assaults of an overprotected adversary. Yes indeed, Kon Teke faces you in a splendid way."

Tamatoa felt warm blood flush his face. His eyes glowed with savage inner fire, and his anger turned to fury. Then his son Tera came to him.

"Father, let me race against that man with Taatamao."

"You too my son!" Tamatoa exclaimed. "What is wrong with all of you? Don't you see that we are the victims of a well-planned plot?"

Tamatoa's words were very convincing for his people. At this moment, Kon knew it would not be simple to convince Tamatoa, who was a fine strategist, but Hina asked an incredible question, a question Kon himself would never have attempted.

"Are you afraid of Kon Teke?" Hina asked with a humiliating grin.

This time it was too much for Tamatoa. It was the ultimate insult to be humiliated by a woman, especially in the face of all his people. Tamatoa walked slowly toward Hina. In silence, he looked at her with burning eyes. She lifted her chin, and stared at him with defiance. He was proud, but so was she.

Her unthinkable attitude had the effect nobody expected. Tamatoa suddenly realized he was dealing with no ordinary adversaries, with those far above the cruel cowardice of the Pora Pora people. Perhaps, his strategy was not right. This alien and this young woman brought something different to his dull life. He felt in them a sense of moral values, something he had never dreamed of.

Once more, Tamatoa looked at the dazzling black eyes of

the young priestess: She was not afraid. Then, he looked at the mysterious blue eyes of this nonviolent alien: A strange power was in them. Finally, he noticed his people looking at him, waiting for a gesture from a true king, their king. They all wanted to be proud of him, and Tamatoa was smart enough to clearly understand the subtlety: They all wanted the race. He walked away toward the edge of the galley. Alone, he looked at the sea, where he looked at seabirds. He had not looked at any bird for a long time.

Everyone knew he was going to make his decision, and everyone knew it would be unshakable, final. It was the moment of truth, the moment that would change the course of history.

Tamatoa turned around and looked at Kon, straight in the eyes. The tattooed giant slowly walked to him, each step thundering on the deck. He stopped and saw himself inside the glittering gold. He glanced at the red condors and suns woven on Kon's headband, and raised one hand toward the Son of the Sun, who did not flinch. The awesome hand landed on Kon's shoulder.

"I don't understand who you are," Tamatoa said. "But, you will race against my three best warriors. You will race against Taatamao, Tehau, and my son Tera."

Everybody on both ships exploded in joy and euphoria, but Tamatoa's thundering voice froze both camps.

"On two conditions!"

They all looked at him, and once more, time had stopped. They waited.

"First, my three men must go for a reconnaissance to the top of that mountain, today and tomorrow. And you, man from another world, shall go with them and show them the way."

"I accept," Kon said.

"Second, I will watch the race near its finishing point,"

Tamatoa said, walking to Hina, placing his huge hand on her shoulder, and looking at Tupua. "I shall take this young priestess as a hostage. She will remain close to me all the time. And, if there is any malice from your part, people of Tahiti-nui, Hina shall die from my own hands."

Tupua protested vehemently, but was instantly astonished by Kon's answer.

"I accept this condition," Kon said.

Everyone became silent. Tamatoa smiled: He was in control. Hina glanced at Kon in dismay, but she knew him, and many details spun in her head. All along, it had been Kon's plan. All along, he had wished for that moment, and that was her true mission. All the pieces of the puzzle suddenly fell into place. Now, she knew there would be two races. One would be Kon's race against Tamatoa's warriors. The other was Hina's race against time, against Tamatoa, and it would be a far subtler race.

Instantly, her destiny assumed another dimension, and her life had a formidable purpose she had never expected. She had been to the top of Mount Orohena, and as Kon had told her many times: "There is a purpose for everything, because you serve the cause of an unknown force." Indeed, she was well prepared, a good climber, and she had a knowledge of the Mountain. A complex scenario was taking shape in her mind.

Her eyes crossed Kon's eyes: They understood one another perfectly.

Reluctantly, Tupua accepted the conditions.

Hina went to her father.

"Today, life goes on for Maohis," she said. "I heard the voice in the wind call my name."

With style, the young priestess pulled out three more sacred tiare flowers from her clothes. She gave one to Mahine.

"Welcome to Tahiti-nui; this flower will bring you good luck, because you have a peaceful soul."

"I have nothing to give you," Mahine answered, obviously touched.

"Yes, you do," Hina said. "You can give me your innermost generosity."

Then, Hina of the Valley gave one flower to Mato.

"From priestess to priest, receive this modest present, because modesty is our true grandeur," Hina said to the old man, who was charmed by the music of her words.

Finally, Hina the priestess went to Tamatoa. She looked at the tiny flower in her hand.

"One day shall come, when I may give you one of these," she said. "But, for now their beauty cannot reach you."

She let the flower fall into the sea. The current took the flower away. She stared at the eyes of the giant, in a gentle manner.

"You are the pillar of an empty space," she said.

He knew what she meant.

****

CHAPTER 20

"As the sandpiper follows the receding wave, and runs away from the rising one, many stories have no end or beginning: So goes the life of Maohis. Only the stations where the bird stops feeding count. For Maohis, only the events worth remembering count. The rest can be the past,the present or the future; it makes no difference."

Hina of the Valley

Tupua went to Papenoo, and called his people back from the deep rain forest: There was a race to prepare, to witness and to win.

Kon and Aru went to the mountain with Taatamao, Tera, and Tehau, to show them the exact path of the race.

Hina was told to stay close to Tamatoa and his followers, who established their camp at the Teauroa Point, so familiar to her. She had plenty of time to observe, and wait for opportunities. For her, Mount Orohena had been a formidable conquest, and most certainly Tamatoa would be an equal challenge. She walked on the beach, to the tiare shrubs. She saw a sandpiper running after the receding wave, then running away from the next rumbling, giant wall of foam. To the tiny bird, the awesome mass of the waves was of no concern. It was part of its life and predictable: There was no giant.

Hina laughed at the bird. Mahine was behind her, and asked what was so funny.

"This bird reminds me of Vana, our great priest." Hina giggled. "Sometimes, he walks like this bird, when he is in quest of a sign."

They both laughed and scared the small bird, which flew away, emitting a plaintive whistle.

This was not the reason why Hina laughed. She laughed because the waves were Tamatoa, and the fragile bird was Hina. Tamatoa was powerful, but she would manage, survive and indeed send a plaintive message to the heart of the Maohi people.

When the evening came, Hina helped Mahine and several other women prepare the meal. At some distance, Tamatoa, Mato and two other men argued about the best strategy for the race. She listened to every word, and what struck her most was the speed of Tamatoa's replies. It was no accident that he was the king. His judgment and logic were impeccable, and inspired his people. They were obedient, and they admired him.

Hina saw Mahine taking some food for Tamatoa and Mato.

"May I ask you a favor?" Hina said.

"Of course, Hina." Mahine smiled

"Let me take this food to your father and Mato. I would like to do that."

Mahine hesitated a little, then let Hina proceed.

Hina went to Tamatoa and just looked at him, then went to Mato, squatted, and gave him warm breadfruit and raw fish. Mato accepted with noticeable pleasure.

"This young woman hates me so much," Tamatoa said, with open amusement, "that she would make sure she serves Mato first."

Hina served Tamatoa, and looked at him straight in the eyes.

"I don't hate you. I hate nobody," she said. "I don't like you, but I still respect who you are."

She stood up, and walked away.

"This girl is skilled with words," Mato said.

"She does not sound like a Maohi," Tamatoa remarked, "she sounds like this alien."

"This is true," Mato said, "and they are fond of one another."

"Why am I doing this?" Tamatoa asked, eating his breadfruit.

"Because Kon Teke challenged your honor," Mato said. "Or, perhaps, for the fun of it."

"But, I don't trust any of them," Tamatoa said, with a mocking tone.

"Perhaps I should remind you that we are the invaders," Mato added, his eyes glittering with malice. "They were living in peace."

"Perhaps, I should remind you not to annoy me," Tamatoa replied. "Only my people count."

"Let's not quarrel on this subject," Mato said. "Let's simply notice that Hina was nice to you."

"In a way she was, in a way she was not," Tamatoa murmured, looking at the fronds of coconut trees moving in the wind.

After all the men were served, Hina and Mahine sat side by side, near a tiare shrub. Silent, they ate their meal, and felt the warmth of friendship each time they glanced at one another.

"I like you," Mahine said.

"How can you tell?" Hina asked. "You were told to hate us."

"We were not told to hate you," Mahine objected. "My father is not as bad as you may think, and he suffered very much when he was a boy."

"Do you suffer, right now?" Hina asked.

"Yes!" Mahine answered, with tears in her eyes.

"Do you have friends?"

"No, I only have a mate, Taatamao, who is always with my father. I rarely see him."

"Then, let me be your friend," Hina said gently.

Mahine stared at Hina, as nobody before had said these words to her. The only friend she knew was old Mato, but in her eyes, he was not really a friend. He was too old, and a living shadow of the past. Plus, because of his status as the great priest, she was not always comfortable with him. In a sign of recognition, Mahine laid her head on Hina's shoulder, and they both admired the sunset. At some distance, Tamatoa watched his daughter. There was no emotion in his eyes, no surprise or sympathy: He was a warrior.

"I don't like for my daughter to become friendly with this priestess," Tamatoa said, frowning. "Maybe you should talk with these two girls."

"I may just do that." Mato replied.

The old priest sat on the black sand, facing the two young women. Slowly, the tide was coming up. Silent, the three of them enjoyed the tranquility of the lagoon at their side. The sour smell of dead corals was everywhere. In the trees, restless parrots argued. At times, when the breeze came from the mountain, they could smell fragrant frangipani and tiare flowers closing their flowers at the end of the day, which was a reminder we were all part of an ephemeral universe.

"You like this Kon Teke very much," Mato said, looking at Hina, who did not answer immediately.

She turned around and glanced at Mount Orohena. She worried about Kon being with the others, on the mountain. At least, she was happy Aru was with them. Then, she looked at Mato.

"I cannot describe to you, nor can you comprehend who Kon Teke is," Hina said. "You have to spend time with him, alone, when you can. He would give you unforgettable moments to remember. He is a pillar supporting space filled with treasures beyond imagination. Yet, he is simple, humble."

"I don't understand," Mato said, disoriented.

"I care for this man," Hina said. "I love him. He taught me that there is another life beyond flesh and blood, and there is no need to wait for death to find out what it is. Right here, in our minds, there is an incredible world, as vast as the awesome sea, where our soul waits for us. Yet, we lose our time in futile conflicts and pitiful jealousy, so we never take the time to find this island of beauty."

She stopped, waiting for Mato's questions.

"Continue my child," Mato said, "your words are most interesting."

"Our soul is full of stars, and each of them has the energy of our sun. Our soul is all light, and pure energy. In each of us, there is an infinite force, far beyond the reach of those flirting with mediocrity. But, any of us can learn and use this force, honor it, add to it and hand it to our children. The result would be a lasting peace, in harmony with everything around us, and a tribute to the extraordinary beauty of these islands."

Mato placed his shaking hand on Hina's thigh.

"Where did you learn these words?" Mato asked with glowing eyes. "How can you speak like this, at your age?"

"It was not difficult," Hina replied. "Everybody can do it. Just be who you want to be, and be honest with those with whom you speak. Sincerity shall make the words flow, like blood in our veins, like light through the universe."

At some distance, Tamatoa watched the small group. He

saw the interest with which Mato listened to the priestess. More than ever, he thought the world of priests was a strange world in which he had no interest. More than ever, he was emotionless, with no fantasy or sentiment: He was a pragmatic man.

Later, when Mato and Mahine left, Hina lay on the sand and tried to get some sleep. She could not sleep. She heard the steps of someone walking. She did not look to see who was behind her, but she kept her eyes open, listening. He sat close to her: She knew who he was.

"My daughter and Mato were fascinated by your words," Tamatoa said. "Could those words entertain the king?"

"Mahine and Mato are nice persons," Hina said, without looking at him. "They have the class of Maohi aristocrats."

A deep silence took place for a moment, then she turned around and looked at the king.

"You are strong, and invincible," Hina said. "For this, history will remember you. But, sentiments and magnanimity count most, and for this history may curse your name."

"Are you trying to insult me?" Tamatoa asked.

"Not at all!" Hina replied. "I want to put some light in your dark ways, and help you to open your eyes and see the Maohis."

"I know everything about Maohis."

"You know them, and they know you," Hina said. "Yet, you don't see them, and they don't see you. There is a difference."

"My people like me, respect me and I serve them," Tamatoa said.

"Don't you wish all Maohis could say that? Is not that exactly who you want to be?"

Tamatoa stood up, and walked away.

At dawn, Tamatoa and Tupua agreed that the start of the race would be in Papenoo, and Mato and Vana would referee it.

Observers from both camps would be dispersed all along the path of the race. No fighting between the racers would be allowed during the entire contest. Tamatoa would go very high in the mountain to witness the final phase of the race.

Moments later, Tamatoa, with a dozen of his people, Mahine and Hina started their long journey through the hills.

"I suppose Hina could show us the way," Tamatoa said with sarcasm. "Unless you cannot follow. In which case you would have to stay with my warriors on the lower hills."

"I will show you the way," Hina replied, "to the top of Mount Orohena. But, none of you is dressed to sustain the cold at the top of the mountain."

Tamatoa glanced at Hina, turned around and ordered some of his warriors to go back to the camp and take more clothes.

"At night, it can get very cold up there," Hina said.

"Why shall you care about us?" Tamatoa asked.

"This is my land, and for the time being, you are my guest," Hina replied.

Tamatoa looked at Hina climbing. Her steps were firm, precise and revealed her will. He thought she had more capabilities than he originally suspected. He liked her, but he could not explain the reasons yet. Perhaps it was because she was a daring person, with no apparent malice. Or, perhaps it was because she was aggressive, with no hate. She was no ordinary Maohi. Puzzled, Tamatoa asked his first friendly question.

"Do you really think this Kon Teke stands a chance to win the race against my three best men?"

Hina stopped and looked at Mount Orohena.

"He is the mountain," she said. "He is Mount Orohena. He is a giant, and your warriors do not stand a chance."

The sudden force of her words impressed Tamatoa.

"But, you don't really know how good my three men are."

"For Kon Teke, this is irrelevant," she said. "Our best climber thought like you, and he lost, decisively"

Hina stopped talking, thinking she would annoy Tamatoa. She did not want to destroy what she had built so far, but Tamatoa was not who he was for nothing, and he understood her concern right away.

"During this trip, you may talk freely," Tamatoa said. "You words will offend me no more."

"Why the change?" she asked, taken by surprise.

"Because, I would like to hear what you have to say."

Hina stopped, a bit confused. She had not expected such a statement, at least not so soon. She thought that it might be a trap. Aware of her surprise, Tamatoa showed amusement on his face, and she thought he had a beautiful smile.

"You are the king, I am only a humble priestess," Hina said. "But, I see two persons in you: the warrior with all his might and glory, and the protector of his people. If you could enlarge these two persons for all Maohis, you would be a better king."

He laughed at her impertinence. She indeed had courage, and he liked the quality. Her self-confidence had surprising strength, and there was no hesitation in her answers, as if she had the opportunity to prepare them, but Tamatoa was most puzzled by who she was, so young. She was a fantastic anachronism.

"How long has this Kon Teke been here?" he asked.

"About two sun-cycles."

"How long have your people known him?" he asked.

"A little less than one sun-cycle."

"How long have you known Kon Teke?" Tamatoa asked with a grin on his face.

Hina blushed, embarrassed. How could he know? Suddenly,

she realized Tamatoa was a fine strategist, and effective in getting the information he wanted.

"For two sun-cycles. I met him the first day he came on the island." Hina replied.

"I see!" Tamatoa exclaimed, touching her shoulder. "You are honest, and I like that. Then, you taught him our language."

"Yes."

"Then, you are a good teacher. But, you were very young and of royal blood. How did you keep your secret for so long?"

Hina could not take it anymore. She stopped walking, faced the king, and gave him a black look.

"Why should I answer these questions? Those things do not concern you. Indeed, I may share them, but only with people for whom I have esteem."

"I did not intend to annoy you," Tamatoa apologized.

Silent, she glanced at him, more perplexed than before.

When they reached the long ridge leading to Mount Pitohiti, Hina decided to give a lesson to her adversaries. She accelerated her pace. She knew the mountain and every stone of it. She knew where to place her hands and her feet. Tamatoa and his people struggled behind. The king observed Hina carefully, turned around and saw everybody huffing and puffing. Mahine was far behind, trying to memorize Hina's path. In spite of himself, Tamatoa chuckled.

"You enjoy this, I suppose," he said.

"This is the mountain," Hina said with defiance. "You learn to live with it, or you stay away from it. You wanted to come, then follow me."

"You stop and wait," Tamatoa roared. So, she did.

After Mahine caught up with them, Hina started climbing again, but she changed her strategy, going more slowly and concentrating on her skill: She wanted to present a good image.

"How did you learn to climb so well?" Tamatoa asked.

"Kon Teke taught me," she answered with a grin. "I told you, you cannot win this race."

"Well, we are not the champions," Tamatoa argued.

"Well, I am not Kon Teke," Hina replied.

They both laughed with good humor.

Halfway up, Tamatoa stopped and surveyed the mountain. The more they climbed, the more the mountain looked gigantic, and inaccessible. He smiled, thinking that he may have been a little quick to accept the challenge, and that Kon Teke knew exactly what he was doing, but Tamatoa would be a good player. He knew it was too late, and backing out would be disastrous for his reputation.

At some distance ahead, they saw the five men coming back from their reconnaissance. Taatamao came close to his master, who told him to do so with a hand signal.

"Who will win the race, tomorrow?" Tamatoa asked.

"I will," Taatamao answered.

"How good is this Kon Teke?" Tamatoa asked his son Tera.

"He is an outstanding climber, but not as good as we are."

Kon and Aru came close to Hina.

"How are you doing?" Kon asked.

"Believe it or not, I am having fun," Hina replied, kissing the man she loved.

Kon glanced at Tamatoa.

"We shall meet again, tomorrow evening," he said to the king.

"Only if you win!" Tamatoa said with a mocking tone.

With no further comments, the two groups separated.

Hina and her followers were on the sharp spine of the ridge, trying to find their way through rocks, mud, shrubs, and giant ferns. Hina knew the place perfectly, and the higher they went, the slower their progress became. She was happy, and for her it was easy. With great satisfaction, she watched these people fighting the ferns, struggling on slippery ground, and suffering to their bones. She felt sorry for Mahine, who was determined to follow. Hina understood her will: Taatamao was her mate, therefore she wanted to see the end of the race, but there was something Hina did not know. Mahine remembered her horrible vision of Taatamao falling from the mountain: She never told anyone about this, except Mato. Alone, she agonized, and prepared herself for the final moment of truth. She thought she had found a friend, but Hina was more preoccupied by her contest with her father. It never occurred to Mahine what Hina was up to.

The last pinnacles before the summit of Mount Pitohiti challenged them.

Hina saw Mahine lose her balance several times and hurt her legs: She had bleeding scratches everywhere on her body.

"You should help your daughter," Hina said. "She is very brave, but it is becoming dangerous for her, and we must keep going before nightfall. We will stop in a cave, well protected from the cold wind."

Several men helped Mahine. Near the top of Mount Pitohiti, everyone was silent, covered with perspiration, cuts and blood. The mountain was tough, and so were they. Hina reached Mahine's hand and pulled her to the top of the mountain, where she collapsed. When Tamatoa took his last step, he looked at Hina, who took his hand and pulled him as hard as she could.

"Welcome to Mount Pitohiti," Hina said. "This is Orohena's tiny brother."

"Is your cave still far?" Mahine asked, out of breath.

"It is close," Hina replied. "You will be comfortable soon."

"Why are you concerned for our comfort?" Tamatoa asked, irritated.

"I walked all day with you," Hina replied. "I actually enjoyed my time with you, and I like Mahine. All this goes against your plans to eventually execute me."

Tamatoa felt a mysterious current surging through his body, and for the first time felt superiority coming from somebody else. He quickly glanced at the priestess, shook his head, thinking he was losing his mind. The idea of executing Hina of the Valley was intolerable.

At some distance from the cave, Mahine collapsed on the ground, sobbing.

"I cannot walk anymore," she murmured.

"Yes, you will," Hina ordered, "you shall not quit, so close to the cave."

Mahine stood up, and managed to walk. Tamatoa observed the scenario and smiled, but did not say anything. A cold breeze blew in the ferns, and it was the only noise they could hear, besides their footsteps and their pounding hearts. It was Tamatoa's first experience with high mountains. He was short of breath, but felt something fascinating: He could see farther out to sea than he never imagined, and to his surprise the horizon was curved. The sunset above Moorea was beautiful beyond imagination. At this moment, he felt something he had never felt as a warrior. It was as if someone entered his body. Suddenly he thought Tahiti-nui's spirits possessed him, but quickly dismiss the idea. He looked at the awesome sea, and felt free and content.

When they reached the cave, Tamatoa stopped for a moment, and watched Mount Orohena.

"It is majestic," he said.

"Here, you can find who you want to be in a special way," Hina said. "Nowhere else can you feel that way."

"Oh yes I can!" Tamatoa argued. "I felt like this many times on my ship at sea. It is like a sentiment of peace."

"Of peace!" Hina chuckled. She stared at him, judging the man. She walked away, shaking her head.

Moments later, Hina came back with a gourd of water. Cautiously, she cleaned Mahine's bloody legs and arms. She did the same for two men who were in no better condition. Tamatoa himself had a deep cut under one knee.

"May I?" Hina asked, looking at the king.

"Yes."

As she cleaned his wound, her eyes caught Tamatoa's eyes. She stared at him for an instant, then smiled with serenity.

Outside the cave, the men prepared a fire. Hina saw one of them bend over the ground, revealing a long cut in his back she had not seen. She pulled on his arm and told him to sit down. The man complied with no resistance, and she did what she had to do. But, the man became interested in her in a way she had not anticipated, and his intentions became obvious. She felt a flow of blood rush through her head. She was not prepared for something that could bring shame on her royal rank. She was frightened, but Mahine noticed Hina's problem, and put one hand on her father's arm to give him a silent signal. Tamatoa's thoughts were lost inside the flames of the fire, and he had not noticed anything. When he felt Mahine's hand, he looked at her, and with her head she pointed at the man close to Hina. Tamatoa saw Hina's silent agony.

Suddenly, like an explosion shaking the entire cave, the thundering voice of the king instantly paralyzed the young man and Hina as well. Tamatoa took his arm with one hand, and everyone could hear his joints cracking.

"Leave Hina of the Valley alone. Nobody shall touch this woman. She is of royal blood, therefore you shall respect her."

Never in her life, had Hina heard such a voice. The tone was precise with her full name, echoing and impressive. It had been an order with irresistible power. Deep inside herself, Hina was grateful; she thought Tamatoa had changed since they met and became increasingly protective of her. He saw the glowing depth of her black eyes looking gently at him.

During the night, Hina could not sleep. Against her back, she felt Mahine's body, and she was not sleeping either. The night was dark and there were no clouds. Hina pulled away from the bark-cloth cover, and invited Mahine to do the same.

"Come, I want to show you something," Hina said.

Discreetly, they tiptoed outside.

"Look at the sky," Hina murmured.

The sky was almost white, at its best, silent in its timeless infinity. The starlight entered Mahine's wide-opened eyes, and went straight to her soul. Never before, had she seen such scenery.

"Why are they so many, today?" Mahine asked, stunned by a display of beauty she would never forget.

"Because you are high in my kingdom." Hina replied. "It is yours as well. Drink its beauty, its light, its message, and never become tired of it."

Hina felt two massive hands weighing on her shoulders, and for an instant her body froze in terror.

"I like what you said," Tamatoa murmured. "I never thought about stars in such a way."

Hina felt instant relief. The tattooed giant was friendly. Then, they heard Mahine sobbing.

"What is it, Mahine?" Hina asked.

"I am thinking about the race tomorrow, and I fear for Taatamao."

"Don't fear about life, or the flow of time." Tamatoa said. "Always be prepared to accept your destiny, which we cannot change."

"But, why is this race necessary?" Mahine asked.

"You are the one who pushed for it, remember," Tamatoa argued.

"Don't be harsh with her." Hina said. "It is hard for all of us. Between now and the end of that race, each of us may become confused. Nevertheless, I know why the race is important."

"You do! And why is that?" Tamatoa asked, amused by Hina's statement.

She stayed silent for a moment, looking at the stars. She knew the time was right to express her prediction.

"Because, tomorrow night, there will be no loser, only two winners."

****

CHAPTER 21

"Like the sandpiper running down the beach after the receding wave, observe your adversary and understand him. Like the sandpiper running up the beach ahead of the proceeding wave, make sure your adversary does not reach you before he shall recede. Either way, you may change the world."

Hina of the Valley

At dawn, the four racers were aligned on the beach near Papenoo. Along the path of the race, a crowd waited. As Mato gave his last recommendations to his three champions, Vana took Kon aside.

"Our fate is in your hands," Vana said, "you cannot lose the race."

"I had a vision," Kon replied, firmly. "Trust me, and remember, somewhere on the mountain a priestess is leading another race."

Vana shook his head: He did not comprehend Kon's words.

Aru put a friendly hand on Kon's shoulder.

"I wish I could follow you," Aru said. "But, Tupua asked me to remain here. Orohena's spirits are with you."

Fenua came, gave Kon a charming smile and kissed him, sending a shock wave through his body. She was amused at what she had done.

"This was the spirit of my sister living in me," she said gently. "After the race, take good care of her."

She turned around, then stopped as if she had forgotten something.

"It was not by chance that you were sent here," Fenua said. "Look at what Maohis are doing today, for the idea of a stranger lost at sea."

Atea came: heavy, authoritarian and confident.

"My son, Mana is with you," she said. "We trust you to the end. But, along the way, if you see some tropicbirds, please do not look at them for too long."

They all laughed at her comment.

The four men were ready. Mato and Vana waited for the first flamboyant beam from the sun to pierce the eastern horizon. It came, dazzling. The two priests raised their arms above their heads.

"You may go; the spirits are with you," they both yelled.

At the same instant, drums and conchs sent their signal across mountains and valleys: The race had started. Each man had a gourd of water and a little food tied around his belt. The three Maohis raced barefooted, but Kon had on his sandals as usual. They were on the trail of what would remain a famous journey.

It did not take long before Kon understood the strategy of his adversaries. Tehau took the lead, setting the pace, while Taatamao and Tera conserved their energy. Tamatoa's two best climbers worried about the last part of the race, but at the same time they wanted the pace to be fast enough, they hoped, to wear out Kon Tici. Kon thought they were naive: If he would wear out, so would they. He knew Tehau would be devastated soon by his efforts, but this time, Kon would remain careful, recalling his mistakes against Aru. These men were tough, far better trained than Aru at combat, therefore with more ability to withstand hardship. To win, they would be willing to take enormous risks. Atea's comment had been most appropriate. After their long reconnaissance on the mountain, Kon knew his most dangerous adversary was Taatamao, who would remain with him until the last phase of the race.

Very high in the mountain, Tamatoa's group left the cave, and Hina guided them to the small lake where the sacred red ducks lived. Suddenly, they heard the deep sound of the drums and conchs. Hina looked at Tamatoa with excitement.

"They are on their way," she said. "We can stay around the lake until they appear at the top of Mount Pitohiti, late in the afternoon. Afterward, we may approach a little closer to Mount Orohena to have a good view of the last phase of the race."

Tamatoa nodded approval, but did not say one word. He sat near the clear lake, noticed a few ice crystals, something he had never seen before. Then, he looked at himself through the water. Somewhere, he heard the soft quack of a duck.

"There are ducks here, too!" he exclaimed, looking at his daughter.

"I saw one with Hina," Mahine said. "They are not the same ducks as those we saw in Moorea. Those are red."

"They are called Moorauras." Hina explained. "They are sacred, and this is the only place where we find them. The priests cut their red feathers, but never kill them."

"Here is one!" Mahine whispered. "Isn't it pretty?"

"Yes indeed," Tamatoa said, admiring the duck swimming.

"It does not look disturbed by our presence," Mahine said.

"Well, it is brave above the surface, paddling like crazy under it," Hina chuckled.

They all roared in laughter, frightening the duck away.

Tamatoa observed the unusual surroundings: He had seen similar places before.

"I wonder how this lake was formed," He said.

"Vana, our great priest," Hina said, "told me that in the beginning, when Taaroa, the Creator of everything, made Tahiti-nui, this lake expelled fire at great distances."

"I saw such places, far in the west," Tamatoa replied.

"How does that look?" Hina asked, puzzled.

"When the mountain is awake, the display of power is frightening: You cannot approach the island. And, at night, beauty and fear become the same word."

"I would like to see such a place," Hina said, fascinated. "What is the fire made of?"

"It is molten rock," Tamatoa replied. "The entire mountain was once molten rock: red, flowing, incredibly hot. When you watch this, you feel like a grain of dust lost inside the fury of Mother Earth. You become insignificant, and humble."

Hina threw a small stone into the lake, and looked at the concentric waves crossing its quiet surface.

"There are so many things we don't understand," she said. "This is what we are, just a grain of dust. Priestess or king, we are still a grain of dust, and we indeed should have the right to remain humble."

He looked at her, amused by the way she used his own words against him.

"Is this a sarcastic comment?" Tamatoa asked.

"No, it is a fact," Hina replied. "I will die, you will die, we all die. But, the Earth continues its course with its seas, mountains, rivers, floods, storms,...."

She paused, but did not hear any comments.

"So, what are we, besides an insignificant grain of dust?" she asked.

Tamatoa's eyes were lost along the cliffs of the grandiose Mount Orohena.

"Is this a lesson in humility?" he asked. "Too much humility leads to depression, then you become weak."

"I disagree," Hina said. "Humility is a perspective of wisdom. It is a silent force that gives you inner grandeur and control over who you want to be. It is the bond with Mother Earth."

Tamatoa smiled, but did not answer.

Mahine listened, worrying about the conversation. Nobody had ever argued with her father the way Hina did. Yet, she was amazed to see a smile on her father's face. He was happy to talk, and was not offended by Hina's words.

"I am going to tell you something, Hina," Tamatoa said. "I never let anyone talk to me the way you do. You have strong words, yet you know how to speak with elegance: You give me ideas."

Hina blushed with pleasure. Even in her dreams, she never expected such a compliment from the tattooed giant, from this terrifying warrior. Now, she was convinced Tamatoa was not the horrible man everyone described. Once more, she realized how right Kon had been. Our attitudes create our enemies. Suddenly, she recalled she had a mission. Restless, she threw another stone into the lake. She did not even know what that mission was. At least, she was sure of one thing. She would remain in Viracocha's line: be who she wanted to be, honest, and smoothly elegant. Her next comment was going to spark a dramatic course.

"To argue in style is an enriching process," she said. "Man loses his dignity when he can no longer disagree, first because of fear, later because he does not remember how to disagree properly."

Then, the unexpected question came, clear, and appropriate, the question Hina would turn around with devastating force.

"Do you disagree with the way I lead my people?" Tamatoa asked.

"No, my father!" Mahine exclaimed. "Your question is unfair to Hina."

"It is all right, Mahine," Hina said, gently. "I will answer your father's question. However, I want to think about it first. May I?"

"Take your time," Tamatoa smiled. "We have all day."

Tamatoa was amused by his own question. She was not. She knew her answer, but she weighed the risk attached to it. She sat down, put her head in her hands and closed her eyes. She wished Kon could help her. She was afraid to make a terrible error in judgment. Then, she recalled Kon's words: "Be kind to your adversary; make sure he understands the reasons for your kindness, yet remain firm. In return, do not ask for his kindness, but wait and see. The result will be a measure of how honest you were."

Those were her favorite words from Kon Tici, but for the first time she had to apply them, and for the first time she envisioned their depth. Yes, this was her opportunity, her achievement of the day. She had been kind enough, so now she could be firm and take a risk. She decided to give Tamatoa her answer. There was no turning back.

"I am going to be kind to you," Hina said, "not because you are the king, but because you are a father, and a good friend of a remarkable old priest."

"I am listening," Tamatoa said.

"Do Mato and Mahine, two persons very dear to you, agree with the way you lead your people?"

All traces of a smile left Tamatoa's face. Hina's weapon of words went straight to its target. Tamatoa had known the answer to this question for some time. Mato and Mahine had been the two only persons who dared to challenge his ways, but he had ignored them, because it interfered with his goals. How many others thought as they did? How many others agreed with him, just because of fear? These questions were an obsession for him.

Tamatoa glanced at his daughter. She stared at him, delighted. He knew exactly what she was thinking, since she dared him on Havaiki's beach. All his life, he would remember these words from his daughter: "Your war is dirty. You are killing innocent Maohis who are brothers and sisters of blood. You will have no rest, no victory."

Mahine's words echoed across the lake, in the mountain. Mount Orohena laughed at him, silent, waiting. Then, he recalled some of Mato's words: "May the spirits inspire you, Tamatoa, for the best. We are all tired of this life. Do what you have to do, conquer the most beautiful island in the world, but do it fast." He knew they were the words of wisdom, with a sarcastic subtlety.

Tamatoa glanced at Hina. Total triumph was in her eyes. The beast inside the man was attacked from two sides. He knew Hina's spear had wounded the beast, but he also knew the beast would never die without the unconditional acceptance that he had been wrong, that he had gone too far, that he had been the prisoner of his revenge.

Tamatoa now measured the young woman he had just met, two days earlier. Hina of the Valley was not a priestess because of her royal blood, but because of her pride as a Maohi, her wisdom and her intelligence. Under the facade of a gentle, charming beauty, she was a giant. For the first time in his life, Tamatoa felt defeated by a woman who told him he was not who he wanted to be. He suddenly doubted himself, and was afraid.

However, the daring priestess was kind: It added to her superiority. Hina knew his dilemma, and the only thing she wanted was some bond to develop between her and Tamatoa. So, she came to his rescue, with style.

"Could you give me your answer after the race?" she asked.

He approved with a nod of his head, but stayed silent. Hina took Mahine by one hand, invited her to walk around the lake, and to take a closer look at the sacred ducks.

At the foot of Mount Pitohiti, the race gained momentum, with Tehau still leading, but his steps were no longer as accurate, and fatigue slowly diminished Tamatoa's young champion. Kon was behind Taatamao and Tera, who were in excellent condition and determined to wear Kon down before they reached the hardest part of the race. Kon did not worry, followed them the best he could and centered his thoughts away from the race. He thought about Hina, and wondered how she was handling Tamatoa. As resourceful as she was, he knew she would give her best. The thought gave him courage and energy: He was not alone.

They went through mud, streams, forest, shrubs, ferns and cobwebs. The first part of the race was not dangerous, but long and exhausting, with a confusing path. Observers became scarce, and the mountain was looming, silent, impressive. The four men ran almost hand in hand. In their struggle among the formidable cover of giant ferns, they respected one another, at least for the moment.

Later along the sharp cliff, Kon suddenly felt the pain in his legs and chest go away, and the discomfort of short breath vanished. His body attained its maximum performance; his breath became regular, deeper, and his pulse slower. There was no more fatigue. Kon gained his second wind, much sooner than usual:

Tamatoa's men had unintentionally given him a favor.

Immediately, Kon put more pressure on his adversaries. Tehau, who had given too much, too soon, was near total collapse. Kon passed Taatamao and Tera, who were quite surprised. Then, he passed Tehau. Shocked by Kon's aggressiveness, Tehau recovered enough energy to take the lead again. Kon did not expect this rebound of energy, but he knew it would soon be the end for Tehau, who had been brave. The onset of fatigue could be delayed no more. Tehau became short of breath, his pulse rate accelerated, he collapsed on the ground and lay his head in his hands. He was devoid of any form of energy. Weariness literally brought the young man to his knees, to rest.

"Two more to go," Kon murmured, when he passed Tehau.

"You did well," Taatamao said when he passed Tehau.

Taatamao glanced at Tera.

"You or I?"

"I will take the lead," Tera replied. "You have a better chance at the end."

Along the formidable cliff, Taatamao and Tera caught up with Kon, and about halfway Tera took the lead.

"Go ahead," Kon murmured in his native language. "Be my guest."

Two details worried Kon. First, he saw Tera was trying once in awhile to loosen some rocks, hoping they would fall on Kon. For safety reasons, Kon took a slightly different, more complicated path. Also, Kon noticed Tera was not short of breath. Tamatoa's son had far more endurance than Tehau, and would not give up soon.

The cliff became much sharper and more hazardous, the ferns scarcer and the path more challenging. Taatamao and Tera were concerned that Kon had expended very little energy to keep up with them. The temperature was dropping fast, which was a relief for the racers. Far behind, Tehau followed the best he could, after he had taken a long pause.

Just under the most difficult part of the cliff leading to the summit, Tupua, Taaroa and a few other men sat on a narrow ledge. They had struggled their way to this place, but it would be their limit. They would have to watch the race from here, where they had a good view of Mount Orohena: They would be in a position to see who would be the winner. They knew it would be unmistakable: Tamatoa's warriors had white garments, and Kon was dressed in all dark blue.

Kon was amazed to see Taaroa with Tupua. He had never thought Taaroa capable of such a physical effort. His feet battered Taaroa smiled at Kon when he passed nearby.

"Remember what you told me," Taaroa said. "There are no limits for a well-born soul. Today, we shall see."

Tupua was not smiling. He was worried, and it was Taaroa the leper, who gave courage to the king.

"Kon's victory is going to be awe inspiring," Taaroa said, in his croaking voice.

Tupua looked at his old friend. At this moment, he would have given anything to stop Tamatoa's madness, even his rank as the king, but for nothing in the world would he have given away his friendship for his old companion. Kon Tici had showed him how much he loved Taaroa, and at this moment, those sentiments came back strongly to his mind. Without noticing, Tupua placed one hand on Taaroa's shoulder. In times of despair and hopelessness, the illness of your friend does not matter. What counts most is his presence.

Tera approached the summit of Mount Pitohiti. In the blink of an eye, he saw his opportunity. Under his hands, a large rock was loose. With no hesitation, he jumped on it, pushed it down with one foot. The boulder started rolling, and Tera screamed his pleasure at the very instant he reached the summit.

Kon saw the stone coming and Taatamao on his left, terrified.

"Jump in the ferns," Kon screamed.

They both landed among a cluster of giant ferns, on one side of the cliff. The boulder landed on the cliff near them, sending a shock wave through the ground. Part of the cliff went down, tumbling into the valley with awesome power. The two men glanced at each other. Taatamao spit in the ferns, and expressed his anger to Tera with vehemence. At this moment, Kon knew whom he was dealing with. He knew it would be a fair race to the end, against Taatamao.

They both reached the summit, and Kon immediately started running. He knew exactly where his feet should land. Taatamao stayed behind him, in his tracks. They were closing on Tera, fast. When they reached the lowest point between Mount Pitohiti and Mount Orohena, Kon passed Tera with dazzling determination. Surprised by Kon's energy, Tera lost his momentum, and his will.

Taatamao passed Tera, still furious at him.

"In due time," Taatamao said, "we shall talk about your attempt to kill our adversary."

Now, it was a two-man race.

Hina and Mahine spent a long time talking, while strolling around the lake. Tamatoa was in a bad mood, and venting his frustration against his men. Hina decided she would not talk to him anymore. He would hear nothing of what she had to say. The atmosphere deteriorated further as the race neared the end. Hina herself lost confidence in what she had done. She wondered if she had only made Kon's work more complicated. It may have been better if she had not been with Tamatoa for three days.

A soft quack came from a cluster of tall grass. A sitting duck became upset as the two women approached. Hina stopped Mahine with her hand.

"Let's not scare this mother," Hina said.

They circled the nest from a distance.

"You like this place a lot," Mahine observed.

"Yes, I do, for many reasons. During the day, the mountain is a crown above my soul. During the night, the stars are the light above my crown."

"This is why you are a priestess. How does it feel to be so?"

"I am the same person as before I became a priestess," Hina replied, taking a blade of green grass in her mouth. "You are who you want to be for yourself, and you become who others want you to be. If you reach the point where these two persons can be the same, you reach happiness and serenity."

"You mean I have to work hard to please others."

"Not at all," Hina said. "You have to work hard to demonstrate how valuable you are, the way you are. But, who you are must remain your choice, not the result of fate or the idea of someone else."

"I wish I could spend more time with you," Mahine said with a touch of sadness. "I wish Taatamao could spend more time with Kon."

"Such a time may come soon," Hina said, pointing at Mount Pitohiti. "Here they come!"

"Tera is leading!" Mahine exclaimed.

"Not for long," Hina said. "They are still far from here. Let's swim."

"Swim in the lake! It is too cold," Mahine objected.

Hina removed her clothes and dived into the clear water.

"Come, it is not that cold."

Mahine undressed herself and dived into the lake.

At the sight of the two women playing in the water, while racers approached, Tamatoa became irritated. For him, it was as if they did not care about the race. He had two reasons to be humiliated: Hina told him all the way Kon would win the race, and now, Kon Tici was taking the lead. Hina looked at Tamatoa as she swam. Her lips spread into a smile, and Tamatoa was a glowering mask of rage. He went to the lake, told Hina and Mahine to get out, and to stay with him and his men. He was perfectly aware that Hina knew all the details of the mountain, and in due time, she could easily vanish if not given the proper surveillance. Both women complied. Tamatoa threw their garments in their faces, as they shook in the cold wind.

"Get ready," Tamatoa ordered, "we must walk closer to the summit.

Kon increased his lead on Taatamao, and Tera struggled far behind.

Hina watched Tamatoa's face. His eyes glowed with an inner fire. When Kon passed nearby, the giant realized the mountaineer was not suffering, his breath was regular, and his steps long and precise. Taatamao came, showing obvious signs of great fatigue: Tamatoa's best man was in deep trouble. Mount Orohena loomed in front of them: silent, far away and inaccessible.

"Taatamao does not stand a chance," Hina said with cold triumph.

"Along the sharp peak, everything is possible," Tamatoa said, without flinching.

"Yes, along the peak, you are going to find out who is the master of the mountain," Hina said with pride.

"You knew all along that the race would not be fair, in the last part," Tamatoa said, angry.

"Tell me anything, but not this," Hina replied violently. "One of your men lost the race long ago, a second one looks pitiful and the third one is struggling. The three of them had a fair chance to measure the challenge during the reconnaissance."

Tamatoa did not answer. He knew his comment had been inappropriate.

"Remember," Hina said with dignity, "at the end of the race, you will show if you really are the king you think you are."

Mahine, still shivering from the cold, listened to the argument with mixed feelings. On one hand she wanted Kon to win because his victory might bring an end to her father's madness. On the other hand she wanted Taatamao to win because she loved him and was proud of him, but deep inside, she still struggled with the vision she had several days earlier, in which Taatamao fell from the cliff. Now, her eyes were on that cliff, and it perfectly matched her vision. She waited, in pain.

"If something happens to Taatamao, I will hate you for the rest of my life," Mahine said to her father.

"If anyone dies with courage, I will remember the man, and make sure he did not die in vain," Tamatoa said, fascinated by a sudden recovery from Taatamao.

Hina recalled Vana words: "Nobody can climb Mount Orohena. Therefore, to protect the people from deadly danger, the mountain was declared taboo." She recalled how Kon helped her to climb the forbidden Mountain. She recalled that without the ropes, it was tantamount to suicide. Kon had done it several times, alone, but nobody had his skill. She knew Taatamao was heading to a certain death, and felt sorry for Mahine.

"Go! Taatamao, go! go!" Tamatoa roared into the evening breeze.

The powerful voice of his master gave courage and energy

to Taatamao, who instantly came closer to Kon. Now was the moment of truth. Now, the mountain was changing for the worse. Now, it was the forbidden part - too steep, dark, slick, full of crumbling stones and unpredictable.

Mahine saw the drama coming, slowly collapsed on the ground, put her head in her hands and wept aloud rocking back and forth.

"Stop the race," Hina said to the king. "Don't murder this poor man. Please, for your daughter!"

"Go! Taatamao, go! go!" Tamatoa roared.

Kon came to a stop. Ahead of him was a large crevasse. He had to jump across, but the other side was covered with crumbling stones. Kon took a deep breath, jumped across, and landed on the top of a boulder that immediately rolled down. He had enough momentum to reach another boulder, which started rolling as well. Just in time, he reached the cliff with his hands and held it firmly. He looked behind, at the avalanche of rocks thundering into the deep valley.

In turn, Taatamao stopped at the edge of the crevasse, hesitated for a moment, held his breath and jumped across the deadly obstacle. He was more lucky than Kon and landed on a firmly anchored boulder. The two men were on their way to the summit, jumping from block to block. New avalanches shook the Mountain.

Soon, Taatamao realized he was losing the race. In a formidable rebound of energy he jumped faster and farther, but the Mountain waited: silent, implacable. Taatamao jumped once more. Suddenly, his foot landed on the forbidden spot. Everything collapsed under his foot. He lost his balance, and fell sideways. Taatamao screamed and knew he was going to die.

Kon heard him, then heard the familiar rumbling avalanche.

He stopped, and looked behind. He saw Taatamao tumble behind the falling rocks. Desperately, the young man attempted to hold on to boulders, cliff, ferns, but nothing was anchored strongly enough to hold his weight. The abysmal emptiness of the forbidden side of the mountain was coming fast.

In the blink of an eye, Taatamao saw a cluster of larger ferns. It was his last chance. First, he hit the ferns with his feet, went through them, grabbed them with his right hand, broke his wrist, grabbed them with his left hand and came to a stop. The silence came back, implacable. Taatamao was hanging by one hand above a terrifying world, with no place to rest his feet. It was the world of birds, where no man dared to venture.

Kon looked at Taatamao, quickly recalled the words of the Light: "When you hear the man screaming, give him a friendly hand of mercy. Between your fingers, a bond will develop, so strong that nobody would ever destroy it." Who was this inner being, guiding Kon Tici Viracocha? Kon himself did not know the answer. He only knew he would obey, follow his common sense, fulfill the will of his Creator.

Mahine screamed, beating her father. Tamatoa came closer to Hina, and grabbed her neck with one hand. She felt the powerful fingers of the tattooed giant pressing on her carotid. She thought her life had come to an end. From now on, Tamatoa's madness would be insurmountable. At that moment when she was losing faith in the meaning of the race, never would she have imagined the scenario that would follow.

Kon saw Taatamao in a very awkward position, unable to use his right arm. There was no possible support of any kind for his feet. Taatamao was hanging above the deep ravine, and would not have the strength to hold on very long. Tamatoa's men were too far away to rescue him. Kon knew he was Taatamao's only chance. Tera was already climbing among the crumbling blocks, paying no attention to Taatamao. Kon had two choices: either to continue, win the race, and condemn Taatamao to a certain death, or to help him, lose the race, and condemn the people of Tahiti-nui to live a nightmare.

For the common man, this could have been a dilemma, But for Kon Tici there was no choice. Yes, Kon Tici would stop racing, would give the victory to Tamatoa's son, and help a courageous warrior from being a victim of monstrous futility. Slowly, Kon found his way down toward Taatamao. Now, nothing could stop Tera from victory, and he knew it, so he slowed his pace and became very careful about each step. Kon had lost the race, but sometimes, small details may have the power of changing the world.

Tamatoa suddenly stopped walking, and an enigmatic grin came to his face. He saw Kon attempt a desperate rescue for a man who was a stranger, an adversary and an enemy. His mouth dropped open, and he recalled Kon's words: "I have no enemy."

"I don't believe this!" Tamatoa exclaimed, releasing Hina from his grip.

"Now, with your own eyes, you can see the real Kon Teke Viracocha," Hina said, with her lips trembling.

"I just cannot believe this!" Tamatoa murmured.

When Kon heard Taatamao groaning and some rocks fall beside the wounded man, he was afraid he would be too late.

"Hold strong, Taatamao. I am coming," Kon said.

His words gave energy and hope to the young man, who was almost at the limit of what he could endure.

"What is wrong with your right arm?" Kon asked.

"Broken!" Taatamao whispered.

Kon stopped just above Taatamao, secured his feet on the ferns, then reached Taatamao's uninjured wrist. Taatamao instantly gave up his grip on the fronds, and Kon felt the heavy weight of the man. He slowly moved Taatamao to one side, searched for a new anchor, found a narrow ledge, swayed Taatamao, who felt large ferns against his legs. Taatamao instantly wrapped his legs around the ferns, and Kon felt a relief on his arm. Taatamao was on solid ground. He was safe. The young warrior lay among the ferns, on a gentler slope. Kon would have to wait for the help of Tamatoa's men to bring him to safer ground. They waited, silent at first. Two large black eyes met two deep blue eyes. In them, there was joy, compassion and friendship: A powerful bond had taken place.

"Why did you do this?" Taatamao asked.

"Because, you and I are the ones who won the race," Kon replied with a smile.

Taatamao returned Kon's smile, but it was mixed with pain.

"Where do you hurt?" Kon asked.

"I broke several ribs," Taatamao said, grimacing each time he took a deep breath.

Taatamao was shaking from cold and from shock. Kon removed his garment and tightly wrapped Taatamao's chest with it. They both watched Tera progressing slowly toward the summit.

"Your master is going to be proud of his son," Kon said, with a sarcastic smile.

"Tera's victory is irrelevant," Taatamao said. "You don't know my master, and he is not the man you think he is."

Tamatoa glanced at his son, hesitated, then raised both arms toward the mountain. His thundering voice echoed everywhere, sending a shock wave strong enough to displace some gravel that had not found a stable place yet.

"Stop the race," Tamatoa screamed. "There is no need for a race."

Tera stopped, paralyzed by his father's words. Tamatoa glanced at Hina. She met his smile, and his hand that was offered to her. She took his hand, and returned his smile with a beautiful expression. Mahine was with Tamatoa's men who were rescuing Taatamao. Hina was alone with the king.

"Don't you think this race was worth something?" Hina asked.

"As you said earlier, tonight there are two winners, Kon Teke and Taatamao," Tamatoa replied.

"You have it all wrong," Hina argued. "Tonight there are two winners, your people and the people of Tahiti-nui."

"You have it all wrong," Tamatoa smiled. "Tonight, there are two winners, the Viracocha people and the Maohi people."

As soon as Taatamao was on safe ground, Mahine wrapped him in her arms, and she cried and laughed at the same time. Taatamao had fallen from the mountain, but he was alive and well: She was blissfully happy. Hina covered Kon with a bark-cloth and kissed him with passion. For a short instant she had almost lost faith in what he had been trying to do, but once more, she learned that Kon Tici could not be challenged on the Mountain: O the mountain he attained peace.

Kon walked toward Tamatoa.

"Shall we meet again?" Kon asked. "Even if I lost the race."

"You don't need to be sarcastic, young man," Tamatoa replied, putting one hand on Kon's shoulder. "I like your skills, your courage, and most of all, I like your magnanimity. Magnanimous people will never be my enemies."

A deep silence fell. Everyone glanced at one another, wondering if they had understood Tamatoa's words well. Tera still struggled among the crumbling rocks, on his way back.

"Why did you stop Tera?" Kon asked. "It was his race. He would have been happy to win it."

"I said there was no need for a race," Tamatoa roared. "The last few moon-cycles I let revenge control my mind. I had my revenge, and I let madness control my way of thinking. Then, I came here, and met remarkable people, who deserve my trust. For the first time, the word "peace" means something."

Hina could not believe what she heard, and she shook her head to make sure she was not dreaming. No, it was real, and Kon's plan was a total triumph.

"Hina is a wonderful young priestess," Tamatoa said. "Even before you rescued Taatamao, just because of her, I was already tempted to stop the race."

Hina felt tears rolling down her cheeks; she had a few compulsive sobs, jumped in Kon's arms, tied her legs around his waist, tousled his hair with her hands and kissed his head and long ears. The man she loved was an ambassador of peace.

"I have been unfair to you, my father," Mahine said.

"I have been too far away from you, my child," Tamatoa replied.

He took his daughter's hand, and pulled her against him. She buried her face against his massive chest, and for the first time in many years, Mahine felt the warmth of her father's love. She knew it was the beginning of a new era, and she trusted him greatly. She knew he would acknowledge his mistakes with honor, pride and style. It took a lot of skill for Tamatoa to look good for his people, as a winner against the Pora-Pora enemy, but it would require far more ability from Tamatoa to give back Havaiki, Huahine, and Moorea to the people who never were his enemies in the first place: It would take magnanimity.

Since dawn, the beast living inside Tamatoa had been pierced twice, by Hina's firm kindness, and by Kon's unshakable generosity. Tamatoa put his arm around Hina's shoulders.

"Mato and Mahine did not agree with the way I was leading my people," he said. "This is the answer I was supposed to give you this morning."

With infinite pride, she raised her chin and stared at him. Her eyes were shining with Mana's power. She was a superb priestess.

Slowly, she pulled something from under her garment. Tamatoa saw the delicate, sacred tiare flower between her fingers. It was the gift he wanted most, just this tiny flower she had shared with other people, a few days earlier. She put the flower on his ear, bent in front of him and murmured the magic words.

"You are indeed a king."

****

CHAPTER 22

"The fundamental rule of those who build a wise community calls for the respect of everything that lives in its environment. If we fail to comply with this rule, we do not deserve the ownership of what was given to us by the Creator. If we fail to look at beauty with silent humbleness, we are only a manure generator."

Kon Tici Viracocha

A few days later, after stormy negotiations, the kings of Havaiki and Huahine were allowed to take their kingdoms back, but they would remain under the control of the great Tamatoa, who agreed to give them ample freedom to rule their affairs, as long as they would not interfere with the interests of the new Pora Pora people. The islands of Pora Pora, Tahaa and Maupiti were parts Tamatoa's sacred kingdom whose inhabitants were called the new Pora Pora people. To everyone's surprise, Tamatoa was not the tyrant they had expected, and he did not rule with oppression or brutality. Tahiti-nui was free, and would keep the island of Moorea under its jurisdiction, as in the past. Everybody agreed it was time to prepare for the great gathering of the Maohis that would take place in Havaiki, at the Taputapu-atea Marae.

One morning, Tupua had the right words to describe Tamatoa: "His appearance is always stately and dignified. He is magnanimous and has a ready wit, but when necessary he can be stern. He is a man of honor; I like him." His words were the basis of a new order.

A few days later, at dawn, Kon and Hina went on an excursion with Tupua, Vana, Mahine and Taatamao. Mahine was delighted to be with Taatamao for the time it would take for his recovery. It had been Tamatoa's request that they would stay for some time in Papenoo, with Kon and Hina, and Tupua thought it had been a wonderful gesture of trust from his powerful neighbor. It had been Tupua's idea to take the small group of friends to a long journey to the magnificent and mysterious Vaihiria Lake. It would be a tribute to the splendor of the rain forest, and to all their efforts to maintain a precarious peace among themselves. The lake fascinated Kon, when he went there once, before he met Hina's people. Before they left Papenoo, they met a short time with Taaroa, who wanted to tell them a legend about the lake.

"I cannot go on such a long journey," Taaroa said. "But, when you are at the lake, I want you to remember me."

"So, you want to tell us about Tahiti-nui's legend," Hina said

"A long time ago," Taaroa said, "on Havaiki, there was a sacred ceremony held every sun-cycle, at the Taputapu-atea Marae. For two days, a strict taboo was implemented during which men and women were not supposed to walk or talk, roosters were not supposed to crow, dogs were not supposed to bark. One day during this ritual a young woman called Terehe did not respect the taboo and went to the river take a bath. Irritated, the gods punished Terehe and a huge eel attacked her. Terehe was so terrified before her death that her spirit left her body before the eel swallowed her, and became a wandering vortex of dust, but the eel was possessed by Terehe's body, and became a monster that went to the sea far away from Havaiki. After a few days, the monster developed roots and anchored itself where we are now, and became Tahiti, which means the separated one. Tahiti-nui was recognized by Orohena, which means the largest fin of the monster. Tahiti-iti was recognized by Moorea, which means the small fin of the monster. Deep inside the monster, the mouth, which is Lake Vaihiria, gigantic eels still live and are the object of many legends. Around Orohena and Vaihiria, you can still see Terehe's wandering spirit that often takes the form of a powerful vortex of dust."

Later, Taaroa watched his friends until they disappeared. It took them two days to follow the Papenoo River, then the Vaituoru River all the way to its springhead. They climbed the western flank of Mount Urufa beyond which Vaihiria was hiding. They followed a narrow trail within an incredible canopy of vegetation. At times, they were in total darkness, under the thick canopy of giant trees.

When they reached the divide between the northern and southern valleys, they saw spectacular jagged cliffs spreading their roots to the sea, making the monster look as if it was alive again. Then, straight down, not far away, was the beautiful blue Vaihiria Lake.

"Every time I see it, I cannot believe my eyes," Kon said, kneeling on the ground with respect.

"This is sacred land," Tupua said. "Only high dignitaries are authorized to approach the lake. It is Terehe's and Vaihiria's world, a weird one."

Kon took his time to admire the green hills surrounding the lake like half-circles. He observed the many creeks feeding the lake, and the numerous waterfalls plunging majestically from the jagged mountains. Quiet and silent, Vaihiria was set between the mountains like a dark blue jewel. With caution, they descended along a narrow ledge, until they reached a deep valley, where the lake disappeared from sight. Above the living canopy of trunks and branches, a few birds chirped in peace. When they found a spectacular arching waterfall foaming between giant ferns and enlightened by the magic of a rainbow, Kon stopped, astonished. Vana's face showed a mixture of pride and joy, and they all stared at the stunning scenery, silent. The continuous powerful rumble of the waterfall was a reminder of nature's force, like a timeless presence for an unknown purpose. They took a quick bath in the clear pool, and enjoyed the cool luxury of the mist washing their face. Then, they followed a creek, and finally reached a flat, enchanted botanical garden. It was not like the forest, but like a plantation created by the gods. There were trees of all kinds, fruits everywhere, and thick carpets of moss and ferns. The smell of flowers was a delight all along the trail, until, right in front of them, the blue lake was there, with its beauty, its peace and its appeal. When they reached the bank, they sat on a cover of moss whose cushion for their tired legs was refreshing.

"Is anyone living in such a beautiful place?" Mahine asked.

"This place does not belong to men, as Taaroa explained," Vana answered. "We can look at it, taste it and enjoy it for a short time. Then, we must leave, and nothing shall reveal that we have been here."

"A place like this deserves total respect," Kon said.

Beards and coats of ferns, moss and lichens mantled trees and shrubs. Everywhere on the ground, death and decay of plants inexorably recycled what was necessary for a new life. Time was not important. Man was not important. Man did not exist. A few ducks paddled nearby, ignoring the group: In their environment, nothing was questionable.

Mahine raised her hand toward a cluster of pink orchids.

"Don't!" Vana ordered. "You shall not pick flowers in this area. You can eat fruits, but just what you need."

"May I swim in the lake?" Mahine asked.

"Yes," Hina answered, "I am going with you."

Both women undressed and entered the blue water with respect. Hina swam far away from shore. Mahine, less adventurous, followed the bank at a short distance. Somehow, she did not feel comfortable in this very deep, legendary lake. She swam and walked in the water, and watched a mother duck, followed by seven newborn ducklings.

From a distance, Hina swam on her back, watching Mahine, and seemed to be waiting for something to happen.

"Why are you staying close to shore?" Hina asked.

"I fear these deep waters," Mahine replied. "Taaroa scared me with the legend."

"There is much more to fear in the lagoon," Hina said.

"I know," Mahine said, "but I know what to expect in it."

Hina continued watching her friend.

Suddenly, Mahine gasped with anxiety. She distinctly felt something sleek caressing her calf, and jumped aside.

"Are there large fish in this lake?" Mahine asked, quite disturbed.

"Oh yes!" Hina replied. "There are indeed strange fish in this lake."

"You try to scare me," Mahine objected.

"No, I am trying to tell you that where the water is deep could be less frightening for you."

"What do you mean?" Mahine asked, more concerned than ever.

"You are going to find out soon," Hina said, with a grin on her face.

"Tell me! This is not fair," Mahine said.

Hina continued to swim on her back, ignoring her friend. Mahine slowly walked toward the bank, where she could see the bottom of the lake. Through the clear water, she saw small fish, stones, sand, dead branches and finally a black tree trunk decaying in the water. Because of the waves she created, the trunk swirled slowly. Or, that was what she thought. Her instinct told her to stop. At the end of the trunk close to her, she saw two large black leaves, one on each side. The symmetrical way those leaves grew sent a signal to her mind: Something is not right. The trunk is not a trunk. She backed off slowly, and the long, dark mass swirled in her direction. She gasped, panting with terror. The thing was alive, crawling, impressive and awful. Total panic engulfed her and she screamed for help.

The men ran to her, and helped her get out of the water. She was shivering, and her eyes widened with fright.

"Have no fear my, child," Vana said, "you saw King Vaihiria. It is a harmless creature, and indeed a spectacular eel."

Hina laughed in sheer joy in the water.

"It is not funny!" Mahine protested. "Why is it that nobody told me anything? You waited for this to happen."

"Don't be angry," Tupua chuckled. "We laugh because it happened, but there was no malice on our part."

"You maybe, but I know Hina was waiting for this."

Taatamao glanced at Kon and giggled.

"You, too, you are making fun of me," Mahine said, with fire in her eyes.

"Don't make me laugh," Taatamao said, "it hurts my ribs."

Hina came out from the water and took Mahine's head against her shoulders.

"Don't be angry with me," Hina said. "You are my friend,

and one day you may rightly tease me."

Mahine released her fear on Hina's chest, with a few tears in her eyes.

"I hate that animal," she whispered gently. "It was larger than my thigh, and another one crawled between my legs."

Tonight, I will tell you about the Vaihiria legend," Vana said with a gentle tone.

"Another one!" Mahine objected.

They walked around the lake, circled the roots of sharp cliffs that made their progress difficult. They struggled through vines, leaves, trunks, creepers and swamps. They reached the point where, on rare occasions, the lake overflowed toward the southern valley. By midday, they found a small Marae, surrounded by two modest dwelling houses, an ultimate retreat for priests in search of inner peace.

"How deep is the lake?" Kon asked.

"Nobody knows," Vana replied. "Taaroa pretends there is no bottom, and this is why those eels are so big: They come from the center of the earth."

"The lake rarely overflows," Tupua said, "yet it is always full."

"With all these waterfalls, this surprises me," Kon said.

"The spirits of the depths regulate the level of the lake," Vana said.

"This is the reason we shall not alter anything around it," Tupua added.

"What a magnificent harmony between mountains and valleys," Kon said, "between vegetation and water, and between life and death."

"What would your people do with a place like this?" Tupua asked.

"It would be a sanctuary for man," Kon replied. "We would

build a Marae as you did, for our children to learn what beauty really is. Beyond the Marae, everything would be left to the wisdom of wilderness."

"So," Hina said, "if there is wisdom in wilderness, this means it is organized."

"Yes," Vana smiled with approval, "I recognize the child you have always been, who often came with impossible questions. I always enjoyed them."

"The chaos of nature is only an illusion created by man," Kon said. "Our notion of order is a product of primitive naivete. The true order is immensely complex which makes it look like chaos for the uninitiated. It is our pride, our arrogance, our neglect and our thirst for possessions that lead to true chaos."

"I like what you said," Vana murmured, looking at the lake with melancholy. "It is so true."

Hina sat, and gently caressed the fragile moss on the ground, with the tip of her fingers.

"So, one day, we may destroy this place," she said.

"Perhaps we will," Vana said.

"It all depends if we can reach the valley of self-discipline before it is too late," Kon said.

"What do you mean?" Hina asked, puzzled.

"Self-discipline is an immense valley," Kon replied, "like this lake and its surrounding gardens. On each side of the valley you have two worlds: The world of which you were at birth, and the world of which you want to be."

"These two opposite worlds drain water, and give life to the valley," Vana said.

"Precisely," Kon pursued, "let's cultivate our garden in the valley, with harmony to its surroundings, and one day raise our head as a winner."

"Otherwise, it will be fire, dirt, blood and chaos," Vana added.

"But, victory can be ours," Kon said. "For the first time, we will understand the purpose of being. The Light, this incredible force which is waiting for a sign that we have reached wisdom, will finally speak to us."

"The Light will speak to us as a group, or as an individual?" Hina asked.

"As an individual." Kon replied. "Our experience with the Light is a personal one: It is a task for each of us to perform. It is not difficult: With honesty and kindness be who you want to be."

Everyone looked at one another and took a pause.

"So, there is incredible power in peace and beauty," Hina said.

Vana looked at her, and pointed a finger at Kon.

"You see what I meant," Vana said, "this child is gifted. She has a wonderful ability to turn words around."

Kon looked at the golden pendant on her chest, glittering through her hair. She was indeed a wonderful keeper of this condor and this sun. He smiled at her, and looked at the summits.

"Hina of the Valley," Kon said with a loud voice echoing across the lake, "If I find my people, would you help me build a society where your people and mine would live forever in harmony?"

She smiled, showing her white teeth and a radiant face.

"Yes, I will, Kon Tici Viracocha. But, I belong to Tahiti-nui."

Vana did not notice any difference in her voice, or the subtlety of her statement, but Kon most certainly did. It was the first time she had pronounced his name entirely right, which added tremendous lucidity to her statement: Hina would not leave her valley, her people, her island. He knew she was absolutely sincere. He knew they would have a tough life, and there was no need for further words. They were all at peace with themselves, and silently, they listened to many hardly noticeable sounds: duck and ducklings, a fish and a splash of water, a parakeet and a broken nut, a flying insect and a flower dripping water, a tiny peeper and its shrill song, a faraway tropicbird and its flapping wings, the distant thunder of waterfalls,... Even for the blind, it would have been a paradise.

At dusk, when they heard the chirp of crickets and saw the first stars, they went back to the nearby Marae. Under a dwelling house, Tupua and Taatamao had prepared a fire, and Mahine worked to prepare the evening meal.

"You did everything," Hina said to her friends. "You worked hard when I was enjoying myself."

"I did not work hard," Mahine replied, "I enjoyed myself preparing something that would give you pleasure."

Mahine's modesty was equal to her beauty. She took a stick, and removed two breadfruits from under the embers. She unwrapped the many layers of charred banana leaves protecting them. With Hina's help, she removed the hard shell of the fruits. Then, the yellow, tender, steaming flesh was sliced and passed around to everyone. Mahine gave empty half coconut shells to her friends, and from a heavy gourd poured a thick beverage she had prepared with coconut milk, crushed vanilla beans, and a pasty mush of taro and wild sugarcane. She unwrapped a large bundle of burned banana leaves inside which were steamy giant bananas with purple flesh, starchy taro tubers, and mape chestnuts. Finally, she brought a plate with colorful berries, young fern fronds and tiny green gherkins.

"As you did not know this place, it shows how resourceful you are," Tupua complimented, looking at the food with widening eyes.

Vana ate some breadfruit, then raised his arms.

"Now comes the time for you to listen to the Vaihiria legend."

"Are you going to talk about this horrible eel?" Mahine asked with concern.

"Do not fear my child," Vana said, "you will like the story."

"I have heard several versions of this legend," Hina said, "only one is a good story."

"This is precisely the one I chose," Vana smiled.

"A long time ago, the Sun and Moon's daughter, whose name was Hina, was taking a walk around Vaihiria Lake," Hina started. Then, she stopped when she saw a vague hint of disapproval on her father's face.

"Hina swam in the lake," Vana continued, "until she met King Vaihiria. She had heard about the king, but it had never occurred to her that it would have been a horrible giant eel from the earth's depths."

Mahine sat near Taatamao, and rested her head on his thigh. The wounded warrior caressed her cheeks gently.

"When Hina saw the monster crawling in her direction, she jumped out of the water, and ran away inside the rain forest, terrified."

"Are you sure her name was not Mahine?" Mahine asked.

"But the awesome eel followed Hina; the eel was in love with Hina."

"Great!" Mahine murmured. Tupua looked at her with a hint of disapproval.

"Hina went to a distant island that had been found by Maui, king of navigators. Maui took Hina under his protection. The eel went to the abysses of Vaihiria Lake and easily reached the forbidden island. Aware of the danger, the eel watched Hina in secrecy from a distance, for a long time."

Vana looked at the two young couples, and pointed a finger at them.

"Beware of passion. There are times when emotions such as love or hate may govern your actions. Then, you may be pushed by inner forces to do things beyond your control. The eel from Vaihiria loved Hina, but could not have her. Love became passion, with willingness to kill, then possess. There were two solutions for the eel: either killing Maui and taking Hina, or killing Hina to make sure nobody would possess her. The eel nurtured the ideas for a long time, until one day, along the bank of the river where it was hiding, it met Hina by accident."

"I know you love me," Hina said to the eel, "but I am not one of yours. Don't kill me because you cannot possess me. Don't kill Maui because he wants to protect me. Be magnanimous, and do what courage alone can do. Then, and only then, you will be in my memory as a hero for eternity."

"Moved by Hina's words, the eel went to the darkness of the rain forest, and fought its passion for days, for moon-cycles. One day, the eel took the ultimate step, went to Hina's house during the night, dug a huge hole near the house, until it could hide its enormous head inside. The eel from Vaihiria entered the darkness of the earth forever."

Vana drank some of Mahine's beverage, and glanced at her.

"Do you know what happened to the eel, after that?" Vana asked.

"I would prefer to know what happened to Hina," Mahine replied.

"The next morning, Hina walked outside her house, and saw the dead eel. From its head sprang many roots. Its body was growing straight to the sky. Its tail developed fronds that flowed in the morning breeze. This is how Hina found the first coconut tree, and took care of it for the rest of her life. A long time after that day, Hina brought some young coconuts from that tree to Tahiti-nui, and planted them around this lake. This is why Vaihiria Lake has the most magnificent coconut trees."

"After all, King Vaihiria is a nice creature," Mahine said, with compassion in her eyes.

At some distance, they saw a vortex of dust wandering near the lake.

"This is Terehe's spirits," Vana said.

"I am not so sure," Mahine said. "I saw this several times, and Kon is always present in it."

"What do you mean?" Kon said, with amusement in his eyes.

"I saw you in the vortex, several days before we met, at the Taputapu-atea Marae. I was sitting on the white monolith."

"Were you asleep?" Kon asked.

"I was in deep meditation, doing what Mato taught me."

"So, you are not sure you were fully awake when you saw me," Kon said.

"I am not sure," Mahine replied.

"I saw it several times," Hina said, "but I always thought the wind was doing this."

"If you are awake when you see it," Kon said, "there is never anything special about it. But, if you see it in a dream or in a meditation, there are often pertinent visions associated with it. I experienced this myself, many times."

"There are spirits," Vana said, raising his arms. "I keep telling you there are spirits everywhere in our lives."

Suddenly, they heard the strong wind between the coconut trees, dust flew everywhere, the roof of one dwelling house ruffled violently, ash from the fire swirled into the air: The vortex was here, stationary on the fire. They all watched, astonished. Then, the vortex became smaller, moved toward the lake and vanished above the water.

They all looked at each other, wondering what that thing was trying to tell them. For a moment, they remained silent. Kon himself seemed puzzled, and challenged by the force of something unknown, but something else awaited that night. They heard the rain falling on the roof of the dwelling house, and it was the only rumble they could hear until they finished their meal. Then, the rain stopped. Right away, they thought something was unusual. Vana went outside, and looked at the sky. There was no moon, and no stars. The silence was total.

"Do you hear anything?" Kon asked.

"There is nothing to listen to," Vana replied, "the cricket is gone, the peeper is gone,...,; they know."

"What do they know we don't?" Hina asked.

"They know the time when earth awakes with destructive fury," Vana said. "They know the season for hurricanes has arrived, and you saw a sample of one. There is a storm coming."

"Are you sure?" Mahine asked, concerned for her seafaring parents.

"Yes," Vana said, "when the cricket and the peeper turn silent, it presages for a very bad storm."

"I knew it!" Tupua said. "I knew he would talk about omens. He cannot say anything without mentioning them."

Everybody laughed in a jovial way. Then, they became silent, and listened for the cricket and the peeper. There was neither cricket, nor peeper sound.

"How long from now?" Tupua asked, pointing a finger on Vana's chest.

"Two days, maybe three," Vana replied.

"We shall leave at dawn," Tupua said with resolve.

That night, Hina and Kon could not sleep. They sat near the fire, and Hina laid her head on his thigh.

"Today, you said something I don't understand," Hina murmured. "The world of who we are at birth, and the world of who we want to be."

"You may think you came into this world knowing nothing," Kon said. "In fact, you were born with a treasure of knowledge. As you grow by necessity, and mature by circumstances, this treasure fades away, swamped by what you are told to learn. Either by deliberate choice, or because of others, you forget who you are, until you discover who you want to be."

"Who I am, and who I want to be, can be very different," Hina said, with her eyes lost in the fire.

"As you learn, you may forget who you are for some time," Kon said. "New knowledge must be digested, transit through yourself as needed, and used by forces living in your mind. Then, and only then, you may trigger a powerful surge of creativity and become someone you would like to be."

"I still don't know what the treasure is I was born with," Hina said.

"The treasure is your ability to be creative," Kon said. "Some people learn all during their lives, but create nothing: They go by, unnoticed. They were born that way. "Am I creative?" Hina asked, with a frown on her face.

"You are very much so, and you should remain that way. This is why Vana and many others like you so much. At birth, it was a faint star living in you, later in your life it must become the shining sun, and at the evening of your life it must spread its fantastic energy to others: This is who you want to be."

"So, what I learn is only some kind of food for my mind. It is only half the story. The other half is what I am going to do with it: It must be new, it must be useful to others, it must make those who live near me happy and those who are far off attracted."

"Beautifully said!" Kon concluded.

Two days later, Hina left her Marae and went to the beach. It was very cloudy, there was no wind and it was hot. Far away, she saw Kon walking toward the Teauroa Point. She took her father's outrigger, and paddled in Kon's direction. She looked at the quiet lagoon. Her land, her mountains, her valley and her lagoon could never be the same again. Now, deep in them, the name of Kon Tici Viracocha was an eternal presence, and she realized how important he had become in her life. Still, she knew that one day he would leave, searching for his people. She feared for that day: It would be the impossible day.

Again and again, she reflected on Kon's words, and in her mind a faint star was shining. It was the star she was born with, the star she would cultivate and cherish. Never before had she seen it, and it was so faint that the beautiful priestess was afraid to lose it forever. Surrounding this humble light was a tumultuous, spiraling storm of many dazzling stars: It was the others, and what she had learned from them. Was it too late for the faint star to take command, and bring Mana in everything she did? Hina wanted to know, and she would.

Kon heard the familiar lapping of a paddle in the clear lagoon; it was unmistakable and music to his ears. He knew it was Hina and did not have to turn around to find out. The lapping stopped, the outrigger slid on the sand, then he heard nothing, but he felt a warm presence behind him, and Hina put her hands on his shoulders.

"Since the race, you have been talking to Tamatoa often," Hina said. "Do you find the man interesting?"

"He has traveled to places unknown to me," Kon replied," and I have seen places unknown to him. We concluded this world is much larger than we ever imagined."

"Do you think you may travel with him?" Hina asked.

"Maybe I will," Kon replied, surprised by her question and the tone of her voice, tinted with concern. "But, I will always come back to you."

"Perhaps you will," she said, "if the awesome sea permits."

Hina looked at Mount Orohena, turning her back to Kon, so he did not notice blinding tears in her eyes. She remained silent for a while, then looked at the sea and wondered what was most dangerous for both of them: the mountain or the awesome sea?

"The mountain and the awesome sea!" she whispered.

"What did you say?" Kon asked.

"The mountain and the awesome sea are your two loves, and your two reasons to live. Both possess you, and caught in the middle, there is a tiny flower who also wants to share some of your time. Would Kon Tici give some of his time to the little flower?"

Kon finally understood her emotions and her drama. He saw spreading agony in her eyes, fright in her tormented face, and he heard the pain in her trembling voice.

He went to her, held her face gently in his long hands, and kissed her with passion. Hina's head spun, and for an instant, the world was theirs. She pushed him aside, then undressed herself slowly, worshipfully, until she was Hina, only. She was magnificent, with her long black hair for her only dress, hanging in graceful curves over her shoulders and above her breasts. She took his hands, pressed her lips against hers, and looked at his deep blue eyes.

"My life crossed the most unique being on this earth," she

said. "I am perfectly aware of what you will do, and where you will go, Kon Tici."

She looked at the sea with a mysterious depth Kon knew well, and he immediately saw the uprising tide of Hina's sentiments. She was unique in her ability to turn over situations in unpredictable ways. In a short instant, she could rise from the abysmal depth of despair to courage and dazzling determination. Now, she was the gracious, genial priestess, and showed reassuring satisfaction in her eyes.

"Kon Tici, let me give you a few facts," Hina said, with her eyes shining, large and charming. She was an integral beauty, with her mind in superb harmony with her body. "Your triumph of the last few days is only a short leap in your destiny. You conquered this mountain because it was our only way to this peace of the moment. You saved the life of an adversary because it was the sacred sign given to you by the Light. Now, your adversary shall become a powerful friend at sea. Somewhere, beyond the eastern horizon, Viracocha's men and women are still fighting the elements for survival, and they wait for you. This is your destiny, Son of the Sun!"

Kon looked at her, surprised she had thought about an idea he himself had nurtured for some time.

"Tamatoa is the man with whom you will achieve everything," she said. "He must be your friend. With your mind and his mastery of the sea, you will find your brother Illa."

Kon wrapped his arms around her midriff; her head fit in the hollow between his shoulders and neck, and she saw herself inside his shiny golden earplug.

"Would you come with me?" Kon whispered in her ear.

"No, I will not," she replied. "I belong to Tahiti-nui; in Tahiti-nui I shall stay."

Hina's words were exactly what he understood she had said at Vaihiria Lake. He was not surprised, but her words sent pain to his soul. He closed his eyes, and felt his heart pounding and aching.

"But, I will have your children," she said. "I will name our first son Maui. He will become the most extraordinary navigator of all time. He will be the king of the sea, educated by Hina of the Valley and the Son of the Sun. At times, I will lose you both. But, you will be back, richer, and stronger. This is the prophesy of a priestess."

She walked to the outrigger, her breast thrust forward, and her long hair waving in the freshening hot breeze.

"I have this vision of someone mastering you, the ones you love, Tamatoa,...," she said. "All this is to give birth to a new world and a new order."

Kon came behind her, put his hands on her shoulders, and she buried her face against his chest. He felt the sweetness of her warmth, and his body instantly melted against hers. She felt his desire intensifying. She showed her beauty, but would keep her desires for later. She turned around, ran on the hot sand, retrieved her garments and dressed herself.

"Tonight, I will show you another side of your destiny," she said, with passion in her eyes.

A frigatebird came above them, sounded a few grunts, and made graceful soaring circles. Kon caught a small crab, and presented it to the bird. The deeply forked tail of the majestic bird opened up. The bird rapidly maneuvered in flight, and plunged at amazing speed toward the lagoon, soared just above the water, and came straight to Kon, picking up the crab at full speed with its long, sharply hooked bill.

"That bird trusted you," Hina said. "It would never come

right away like this to anyone else."

"Why do you think I should be any different for that bird?"

"Because you are different," Hina said, gently. "Because the bird is like me, and noticed this unmistakable signal of peaceful force the first time it saw you. It is obvious when you talk, walk, sleep or do anything. Others noticed this too; my father did, Vana did, Taaroa did, even Tamatoa did. They all know Kon Tici is a shooting star passing through the clear sky of Tahiti-nui. It is beautiful, enlightening and inspiring, but it passes too fast. So, they come and listen, afraid to let this unique opportunity go by."

She put her belt of shiny cowries around her white robe. She had the serenity of gifted people, and looked royal. Kon knew he had never met anyone who learned so fast, and created so much on her own: He loved everything about her. He took her hands and felt her warmth drifting from her fingers into his entire body: Something in her was Viracocha. Mana was with her.

Here he was, very far away from his home, alone in a land completely different, with people even more different. Yet, he knew Hina was his final destination. He felt that from now on, nothing could be done without her, but he would have to leave, and she would have to stay. Something was not right. Intuitively, Kon knew something was still missing, and he would soon find out what it was.

They jumped in the outrigger, and paddled across the lagoon. Behind the reef, the deep blue sea was calm. They went through the pass, and stayed nearby the sunken barrier of corals. There was neither current, nor waves. The tranquillity and transparency of the underlying world fascinated them. They stopped paddling, and enjoyed a silent and slow drift.

Suddenly, at the instant they expected it the least, and with the majestic power of its slick body, a dolphin jumped up in the air, flipped once, then twice, and came down in a huge splash. Instants later, the dolphin came out of the water just ahead of the outrigger. This time, Kon and Hina felt the splashed water in their faces, and they laughed in sheer joy.

"This animal is beautiful!" she said. "Do you think it was also born with some knowledge, like us?"

"It must be," Kon replied. "What a jump! It is playing."

Hina thought the dolphin's majesty was a tribute to their earlier conversation, and to everything they had said since their trip to Vaihiria. Nothing more beautiful than the formidable jump of the dolphin could translate as accurately the state of their minds. Anyone could see in this jump the connection with their visionary ascendant. Kon understood it silently and Hina understood it with a radiating smile of triumph. She was so alive, so energetic, and felt the urgency of giving, of learning, of creating, of loving, that for the last time the powerful animal went into the depths, disappeared in the dark blue abyss, and suddenly Hina jumped in the outrigger.

"It is coming back!"

For the last time, the dolphin broke the surface at full speed, heading for the sky. It flipped once, twice, and a third time, before raising into the air a screen of water and white foam. They could distinctly hear its strident calls as it touched the sea. The dolphin did not come back, but Hina and Kon were enthralled with what they had witnessed.

"This was in your honor," Kon murmured.

She smiled, took the paddle and firmly stroked the calm water.

"Let's go home," Hina said. "The little flower showed you what the beautiful is, and the dolphin just showed you what the sublime is. It is enough for one day."

****

CHAPTER 23

"My ship is more than a ship, it is my home and a friend that takes me across the awesome sea. It has a soul and possesses me completely. If it dies, I may willingly die with it."

Tamatoa the great

The rain poured with force on Tupua's house. In a corner of the main room, Hina wove vegetable mats with her mother, her sister and Mahine. Taatamao, still recovering, sat on the ground near the entrance, and watched the men outside, preparing the village to survive the violent storm. Vana came with Mato and Taaroa, and laughed at the way their clothes were soaked. Hina brought them dry garments.

"Did you see Kon and my father?" she asked.

"They are coming," Vana replied.

In the middle of the room, Atea placed a few breadfruits under the embers of a fire. The evening would be long and, as customary, children would listen to Vana's stories with eyes wide open. Hina recalled these moments when she would challenge the high priest with difficult questions for the fun of it.

"What legend do you want me to tell?" Vana asked.

"Long ago," Hina replied, "you told us about the ghostly spirits living in the strait of madness between Tahiti-nui and Moorea, during storms. Many of us would like to hear why the channel between the two islands is so dangerous."

Vana's face became sad, and his eyes looked straight in the embers. Kon recalled the famous storm he had been through the night before reaching Tahiti-nui.

"Kon Teke," Vana said, "you were fortunate not to be driven into the channel. If you had been, today you would be in the world of spirits."

"I was protected by the tropicbird," Kon replied.

"What is happening between the two islands during storms?" Mahine asked with a concerned face.

"Do not fear, my child." Vana replied. "Your father knows the sea very well, and at this time he would never cross the channel."

"A few days ago we were in the channel," Taatamao said, "and I noticed swift, swirling currents."

"Yes, swirling currents!" Vana said "Eastern currents meet western currents leading to a fight between two giants. As a result the channel is never quiet. During storms, all this is magnified and the sea becomes a devastating force able to swallow anything. It is a living spirit feeding on the unwary traveler in a terrifying way. You would hear voices at night calling for help, you would hear breaking outriggers crushed by the jaws of unforgettable sea swells, and you would have visions of ghostly ships long gone. Those who die in the channel are condemned to scream, lament and fear for eternity. Their soul is caught in a spiral of incredible force that would never release its grip. It is something unknown anywhere else. In such a place, the question is not how to escape death, but how long it would take to die. From such a place, you never return and you vanish without a trace...."

Earlier the same day, Tamatoa went back to the Paopao Bay in Moorea where his wife, Tehani, waited for his return from

Havaiki. For some time, she had noticed profound changes in her husband's attitude: He was more relaxed and calmer than usual, but above all, he was kinder. She kept wondering how such a thing was possible. She went to his ship, and talked with him for a long time. They ate and drank together, a luxury she had forgotten for many moon-cycles. He complimented her with gentle words, an act she never thought possible from the man she loved. At this moment she wondered if she was with someone else. She finally realized the immense suffering and harshness they had been through had come to an end. Tamatoa was prepared for a peaceful time, but no one else ever thought it would come so soon, so fast, so unexpectedly. She could not help being incredulous.

"What kind of man can cause such deep changes in you, in so short a time?" she asked.

Tamatoa looked at the dark sky in the northwest.

"It is not just a man, but a context," Tamatoa replied. "It is Kon Teke and his magnanimity. It is Hina of the Valley and her ability to make a tiny flower look like a kingdom. It is Vana the great priest and his humor. It is Tupua the king and his kindness. It is Taaroa the ill and his willingness to suffer if he can see the good health of others. It is the mountain and its beauty, the stars at night I saw for the first time, and the song of birds. It is also the nobility of my daughter's heart, the unconditional support of those who work for me such as Mato, Taatamao, my sons and you."

He paused for a moment, still looking at the approaching storm. Tehani was astonished by his words.

"Many of these things are not new," she said, putting a friendly hand on his shoulder. "I still wonder who is the man who can let you see this just now, at the right time."

"We are going to leave now," Tamatoa said. "We may reach

Tahiti-nui before the storm arrives."

This was the time when Tamatoa made his greatest mistake at sea.

As the fleet left the Paopao Bay, the wind was still blowing gently. It was early in the afternoon, and still sunny at times. Tamatoa's ship led the fleet as they turned southwestward, followed by Tehani's ship on his north side, and the ship of his son Mehao immediately behind her.

They were still close to Moorea when they encountered unusually large sea swells. For an instant, Tamatoa thought he may not have been wise to leave Moorea on that day. He turned around and saw Tahiti-nui on the horizon. He shook his head, and rejected the idea of reversing course.

Later, at about one-third of their journey, Tamatoa noticed details on the sea that had escaped his attention the first time he had crossed the channel a few days earlier. He clearly saw that counter currents were responsible for the massive sea swells. Several times, he saw waves run into one another, resulting in high columns of water immediately collapsing into huge, swirling pools. Surprised and silent, he glanced at the sky and did not like what he saw. He took his conch, which he blew powerfully, giving the signal to all ships to paddle full speed toward Tahiti-nui.

Thick clouds encircled Moorea, whose mountains were no longer visible. Suddenly, the wind increased and became a brutal force. The rain poured, and within an instant the sky became very dark. Sea swells increased in size and dangerousness. Tamatoa realized the extent of his mistake, with many of his best ships at sea. He looked at Tehani's ship, too close to Mehao's ship. With his conch he tried to tell them to put more distance between them, but nobody looked at him or heard him: The wind rumbled with power, and each ship was on its own.

A tall steep wave assaulted Tamatoa's ship, which climbed to the edge like a wood chip. One warrior fell into the sea. Just in time, Tamatoa grabbed his arm and brought him back on board. Everyone secured themselves to the ship with ropes.

Suddenly, Tamatoa's ship was caught in a large, swirling pool. Warriors tried to paddle outside this frightening phenomenon in which they would lose control of the ship. Next, they saw a rolling hill of water coming, growing, climbing, and passing under the ship. Another one came, immense, steeper, and took the ship to its crest, then passed. A third one came, awesome, its height not seen before. Some warriors screamed, terrified. Time came to a stop. Climbing the wave was an eternity: Would the crest turn the ship over?

The ship went through the crest, and cracked violently in the middle. Several men tried to add structural ropes attaching the two hulls of the ship to one another. Tamatoa knew more waves like this one would come soon. Now, the visibility was nil, and the ship went in circles several times: There was no direction to follow. The pattern of waves was completely erratic, and no longer a reference. Nothing could give them a clue as to where they were between the two islands. They were trapped in the legendary channel of no return, between two deadly barriers of coral on which they could crash at any time. Tamatoa remained calm and concentrated on his options: There were none. He thought his fleet was about halfway between the two islands, therefore fairly far from the barriers of coral, at least for now. For the first time, the powerful warrior felt vulnerable at sea.

The storm was at its full strength. It should still have been daylight, but it was dark as night. The wind was so powerful that a huge quantity of water climbed in the air at the crest of waves, creating thick mist, rain of salted water, and total loss of visibility. Tamatoa had no fear of death; he never did, and never would. Yet, he was devastated at the thought he had taken his wife and one of his sons into a deadly trap from which it would take a miracle to escape alive. For a moment, he saw his life in perspective and realized how precarious were all the values to which he had given his tremendous energy and passion. How much time had he given to the woman he loved? None! The word rang in his ears with each giant rolling wave. He thought his head would explode. Desperately, he tried to find Tehani's ship through the fog, and indeed, the spirits would give him satisfaction with a vision that would destroy his mind.

For a faint moment, he saw another ship crash violently against Tehani's ship, and many people fell into the sea from both ships. Then, a powerful wave took Tamatoa's ship in a swirling course. He tried to recall in which direction he had seen the ships, but another wave almost turned his ship upside down, then another one, and another one....

The sea was mad and empty. He never saw a trace of his wife. Worse, he was almost sure the other ship had been Mehao's ship. He heard the ululating wind call their name. He heard the fury of the night call Tehani,... Mehao,... He heard the ghosts of darkness laugh at him. He realized the tremendous price he would pay for his mistakes. He kneeled on the deck, and surprised himself murmuring unbelievable words:

"Kon, Hina, help me!"

With humbleness and respect for the awesome sea the tattooed giant raised his arms toward the sky, and saw something coming to him. At first, he thought he was hallucinating, but he was lucid, and the shadow became real. The phantom took form and color. The bird of luck was right here. It was a white-tailed tropicbird, looking for refuge, exhausted. It landed on the deck, and walked by Tamatoa's side. He observed the bird and found it to be pretty. He, the great Tamatoa, who never paid attention to birds, was seduced by the sacred bird. In the storm that tormented his mind and crushed his pride, he found a bird and cared for it; he found a beautiful being and protected it; he found the meaning of life and the reward of giving. He sat on the deck, took the tropicbird under his flowing red robe, and the bird looked at him with trust. Tamatoa began a very long night during which he listened to the wind, watched the rain smashing the deck and the lightning showing the surroundings for very short moments. He wanted to cry, and expel his suffering. He wanted to give his love to the woman he had forgotten for so long. He wanted to give up all his ambitions. He was submitting, unconditionally.

Later in the night, the storm calmed down, and Tamatoa noticed there were no swirling currents. Then, the wind ceased. He knew it was a false signal. The storm would be back, blowing in the opposite direction. Indeed, it did not take long before the wind whistled slowly at first, then accelerated to incredible power, breaking masts, pulling planks from the deck, destroying everything. Again, for the rest of the night, Tamatoa and his men were the prisoners of the roiling channel. The bird was still here, waiting, and resting.

At dawn, the storm calmed down, at last. The sea swells were still impressive but not dangerous. The visibility became better, and good enough to avoid crashing on the reef by surprise. Tamatoa inspected his ship and found all his men. A few waved at him, but none had the strength to paddle, and none dared to untie themselves from the ropes yet. With his usual thundering voice, Tamatoa gave orders to take control of the ship, but his voice did not reach them. His words got lost among much louder howling spirits. He would have to wait a little more. Maybe, the best thing he could do was to rest, recover and listen for the reef, like the bird. Soon, he knew he would be able to organize his search.

By midday the wind diminished, the sea calmed down and the tropicbird took its flight in the direction of Tahiti-nui. It was enough for Tamatoa to guess in which direction the island was. Slowly, the daylight became more intense and the visibility improved. The hills of Tahiti-nui were visible under a thick cover of clouds. Not far away, the barrier of coral roared with fury. Tamatoa followed the dangerous reef to the first pass, and he found out that most of his ships had survived the storm. However, there was no trace of Tehani and Mehao's ships. Tamatoa regrouped the greater part of his fleet, and went back to the open sea, searching for wreckage. He went back to the legendary channel, now much calmer. They indeed found many pieces of wood and clothing on the surface of the sea. They wandered for three days and three nights, until it became clear to Tamatoa that it was hopeless to continue the search. He had lost his loved ones, and he was the only one to be blamed for it. Reluctantly, he stopped the search, and sailed to Papenoo, heartbroken, humiliated and looking older.

When Mahine saw her father, she did not ask questions, and she wept in his arms, devastated. He gently caressed her hair, and kissed her forehead.

"They died with honor; I survived with pity," Tamatoa murmured with a trembling voice.

Hina and Taatamao came to ease Mahine's distress. Tamatoa went to the beach, alone. He did not want to share his suffering with anyone, but he felt a presence behind him, and a friendly hand landed on his shoulder. He turned around, and saw compassion on Kon Tici's eyes.

"Sometimes, when you have no proof, you may wrongly

assume everything is hopeless," Kon said. "May I convince you to go to sea, and try again?"

"I don't know," Tamatoa said, looking at Kon with empty eyes.

"They vanished in your mind," Kon said. "But, the sea is immense, and they may still be desperately waiting for you, somewhere."

Tamatoa came close to Kon, looked him straight in the eyes, still perplexed.

"Why should you care about them, or about me?"

"Because I like tough adversaries," Kon replied with firmness, and no hesitation. Once more, Kon Tici's magic was at work.

Tamatoa looked at the sea, took a few steps into the water and turned around.

"Would you come with me?" the great warrior asked.

"Of course!" Kon replied. "Take your twelve best ships. Enhance their mast with a long bamboo pole, so we can climb higher and see farther at sea."

Tamatoa looked at the masts of his ships anchored at some distance, and looked back at Kon.

"I like your idea. What else do we need?"

"We need Vana with us," Kon said. "He knows the complex pattern of the currents around these islands."

"I thought about asking for Tupua's help," Tamatoa said. "But my stupid pride told me not to."

"Let me take care of this," Kon said.

"No!" Tamatoa replied, stopping Kon with his hand. "I must do it myself. It is important. Take me to him."

While sitting on the trunk of a old coconut tree, Tupua saw both men coming.

"I wonder what they are up to," Hina said to her father.

"I need your help," Tamatoa said, with a moderate tone.

"What do you need?" Tupua asked, with visible pride.

"I need Kon and Vana to come on my ship for another search at sea. It may take a few days."

Tupua did not look surprised: He knew it was Kon's idea.

"You may take them with you," Tupua said.

"I will go with you." Hina said.

"No Hina..." Tupua started. He saw his daughter staring at him in a way that paralyzed him instantly. Hina's personality had greatly changed, and she had the remarkable talent to impose her views without saying one word. It was all in her eyes, with the Maohi's pride and the Viracocha's magic.

Surprised, Tamatoa glanced at Tupua, then looked at Hina. Kon smiled, amused: They all knew she would be part of the search.

Later, at dusk, Hina had a long discussion with her father, Vana and several other dignitaries. Nearby, Atea and Fenua prepared the evening meal.

"Did you notice the tone of your sister?" Atea murmured. "They all respect her."

"Hina likes to be with men," Fenua replied. "With us, she is bored."

"You should not talk like this about your sister," Atea said.

"I am not criticizing, mother; it is a fact. We just don't measure up to her, but I love her the way she is."

Atea nodded with her head as a sign of approval. As a mother, she had witnessed Hina's changes, and she was proud of her wild child, but it was increasingly more difficult to be close to her. Hina was becoming the center of the world for many people. Everyone wanted to be with her, to talk with her, and share her life. From young children to the elderly, from warriors to priests, from the ill to the king himself, they all wanted her attention. With wise patience, she would listen to everyone, and give herself completely. Sometimes, when she was in a hurry, with just a few words she would enlighten someone and vanish to other duties. Atea saw all this, and she developed deep respect for her daughter.

Fenua brought a piglet she had killed earlier, and filled it with taros, bananas cut in cubes and spices from the valley. She rubbed it with thick coconut milk, and wrapped it inside several layers of green banana leaves. With Atea's help, she dug a hole inside the embers of the fire, placed the piglet inside, and covered it with red embers. They repeated the same scenario with several tuna filets, parrotfish, and lobsters. Then, they wrapped several breadfruits and placed them on the fire.

On such occasions, Kon would always be close to Atea and Fenua. He loved their food, and they were most honored to make him happy. Atea considered him as her own son who brought order in her family, and she was immensely thankful for it.

All night, Tamatoa's men performed essential repairs on the twelve selected ships, and installed the long bamboo poles to extend the existing masts, as Kon had suggested. At dawn, Tamatoa was ready and behaving as the great leader he was. Tupua gave his last recommendations to his children. Hina saw Taaroa standing at some distance. Timidly, the ill man called Hina with his hands: He wanted to give her something. She went to him.

"Take this with you," Taaroa said in his usual croaking voice.

"What is this?" Hina asked, surprised.

"It is a gourd filled with the sacred water of the valley. Keep it attached to your belt at all times, and use it only in case of emergency."

"Why? Do you think we could become thirsty on these huge ships?" she joked.

"Do as I say," Taaroa replied, with wet eyes. "I saw signs in the sky. Go to your destiny, my beautiful child."

Hina took the gourd, attached it around her waist, and went to Tamatoa's outrigger, puzzled. As the outrigger glided toward Tamatoa's ship, the horizon was already red. Hina saw Taaroa's shadow slowly vanish in the darkness behind the trees at the top of the beach.

"I respect the wishes of this old friend," Hina said.

"Through you, he still fulfills his role of great priest," Kon said. "Through you, he is at his best."

All twelve ships cruised in the area where Tehani and Mehao had vanished, on a relatively calm sea. There were few clouds, and the visibility was outstanding. Kon climbed to the top of one mast, and tested the reliability of the bamboo extension. Then, he slowly climbed along the many joints of the pole. A rope around his waist and around the pole helped him maintain his balance. When he reached the top, the ship appeared much smaller and far below. Long swings from one side of the ship to the other were uncomfortable at first, then became part of a new routine he had never experienced. He recalled the time he had been at the top of the mast on his crude raft, looking for his brother Illa. With a mast of this height he would have followed him for much longer, but could it have made any difference? He would have lost his brother anyway. Would he find him? Kon recalled his promise, and repeated it to himself, slowly, as determined as ever.

"I will find you, my brother, even if it takes a lifetime."

On the deck, Hina observed him, and she knew his thoughts. She knew they would not find any trace of Tehani or Mehao in this area. She knew Kon's mind was much farther away, on a distant island where the sun rises every morning.

"What do you think our young man is thinking up there?" Vana asked.

"Kon is with us," she replied, looking at Vana with pain in her eyes. "But his mind is far away beyond our world, on an unknown island where his brother might be."

"If such an island exists," Tamatoa said, "it would have to be far beyond Mangareva, the last known island in the east."

"You and Kon have something in common," Hina said.

"Such as?" Tamatoa asked.

"He is looking for a lost brother; you are looking for Tehani and Mehao," Hina replied. "He is helping you," she added with a smile, emphasizing every word.

"Does that mean I should help him to go beyond Mangareva?" Tamatoa asked, perplexed.

"Let's find Tehani and Mehao first," Hina replied. "In due time, Tamatoa the great will decide if Kon Tici Viracocha is worth his compassion."

CHAPTER 24

"Taaroa gave me the sacred water from my Valley. I heard its gentle lapping inside the gourd hung on my belt, which gave me confidence and security. As a priestess, I knew something of great importance would materialize soon."

Hina of the Valley

Vana checked the direction of the wind by looking at Hina's hair flowing in the afternoon breeze.

"Stop paddling, bring the sails down and let the ship drift on its own," Vana ordered.

Hina came close to the old priest, so he could look at the current and at her hair at the same time. She had faith in his vast experience of the sea currents in this area. Vana bent on his knees and scrutinized the waves for a long time, comparing their shape with the direction of the wind. Several times he checked the alignment of one mast with Mount Orohena. He finally looked at Tamatoa.

"They have been at sea for five nights and five days, haven't they?

"Yes," Tamatoa replied.

Vana pondered for a moment, checked the alignment of the mast with Mount Orohena, and looked once more at the waves and at Hina's hair.

"If they have been drifting ever since," Vana said, "by now they are beyond the Tetiaroa atoll. We waste our time around here."

Immediately, Tamatoa roared orders and blew powerfully in his conch shell. Warriors brought up the sails, and others started paddling. Twelve ships cruised at high speed toward Tetiaroa.

"It may take all night and all day before we catch up with the drifting wreckage," Vana said.

"Can anyone survive seven days with no food and no water on a drifting piece of wood?" Hina asked.

"It depends on many things," Vana replied. "They may have collected enough water from the rain. Yes, they could be alive."

The next day, in the afternoon, they sailed very close to the Tetiaroa atoll. Tamatoa sent one ship to check the atoll, then they kept going. At the top of the mast, Kon scrutinized the sea as far as he could. His thoughts drifted between his brother Illa and Hina. How could he convince her to come searching the awesome sea with Him? He knew her place was in Tahiti-nui. Did he have the right to even attempt to take her away from her paradise? He knew the answer, and he would have to leave without her. Would he ever be able to return? He also knew the answer: The chances for a return were slim. Frustrated by an impossible choice, he closed his eyes for an instant, and explored his memories. Visions started spinning in his mind. Suddenly, everything stopped all at once, when he heard Hina on the deck talking to him.

"Are you taking a nap?" she joked.

He knew exactly what she was thinking. He knew she would stay. He was a fool, but there was no choice. There had never been any choice. He would leave, and she would stay. It was sad and simple.

Now the night was coming. Kon slid down to the deck, went

to rest close to Hina, and laid his head on her thighs. He felt her warmth as she slowly caressed his long hair. She knew she would be with him until the great gathering of Maohis in Havaiki. That time was near. Then he would meet some of his people, and they would organize a long search toward the east. At that time, she knew she would lose him. They looked at each other, saying nothing. There was no need for words. They both had sharp pain in their hearts. Tamatoa came close to them, and laid his hand on Hina's head.

"Tonight, they will paddle slowly," Tamatoa said, "and I brought the sails down. You both should sleep."

With no further words, the giant went to the front end of the ship, and scrutinized the night. Everything became quiet. Later, the paddling warriors started singing to keep the evil spirits of the night away from the ship, and to forget the pain in their blistered hands. On the horizon, the moon would rise soon.

Kon put his arm around Hina's neck, and pulled on her gently, until their lips met with passion. Their faces were completely surrounded by Hina's hair. Inside this beautiful shelter, they were in a world where only they could travel.

Much later, Hina could not sleep. She watched the moonlight reflecting on the sea. Only she and the paddling warriors were still awake. She walked around the ship, and listened to their song. She thought the meaning of the words was superficial. Nevertheless, she was fascinated by the rhythm, which was a clever mix between an intriguing melody and a necessity to survive. She went to the rear of the ship, climbed on a narrow platform, and sat looking at the track of the ship visible across the long, golden alley of the full moon reflecting on the sea. The night was so clear that she was surprised no one tried to look for wreckage. She had a feeling that something was about to materialize, and she decided she might as well do something useful, and began searching the night. A gentle breeze was blowing from the west. It was warm. Suddenly, she heard a bird. She thought it was most unusual at this time of the night. She concluded that, perhaps, some seabirds kept flying at sea during clear nights. For an instant she wished the warriors would stop their song. She would have loved to listen to the subtleties of the silence, at sea. Then, a meteor crossed the sky, silent, mysterious.

At some distance, ahead of the ship, she saw a dark object floating. As the ship came closer, the object grew larger. For an instant, she hesitated to awaken the others. The warriors were still singing and looking down at their legs as they paddled. She concentrated her attention on the wreckage as it passed nearby the ship. Suddenly, to her astonishment, she distinctly saw at least two human bodies lying on the drifting part of what used to be a deck.

Hina screamed to alert everybody. Then, without hesitation, she plunged into the sea and swam toward the wreckage. At that time, she stopped, paralyzed by a horrifying thought. She turned around and looked at the ship fading away into the night. From all the strength of her lungs she called for help, but it was useless. Because of the warrior's song, nobody heard her. The ship completely vanished. She was alone. Her blood ran inside her head. Her mind spun in distress. She had no idea what she should do, and fully realized the consequences of her incredible mistake. There had been no need to plunge into the sea, and she had all the time to awaken Tamatoa and Kon. It would have been easy to find the wreckage under the moonlight. She hit on the water with her hands, and cried with madness: It was too late.

Slowly, she regained her composure and searched for the wreckage. There was nothing. Perhaps, it had been a dream.

Again, she looked carefully all around, and saw a distant shadow on the sea. That was it, but it was drifting away fast. She swam as fast as she could, but the breeze was pushing the wreckage faster than Hina, who only exposed her head to the wind. In a surge of energy she swam as fast as she could. Would she have the strength, and the stamina? The wreckage was close, but she was out of breath, incapable of exerting more effort, and she looked at the wreckage going away. Desperate, she gave everything she had. Then, she realized she would not have enough energy. She slowed down, but kept swimming, and kept her eyes on her target. She felt a cramp in one leg, but kept swimming. She was determined to survive; she would not give up. The wreckage was her only chance. In her mind she saw a few flashes. She saw Hina fighting with Mount Orohena, she saw Hina fighting with the great Tamatoa, and she saw Hina the priestess. The thoughts gave her more energy. She swam with better technique, more efficiently, and she had Mana in her eyes.

At last, she succeeded to grasp a piece of rope. She held it with both hands, pulled to make sure it was well attached to the wreckage, and it was. She was safe. She let herself drift, resting for a moment, but she was in the mood to get things done quickly, and she strongly climbed on the wreckage. It was the entire rear end of one of Tamatoa's ships. She recognized the characteristic carvings she had admired a few days earlier. She saw two men attached to the deck with ropes, and she recognized one of them. He was Mehao, Tamatoa's son, whom she briefly met after the race on Mount Orohena. She checked the pulse of each: They were alive, but unconscious. Their breathing was weak. She looked at her belt: She had very little food, and Taaroa's gourd of water. She took the gourd, and put a few drops in Mehao's mouth, who slowly awoke. Then, she realized he had been only sleeping.

Instantly, Mehao grabbed the gourd and drank. The other man woke up, and also took a drink. Then, firmly, Hina took the gourd back and attached it to her belt.

Only then, did both men look at her, with astonishment. They slowly untied the ropes from around their bodies and looked at one another. They carefully looked all around. The night was empty. There was only Hina and the wreckage. Their eyes widened with terror: How did she come, and who was she?

Hina suddenly realized what their problem was, and started laughing, but they did not share the same pleasure, and they were convinced she was a living spirit.

She was something they had heard of, but never thought they would see. They backed up, ready to plunge into the sea.

"Don't!" she said. "I am not a spirit. I am in trouble like you are. Let me explain how I came here."

They did not listen at her. They were ready to jump, when Hina grabbed Mehao's arm. Instantly, both men were paralyzed from fright, and sat on the deck, protecting their faces with their hands.

"Mehao, let me help you," she said gently. "Your fatheris nearby looking for you."

They were the magic words, and Mehao finally regained some courage, touched Hina's hair, held her hand and touched her face.

"You are real," Mehao murmured. "You are Hina of the Valley. But, how did you come here? No! It is impossible, you must be a spirit."

"Don't be afraid, Hina replied. "I was on your father's ship looking for you. I saw you, but everyone was sleeping or paddling and singing. I was at the rear of the ship. I called them, and jumped into the sea. Nobody heard me. I made a terrible mistake, and I had a very hard time to swim to you. I hope they will find us in the morning."

"My father is dead," Mehao said. "Nobody can survive the swirling sea of madness during a storm between Tahiti-nui and Moorea. If you were on his ship, then you are a spirit."

Hina grabbed his arm again. This time she was angry.

"Let me tell you something, Mehao, go ahead and jump. But, remember, there is a father somewhere who is looking hard for you, because he loves you, because he needs you, because you still have a chance of finding your mother alive."

This time, Hina chose the right words. Both men instantly became more confident, and friendly. Mehao tried to take her gourd.

"Wait!" she said.

She took her gourd, opened it and filled it with seawater.

"What are you doing?" Mehao asked, confused.

"I learned this from Kon Tici," Hina said. "You may drink again. Tomorrow, I will put more seawater in this water from my valley, so the valley will meet the sea in equal amounts. After this, we would have to drink only what we have, until they find us."

The charming priestess had spoken, so they complied. She gently talked to them, until they fell asleep. Here she was, in the middle of the sea, alone with her hopes. She looked at the golden alley under the moonlight: There was nothing. "Alone!" Never before had she realized the power of that word.

It rang in her head, like a terrible omen: alone,...alone,...

At dawn, Tamatoa went on the deck, to change the paddling team. He saw Kon and Vana, asleep, and wondered where Hina was. He walked around the cabin, went back inside the cabin...

Furious, he came out and grabbed Kon's arm.

"Where is she?" Tamatoa roared. "She is not on the ship."

Kon became anxious instantly, and jumped to his feet. Tamatoa questioned the paddlers who should have seen her. They told him the last time they had seen her, she was walking toward the rear of the ship where the cabin is.

Kon climbed the mast, and Tamatoa ordered his twelve ships to reverse their course and keep more distance between themselves. It became instantly clear that Hina was lost at sea.

"Where are you, Hina?" Kon murmured, scrutinizing the morning sea. The weather was clear, and he could see for a great distance.

"Put even more distance between the ships," Kon ordered. Tamatoa immediately complied.

"How is it possible that you fell into the sea, with weather so calm?" Kon asked himself. "Is it possible that you fell as you were asleep? No, this is not Hina. There must be another reason."

"Kon, can you come down?" Tamatao asked.

Kon looked at the deck below, and saw a warrior ready to take his place.

"Vana may have an explanation," Tamatoa said.

Kon went down, and joined Tamatoa and Vana.

"Hina saw something last night," Vana said. "Then, she deliberately jumped into the sea to rescue someone."

"This is impossible," Kon said. "The first thing she would have done is to awaken all of us."

"Maybe she tried," Vana said. "Maybe she called as she jumped. But the paddlers were singing loudly, and she was at the rear of the ship. Nobody saw her jump, and nobody heard her. She assumed otherwise, and that was her mistake."

"This is Hina," Kon concluded.

Tamatoa nodded his head, took his conch and with all the power of his lungs sent a message of distress to another ship. Soon, one ship left the fleet, and headed full speed toward Tahiti-nui. Kon immediately guessed the message: Tamatoa was asking for more ships, but it would take this ship at least three days to reach the main island, and three more days for the new ships to come: There was nothing they could be cheerful about, and they knew time was too valuable to make any mistake. The remaining eleven ships formed a large crescent from one horizon to the next, and zigzagged across the same path they had traveled during the night.

By the end of the day, the only things they had found were pieces of wood, pieces of cloth, nothing else. In a way, it was a confirmation that Vana's theory was right. Nevertheless, there was no trace of Hina: She had completely vanished.

Kon remained at the top of the mast until sunset.

"Come down; drink and eat something," Tamatoa said.

"I am not thirsty or hungry," Kon replied.

"Drink and eat anyway. We must remain healthy and strong; crucial decisions depend on it."

Kon glanced at the Maohi: He was right. It was not the right time for despair. Now, both men had a lot to lose. Kon's dark blue eyes met Tamatoa's black eyes. Silent, they understood one another. The tattooed giant put a friendly hand on Kon's shoulder, and without saying a word, walked toward his warriors.

The next morning, they found large pieces of a wrecked ship.

"This is part of Tehani's ship," Tamatoa said.

"Now, I am convinced Vana was right," Kon said.

"At least, we know we are in the right area," Vana added.

Three days after Hina found the two men, she had no food left, and no water. Worse, Mehao was ill. With a few pieces of wood and ropes, Hina built a small mast. She removed her clothes and hung them at the top of the mast. Perhaps, someone would see them from a greater distance. She looked at her creation, shrugged her shoulders, thinking it was better than nothing.

Mehao looked at her for a long time.

"At least, I will have the satisfaction of seeing a beautiful woman before I die."

"Mehao shall live!" Hina replied. "We all shall live, even if we have to swim all the way back to Tahiti-nui with this piece of a ship attached to our feet."

Mehao smiled at her resolve, turned aside and went to sleep. Hina put her hand on his head: He was warm, too warm. The other man looked better, but lacked energy. She was on her own, and she would see them die. Then, her time would come. It was dusk, and she had to save her energy and try to sleep. Reluctantly, she checked the horizon once more, curled on the deck and glanced at her clothes floating in the gentle breeze.

"Where are you, Kon?" she murmured. "Perhaps, tomorrow you will see these clothes from the top of your mast."

She tried to sleep, but could not. She sat and looked at the golden reflection, as the moon climbed slowly above the eastern horizon. The sea was calm, unusually so. The breeze was warm and caressed her body, which was burned by the sun and dried by the salt. She felt abandoned and powerless, but rejeced the idea of death. She knew her days were numbered, unless rain came. She glanced at her companions, and wondered how long they would survive. She knew Mehao might not last two more days.

She let her hand hang in the warm sea, and thought it was ironic to die of thirst with so much water around. She tasted a few drops, and wondered how so much salt could hold so much life. Puzzled, she tasted a few more drops.

Early in the morning, a bird came nearby. Hina did not move. She watched it with a look in her eyes she never had before, a look she never thought she would have. Suddenly, by necessity, she was a hunter. It was a young, brown and white tern, tired, looking for somewhere to rest. It landed near Hina. Slowly, her hand crawled toward the bird. Then, she violently struck the bird, and grabbed his neck. The tern flipped its wings, but she squeezed its neck harder, until life left the poor creature.

She gave the blood to the two men. She plucked the bird, removed its guts and they ate its warm flesh. Later, in the morning, they ate two flying fish that accidentally landed on the wreck.

"I wish it would rain," Hina said. Then, she realized no one had heard her. Both men were asleep. She stood up, holding the mast, looked at the horizon, all around, several times. There was no land, no ship, no birds, nothing. She looked for clouds. There were none. She sat on a broken piece of wood, then she lay down, and touched the ocean with the tip of her fingers. Once more, she tasted a few drops of salt water.

"I am the priestess!" she murmured.

"I am Hina of the Valley!" she said.

"I was meant to die here! Is this conceivable?"

"No! It cannot be," she cried.

She glanced at her legs and at her arms; they were strong. She looked at the mast, and she had hope. She dared the sea, and became arrogant.

"I am a Maohi," she said loudly, "and Maohis don't die easily at sea. As long as I have life in these veins, I will not surrender."

Two more days went by, and morale was low on Tamatoa's ship. Kon and Vana desperately developed search strategies, and Tamatoa willingly tried each of them, but they looked older, defeated. Kon could not accept the idea of giving up the search, and they all agreed that they would pursue their efforts until Tupua's ships arrived.

Kon had bruises around his legs from staying all day at the top of the mast, and he suffered from sunburn, but once more, he made a commitment at sea.

"I will find you, Hina of the Valley," Kon said, with a gesture of defiance to the awesome sea. "I swear I will find you."

Tamatoa and Vana looked at him with sadness.

"Have will power, my friends!" Kon said. "The search only begins. Put more distance between these ships; I don't want to see them unless I am at the top of the mast."

Tamatoa looked surprised at Kon's renewed energy, and realized his words had been an order. The great warrior smiled, and executed the order.

Later in the afternoon, Vana came near Kon, and poked his forefinger on his chest.

"A long time ago, you told me Viracocha's sons could read words through the wind."

"Yes, they can," Kon replied.

"Then, why are you waiting to experience this at sea?" Vana asked. "This girl is screaming for you."

"I tried, but it does not work," Kon said.

"And, why is that?" Tamatoa asked.

"There are too many people around me, too much noise," Kon replied, restless and irritable, "I cannot concentrate."

"You are a man of many talents, Kon Teke," Vana said. "Tonight, you shall try again."

"I will keep everyone away from you," Tamatoa said, "and you will hear your heartbeat."

"I will do as you say," Kon murmured, humiliated by his fate.

As planned, when the moon rose above the horizon, all

these sailors became silent, and still. Tamatoa sat on the deck and looked at the golden reflection. Vana looked at the stars and wondered if the good spirits would help them. Kon sat, cross-legged, at the rear of the ship, from where Hina had vanished. Tamatoa's ship became a silent shadow, lapped by gentle waves. Soon, the shadow became a drifting phantom in a maze of mystery. Time had stopped. Kon felt extraordinary energy fill his veins, something he had not experienced for a long time. Something new was happening. He went into deep trance, saw light everywhere, and an old man floating in the clouds, looking for him. A Viracocha spirit was around, observing in mysterious ways.

From a distance, Vana watched Kon's face, as he often did in the past. He knew Kon well enough to notice that something was happening. He had made contact with someone, somewhere, in a faraway dimension.

"Have a long journey, son from another world," Vana murmured.

Hina held Mehao's face on her lap. She knew he would not live one more day without fresh water, and there was nothing she could do. The other man was completely demoralized at the sight of his master, and was giving up any hope. Hina herself was weaker, and extremely thirsty. She realized she did not know the name of the other man.

"What is your name?"

"Taa," he replied, keeping his eyes closed.

She took his hand on her lap, and caressed his hair, but she did not say anything. They waited for the last time they would go to sleep. Mehao would go first, then it would be Taa, and at last it would be Hina. It was their fate; now they knew it.

In the evening, after Taa went to sleep close to his dying

companion, Hina scrutinized the spectacular western horizon once more, very slowly, once, twice, three times.... She tried to distinguish the distant land of Tahiti-nui. There was nothing. They were alone, lost on the awesome sea.

She sat, cross-legged, put her face into her hands, and deeply thought about the man she loved with great passion.

"Where are you?" she murmured. "Why is it taking you so long? Why can't you find me?"

She tried to concentrate strongly on his face, his hair and his blue eyes. Her fingers reached the gold necklace. Her fingertips touched the rising sun, and the flying condor. She felt energy coming from the condor, and vaguely saw the outline of an old man, with a long, white beard. She opened her eyes, and realized she had been dreaming.

"Kon Tici Viracocha... wherever you are, I know you are searching for me. Don't let me die."

Tears ran down her cheeks, but she was not afraid. She was immensely frustrated, because there was nothing she could do. The shiny condor was her last resource. Yes, she would rely on the unthinkable. She would rely on concepts she did not comprehend. She was, for the first time, willing to believe in the secret world of spirits. She looked at the stars, holding the condor pendant in her fingers. She stood up, lifted her arms and felt a powerful sense of soaring.

"Viracocha!" she screamed with all she had in her lungs. "Come to me!"

The sacred name of the supreme ancestor rang across the sea, from west to east, with the suppliant demand of a broken heart, with the serene beauty of sincerity, with the thirst for life. She smiled, and drank her own tears.

CHAPTER 25

"I heard the breeze of the night call my name. I knew the ghost of my wandering grandson was searching for me. The surrounding air was filled with perfume from unknown flowers, and with the unmistakable moving force of Kon Tici."

Taranga Tici Viracocha

Somewhere in the northeast, six ships were gently gliding in the golden reflection of the moon. They were from the distant land of Hiva. They were going to the Maohis' great gathering held in Havaiki.

On the leading ship, an old man searched the surface of the sea. He was tall, thin, with white hair and a long white beard. He was dressed in his traditional, plain white robe. His deep blue eyes showed immense wisdom mixed with kindness. He had been meditating all day about their encounter with wrecked ships from which they had rescued many survivors. He wondered why these men and women had been surprised by a storm in waters they knew well. Those who were able to speak did not make much sense: Most of them were exhausted, ill or dying, but he knew something was odd, instinctively worried that something bad had happened at Havaiki, and wondered what kind of string of events would soon unravel.

A young girl, about eight years of age, sat near the old man.

She did not speak, and put one hand on the ancestor's lap. In turn, Taranga gently caressed the child's head. Attached to her belt, were two sacred rosewood tablets on which a treasure of knowledge was carved. She had cherished these tablets for many moon-cycles.

"Did you memorize all these signs?" Taranga asked.

"I know them all, Kukara answered. "I like to look at them. They are so beautiful."

"It was an immense honor for me to receive this treasure from Hotu-Matua, king of Hiva," Taranga said.

"Hotu-Matua liked you the first day he saw you," Kukara said.

"How do you know this, my child?"

"Because he told me."

"All your life, this treasure shall puzzle you," Taranga said.

"How far is the land where Hotu-Matua found this treasure?" Kukara asked.

"He never saw the land," Taranga replied. "He received these tablets from other travelers as a present, far away from Hiva, in the northwest."

"Hotu-Matua taught you the meaning of all these signs," Kukara said.

"He only remembered the exact meaning of a few, and guessed the others," Taranga said.

"When he reads them, the story makes sense," Kukara said.

"Perhaps, but when he reads them twice at several moon-cycles intervals, he tells two different stories," Taranga joked.

"Then, how did you learn their meaning?"

"I know the signs where he is consistent, and I also guessed the others."

"What am I supposed to do?" Kukara asked.

"Honor these tablets, learn what they say, discover what they mean and ultimately add to them."

"I see," Kukara said, looking at the stars, and grabbing Taranga's hand.

"Are we going to find Kon?" she asked.

"Perhaps. Why do you ask?"

"Because you are thinking about him," Kukara replied. "I want to find him."

"We will find him," Taranga said. "The man who adopted you is already with us."

"Did you see him?"

"Yes, my child," Taranga replied. "Mana is with him."

Kukara had grown up, physically and mentally. She remembered the promise she had made the day she lost contact with Kon Tici. Through Taranga's words, she knew he was still alive. Suddenly, she heard Viracocha's name in the air, in the water and inside herself. Viracocha was everywhere, and all the phantoms of the night sang his name. Was it her imagination, or was she hearing voices?

"Someone is calling Viracocha," Kukara murmured. "A woman!"

"His name is in the wind," Taranga said.

"His name is everywhere," she added.

Behind them, the honorable king of Hiva listened. He had deep respect and admiration for the old friend he had saved several sun-cycles before. He would always recall that day when Taranga and his followers reached his shore, dehydrated, hungry, coming from the east on a rotten, sinking raft. Several moon-cycles later, he had found two more rafts on an isolated atoll. Among the few survivors was Kukara.

Kukara had transformed Taranga's life. After losing so many

people at sea, she gave him courage and the will to endure. Hotu-Matua, king of Hiva, quickly grew to love her. In her, he saw the class of royal blood. In her, he saw the daughter he never had. All his children were young men, already traveling across the awesome sea, in search of new lands. Would he ever see them again? He was not sure. He had extraordinary patience with her many questions. Her favorite game was to read the Kohau Rongo-Rongo tablets with him. Each time, he would carefully have to be consistent with what he had said before.

"What does that little circle mean?" Kukara asked. "It recurs on both tablets."

"It is the sign of ultimate knowledge," Hotu-Matua replied. "For example, if you see it representing the head of someone, he or she is a respected master in a given field."

"Here, it represents an eye," she said.

"Then, this person is looking at the stars, where so many mysteries hide."

Kukara's finger precisely slid on each line, as if she was reading. Then, her finger stopped, where one circle was set above waving lines, and under the lines was a sign very much like a mountain.

"What are those?" Kukara inquired.

"The circle is the Sun, source of life. The waving lines are the awesome sea, source of clouds, rain and rivers. The broken line is the mountain, source of islands, where water shall create life."

The small girl's large blue eyes expressed calmness. Two moon-cycles earlier she had asked the king exactly the same question, and Hotu-Matua had given the same answer. She was content.

Kukara wanted to confound the king with an impossible question. It was a game, for her and for him.

"What does Kohau Rongo-Rongo mean?" she asked.

Hotu-Matua caressed her long, black hair, obviously impressed by her provocative question. Taranga glanced at him, amused.

"It is the sacred tool to transmit knowledge," Hotu-Matua replied. "Kohau Rongo-Rongo shall help you remember everything. Faraway priests created these tablets to cure man's aging memory."

"With these tablets, knowledge becomes immortal," Taranga added.

Kukara looked at them with surprise in her eyes.

"Shall I add to these tablets, after I learn how they work?" she asked, with hesitation.

"Yes!" Taranga replied. "Then, all our knowledge could be transferred to the future generations in a more reliable way."

Kukara's fingers gently slid on the signs, and came to a stop.

"Is this a bird?" she asked, excited.

"It represents the travelers of the sky," Hotu-Matua replied. "It can be a booby, a tropicbird, or an albatross."

"Or a condor!" she said.

"Birds will always remind us, with magnificent modesty, that there is someone above all of us," Taranga said.

"But this has always been Viracocha's way," Kukara said.

"Then, Viracocha was in touch with something unusual," Hotu-Matua said with a humble voice.

"But, so did other people, in other places, at other times," Taranga added, looking at the stars. "Somewhere, there are forces beyond imagination."

The old Viracocha and the young girl went to the other end of the ship, away from everyone, and they listened to the night.

"Listen!" Taranga said. "You have better ears. Tell me what

is in the wind."

"Could it be my father?" Kukara murmured.

"I don't know. At times I think I hear a man, but I also hear the laments of a woman. Close your eyes, listen and tell me what you hear."

Kukara complied, lowered her head in her hands, and went into a trance with extraordinary ease. At some distance, Hotu-Matua was observing her. With a sign of his hand, he brought absolute silence on the ship. Kukara was gone, far away, traveling with seabirds.

She saw a magnificent mountain, similar to the silent peaks around the City of the Sun where her brother had been murdered. Then, she saw Kon Tici climbing the mountain. The mountain slowly vanished and became a beach of black sand, on which a woman of remarkable beauty was walking. Her long, straight black hair ruffled in the breeze. Ahead of her, a sandpiper was feeding after the receding waves. She seemed to be amused by the bird. The woman climbed the beach, followed a river and vanished in the rain forest. Then, the mountain came back, and a tattooed giant was watching men racing to the summit. Suddenly, the beautiful woman brought the giant to his knees. Finally, she saw Kon Tici taking the hands of the woman, but they immediately vanished into the mist of her dream. However, Kukara had enough time to notice a small detail on the woman's chest, a detail she thought astonishing. She opened her eyes, and saw Taranga's eyes full of questions.

"My father is alive and well," Kukara said. "A beautiful woman helped him to pacify his adversary who was a frightening tattooed giant."

"You did well," Taranga said, caressing her hair gently.

"I saw something else," Kukara said.

Taranga looked at her, puzzled, and Hotu-Matua came closer to listen.

"The woman was wearing Kon's necklace with the golden condor."

The old Viracocha wrapped her shoulders with his arms.

"Indeed," he said, "we are going to find Kon Tici."

Kukara looked at the Rongo-Rongo tablets with melancholy.

"Everything is written in them," she said, "yet I don't know how to read them."

"You most certainly will," Taranga said, "in due time."

Later during the night, they were still searching for signs that would lead to Kon Tici. Viracocha's children did not know the words "failure," "despair," or "death." The only words they knew were "courage," "self-discipline" and "kindness." They were good people, searching the awesome sea for one of their own.

Farther to the south, another Viracocha was traveling in time and space. In his dream, Kon Tici saw Kukara for a short time. She had grown up. She was with other people, but he could not see them well.

"You gave your necklace to a beautiful woman," Kukara said. "I saw her call Viracocha's name."

Kon Tici opened his eyes, and smiled.

"Don't ask!" he said. "But keep searching."

CHAPTER 26

"A white-tailed tropicbird wandered around, showing off fast and continuous wing beats, interspersed with a few glides. It suddenly twisted, turned in flight, paused on a wave and swam with a cocked tail. I was not aware this bird would change the course of my fate."

Hina of the Valley

At dawn, long before sunrise, when dark red light was barely noticeable on the eastern horizon, Hina heard a bird flying around the wreck. Taa was asleep and ill. Mehao was in a coma, and only his heartbeat was proof that he was still alive. Dehydration would kill them soon. Like a hunter, Hina watched for the bird, but it remained elusive, at some distance in the dark.

Her thoughts wandered with the sea swells and the current. She recalled her rank as a priestess and wondered if she had filled her short life with enough wisdom. She wished she would survive, knowing this suffering would help her to realize her priorities, but nothing could make a difference. She heard the bird again, and now she could see it.

"A tropicbird!" she said, standing up in euphoria.

She raised her arm. Immediately, the white-tailed tropicbird landed on her wrist. Wrapped in the majesty of its colors and long tail, the magnificent bird looked at her. Hina would never kill such a beauty, no matter how hungry or thirsty. Furthermore, it was the sacred bird of good luck for people lost at sea. She always thought it had been only a superstition perpetuated by Vana's stories. Today was the perfect time to test the truthfulness of the legend.

Quite fond of the bird, she gently caressed its head. Dissatisfied by her behavior, the bird pecked her hand with its sharp and powerful orange bill. Pain filled her eyes. The bird jumped away to the other end of the wreck.

"I suppose this is how good luck must start!" Hina murmured, licking her bleeding finger.

She took her necklace, and admired the shiny golden condor.

"In Kon's land, the condor is the sacred bird. Here, it is the tropicbird. Different worlds, different birds, but the idea stays the same."

She wondered why birds were so important to humans, and why some should be sacred. Perhaps, they held the mysteries of life, at the heart of our troublesome solitude. Depressed, she forced herself to find another explanation. Birds flew; humans did not: That was the likely explanation. Humans were fascinated by something the bird could do that they could not. Then, if the bird was also gifted with elegance and beauty, it became the sacred bird. There was nothing that bird could bring her as good luck. In despair, she strongly squeezed her necklace.

"Oh, Viracocha!" she said in a weak and tremulous whisper. "Why did you abandon me?"

The tropicbird uttered a harsh, rasping scream. She looked at the black stripe behind its eye. She thought the bird was ready to take off. The bird screamed again, looking at the sky with one eye.

"Are you trying to tell me something?" she asked, looking at the sea all around.

The bird gave another strident call and spread its wings in a royal takeoff. She saw its bright white belly, and its characteristic, long white tail streamers. Just above her, the bird flapped its wings rapidly, called twice and flew toward the northwest.

She followed the bird as long as she could. It soon became a tiny dot above the horizon. Suddenly, she saw it plunging toward the sea. She stood up to search for it, but could no longer find it. Instead, she saw a fuzzy shadow, just at the horizon. She instantly felt blood pounding everywhere in her body, as never before in her life. She looked away, wondering if she was dreaming. She looked all around, at the horizon, making a perfect circle, and came back to the fuzzy shadow of hope. There was no doubt. It was a boat; it was someone; it was Kon.

She regained her full strength, and grabbed the makeshift mast where her clothes were hanging. She desperately waved with the mast, as high as she could. It was her chance, probably her only chance. She started yelling, fully aware that the boat was still too far for anyone to hear her call, but the fuzzy shadow became larger, and she saw the tropicbird circling the boat. With the resources of a mysterious force someone finds for survival, she made large circles with the heavy mast. Once, she lost her balance and fell in the water. Instantly, she was back on the wreck as if nothing had happened. After she saw the boat coming in her direction, she calmed down. She saw the bird going farther north, and at this moment, she saw the most incredible sight of her life. There were two, three, then at least five other boats spread on the horizon, all coming in her direction. She smiled, and was filled with joy she could not describe. She would live. She was safe. Hina of the Valley would turn despair into triumph.

"This is not Tamatoa's ship," she said, "or my father's ship.

Who are they?"

At this point, she did not care. She knew they were on their way to the great gathering. She clung to reality, and a smile trembled over her lips. Then, tears quivered on her eyelids, sweet tears.

"Thank you, Great Spirit," she whispered. "Thank you, Viracocha. You heard my call."

She glanced at the two men, and suddenly realized that if she could save them, Tamatoa would treat her with respect always. He already did, but she would seal an unshakable bond between herself and the tattooed giant. Because of what she had done to save his men, it would make her rank as priestess unquestionable for her lifetime.

What she felt was new, a mixture of pride, joy and humbleness. It was a sacred instant when realizing that courage, suffering and hope, are the same thing along the trail of life. She felt she had aged, but she was stronger. She felt she had reached maturity in her soul, but she was happy as a child. She was ready for an unforgettable encounter with her people.

The tropicbird came back, flew above her and landed on her arm.

"Oh yes, Vana!" she cried. "Your legends are true."

She sent the bird toward the sky. It circled the wreck and the first boat a few times, as if it was pointing at Hina, then vanished to the southwest, toward Tahiti-nui.

Hina wanted to share her joy with her ill companions. Taa was too weak to stand up, but managed to smile. He knew he would live. Once more, she put her ear on Mehao's chest, and heard the heartbeats: She was content.

She took another good look at the approaching ship. She waved, and they waved back to her. She exchanged a few words, and from their accent she knew they were from Hiva. With determination, she told the sailors to hurry up. They immediately understood her concern for Taa and Mehao.

As the ship came in contact with the wreck, Hina felt two strong hands grab her arms. She looked at her feet landing on the deck of the ship, and found the contact with the shiny planks most delightful.

"Are you all right?" one man asked.

"I am fine," Hina replied, but pointing at Taa and Mehao.

A tall, well-dressed Maohi came to her, and took her hand.

"Don't worry about these two men," the dignitary said, "we are going to take good care of them."

His words were immensely comforting to her, and she suddenly realized she had been rude with her rescuers.

"I am thankful," Hina said, with respect. "My name is Hina of the Valley. I am a priestess and Tupua's youngest daughter. He is king of Tahiti-nui."

"My name is Hotu-Matua, and I am king of Hiva."

He slowly removed his magnificent red cape, and wrapped it around Hina's naked body.

"This looks a lot better on you than on me," the king joked. "Long ago, when I was a boy, I met your father at the great gathering, and we had a wonderful time."

"My father has spoken about you many times," Hina said, with a shy smile.

Behind her, she heard the voice of an older man, with a much different accent, with a familiar accent.

"Drink this water," the voice said.

Hina turned around, and with no further formality, grabbed the gourd from the old man and drank. She closed her eyes with intense pleasure when she felt the fresh water flow in her body.

As she drank, Taranga saw the necklace with the golden condor on her chest. His eyes opened wider, and he was too startled to say anything. On his side, Kukara also noticed the condor, looked intently at the exhausted woman and pulled on Taranga's robe.

"She is the beautiful woman I saw in my dream," Kukara murmured in the ear of the ancestor.

Hina stopped drinking, and poured the rest of the water on her salty face. She opened her eyes, looked at Kukara's deep blue eyes, and gasped with astonishment. Then, she met the warmth of Taranga's smile. He was exactly as Kon had described. There was no possible doubt in her mind regarding the identity of the girl and the old man. She regained her composure, raised her chin and stared at Taranga with a mixture of Maohi pride and sweet delight. Then her words echoed in everyone's mind, with the full force of surprise.

"Your name is Taranga Tici Viracocha, and yours is Kukara Tici Viracocha," Hina said, emphasizing on each syllable in Viracocha's language.

A long silence followed her words, and she instantly became the center of attention for the entire crew. Taranga and Kukara stared at her, speechless and baffled. Their surprise was great, yet because of the golden condor they almost expected to hear what she had said. Indirectly, Hina had told them she knew Kon Tici. They had so much to ask, and she had so much to say, that a moment of silence became an eternity to all of them.

"Did my father gave you this necklace?" Kukara asked.

"Yes, he did," Hina replied. "Kon Tici is with us; Kon Tici is well."

Taranga could not resist any longer. With compulsive sobs on his old face, he hugged the young priestess.

"Thank you for loving him," he murmured.

Kukara gently eased her head between the old man and Hina, holding their hands with her fragile fingers.

"I love him, too!" the young girl said, her eyes brimming with tears.

They were tears of joy, and of triumph. On her chest, two small Rongo-Rongo tablets clapped against one another, and seemed to say: "We told you so!"

With red eyes, Taranga looked at Hina's face, tilted his brow and observed her from head to toe, keeping his hands on her shoulders: She was magnificent. She was quite different from most Maohi women he knew. She was taller, with lighter skin, and her healthy long hair was straight, still full of water. She showed inner peace and graceful self-confidence. She looked intelligent and well mannered. From a short distance, her eyes were bright brown, though they seemed black from a distance. Taranga touched the golden condor hanging on her breast and admired it for a moment.

"Dear Kon, we have so much to do," he murmured, coming back slowly to reality.

"What were you doing, lost on this piece of broken boat?" Taranga asked. "How did you come here? Why is it that the two other men are near death, and you are fresh and healthy? Where is..."

Struggling to remember all his questions, Hina put one finger on his lips, and gave him an affectionate smile.

"It is a long story," she said, in his language. "I don't really know where to begin."

"Take your time," Hotu-Matua said. "Come in my cabin, sit comfortably, and start at the beginning, when you met Kon Tici the first time."

They listened to her story until midday. Kukara had been

silent, very close to Hina, observing her, and studying her. Several times, Hina looked at her blue eyes. Kukara penetrated her mind in depth, as Kon had done so many times. Hina thought she liked the girl very much.

"Where is my father?" Kukara asked, with concern on her face.

"Kon is somewhere around," Hina replied. "I know he is searching for me, on Tamatoa's ship."

Hina noticed that each time she mentioned Tamatoa's name, Hotu-Matua was annoyed. She concluded that he knew who Tamatoa was, but she decided to wait before attempting to appease the king. Her long story gave him enough information to understand that he should not fear Tamatoa.

"The great gathering should be most interesting this time," the king said, with his eyes wandering around Hina's shoulders. Then, he left the cabin, and Kukara followed him.

Taranga was alone with Hina for the first time. They smiled at one another. It was like meeting again, but this time far more in depth. The old Viracocha caressed the golden condor on Hina's chest, with amazed wonder. Instantly, she felt a familiar current enter her body. She looked at the sky and shivered.

"Many times, when Kon touched me, I felt the same current," Hina murmured.

"It is Viracocha's fluid," Taranga replied. "It is like the fresh water draining your valley. It is like the rain offering life to the forest. It was a gift from the stars, given long ago to my ancestors. It is Mana and its incredible force. When it touches your body, you instantly become Mana itself, and capable of anything."

"The condor reminds you of many fascinating memories," she said.

"There were only two possible reasons for Kon to give you

this necklace."

"What could they be?" Hina asked with good humor.

"You must have achieved something extraordinary with him. It is a prerequisite in Viracocha's society before anyone can wear the golden condor."

Hina waited, and he saw she was waiting.

"Oh yes, I forgot," Taranga said. "You must also have been very dear to him when he gave it to you."

"No, you did not forget," she said, amused. "You were testing me, to know if I was listening."

Without a word, he apologized with a smile. Hina was startled by the accuracy of his words.

"You are right on both counts," Hina said, still overwhelmed. "I conquered the impossible Mount Orohena with him. It is a forbidden mountain from which no one can return alive. Also, in a secret cave on Mount Orohena, Kon and I shared the ultimate pleasures of life."

Taranga blushed, amused by her honesty, and fascinated by the purity of her attitudes. She was always straight to the point, with enchanting charm. Taranga knew that in the mind of the young priestess, there was no place for malice. She was Maohi by blood, pride and freedom, but she was Viracocha in her attitudes.

"One day," she said, "you will tell me who gave Mana to your ancestors."

"That day," he replied, turning away from her, "you will see a powerful vortex of purple light."

Hina was surprised and puzzled by his answer. She left the cabin, and took a walk on the deck. At the bow of the ship, she saw Kukara standing alone, looking at the southwestern horizon. Kukara did not turn around, but she knew Hina was behind her.

"He is not my true father," Kukara said, with a sob in her

voice. "But I love him as if he was."

"I know that." Hina said, putting her friendly hands on the shoulders of the child. "Kon told me."

Devastated by inward pain from ancient memories, Kukara managed a few words.

"I lost my parents, my brother, everything. Without Kon I would have not survived the great trip across the awesome sea."

Kukara turned around, looked Hina straight in the eyes and asked the question the priestess would never have thought possible.

"Kon loves you. So, could you be my mother?"

Hina's eyebrows rose in amazement. She was startled by what Kukara already knew about her. She was intrigued by her own attraction to the girl. Most of all, she was unable to resist Kukara's need for love and affection. Hina was bonded to her by Mana's force, for unknown reasons. She combed Kukara's long black hair with her fingers, and held her face against her chest. She felt Kukara's head pushing on the golden condor, and a powerful current of energy entered her breast.

"Yes, Kukara, I will be your mother."

CHAPTER 27

"I found my father, and a beautiful priestess who agreed to be my mother. Satisfied, I became willing to look at my future, and search for the secret of the Rongo-Rongo tablets: I knew it would take all my life."

Kukara Tici Viracocha

Kukara sat on the deck. Her hair was sprinkled with salt crystals and waved in the breeze. Her hair blew across her face so she could barely see around. She concentrated her attention on the characters carved on the wooden tablets. She had already established a parallel between the secret meaning of the characters and her destiny. In a way she was a happy young girl, but she felt the pain in her chest generated by brutal and cruel memories. As a result, she was too mature for her age. She questioned everyone's actions, and often kept the answer to herself. She judged people, but kept the criticism, or the approval, as an engraved secret within the Rongo-Rongo tablets. Unconsciously, she added as much to the original meaning of the tablets as she was discovering. She was quiet, easygoing, and often forgotten by most people, but now, she knew someone was watching and studying her in depth. She raised her hands, pulled her hair behind her head and glanced at Hina, who smiled at her. She smiled back and let her hair fall around her face. A warm drop of salty water fell from her eyes on the top of one of the Rongo-Rongo tablets. Suddenly, in the middle of an ocean of mysteries, Kukara saw the island: The salt drying around her tear was the coral reef encircling the island. With time, the island became smaller and smaller, then vanished. She erased the salt from the tablet with her fingers, curled up near a pile of ropes, and took a nap.

Hina spent most of the afternoon near Mehao. When Tamatoa's son opened his eyes, she washed the perspiration off his forehead, and immediately forced him to sip more water. Nearby, Taa was recovering fast. Hotu-Matua could not resist questioning something he would later regret.

"Why are you so protective of Tamatoa's son?" The king asked. "He murdered innocent people."

Shocked, she glanced at the king, as if she could not believe what she had heard. Then, as he left, she jumped to her feet and grabbed his arm to his great surprise.

"Whoever you are, listen to me," Hina said with arrogance. "I am a priestess, and as such I care about whoever is ill, hurt or depressed. Also, a man called Kon Tici taught me how to reach out to enemies with a friendly hand. Furthermore, I happen to have compassion for those who suffer. Finally, I am helping this man because I cannot bear people in a position of power who are naive, aggressive, brutal or selfish. The prime quality of a leader is magnanimity. If you don't have it, you are a dangerous man disguised with a rank that cannot and shall not be yours."

Hotu-Matua was startled by Hina's swift words. Never, had anyone spoken this way to him. For everyone, time came to a stop, and they waited for the king's reaction. He looked Hina straight in the eyes for a long time, and she never flinched. Through Hina, he could not recognize his good friend Tupua.

"Hina, I apologize if I hurt your feelings," Hotu-Matua said in a low tone, pointing a finger at her. "But, you and I will have further words on this matter, in another place, and in due time."

Hotu-Matua turned around, and walked toward his cabin, obviously upset. Hina looked at the sea, wondering if her words had been wise. He was a king, she was only a priestess and she had insulted him in front of his own people, which was a supreme offense in the Maohi society. It was too late. She could not take back what had been said. She shook her head, aware she had made a mistake. She was not supposed to lose her temper.

"Hotu-Matua has been my friend for a long time," Taranga said, still amazed by Hina's courage. "I never saw him apologize to anyone."

"I should not have done this," Hina murmured.

"I would not be concerned about the harshness of your words. He will remember them, and perhaps this will help him, someday."

Hina saw sincerity in the eyes of the smiling old man. She thought she cared for him. She could see the entire universe in his compelling eyes, and she wished for a moment she could travel in Viracocha's mind, and explore other worlds. Some day, she would learn how to do that. Kukara suddenly took her hand, did not say anything, but Hina felt a strange current invade her. She could hear Kukara's voice deep inside her soul: "My mother, you did well."

Hina looked at the girl, astonished, and absolutely certain she had not said anything.

Mehao found enough energy to also take Hina's hand.

"I heard," Tamatoa's son said. "Thank you, princess of the night. You came to me like a phantom from the world of spirits. You saved my life at the risk of ruining yours. I will never forget. My father will never forget."

She smiled, gave him water to drink and breadfruit to eat.

Kukara went to the cabin, pushed aside the curtain over the entry and saw Hotu-Matua sitting, his head in his hands.

"May I?" she asked with a shy voice.

The king raised his head, and smiled at her with pleasure.

"Of course, you always can, my little one."

She sat on his lap, and put one arm around his powerful neck.

"Hina did not mean to hurt you."

"I know."

"Hina told me she would be my mother."

The king looked at Kukara's face, wondering if he would lose her. He was attached to her and loved her.

"She would be an outstanding mother, and a friend for you...."

The king hesitated, and saw Kukara's interrogating eyes.

"You will never be bored with Hina of the Valley," he added. "She is a woman of virtue, and action."

"I know that, but this is not what you were thinking about."

He looked at her, sad.

"It would have given me great pleasure to be your father."

"But, you are my friend," she said softly, "I will always be with you."

Kukara was right. At the dusk of his life, in another time and faraway island, she would be the one who would close his eyes for the last time.

"Earlier, you said you found other people," Hina said.

"Yes," Taranga replied, "they are on two other ships."

"Did you find a woman called Tehani?" Hina asked, to Mehao's great surprise.

"I don't recall," Taranga said, "I know there are several women."

The old Viracocha approached Hotu-Matua as he came out from the cabin with Kukara. Taranga repeated Hina's question to him. The King stared at Hina for a moment. At first she stared at him, then lowered her eyes as a sign of respect. With his conch, the king ordered two other ships to come closer.

"Who is Tehani?" Kukara asked.

"She is a great lady," Hina replied. "She is Tamatoa's wife, and Meaho's mother. She is also the mother of my good friend Mahine."

Mehao shook his head, persuaded he was living in a dream.

"What does she look like?" Kukara asked.

"I don't know, I never met her," Hina replied, with a strange feeling that her story no longer made sense.

"Tamatoa and several of his children were in Tahiti-nui," Hina continued, "while Tehani was on another island, with Mehao, waiting for them."

"Still, how do you know she is a great lady?" Kukara asked.

"Because Tamatoa is a great man," Hina replied, glancing at Hotu-Matua, who was obviously irritated. "But, I know mainly from my friend Mahine. You will like her, too."

"I see," Kukara said, with a grin on her face, looking at the Rongo-Rongo tablets.

"Are you going to show these tablets to the priests, at the great gathering?" Hina asked.

"No, I will not!" Kukara replied without hesitation.

Surprised at first, Hina regained her composure, while Taranga and Hotu-Matua walked away, hiding their giggles.

"But, why not?" Hina asked. "You would attract the attention of many knowledgeable men."

"These tablets are unique," Kukara explained. "Nobody understands them yet. Only Hotu-Matua, Taranga and I know the meaning of a few signs. I am not ready to share that knowledge with anyone, but my relatives...like you, Kon, Taranga and Hotu-Matua."

Hina smiled, and put a hand on Kukara's shoulder.

"As you say, young girl. I hope you will teach me the meaning of these signs."

"I will," Kukara said, "with pleasure."

"I know Kon will be fascinated by these tablets," Hina said.

"I know he will help me discover the meaning of many of these signs," Kukara murmured, caressing the tablets.

"I know what it is to protect secrets," Hina said, with a wide smile. "Once, it absorbed my whole life."

"So, can I have my secrets, too?" Kukara asked.

"You most certainly can."

When Kukara walked away, Taranga took Hina's hand.

"I have something to tell you," He said. "You told that girl you would be her mother."

"I did," Hina replied, "and I will."

"Do you know the meaning of this for Viracocha's people?"

"It is a sacred commitment which I shall never forget," Hina replied, with evident pride.

"Good!" Taranga said, holding Hina's hand. "This is what I expected from you."

"Maohis adopt children from others all the time," Hina explained. "It is our tradition to give everything to children. And, I know what my commitment means to Kukara."

"It is a noble commitment," Taranga said. "Only people with a certain class can find the courage for it."

"I disagree!" Hina objected. "I don't need courage to adopt Kukara. Instead, I take pride and pleasure in being dear to her."

Taranga walked away with a smile on his face, and tears in

his eyes. He was silent, and content.

"He is a good man," Hina murmured.

At dusk, another ship came abreast of Hotu-Matua's ship. Hina saw two women standing on the deck, and she took Mehao's hand.

"Can you recognize your mother from here?"

Mehao rolled on one elbow, with feverish eyes. He did not fully comprehend Hina's question, until he saw a familiar woman on the other ship. His eyes opened wide, followed by a radiant smile.

"She is alive!" he said with joy. "She is the tallest woman."

Hina noticed an instant change in Mehao's voice. She knew he had regained enough energy to live. When the two ships met, Hina jumped on the other ship. She looked at a man coming toward her, and instantly blanched from surprise. The man was a Viracocha, and looked very much like Kon.

"Is your name Illa?" she inquired.

"No, my name is Rangi," he replied, shocked by Hina's question.

Kukara jumped on the ship and went straight to Rangi, who took her in his arms.

"Her name is Hina of the Valley. She is Kon's mate, and my mother."

Rangi regarded Hina for a moment, saw her beauty and intuitively knew she was important for Viracocha.

"So, Kon is alive," Rangi said, with sparkling blue eyes.

"Alive and well!" Hina replied. "He often talked about you. But it never occurred to me you would look like him."

The man smiled, and left with Taranga. Hina went to the tall Maohi woman. She was strong, well built, in her late thirties. She was still beautiful.

"My name is Hina of the Valley, Tupua's daughter... Are you Tehani?"

Surprise covered Tehani's face.

"How can you be on this ship? Yes, I am Tehani. But..."

"I was on Tamatoa's ship, searching for you," Hina said.

Tehani looked at the sea, more confused than ever.

"A few nights ago, I saw a wreck from Tamatoa's ship." Hina said. "Two men were on the wreck. I jumped in the sea to rescue them, but nobody saw me, and nobody heard me. I drifted with the two men for several days, until Hotu-Matua found us."

Tehani was still skeptical. Hina's story was unbelievable.

"Come with me," Hina said gently, taking Tehani's hand, "I want to show you someone you may know."

Both women went to Hotu-Matua's ship, followed by Kukara. Immediately, Tehani saw her son lying on the deck.

"Mehao!... Mehao, my son!" she said, her eyes rimmed with tears. She kneeled, and took him in her arms.

"Mother, you are alive," Mehao said, closing his eyes.

"You are ill," the queen said. "I will take care of you."

"Hina saved my life," Mehao said.

Tehani turned around, and looked Hina straight in the eyes.

"Why is it that all of us owe you so much?" Tehani sobbed.

"You owe me nothing," Hina replied. "I am a priestess, and it is my duty to help people."

"If so, we should have more priestesses like you," Tehani grinned. "Whoever can change Tamatoa's mind so deeply as you did, is far more than a priestess."

"He did not change his mind because of me," Hina replied. "Tamatoa is a remarkable man who was in desperate search of himself. At one point, along his tormented journey, he found serenity. It just happened that I was there, with him, at the right place and the right time."

"Modesty is a great quality," Tehani said. "If Tamatoa found serenity in Tahiti-nui, then I want to see the grandeur of your peaceful valley."

"I welcome you," Hina smiled, showing her beautiful teeth, "as my guest and friend."

"You give me a great honor," Tehani said, bending her head in sign of recognition.

Later at dusk, Hotu-Matua ignited a torch of burning oil at the rear of the ship. With his conch, he invited the other ships to do the same. Soon, the night was decorated with six bright spots that could be seen from a considerable distance. Hina understood immediately. The search was on, to find Tamatoa, to find Kon Tici.

"Tonight is the night," Taranga said, laying his wrinkled hand on Hina's shoulder. Before dawn, he knew he would see his grandson. Kukara's eyes were fixed on the southwestern horizon, and she never blinked. Her eyes were tearful with joy and emotion. She also knew she would see her father before dawn. Their inexpressible joy spread to Hina, who wondered how they could possibly know for sure, but Hina knew Viracocha's ways too well. She knew they were both in touch with Kon Tici, and this was a fact.

Somewhere to the southwest, Kon woke up from a one-night and one-day uninterrupted trance. Tamatoa went to him, but a wise hand stopped him.

"Let him finish what he is doing," Vana said. "In due time, he will come to you."

Kon passed the two men, did not even notice them and climbed to the top of the bamboo mast.

"This is behavior beyond my understanding," Tamatoa

chuckled. "I suppose I would become accustomed to it."

"We all did," Vana murmured. "He is from another world."

At the top of the mast, Kon slowly circled the northeastern horizon.

"What can he see?" Tamatoa asked, puzzled. "It is all black. I cannot even see my own ships."

"Kon never does anything in vain," Vana smiled.

Kon surveyed the horizon once more, came to a stop, thinking he had seen something. He closed his eyes, and backed up slightly from the mast. Then, he looked at the horizon again.

"Would it be the rising moon?" he murmured to himself. "No, it is too early, and at the wrong place. This very faint glow is something else."

Suddenly, pointing at the northeastern horizon, Kon Tici gave his order with a calm voice.

"Paddle full speed, this way, and light your oil torches."

He carefully checked the alignment of the mysterious glow with several stars, went down and showed the stars to Tamatoa. Soon, a torch started burning at the rear of the ship. With a thundering blow from his conch, Tamatao instructed the other ships to light their torches and follow him. They raised the sails, and eleven ships went full speed toward an unknown target. Soon, everyone could see the glow above the horizon. Then, the glow became six tiny bright dots.

Kukara watched the horizon with inner certitude the light would come only from one direction. Then, with incredible calmness, without blinking, she looked at Hina.

"There is a light on the horizon that is not one of ours."

Hina jumped to her feet, and saw the light. She quickly turned around and counted seven lights. There was one too many. She counted again with her fingers: There was no more doubt.

Before she said anything, Hotu-Matua blew powerfully in his conch to alert all other ships. Then, they cruised toward the southwest. Soon, there were several lights too many, and Hina was startled by a familiar detail. She knew Tamatoa well. She knew his men were well trained and disciplined. She counted eleven lights, exactly at the same distance apart. She could even guess which one was the leading ship: The oil was burning with a different color on that one. Kon Tici was coming.

In a way, Hina was amused, because Kon could not know she was on one of the new ships. On the awesome sea, finding ships did not mean finding lost Hina. She could already anticipate his joy when he would see her. They would share a sacred happiness she had thought impossible two days before. Touching him again would be a euphoric and unforgettable moment.

Hina could see people on Tamatoa's ship. She looked at the tall bamboo mast, but there was nobody on it. She wondered how many days Kon had stayed on the mast, searching for her. Then, she saw the powerful silhouette of the tattooed giant. Kon must have been one of the men at his side.

"Come closer,... come closer," she murmured, holding Kukara's shaking hand. Suddenly, her eyes stopped on a tall, thin man different from the others. At his side, she recognized Vana. There was no more doubt. She had found Kon Tici. Hina's happiness was such that she could not suppress tears, many tears of joy. Never before in her life, had she felt as she did at that moment. Instantly, she forgot all her pain and suffering. She stepped away from Kukara.

"No, Hina, don't," Hotu-Matua said, trying to stop the young priestess.

It was too late. Hina was already swimming fast toward the

other ship. At the same instant, a man jumped into the sea from the other ship, and swam toward Hina.

"I think Kon found an amazing woman," Taranga said, placing a hand on Hotu-Matua's shoulder. "Look at her, she is swift like a fish."

"She is swift all right," Hotu-Matua joked.

"I hope you don't have grief for what she told you."

"I don't," Hotu-Matua replied. "Being a king does not make me immune from making mistakes."

Hina swam without effort, gliding along with perfect technique. At full speed she reached Kon's hands. Without saying a word, they embraced passionately. His lips parted hers in a soul-reaching contact. She felt his teeth against hers, and the warmth of his tongue searching for hers. The salty water in their mouths added a unique pleasure. They wanted that moment to last forever.

"Come on, children!" Tamatoa said, visibly worried. "This is the open sea. It is not a place to take a bath."

"Right now, nothing can stop them," Vana said, "not even the great blue shark."

Hina backed off some distance from Kon, and smiled at him with a daring quest.

"Swim down with me," she said, "as deep as we can go. Come taste this water I have been drinking for too long."

Kon hesitated, a bit concerned, then nodded with approval.

"Let's go!"

They took several deep breaths, then hand in hand, they dived into the darkness of the sea. It was a mysterious world, with no light, no stars, no air and no breeze. It was not their world.

The pressure of the water became greater, and greater, on their ears, then on their jaws. They stopped their descent, closed their nose with their fingers, and blew to equalize the pressure on both sides of their eardrums. Then, they went deeper, until the water became cold. It was as far as Kon could go. Hina wanted to go deeper, but he prevented her from doing so, by pulling her hand. She knew it was his limit, she complied.

"This is insane," Tamatoa said, restless and irritated.

"This is love," Vana said, openly amused. "We owe them that moment, don't you think?"

Kon caressed her waist, brought her against him, and they swam straight up. The water became warmer. A few dim lights seemed hanging on a moving ceiling. The two ships were much closer to one another. As they broke the surface, everybody cheered them. Hina raised her arms in a sign of victory and said something only one man in the world knew the meaning of.

"Remember the dolphin!" she screamed, splashing back into the sea.

Everyone was puzzled by her words. Only Kon knew exactly what she was referring to. Excited beyond reason, they both climbed on Hotu-Matua's ship. Kon did not have the time to say a word, or look at anyone before a young girl jumped with passion into his arms, all way up to his chest.

"My father!" Kukara said, with deep sobs. "It was so lonely without you, for so long."

Kon closed his eyes, astonished, overwhelmed and content.

"You were in my dreams every day," he said. "I knew I would find you."

With no further words, they embraced, looked at each other and wiped the tears from their cheeks. She caressed his face, and he ran his long fingers through her hair.

"My daughter!" Kon said, immensely happy. "We have so much to talk about."

Kon felt a familiar hand on his shoulder. He turned around and saw his grandfather. The two men hugged each other for a long time. They had sustained many losses at sea, but at this moment they saw only the priceless reward of an awesome saga. They saw only the dawn of a new era on which they would build. The entire Maohi family watched them with compassion. Viracocha was not dead. Viracocha was being adopted.

Tamatoa's ship came in contact with Hotu-Matua's ship. Sailors tied both ships together. The tattooed giant waited for Hotu-Matua's signal. They stared at each other for too long.

"You are my guest," Hotu-Matua finally said.

Tamatoa stepped into his adversary's ship, and Tehani immediately melted into the arms of her husband and king.

"The last few days, I realized how dear you are to me," Tamatoa said.

"I thought I would never see you again," she replied.

"I see our son is with you," Tamatoa noticed.

"Hina saved his life," Tehani said. "Without her, our son would have died a few days ago."

Tamatoa turned around, walked to the young priestess until his chest almost touched hers. She could feel his powerful breath. Tamatoa kneeled, bent his head, and showed emotion and deep respect to a remarkable woman who became a source of inspiration for him.

"Hina of the Valley," Tamatoa said with deep sincerity, "you are who I cannot be, but I shall be who you want me to be. This is how I shall repay you for what you have done."

Hotu-Matua heard Tamatoa's words, and glanced at Taranga, who looked at the stars with a broad smile

on his face. Hotu-Matua glanced at Hina, and she stared at him in return, with expectation. He looked at the moon that had just risen, and the golden reflection on the sea, pondering his thoughts and wondering about the wisdom of what he was prepared to do.

Finally, the Kings put one arm on the other's shoulder. Two solid arms created a new bond between two different Maohi families. They stared at one another with cold eyes.

"During ordinary times, you would have been my enemy," Hotu-Matua said.

"During ordinary times," Tamatoa replied, "I would never have given you the opportunity to see me."

Hotu-Matua knew his people would have been no match for Tamatoa's war machine, but in the eyes of his formidable adversary, he saw unexpected compassion and generosity.

"I may learn how to accept you as a neighbor," Hotu-Matua said.

"Hiva is your land, and I respect that," Tamatoa replied.

The first contact between the two men was difficult, but enhanced with good will.

Later during the night, Kukara was peacefully asleep between Kon and Hina. Taranga covered them with a blanket, went back to Tamatoa and Hotu-Matua, and saw a bright shooting star crossing the entire sky and fall in the east.

"What makes them most spectacular is the silence that surrounds them," Tamatoa said.

"They mean something, but I am not sure what," Hotu-Matua said.

"Perhaps, it a sign for us to go east," Tamatao added.

"If the time is not right, we look at them with curiosity," Taranga said. "But, if the time is right, they become a signal pushing us to fulfill our dreams."

Tamatoa glanced at the old Viracocha, and thought he was a

good man.

"Follow my ship," Tamatoa said. "We should be in Tahiti-nui in about three days."

"The good spirits be with you," Hotu-Matua replied.

Tamatoa jumped onto his ship, and helped Tehani and Mehao to do the same. They untied the ships, and quickly separated.

Hotu-Matua waved at the great warrior, and admired the superb vessel going away. Tamatoa was not the man he had imagined. In a way, he was relieved for the safety of his people, but he pondered if it would always be that way.

"I shall wait, prepare and see." he murmured to himself.

"He owes you the life of his wife," Taranga said.

"This is what worries me," Hotu-Matua replied. "What shall I expect, the day he will owe me nothing?"

"My friend, this greatly depends on you," Taranga said. "This man can be inspired."

At dawn, Taranga sat near Kon.

"Grandson, we have important matters to discuss."

Hina, Kukara and Hotu-Matua joined them.

"I know everything that happened to you," Taranga said. "Hina told us in detail. However, you don't know what happened to us."

Kon crossed his legs, pushed his hair behind his shoulders and looked his ancestor straight in the eyes. Hina laid her head on his thigh, and the golden condor was glittering on her breast.

"Two moon-cycles after we lost contact with you," Taranga said, "we found the beautiful island of Hiva. The balsa trunks of the rafts were soaked with so much water that they sank more and more every day. Our supply of drinking water was exhausted, and we were desperate. When the peaceful islanders found us, we were in poor health. Only three rafts reached Hiva. Several moon-cycles later, we visited the entire Tuamotu archipelago with Hotu-Matua, and found Rangis's two rafts with Kukara. Several days later, we found the remains of your raft, and realized at least one of you had survived because of the tracks of your activities building a small raft with the remnants of the old one. Then, we went farther south, to Mangareva. We found another raft with four survivors. We pursued our long journey to Rapa, and found nothing.... Our losses are appalling, and there are no signs from the largest group, no signs from Illa's group."

"But, Illa and Kama are alive," Kon said.

"How do you know?" Taranga asked.

"I saw them both, in several visions I had," Kon replied.

"If there are islands unknown to us," Hotu-Matua said, "between your continent and Mangareva, it must be far away to the east, because we explored that region many times without success."

"Too many rafts are missing," Kon said. "It is impossible that most of them would have missed the great barrier of atolls."

"Unless they drifted too far south," Hotu-Matua said.

"Then what?" Kon asked, annoyed.

"Then they died in the empty spaces of the west," Hotu-Matua replied.

"Impossible!" Kon said, standing and looking at the eastern horizon. "They are somewhere beyond Mangareva. They are alive."

"There is only one way to find out," Hotu-Matua said.

"I know," Kon replied. "And I already have a plan."

"You may speak," Hotu-Matua said.

"Tamatoa is willing to give me several ships, and he himself would go to the east, as an explorer. Would you do so as well?"

"Yes," Hotu-Matua smiled, "by following a different path."

"I will go with you," Kukara said.

"I am too old for such a trip," Taranga said.

"Hina, would you come with us?" Kukara asked.

"I will not," Hina replied. "I will wait for your return in Tahiti-nui, where I belong."

Kon knew the likelihood of a return was minimal, and the thought of losing Hina was intolerable to him.

"But you are my mother; you said so!" Kukara argued.

"Yes, I am," Hina replied. "But I cannot force you to stay with me."

"If Tamatoa is part of the expedition," Hotu-Matua said, "it would be wise for you to come with us."

"I agree," Taranga said. "You are a strong bond between the Viracocha and Maohi families. Your place is with us."

"I shall think about it," Hina replied. "And I must discuss the matter with my father and Vana. But first we still have a gathering to prepare."

"You are right," Hotu-Matua said, "the gathering will decide many things."

"With Hina or not," Kon said with determination and pain on his face, "I must return to the east."

"Sometimes, a man has to face difficult choices," Hotu-Matua said. "But don't be sad. The rising sun on your bracelets shows the way, and once in my life, I would like to see the continent. So, islands or no islands, it is my wish to go east."

Kon glanced at the king: the Maohi was sincere.

"It will be a dangerous and daring endeavor," Kon warned.

"Across the awesome sea," Hotu-Matua replied with pride, "there is nothing impossible for a well-born Maohi."

"It is not the sea that worries me," Kon said, pondering the king's words. "It is the people on the continent who may not be friendly."

"We are a seafaring race, Kon Tici," Hotu-Matua replied with serenity. "We shall visit the continent, then proceed and search for unknown islands."

Suddenly, Kukara attracted their attention.

"Look at the horizon," she said. "We have visitors."

Moments later, the sea was covered with ships and outriggers of all sizes. Everyone heard Tamatoa's powerful conch announcing the approaching fleet: Tahiti-nui's people had found Hina of the Valley.

There were more people at sea than anyone could remember. They came from every part of the island, on anything that could float. There were warriors, fishermen, priests, women, children, ill people, even kings. Immediately after Tamatoa's call, they all knew Hina was alive, and they all sang for joy. The sea was covered with the sound of drums and an enchanting melody of life. Wrapped in deep sentiment for

their princess, in total euphoria, they offered her the most astonishing gift she had ever dreamed of. Kon came behind Hina, and put his hands around her waist.

"They were told you were lost at sea," he said, " and they all came looking for you."

"There are so many," Hina said, with a choked voice.

"Mother, now I understand what you meant," Kukara said, taking Hina's hand.

"My people," Hina said with tears in her eyes, "you are good to me. I will never let you down."

Deeply moved, Hina looked at the Maohi people, her people, with pride. Her eyes did not blink; the muscles of her face did not flinch, but more tears rolled down her cheeks. She squeezed Kon's hand, and Kukara's hand.

"I shall serve my people for the rest of my life," she said, with a charismatic smile. There was no doubt with anyone that she would do so.

CHAPTER 28

"Our world is a tiny grain of sand with puzzling mysteries, and what we believe we see is nothing more than a supreme illusion. Taaroa's illness was only an excuse for an unknown force to be present among the Maohis, without being noticed. beneath the disguise of a leper, he was a powerful god carrying a message from another world."

Kon Tici Viracocha

Three moon cycles before the Maohis' great gathering, daring travelers from faraway islands would become the honored guests of the Havaiki priests, and would establish their quarters around the Marae of Taputapu-atea. During this time, Kon would wait patiently before making any attempt to prepare a search for his brother, until a spark of light would cross the sky, find a very ill man and deliberately change destiny.

Long ago, Kon gave a helping hand to a leper. The day had come when the leper would repay his debt, and when Taaroa would stop time and seal a bond between Maohis and the Viracocha people for many generations. As Taaroa knew when to give the water of life to Hina of the Valley, Taaroa also knew how to give magical inspiration to Kon Tici.

Kon sat near the bank of the Papenoo River, and watched the running water full of timeless significance. Then, his eyes questioned Mount Orohena. Intuitively, he knew he would meet the sacred mountain once more, before his departure. Somehow, he knew the mountain was a player, omnipresent and above the head of everyone. It was here, sacred and forbidden. It was the domain of the sacred red duck, the tropicbird, and something else, invisible and alien.

"It is here, waiting for you," Taaroa said as he came up behind Kon, who did not turn around.

"I am aware it is waiting for me," Kon replied, "yet I don't know the reason or the necessity."

"The reason is I," Taaroa said, "the necessity is they."

"The necessity is they." Kon repeated, looking at people nearby. "That I understand. But why should the reason be you?"

"Come with me, deep inside the valley," Taaroa said. "There, I will give you the reason."

They went to the heart of the rain forest. Taaroa had no energy, which made their journey very slow. Something was consuming the leper from inside. Taaroa noticed Kon observing him in detail.

"Yes, my friend, my days remaining are few," Taaroa said. "That illness is eating me a little more every day."

"There is still good life in you," Kon said.

"With your help, I want to leave this life with honor and dignity," Taaroa murmured, with a mysterious tone in his voice, which qualified his words as sacred.

Kon knew Taaroa's illness was irreversible and fatal, and the last phase was approaching. Soon, Taaroa would not be able to use his hands, or to walk, or to breathe. He understood the poor man was living an unworthy nightmare.

"What can I do to help you?" Kon asked.

"I recall your words, Taaroa replied. "I recall your desperate search for actions that develop ties between people."

Kon did not answer, but Taaroa knew he was listening.

"The time has come when I can give you an opportunity," Taaroa continued.

The men stopped, and looked at each other.

"Where are you taking me?" Kon asked.

"To the great falls, at the bottom of Mount Orohena, where you raced with Aru once, and amazed all of us with your climbing skills."

"Can you walk that far?"

"Yes, I can. I must," Taaroa replied.

With no further words, they pursued their journey along the river, under the warm rain. Around noon, the rain stopped, and they sat on a large stone partly surrounded by running water.

"Has anyone explained to you the reasons my name is Taaroa?"

"For Maohis, Taaroa is the creator of everything, as Viracocha is for us."

"He was, is, and always will be," Taaroa said. "A long time ago, Taaroa became bored in a vast and dark universe. So, He created light, the stars, the sun, the moon, the earth and the awesome sea. Later,He created the mountains, the valleys, the rivers and the forests. Then, one day, He had a vision of the most beautiful woman in the universe, created her and called her Hina-tu-a-uta. Because of his love for her, He created beauty, flowers, colors, and the legend goes on...."

"What does all this have to do with you?" Kon asked.

"As a child, I was marked by unusual signs, so I became a gifted priest, and people started to call me Taaroa. My real name is Taruia. For many years, I enjoyed being called Taaroa. So, in a way, it naturally became my real name. But I can no longer honor that name."

"Why not?" Kon argued.

"A priest, especially if called Taaroa, must be physically perfect, which I was for a long time. Now, look at me. How can such a thing be called by the sacred name? Look at this, it is disgusting and a repugnance to anyone who sees me. I am a human wreck, and I scare people."

"No, you do not!" Kon objected. "You are who you are, because you are meant to be that way. There is a reason for your illness. There is a reason for everything: The Light has chosen so."

To Kon's surprise, Taaroa looked at him with a broad smile.

"You are right! You know about the Light! Do you know the Light inhabits that prohibited cave on Orohena's flank, where you went once?"

"I know there is a force in there; I saw it under the form of a vortex of dust."

"It is the same thing," Taaroa said. "In total darkness, it becomes a vortex of purple light."

Kon looked at him, waiting for more.

"The Light gave me the reason for my illness," Taaroa said with dignity.

"What is it?" Kon asked, raising his eyebrows.

"I will tell you, but only in due time."

They continued their journey, farther into the heart of the valley.

"What is the meaning of Hina-tu-a-uta?" Kon asked.

"I thought you would never ask," Taaroa replied, amused. "It means Hina from the depths of the valley. It is a beautiful name symbolizing the completeness of Taaroa's creation. In the depth of the valley, Taaroa created beauty that could reproduce itself. As a result, Hina symbolizes life at its best. Our Hina should be honored to be called Hina of the Valley."

"She does honor her name," Kon said.

"Oh yes, she does," the old priest said in a low tone, watching a bird at the same time.

"What is your favorite animal?" Kon asked.

The leper looked at Kon Tici with a dark frown.

"How can you ask me this question, at the moment I was thinking about my favorite animal? Who are you, young man?"

"As a Viracocha, I have great clairvoyance," Kon said.

"My favorite animal is the great blue shark." Taaroa said.

Each word pounded in Kon's mind: They were unbelievable.

"The great blue shark!" Kon repeated with disgust on his face. "I was convinced it was a bird!"

Taaroa started walking, with a smile showing decayed teeth and bloody gums. He was satisfied: Kon had not known the answer.

"Man comes from the sea," Taaroa said. "After Taaroa created the earth, man lived among fish for a very long time. In the beginning, there was a large blue shark living near the beach of the Motuau islet, near the Teauroa Point, where you reached this island. It was called the great blue shark, was Taaroa's friend, and often played with children. When I was a boy, the great blue shark saved my life. One day, in the Fautaua Valley, where my parents lived, I went to the wrong place, at the wrong time. A patrol of warriors followed the tracks of another boy accused of killing the young sister of the king of a nearby district. No one knew for certain who that boy was. When the warriors found me, I was at a place where my father had killed a wild pig, the day before. When they saw the blood on the ground, they looked at me with suspicion, took me to the king and I was condemned to die because I had murdered the young girl. I did not know her, and I had never seen her. I tried to explain I was not the murderer, but nobody listened. I quickly understood it was pointless to deny the abomination, and forced my mind to give me the words: 'If you kill me and bury me, I will come back as an evil spirit to make you pay for this injustice. But, if you tie my body with a rope, and throw me into the sea, my spirit will leave this island forever.' At this instant, someone hit my head from behind, and everything was darkness. They put my body in a bag loaded with heavy stones, and took me to the sea, beyond the reef. Then, the warriors saw a shark, circling their outrigger. They thought the odor of my blood, dripping slowly from my head, attracted it. They dumped the bag into the sea, and I sank until my ears hurt so much that I regained consciousness, and struggled inside the bag. When the warriors came back to shore, they learned the king's young sister was alive, and that nobody had murdered her. She had only been lost in the valley for five days. Soon, everybody on the island learned about a young boy who had been sentenced to death by mistake, and because of prejudice.

"But, I was not dead. The great blue shark took me with his powerful jaw, and in no time, I was out of the bag and swimming. When I reached the surface, I took a deep breath, looked around and saw the warriors already far away. I held the powerful fin of the sacred shark, and swam with him to the Motuau islet. I stayed on the islet for two days, where I hid and recovered from my wound. The third night, I left the islet and went to my parent's house. When they saw me, they did not recognize me and thought I was a ghost. It took me most of the night to convince them I was alive. At dawn, they took me to the king, who was delighted to see me. He asked me what I wanted to forgive his mistake. Again, my mind took control of my words: 'I want to become the greatest priest of Tahiti-nui. My body has been protected by the great blue shark, who was Taaroa's favorite animal.' After that day, I started my long priesthood, and I was called Taaroa."

Kon was astonished by Taaroa's story, but something was still missing.

"All this does not explain the reason for your illness."

"Be patient, my friend." Taaroa said. "But, you are right, I like birds. I am never tired of studying their habits, and marveling at their beauty. My father always told me that people who like birds have a generous heart...." Taaroa glanced at Kon with a smile. "Therefore, you and I must be generous."

Far away at the same moment, at Hina's place, the young priestess hosted several dignitaries. She invited them to rest and meditate at the Marae of Toerau, where day and night they could hear the powerful waves pounding the cliff. Relentlessly, the ground shook, sending a forceful reminder that men were dust, nothing. With all their titles, possessions and ambitions, they were insignificant creatures at Taaroa's feet. Toerau was a place where a king could become humble, listening to the rumble of an infinite force, and where he could expand his vision into the wisdom of peace, into Taaroa's wisdom.

Mahine and Kukara helped Hina to accommodate Tamatoa the great with his old priest Mato, Tupua, Vana, Hotu-Matoa and Taranga Tici Viracocha.

"Without Kon," Tamatoa said, "nothing good can come from our discussions."

"May I say something?" Hina asked him, giving him a drink.

"Of course!" Tamatoa replied. "You are our hostess."

"I disagree with your words," Hina said, confident. "If Kon were here, he would be the center of your discussions. But he is in the valley with Taaroa. So, it is your chance to talk to one another, learn from one another and meditate together. Above all, you should have a good time."

"Conciliatory as usual," Tamatoa said, putting a hand on Hina's shoulder, "but I agree with you."

"I like her words," Mato said. "They fit this unique place, where my buttocks are shaking all the time."

Everyone roared with laughter. Then, Tupua asked a question he had asked earlier.

"So, who will help Kon to sail to the far east?"

"I will," Hotu-Matua answered.

"And so will I," Tamatoa thundered.

"This matter is settled," Tupua said. "Let's have a good time."

"Can I suggest a story about our king becoming weightless?" Vana proposed.

"You, you better shut up!" Tupua replied, suppressing a chuckle.

Far away, deep inside the valley, Taaroa and Viracocha were at work in the mysterious ways selected by the Light. Kon and the leper continued their journey along the river. The day was hot and sunny, and they were at a point where the valley became lush. Among giant trees, ferns from another age, spectacular vines and bushy creepers, birds were discreet and silent. It was a place for the gods, and their selected servants.

Taaroa came to a stop, and pointed at a decaying tree trunk with his gnarled finger. "Did you ever see a kingfisher?" the leper asked. "In some islands, far in the west, these birds indeed fish marvelously. But in Tahiti-nui, the same bird does not like water, and hates fish bones."

Kon came closer to the dead tree, and saw the colorful bird. Its head and back were bright green, its tail was like the deep blue of the sea, its neck was red and its breast and belly were pure white.

"It is beautiful!" Kon said, with admiration.

"In Pora-Pora, the same bird has even prettier colors," Taaroa said. "It does not like the proximity of people, and you will rarely see it around the village. It stays and hides in the valley. It eats small animals such as butterflies, centipedes, spiders and wasps. Once in awhile, it may peck on a fruit."

Kon came closer to the dead tree, and a stick of wood cracked under his foot. Instantly, the bird disappeared inside the tree, but an instant later, it came back and showed his head framed by the darkness of the circular hole.

"When it builds a nest," Taaroa said, "or protects its chicks, it becomes very brave. I saw one follow a chicken and steal several feathers from its tail."

Kon remained silent, admiring the magnificent bird in its privacy.

"This little hunter is very patient," Taaroa continued. "It can stay half a day without moving. But when it flies to its target, it never misses. It stays here in the shade of the forest and rarely goes on the drier plateaus. The faithful couple has a large territory, and does not tolerate any relatives around."

Kon listened with great interest, and was fascinated by the closeness of the priest to all the details of the valley. During his life, Taaroa had accumulated an immense knowledge of the fauna and flora, and it was a constant part of his meditations.

"My brother Illa and I often thought about carving our knowledge on stone or wood," Kon said. "Like those mysterious tablets Kukara is protecting."

"You told me these tablets hold knowledge," Taaroa said.

"But how can one sign carry so many words?" Kon wondered.

"Could one sign lead to an idea, instead of one word?" Taaroa suggested.

Kon glanced at the old man, finding his answer pertinent.

"If so, one tablet can carry a lifetime of memories," Kon said.

"The danger is that one tablet may mean something to you," Taaroa said, "and something different to someone else."

"Therefore, it is not a reliable way to carry knowledge," Kon concluded.

"Only the word of mouth can carry knowledge from generation to generation with integrity," Taaroa ruled.

Deeply involved in their discussion, the two friends did not realize they were approaching the great falls. Suddenly, the magical meadow opened, and they saw the white foam falling from the mountain, sending a fresh mist to the surrounding giant ferns. The falls pounded into the large pond with a timeless rumble, and a rainbow arched its colors on the green background of the forest. They raised their eyes, up and up, until they felt the back of their head touch their shoulders: The giant Mount Orohena was there, awesome.

"We have reached the end of our journey," Kon said.

"Not yet, my friend," Taaroa said, looking at the forest leading to an upper ledge. "I must reach that place where the tropicbird nests. It can be done by crawling through that forest."

Kon was astonished at Taaroa's proposition.

"Don't worry," Taaroa said, "I did it many times before. But, before we reach the ledge, I will show you someone between these giant mape trees who is holding another kind of knowledge."

"Who can live in such a remote place?" Kon asked.

"The bird of priests," Taaroa replied, "the sacred green pigeon."

"It is Hina's favorite bird," Kon replied.

"Hina of the Valley!" Taaroa exclaimed, raising his arms above his head. "She brings out the best in all of us. She did not become a priestess, but she was born as such. One day, I will pass my powers to her."

At this moment, Kon did not realize the full meaning of Taaroa's words. They started their journey through the forest, and immediately, they were in total darkness. It was hot and humid. The immense roots of the mape trees spreading around the base of their tormented trunk, were everywhere, like formidable tentacles covered with ageless lichens and moss. In many ways, it was an uncomfortable world.

"This pigeon is like a ghost," Taaroa murmured. "Its back is shiny green, like young leaves. Its breast and belly are bright yellow like frangipani flowers. You find the bird where no one goes. You can pass nearby it, and never see it, until it calls you hooo...hooo...hou...hou... Maohis are frightened by its call because it is often followed by the swirling ghost of dust. But I can tell you this bird is the most gentle creature on this earth. If we walk without making too much noise, it will come to us, find out who we are, and what we do."

The forest became thicker, and all directions looked the same. The only reference was the gentle slope showing the direction of the mountain.

"This is a place where your body can rot like mine," Taaroa said, taking no unnecessary steps around the giant roots. "It is a difficult world."

Kon felt a slight air draft behind his head, and thought someone was observing them. He turned around, and saw the green pigeon standing on a branch nearby. Taaroa sat on a mape's giant tentacle that spread to the ground like a thick membrane on which the priest drummed with his hands, sending a lugubrious melody through the realm of a forest from another age.

When Taaroa stopped, the pigeon called: "hooo, hooo, hou, hou." Then it flew some distance away, where a swirling vortex of dust vanished behind the trees.

The sight was mostly disturbing to Kon, who distinctly saw a purple glare inside the vortex.

"I hear you, gracious companion of the eternal night," Taaroa murmured. "In your song, I recognize the voice of my ancestors who sleep forever in this green valley."

The pigeon came back, and perched on a small branch very close to them, as if it was expecting something.

"The sacred pigeon likes you," Taaroa said. "You should be honored, my great traveler. Only high priests and kings are friendly to this gentle creature. All others fear what it represents: the living soul of those we loved once, cherished, respected, who now are sleeping until the end of time with the swirling ghost of dust. Look at it closely!"

Kon's eyes were searching what he had seen among the trees, wondering how it could be related to the pigeon.

"If you search for the thing, you will never see it," Taaroa said. "So, focus on the pigeon."

Taaroa raised his arm. Instantly, the pigeon came to roost on it. The leper dug out a few seeds from a pocket, below his waist. The pigeon ate the seeds, one by one, keeping an eye on both men.

"Do you notice something peculiar about this little being?" Taaroa asked.

"Peculiar!" Kon replied. "It is not the only thing peculiar around here."

"About its beauty," Taaroa said, "its delicateness, its fragility, peace and gentleness. Do these words mean something to you?"

Kon thought he was swimming in the halo of a dream, where

reality would slowly mix with mystery. He looked at Taaroa's face and was startled to find beauty in it. It had never occurred to him that such a thought could be possible. The leper was beautiful. The green pigeon, feeding from Taaroa's hand, had never questioned this beauty. At this instant, Taaroa's body did not exist. Kon saw only Taaroa's soul inside a purple glare. Taaroa saw Kon's eyes, smiling at him. Taaroa knew Kon's thoughts.

"The Great Creator gave us a soul," Taaroa said. "It is our treasure with which we can achieve the unthinkable with harmony. Too often, we do the unthinkable and forget the harmony. During the last few moon-cycles, I observed you, Kon Teke, and you did the unthinkable with harmony. What I saw in you made my life complete. From that day when I first saw you coming to my poor house, I knew I would reach the gate leading to the other world, with contentment."

Taaroa placed a few seeds in Kon's hand, stretched his other hand to Kon's hand. The green pigeon walked across the bridge of friendship, went to Kon's hand feeding. Immediately, a purple glare surrounded the joined hands of both men, and Kon felt a tremendous blow of energy enter his body.

"Receive this great gift, Kon Tici," the croaking voice said with power, and pronouncing Kon's name the right way for the first time.

The pigeon cleaned its beak against Kon's gold bracelet, and looked at itself through the golden mirror. The bird cooed gently, convinced it was another of its kind.

"I am adopted," Kon said. "But what it is trying to tell me?"

"Protect me, respect me and preserve the natural beauty of my valley," Taaroa replied.

"So, this world is mine, Kon said. "But it is my sacred duty not to alter its harmony in any way."

"This is said," Taaroa replied, "and it should be done as such."

The pigeon cooed once more, as if it had approved, then flew away. Kon tried to recall all the details of this important moment. He knew something was with them, observing them, something far beyond what he could comprehend. So, he decided to make a strong effort to remain as calm and as lucid as possible. Slowly, the slope increased, and the trees gave way to ferns. They walked under the formidable fronds, and smaller species covered the ground to their knees. They could see neither the sky nor the ground, until a window opened, revealing the majestic Mount Orohena. It was here, close, forbidden and the keeper of an incredible secret. They still had a long way to go before reaching the ledge where Taaroa wanted to go, but they could see it.

It was dusk when they reached the ledge. Far below, they could hear the powerful rumble of the falls. It was a permanent reminder of who Orohena was. A few tropicbirds expressed their defensive views to the two intruders, but they soon accepted their presence. Kon collected dead ferns, and started a fire at a narrow place where they would sit for the night. Taaroa was silent, rubbing his hands bleeding from wounds inflicted during their daring journey through the ferns.

"This fire feels good," Taaroa said, with a shiver.

"Is this the place you wanted to show me?" Kon asked.

"This is the place where you shall know me better."

They ate the last part of the breadfruit they had saved, and some nuts. They savored their last banana, and shared the milk of their last green coconut. Close to the dying fire, they looked at one another, straight in the eyes. It was the end of a long journey.

"You question the sanity of my coming here," Taaroa said.

"It is an understatement," Kon replied with a smile.

"I am doomed," the leper said, with a mask of sadness on his face. "I am not going to live much longer. Now, I must choose the place where I shall rest for eternity."

The last embers in the fire died. Silence surrounded them. The night became so dark they could not see each other at first.

"My death and the reason for my illness seem uncorrelated," Taaroa said, "until you think carefully about the circumstances: I learned that my illness had a purpose for what is happening now."

"So, this is why we are here."

"Yes. My death must generate a historical ceremony, like every high dignitary's death. So, my illness was Taaroa's gift to allow me to terminate my life with no regret, when I wish, when the time would be right."

Kon stared at the leper: There was something terrifying in his words, and the way they were said. They were meant to be true. Kon took the old priest's shaking hands, to keep them warm, and to create a bond of eternal friendship.

He understood very well Taaroa's nightmare, and would never have questioned the leper's ultimate decision. It was Viracocha's way to respect what someone wanted to do with his life.

"Let me go, the way I want, and when I want," Taaroa said.

"And," Kon replied, "no one shall ever dare to interfere with your freedom of doing what you want with yourself, not relatives, or friends, or priests, or the king."

"For my body, and whoever lives in it, we are in charge," Taaroa said.

"The rest of the world shall lower their eyes before you," Kon replied.

"I am asking for your help," Taaroa murmured.

"If asked for help by one who reaches the ultimate decision," Kon replied, "I shall help to the full extent of my capability."

"And," Taaroa added, "you shall not interfere by words."

Kon Tici was overwhelmed and lowered his eyes: He would help Taaroa.

"What do you want me to do?" Kon asked, looking at Taaroa's eyes rimmed with tears.

"For my departure, I don't need help," Taaroa replied. "But, after my death, I want you to take me where I can rest with the spirits of my forefathers."

"Priest of priests," Kon said, squeezing Taaroa's hands, "I will take you wherever you want to go."

"Promise me you will not change your mind when hearing my demand."

"You have the word of Kon Tici Viracocha."

"First, do not follow me during the next few days, and respect my last moment of privacy. Then, you shall mummify my body with precious fragrances, and install me comfortably inside an outrigger I shall select. When you will find me, you will understand which outrigger I have chosen."

Very slowly, deliberately, Taaroa raised his head and pointed at the cave where Kon had been once before. In the dark night, it would have been impossible to see the entry of the cave, if it were not for a faint purple vortex standing in front of it. This time, there was no more doubt in Kon's mind: Something or someone was living in that cave: different, alien and incredible.

"You shall take me in my outrigger to the sacred lake of the red ducks."

"Your demand shall be fulfilled," Kon answered, "completely and unconditionally."

"Two days later, you will bring me down in the outrigger to

the cave, where that thing is."

"As you say!" Kon replied, startled by the demand.

"This is my gift to you, Kon Tici. This endeavor will create ties between former enemies that nothing will ever destroy."

"What is the connection of all this with that thing?"

"Be patient, my friend. Then, Hina shall stay with me for a few days in the cave."

"Why her?" Kon asked, more puzzled than ever.

"She is Maohi," Taaroa replied. "Here, she will discover the identity of the vortex."

CHAPTER 29

"Taaroa's illness could never have altered his pride or his dignity. To the very end of his life, he had been in control of his destiny with class. His act was the result of a true freedom of choice. It was personal, private and the forbidden territory of anyone else."

Hina of the Valley

At the Marae of Toerau, Hina listened to the dignitaries with little interest. Her mind was somewhere else. She was devastated by the idea of losing Kon, but her choice was final: She would not go to the far east with him. Her place was with her people, her village, her valley and Toerau.

When Tamatoa and Hotu-Matua agreed on a joint expedition, she walked out, and went to the nearby tiny garden full of fragrant tiare bushes. Mahine and Kukara followed her, but she told them to leave and accommodate her guests.

Vana had noticed her sudden departure, and he saw Kukara coming back.

"What is bothering Hina?" he asked. "Is she ill?"

"My mother is not ill," Kukara replied. "She is not happy. She likes Tahiti-nui too much. She knows she will lose my father."

Vana frowned with concern, and gently caressed Kukara's hair. Obviously, the small girl was not happy either.

"I should talk to her," Vana said. "You stay here and help Mahine."

He went to the garden that was full of fragrant flowers, and saw the young priestess sobbing.

"Let my words help you," Vana said, with uneasiness.

Hina jumped. She had not heard him coming.

"Come walk on the beach with an old friend," Vana suggested. "Your pain is mine."

Reluctantly, Hina followed him. She did not want to share her sorrow with anyone, especially Vana.

He sat on the warm sand, but Hina kept walking, looking at the sea.

"Come back, Hina, even if you don't care about me."

She came back, and sat near the priest, with a faint smile on her face.

"Kon's expedition will involve many ships," Vana said. "Tamatoa and Hotu-Matua never do things halfway. The round trip may take two sun-cycles. Both are talented navigators, and I am sure you will be safe."

"I will not go. Why are you telling me all this?"

"Because the expedition cannot succeed unless you go."

"I don't believe that," Hina replied, wiping off the salt of dried tears on her cheeks.

"There will be plenty of ill people, physically and mentally, who will need your attention. Hina, dearest, they will easily find courage with you."

"Tamatoa and Hotu-Matua have their own priests," Hina argued. "My place is here, at Toreau, with my people."

"Tamatoa and Hotu-Matua have high regard for you. For them, you are a living legend. They are your people, too: You made it that way."

"So, I made a mistake."

"You most certainly did not!" Vana said, angry, and poking one finger on her chest. "You are young, and a two-sun-cycle trip is nothing for you. You will come back, greater and stronger."

"Are you trying to exile me from my family?" Hina said, irritated.

"Kon Tici is your only family," Vana said. "Be the priestess he created."

"The Maohi people are my only family," Hina said.

"You are still a young girl..."

"No, I am not a girl, I am a priestess," she replied, recovering her pride.

"Yes, you are, and a very good one. I can witness to that. There is grandeur in this expedition; this expedition needs grand people."

"What would happen, if we don't return?"

"It will not be a one-way trip," Vana said. "I don't believe Tamatoa, or Hotu-Matua, or Kon would stay far away from this paradise they have known for so long."

Hina looked at the horizon, then looked at Vana.

"Somehow, my intuition tells me it will be a one-way trip. Kon's brother is a remarkable man. If he did not pursue his trip farther, there must be a good reason."

"Maybe he went too far west, and just missed our islands," Vana said, shrugging his shoulders.

"Not Illa Tici Viracocha," Hina argued. "This man does not miss islands."

"How do you know?"

"Did Kon miss our islands?" she asked.

"No, but he was lucky."

"He was not lucky. He was inspired and guided. There is a

difference."

Defeated, Vana took Hina's shoulders, caressed the green pigeon feather she had attached to the bark-cloth wrapped around her breast. "Dear Hina, the ocean is full of birds, and you love birds. Discovery will feed your soul. The far east will be full of challenges, and you love challenges. You cannot turn your back on your destiny. Kon crossed your path, so it is unthinkable for you to leave his path."

"Why is it that I start to believe you?" she murmured.

"Far away, on another land, you will look at the stars on clear nights, searching for answers where no one has found any. For now, please be positive with yourself. We love you too much to see you suffer unnecessarily."

Hina melted in Vana's arms, and put her head on his chest. He caressed her soft, long hair. Never in his life had he cherished a greater treasure, this one who so often had bitterly argued with him.

"I love you, too..." she said, between sobs. Then she looked at him: "Would you let me consider all this by myself? Perhaps, too many things have been happening too fast. I need a rest."

They walked back to the Marae. Hina washed her face with fresh water. Vana went to a hibiscus tree, and took one of its large, red flowers. He removed the pistil, and placed the lovely funnel-shaped flower on Hina's left ear.

"Hina-tu-a-uta," Vana said slowly, emphasizing every word, "princess of Tahiti-nui, priestess from the depths of the valley, be one of us when Kon and Taaroa will return, as a surprise may change your life."

Two days later, Kon went to Tupua's house and found him carving a wooden mask.

"It is very nice," Kon said.

"No, I am not good at this," Tupua said. "But I enjoy doing it. You look preoccupied."

"I want to ask you a favor," Kon said.

"You ask, and I will give you anything," the King said, dropping his chisel.

"I can tell you what I want, but I cannot give you the reasons, at least not yet."

Tupua roared in laughter, and beat his stomach with both hands. "Another mystery, another secret!... What do you want, son?"

"I want five ropes," Kon replied.

"That is no problem," Tupua said, shrugging his shoulders.

"Each rope must be strong enough to lift a heavy canoe," Kon added.

Tupua raised his head in surprise, and scratched his hair, nervous.

"Simple! Your demand is simple. How long should these ropes be?"

"Long enough to cross the entire village," Kon replied, with a quirk of humor.

The king gave Kon a glance of utter disbelief. "We don't have such things, and to make them would take an entire moon-cycle."

"This is why I ask now," Kon replied. "I will need them one moon-cycle from now."

"I am not sure your demand is reasonable," Tupua said, with a shadow of annoyance crossing his face.

"Do you want me to ask someone else?" Kon said.

Tupua smiled, and put one arm around Kon's shoulder. "Don't. We will make these ropes for you. But, what do you suggest I say, when everyone asks me what they are for?"

"Tell them the great Taaroa needs them to go to the moon."

"Taaroa!... The moon!... Why Taaroa?"

"I will say no more."

Hina saw her father shaking his head, shrugging his shoulders, before disappearing inside his house. "What did you say to my father? I can tell he is disturbed."

Kon laughed and put his arm around Hina's waist.

"Nothing out of the ordinary, I asked him to prepare five strong ropes, long enough for Taaroa to go to the moon."

"I knew it!" Hina said, stepping aside from Kon. "I knew you would find something new to distress that poor man. My mother told me that since you came here, he is agitated at night, talks in his sleep, kicks unfamiliar objects when he wakes up..." She laughed at her own words. "What did you do with Taaroa in the valley?"

"We talked about how to transfer his knowledge to you."

"I don't believe you," she replied, suspicious. "Why should he?"

"Taaroa is dying, and he wants you to be his heir."

"It would take him a lifetime to teach me everything he knows."

"No, it will take him one day, after he dies."

She looked at him for a long time: He was serious.

"You are not going to tell me more," she said.

"In due time, I will."

It was dusk. A shadow followed Kon and Hina, listened to them, but did not want to disturb their privacy. From the corner of her eye, Hina saw the shadow.

"Come with us, Kukara."

Pleased, the young girl ran to them, and took Hina's hand. They went to the beach, and walked on the still hot, black sand.

They heard the familiar "pee-weet" of a solitary sandpiper. They sat, looked at the first stars and listened to the crickets. Silent and quick, a few sand crabs ran sideways. The waves lapped gently at their feet: Everything was calm and in order.

"Are you going to love each other?" Kukara asked.

"You know we will," Kon replied taking the woman he loved into his arms. Hina buried her face against his throat, then pressed her open lips on his.

Kukara crossed her legs, placed the Rongo-Rongo tablets on her lap, and explored the signs, one at a time, with her fingers. Suddenly, she found the sign she was searching for. The touch under her fingers was unmistakable. She had memorized all the signs, by sight, and by touch. Under her finger was a circle for the sun, three undulating lines for the sea, and a broken line for the mountain.

"This is how life starts," she murmured to herself. "My parents are beautiful. They love me, and I love them. We were meant to be here, together, at this moment. Now, I may sleep, in peace, happy. My loved ones, have pleasures."

A little farther on the beach, a tiny shadow ran calling: "pee-weet".

Several days later, as the full moon became a perfect circle on the western horizon, a well-dressed priest left Papenoo. On the beach, he went west, toward the Teauroa Point. He was Taarao. Today, he was the great Taaroa, who walked the same way as when he was young. Calm and slow, with proud posture, he marked each step on the sand, starting the voyage of no return.

A great man he had been, and with the gods he would be remembered. Every step had been planned, and the end result was a certainty. Today was the day he had chosen. It was a day of incredible joy for him.

At the same moment, on her way to her parents' house, Hina noticed the entrance of Taaroa's house was decorated with white tropicbird feathers. It was a sign of good luck for those leaving by sea for a long journey. Intrigued, she went inside the house. Taaroa was not here. All his favorite objects were displayed, making a large spiral on the ground. She knew something was odd. Puzzled, but not worried, she left the house.

When Taaroa arrived at the Haapape village, he went directly to a friend's place. The old outrigger builder had a radiant smile on his face when he saw him. One moon-cycle earlier, Taaroa had asked him to build the best canoe he could, and had told him it would be used for an unusual ceremony. They both walked to the beach. Under the fronds of a coconut tree partially uprooted by a recent storm, was a magnificent hand-dug canoe. The hull was made of a single piece, and a strong and long outrigger was attached to one side. All around the top of the hull, birds, fish, shells, flowers and naked women resting on the beach were delightfully carved. The sight of the canoe overwhelmed Taaroa. It was a dream becoming reality. At the front end of the hull was the best piece of art: the majestic profile of the great blue shark.

Taaroa looked at his companion, speechless and engulfed in emotion. He hugged his friend in recognition, and finally could articulate a few words.

"The Great Taaroa will like this," Taaroa said.

"You have the name of the greatest god of all," his friend said, "what difference would a nice canoe make when you meet him?"

"More than what you may believe, my friend. Your name will never leave the spirit of this canoe, which will be a fortress for my legend."

"How long from now are you going to meet the Great One?"

"I already did," Taaroa replied with a smile, "and I will meet him again tonight."

Four men helped the great priest and his friend to drag the canoe to the water. The tide was low, the water still and the sea at peace. For the last time, Taaroa took a handful of black sand from the beach. His friend watched the sand flow between Taaroa's withered fingers. As the sand touched the canoe, it slightly glowed with a purple color. The men ran away, and Taaroa's friend dropped to his knees.

"You are the Great Taaroa," the man said, humble.

"Not yet, man of a moment!" Taaroa replied, as he climbed into the canoe.

He took a large paddle, and glided toward the Motuau islet, at some distance from the Teauroa Point. There was no wind, no noise, only the lapping of the paddle and Taaroa's heart pounding. He looked at the horizon, with grandeur in his eyes. At this moment, his soul was a giant within a leper's body.

Hina helped her mother and sister prepare the evening meal. Aru brought parrotfish and lobsters. Kon washed the fruits he had gathered earlier.

"Did you see the beautiful moon?" Aru asked.

"Today, it is a full circle," Atea commented.

"Then, today is a great day," Kon added.

"And, why is that?" Hina asked.

"Today, nobody saw Taaroa," Kon replied.

"No, but a while ago, I passed by his house and the entry was decorated with tropicbird feathers," Hina said.

"Taaroa will not return," Kon said, surprising everyone. "We shall prepare. The next few days must be part of an unforgettable legend."

"What are you talking about?" Atea asked, with a shiver.

"All priests shall gather," Kon replied, "and the king shall lead them."

"I will go to find my father," Fenua said.

"How do you know Taaroa will not come back?" Hina asked, intrigued.

"Taaroa told me," Kon replied. "Taaroa showed me a great force living inside Orohena. I gave him my word I would keep his secret,...until today."

Taaroa paddled gently, so the water stayed almost perfectly still. For him, the night was all beauty. He passed the Motuau islet, glanced at the long shadows of the coconut trees on the golden sea. Behind the fronds, the moon was huge and seemed to smile at him. Soon, the islet slowly vanished behind the living canoe. Taaroa brought the canoe to a stop, and wondered if he had passed above the old submerged barrier of corals.

"I think it is a little farther," Taaroa said, paddling again. "This canoe and I are only one body. Nothing will ever separate us."

At times, Taaroa could see the fluorescence of tiny shrimps in the water, and hear the splash of a needlefish chasing them. Once more, Taaroa brought his companion to a total stop. He looked at the light of a fire on the mainland, and checked its alignment with a tall coconut tree on the islet.

"You are not drifting," he said, caressing the hull of the canoe.

Taaroa removed all his clothes, sat on the edge of the canoe, held the outrigger and slowly entered into the sea,...the legs,...the trunk,...the shoulders. Then, he swam away, stopped, looked at the canoe.

"You are perfectly still."

He expelled all the air from his lungs, and dived. It was not deep, and he touched a large block of coral. He checked its shape and size, felt fragile branches breaking between what was left of his fingers. He inspected several rubbery corals, found a deep channel with sand at the bottom. He knew exactly where he was.

The right place is not far away."

He followed the channel that got deeper and colder. Suddenly, the channel vanished. Taaroa faced the abysse. He went back to the surface, took a long breath of warm air and climbed in the canoe with extreme difficulty. He finally crashed inside the canoe, short of breath, and laughing. He paddled for a short distance, stopped and looked around. The sea seemed darker and colder. Again, he paddled for a short time, came to a complete stop and threw the paddle into the sea.

"I no longer need that thing."

He went back into the water, and dived as deeply as he could. There was nothing, just the formidable abysse. He reached his limit, stopped and listened. The silence was impressive, upsetting, terrifying, but not for Taaroa.

"This is my home," he said, listening to his heart pounding. "This is Orohena's home."

"I hear you, my friend, gliding nearby with powerful majesty."

He had found the place he had been once, when he was a young boy.

"Come to me, Great Spirit of the depths, come to deliver me."

Tupua entered the dwelling house, followed by Vana and other surrounding dignitaries. The great Tamatoa, Hotu-Matua, and Taranga Tici Viracocha were waiting for them. Kon, Hina and Kukara were at the center, drinking a ceremonial beverage. Such a meeting enhanced Tupua's status, and he was delighted about it, so he raised his arm and everyone became silent.

"My friends," Tupua said, with pain evident on his face, "tonight is the full moon. Tonight is a terrible time for us. Tonight, we may lose a friend..."

Tupua swallowed hard to control a sob, and immediately Vana came to his rescue:

"Taaroa is gone."

Everyone murmured to one another.

"Is he dead?" Tamatoa asked.

"Not yet!..." Vana replied, embarrassed to find his words. "He decorated his house in such a way that I know he will die soon. But, Kon can tell you more."

Everybody looked at Kon, waiting for the moment of truth.

"All I know," Kon said, "is that Taaroa chose this night to do something he had been thinking about for some time. He chose to leave this life tonight."

Kon's words started a huge commotion. Tupua clapped with both hands asking for silence, and Hina jumped to her feet, obviously distressed.

"Are you saying that Taaroa will end his life himself?" she asked. "Are you saying that we are going to sit here doing nothing about it?"

"Taaroa's will is sacred," Kon argued.

"Never!" Hina exploded. "I will not let this happen. Let's go find him."

Kon stopped her with his hand.

"You will not find him," he said. "Nobody can find him. He told me, at dawn but not before, I shall tell you where he is: in his canoe."

"His canoe! What canoe?" Hina asked. "I know, you were the guardian of his secret. Did you advise him to do such a terrible thing?"

"I did not," Kon replied. "Remember, I am the one who rescued him from his solitude in the valley."

Hina sat down, defeated, shaking her head in disapproval.

"You all know his illness cannot be cured," Kon said. "The last phase is humiliating for an ordinary man. But Taaroa is no ordinary man. He is a great priest, and you gave him the name of the greatest. Therefore, Taaroa has an obligation for his honor. So, Taaroa chose to die with honor. It is his fight, and not yours. You shall not, and dare not interfere."

"We will not," Tupua said, looking at Hina. She approved with a nod.

"What he is doing is the ultimate form of freedom," Kon said. "None of us has the right to alter the integrity of a free Taaroa."

"But..." Vana tried to say.

"There is no but," Kon replied loudly.

Everyone saw authority and persuasion in the deep blue eyes. Kon turned his head, sending his long black hair around his shoulders, and looked at the entire audience. No one challenged his words.

Taaroa climbed in the canoe, dried his body with a clean and soft bark-cloth, and wrapped himself with his most valuable ceremonial costume. It was a magnificent, white tapa, offered to him at the funeral of his father, long ago. He tied a heavy belt made of cowries around his waist. On his belly were two precious golden cowries he had found at great depths when he was capable of diving like no one else could. On his chest, two majestic feathers from the sacred red-tailed tropicbird reminded him that it was the last gift he received from Hina of the Valley.

"Beautiful girl, you are so special to me," he murmured, caressing the feathers with pain in his eyes.

"Young priestess, still a child, I loved you as if you had been my own child. At the moment of my life when I was most vulnerable, you gave me light, joy and happiness. My soul is with yours, forever: This is the Great Taaroa's will."

He put a huge hat on his head, and suddenly looked like the glowing sun. Radiant white feathers from the sacred egret were all around his head, doubled by long, white streamers from the sacred white-tailed tropicbird. It was a gift from Kon.

"Young stranger, man of peace, you are a wandering star passing too fast. Man should learn how to pause and listen, when such a star crosses the sky."

He sat comfortably at the front end of the canoe, took a shark tooth, and made a deep cut across his wrist. His blood flowed into the sea like a pulsing geyser. Taaroa controlled the flow with his other hand.

"Not too fast, just a few drops at a time,...my friend may be far away."

Each drop of blood mixed with the sea. A long strip of this liquid of life found its way to the dark abysse. He watched the surface of the water for any unusual movement, but everything was still, like a pond of golden oil under the moonlight. Suddenly, a tiny wave passed along the hull, then another one. Taaroa smiled.

"Orohena, where are you? These little sharks are showing you the way."

Then, a larger fin broke the surface, and came straight to Taaroa.

"Still too small!"

He watched the excited predators circle the canoe. It was a dance around the place of the ultimate sacrifice. To entice the sharks, Taaroa allowed several bursts of blood to flow from his wrist. Instantly, all the nearby sharks became more active, calling Orohena.

"From Taaroa's will," Kon said, "something from us is required."

They all remained silent, expecting more explanation.

"Deep in the valley, Taaroa and I met a spirit who belongs to the life he will have, beyond."

Extraordinary commotion took place in the dwelling house, until the king recovered his composure.

"Kon, ordinary people don't communicate with spirits," Tupua said.

"Taaroa is not ordinary, and I was only a witness."

"So, where is Taaroa?" Tamatoa asked, impatient.

"I will tell you at dawn. I gave him my word that I will keep the place a secret until then."

"Is there a spirit with him, tonight?" Kukara asked.

"Yes, there is," Kon replied, "and he is looking for Orohena."

The sacred name had a stunning effect on everyone. Only Vana kept quiet, and came closer to Kon.

"Orohena is the name of the tall fin on the great blue shark's back," Vana explained. "What does Taaroa have to do with it?"

"You all know that when Taaroa was a boy, the great blue shark saved his life," Kon replied, "accordingly, you called him Taaroa. It was a daring thing to do."

"Taaroa, the greatest god of all," Vana said, " may not have been pleased with that choice. This may explain his illness."

"I disagree," Kon said, "everything in our life has a subtle purpose."

"Such as?" Vana inquired.

"Your birth is a starting experience," Kon replied, "your life is a training time, and your death a graduation."

"So, the Great Taaroa was pleased with our choice."

"There is nothing anyone can do, without the Great Taaroa's approval," Kon replied.

"Are the Great Taaroa and Viracocha the same spirit?" Hina asked.

"Yes, they are." Taranga Tici Viracocha answered.

"So, the Great Viracocha is not displeased you carry his name," Hina said.

"Of course not!" Kon replied. "It is an honor to him, if you are a good person."

"Therefore," Hina pursued the matter, "tomorrow at dawn, Taaroa and the Great Taaroa may become the same person."

"Taaroa will never die," Kon said, surprised by Hina's comment. "A few days from now, Taaroa will carry an incredible force."

"I am going to the beach," Kukara said, with deep emotion on her face.

Intrigued, Kon and Hina watched her disappear into the night.

One more burst of blood left Taaroa's wrist, and all the sharks swimming nearby suddenly vanished. There were no more waves, no more noise. Only intermittent drops of blood falling into the sea could be heard. Then, it came from the east, awesome.

"Orohena!"

Taaroa's eyes widened. At some distance, a formidable fin cut the quiet surface of the sea, and far behind, the huge tail followed.

"Come on, my friend!"

A swift, powerful swing from the creature's tail made a large wave: Orohena was coming straight toward the canoe.

Taaroa's eyes flashed in a display of pleasure mixed with

impatience.

"It is you. You came once when I was a boy. Now, you come again when I am an ill man."

The giant killing machine was gaining momentum. A crescent-shaped mouth armed with a frightful array of saw-edged teeth snapped one arm of the outrigger as if it had been a twig. The great blue shark, a terror for all living sea creatures, turned around and swam away from the canoe. Taaroa released more blood into the sea.

"Come back, little fish!"

Orohena made a large circle, hesitated for awhile, then found exactly where the blood was coming from. Taaroa looked at the sky, saw the stars and wondered if they were the gates leading to the new world. The shark was approaching fast, compelled by the smell of blood. Nothing could stop its course, and Taaroa knew the time had come for a human sacrifice. Then, Taaroa heard the solemn sound of the drums and the call of the conchs.

"Kon, you did not betray me. Whoever you are, you are a good man. Thank you!"

The leper deeply cut his other wrist, then plunged both arms into the sacred sea. He saw the powerful animal arch its body, and the incredible jaw open slowly. He could see the rows of hand-size white blades. Taaroa closed his eyes. It surprised him to feel only a slight pull. Already, the shark was way below the outrigger. Taaroa opened his eyes: His two forearms were missing, with blood bursting high,... after,... each,... heartbeat....

"I don't feel any pain."

Taaroa found the strength to smile, and sat in the canoe. He moved his legs overboard, and let these deformed limbs hang into the sea.

The shark turned around, and faced the canoe once more.

Taaroa raised his head as high as he could, and saw Orohena above the hull, coming fast. This time, he felt a much more powerful and painful pull. He knew the end was near. Taaroa felt some dizziness and saw a vortex of purple light approaching the canoe. He lay inside the hull, saw the stars, then the vortex entering the boat, and everything became blurry. For the last time, he heard the conchs. He looked at the taller Orohena, rising high in the moonlight. A last time he smiled, as the vortex reached him: Peace flooded his body, then his mind. He found himself floating inside an endless tunnel. The faster he went, the farther away the end seemed to be. Suddenly, he was weightless, and something happened. He looked at himself. He was young again, and had healthy hands and feet, but his body was transparent. At last, he reached the end of the tunnel and was astonished by what he saw.

"I don't believe this!..." He looked, silent, and enveloped by the scenery. He was comfortably sitting among green feathers, protected inside the vortex of purple light. Ahead of him, taking the entire space, was a giant spiraling wheel made of numerous star-like shiny lights. He was approaching its center at incredible speed. Surprisingly, his fear was gone, and the memory of Orohena was fading far away. He wished he could have shown all this to Kon and Hina, but he was not in control of his destiny: He never was. The center of the spiral was too bright at first, then became black, and there was nothing. He could no longer see the vortex, or the feathers, or himself. Taaroa was all spirit, all energy: He was the Light, traveling everywhere with no fatigue, traveling until a new target would materialize as a new world, a new life and a new destiny.

Taaroa was a sleeping young boy. He heard the voice of a young woman he knew well. He opened his eyes, and was instantly terrified by the sight of a giant statue. The giant's deep white and red eyes stared at him, but Taaroa felt the comfort of a familiar touch. Furthermore, Taaroa was no longer his name.

"Don't be afraid my son," the young woman said. "It is only a stone looking at the light from the stars."

The night was falling on Mata-Kite-Rani, and a few stars appeared in the dark sky. The young child looked at them as if they were familiar, and he tried to touch them with his tiny fingers.

"My son, you are already an explorer, just like your father," Hina said. "One day you will be a priest on this lost island, and you will be the living bridge between an extraordinary, vanishing race, and the seafaring Maohis."

Maui looked for safety against the breast of his beautiful mother. Her long, black hair protected him from the cold evening breeze. Hina of the Valley kissed the forehead of her son and started singing words that were floating among the wind and waving dry grass. Her soft voice mixed with some invisible spirits.

"Maui, my son, we have all been touched by the Light. It was written on these Rong-Rongo tablets."

It was another place, in another time.

CHAPTER 30

"I gave my blood to Taaroa, after his death brought light to my mind, so forever he would live in me. Then, a voice told me Taaroa became a force within myself that I would not always control."

Hina of the Valley

At dawn sightseers gathered on the beach, where the royal canoe was pulled into the sea. Tupua stepped inside the magnificent boat, followed by Kon, Hina and Vana. Four men, respectful of the dignitaries, took their place and paddled. With no more ritual, they quickly left in the direction of the Motuau islet, around which Kon thought they would find Taaroa.

"Did you see Kukara?" Hina asked.

"Not since last night," Kon replied.

They circled the islet, then went on the beautiful white beach surrounding it. On the cool coral sand, there were no footprints. Only gray-backed terns took to graceful flight, with their high-pitched screeching signaling their discontent. Kon climbed to the top of a coconut tree, and immediately located the drifting canoe, far away beyond the collapsed barrier reef.

When they reached Taaroa's canoe the beauty of the carvings on the hull astonished them. Hina noticed one arm of the heavy outrigger had been snapped, and wondered what force could have done this.

"I never saw an outrigger arm broken at that place before,"
Tupua said.

Suddenly, they saw who they were looking for, and they
were shocked by what they saw. Taaroa lay inside the canoe, in
a pool of blood. From the mutilations, it was obvious that he had
been dead for some time, and he was entirely drained of his blood.
His body was wrapped inside the most precious bark-cloth. His
forearms and feet were missing. Surprisingly, there was little
blood on his chest. Until the end, Taaroa had the pride to keep his
sacred cloth clean, which made the scenery even more shocking
to everyone. Taaroa was still smiling, showing his triumph over
pain.

"At his last moment," Kon said, "Taaroa was inhabited by
Mana's force. Therefore, he never felt any pain."

Hina was horror-stricken, muffling a few sobs on Kon's chest.
Then, she turned away from what she saw with disgust.

"Why?" she asked. "Why was it necessary for him to do this?
It is infamous. Is it to satisfy our thirst for emotion? Is this smile
the ultimate portrait of terror?"

Vana put a hand gently on her shoulder. "It is nothing like
you said. It was his will, and we must respect that. I have to
admit I would never have the courage to do what he did. In a
way, he won over his illness."

"By cutting his life short!" Hina said with a sarcastic smile.

"Time is no object," Kon argued. "Going now, or going later,
what is the difference? At least, he went away as a great priest,
with dignity and pride."

"It is up to us to make sure he did not leave this way in vain,"
Tupua said.

Kon was silent, looking at Mount Orohena. They slowly

accepted the facts. Hina covered Taaroa's mutilated parts with cloths. She caressed his face, regained her strength and decided she should not agonize over her friend's death.

Surprised by her own thoughts, she looked at the horizon and suddenly wondered if she was becoming insane. Her thoughts spun, and conflicted. She sat on the broken arm between the hull and the outrigger, and glanced at Kon. Would he help her to restore order in her mind? Possibly, but she decided otherwise. After all, she was a priestess and she should take care of herself. She watched the men attach Taaroa's canoe to theirs. She remained silent and motionless. She knew that as long as she would live she would never forget all the details of this horrifying vision. For Hina, it was an aging process. It was the kind of thing that kills innocence and makes a person tougher. She was not sure it was for the best. She put her hands on her stomach and closed her eyes. They had seen enough. Once more, puzzling thoughts went through her mind. She recalled Kon once had told her that incredible forces inhabit our minds. At this instant, she felt them; they were real, but she was not used to them yet. Then, a fearful thought crossed her mind: What would happen if she could not control these forces? What if she was only the physical means by which these forces would perform their will? Was it conceivable that she, Hina of the Valley, could be controlled by some form of spiritual intelligence?

She felt Kon's hand on her head, but she kept her eyes closed. A current of energy entered her head, and went through her entire body. Kon was inside her, aware of her thoughts. It felt warm and agreeable. She opened her eyes, calm and in control of herself. She was strong again. Her fear had vanished. Kon smiled to her and went back to help the others. He knew she was the priestess again.

Hina looked at Taaroa and was attracted to him. Her eyes followed the edge of the sacred canoe, followed the broken wooden arm on which she sat. She inspected the break where a white object called her attention. She slowly entered the cool water, swam along the broken arm, keeping a hand on it. She felt discomfort at the thought of the unfathomable abysse under her: The thing had come from there. She dipped her head under water, and looked down. It was uniformly blue, and not a place to be. She reached the white object, deeply planted inside the hard wood. It took her some effort to remove it from the wood. She looked at it, amazed. Fear glittered in her eyes: Never before had she seen such a large shark tooth.

"What did you find?" Kon asked.

"It is a tooth of the sacred great blue shark," Hina replied.

Vana looked at the tooth, puzzled. "It is like my four fingers," he said.

Hina took the tooth from Vana's hand, and did something that startled everyone. She sat near Taaroa. With the shark tooth, she cut her wrist and mixed her blood with Taaroa's blood. To her surprise, as she made the cut, the shark tooth became bright purple for a short instant, but nobody else noticed.

Her father and Vana were astonished at her act. Kon smiled with an enigmatic approval. Then, she uttered a few ritual words:

"Dear companion, here is my blood. For eternity, your spirit shall be mine. My children shall know who you were once, and you shall be their master, teacher and inspiration. In joy, I shall always remember your words. With Orohena you shall rest. In my sacred mountain you shall be born again. In the cave, I shall be with you, whatever it takes."

Tupua glanced at Vana: They were unsure what she meant. Kon came to the rescue.

"In due time, Hina of the Valley will show you what she meant, and it will be glory for Maohis."

A touch of annoyance hovered in Tupua's eyes: How could Kon comprehend her subtleties, when they could not?

Dismayed, they went back to Papenoo. On the beach, they carried Taaroa's canoe to Vana's dwelling place, where the embalmment ceremonies would take place.

Hina crossed the Papenoo River and went to her Marae. Everyone she saw was silent, respectful for the loss of a great priest. She sat on a stone, beside a tiare bush, and wondered for a long time how she could keep strong ties with Taaroa's spirit. She was almost annoyed at the thought. Why was this so important to her? Why was she always thinking about Taaroa? She gave up, convinced she would never find satisfactory answers. Yet, she was not aware she already had one answer, and would show it to everyone in a powerful way before this day would be over. She looked at her golden necklace, and saw the sacred condor smile at her.

"Is it conceivable that Viracocha is living in me, and masters my thoughts, my acts?"

She smiled to herself. "If this is true, so be it!"

She looked at the cut on her wrist, and noticed with astonishment it had healed to the extent that it was almost invisible. Then, she heard a noise nearby. Someone observed her.

"Is it you, Kukara?" she inquired.

Nobody answered, but dust went into the air, formed a small vortex that slowly turned purple in the dark of dusk, and vanished over the cliff where the sea waves were pounding.

Hina ran back to the river, undressed and swam in the cool water from the valley. Intuitively, she understood strange forces were at work around her. She knew something would happen later, the same day. So far, Kon had not been very active, and she knew his time was coming. She was also puzzled at Kukara's disappearance. So, she prepared herself, and relaxed her mind. In due time, she would have to speak and be part of Kon's mission.

Back to the Toerau Marae, she dressed like a priestess. She wore a long, white robe, split on both sides until her thighs. She tied a belt of golden-ringed cowries around her waist, and a band of golden feathers around her head keeping her hair in the back of her shoulders as Kon often did. On her chest, she pinned three green feathers from the sacred pigeon of the valley: a gift from Taaroa. Around her neck, the gold necklace Kon had given her on Mount Orohena was a reminder of who she was. She caressed it, smiled in silence and felt wrapped in invisible warmth. At the same instant, she heard the drums calling the chiefs, the priests and other dignitaries to the important meeting at Vana's dwelling. Hina stood up, walked to the cliff and listened at the pounding waves. She looked at her cut on the wrist, and noticed it was glowing purple in the dark.

"Taaroa, you are living in me," she murmured.

"Oh yes!..." the receding wave answered.

Then, rumbling, a powerful crested wave slammed the cliff, shaking the ground under her feet.

"This is the way I shall make my point," she said with pride. Hina of the Valley was ready.

"May I come with you, mother?" Kukara asked.

"Yes!" Hina answered, surprised. "Where were you all that time?"

"All that time, I was with you, mother."

They all sat around a fire in the middle of Vana's house. Tupua summarized Taaroa's life, and praised how he braved his illness. The king raised his voice at the end of his long speech:

"...He died with pride. He died with dignity. He died with honor. He died with class."

Tupua swung his long, red robe, and sat cross-legged with the group.

Vana described the embalmment ceremonies, from which Kon concluded it would take a full moon-cycle to prepare Taaroa's body, before the final lifting of it to the forbidden cave. In a way, he was happy about the delay: It would give him plenty of time to prepare for the incredible undertaking. Tonight, he would have to explain what must be done, and he knew his words would create great turmoil.

Vana concluded, turning his head slowly in Kon's direction: "...When the embalmment ceremonies will be completed, this man shall direct us to Taaroa's resting place. Kon, would you explain what is expected from us? Taaroa told you when, how and where. You shall tell us how."

Hina purposively sat at the back of the dwelling, far away from the fire, where few people would notice her.

"May I sit with you, mother?" Kukara asked.

"Of course."

"You are beautiful," the girl whispered.

Kon threw a twig of dry grass he was playing with and took Vana's place. Silent, he glanced at everyone. As for every important occasion, he listened to the silence, and so they did. Only the tiny sparks from the glowing embers, the rolling of the waves on the distant beach, the crickets and a frog could be heard. They all knew Kon Tici was always doing this when he would speak of something important to them. By observing total silence, they showed their great respect for him.

"Taaroa went to a long journey to the stars," Kon said.

They all looked at a hole in the ceiling, where the smoke

escaped, and they could see the moon.

"But Taaroa's spirit is still among us," Kon continued. "For the living, far away are the stars, but the dead can touch them. The dead know no illusion, no dimension and no time. Soon, Taaroa will be born again, with a new name, and a message from the stars. He will be the most formidable seafaring commander that you Maohis will ever know...."

It was too much, and everybody started talking. Tamatoa raised one hand, and his powerful voice silenced everyone else.

"When and where shall that man come, and what will his name be?"

"He will come on a distant island from here, and you will call him Maui."

Every word echoed in Hina's mind. She closed her eyes, raised her chin, and a shiver went through her body. Kukara laid her head on her mother's lap. Hina opened her eyes and gently caressed the long, straight, black hair of the girl. She saw Kukara's fingers reading the Rongo-Rongo signs on the mysterious tablets hanging on her chest. She wondered what her life could be without Kon and Kukara, and found the thought intolerable.

"With Taaroa," Kon said, "I choose the place where his body will rest for eternity."

Kon had enormous charisma. His golden earplugs glittered, his golden bracelets sent beams of light all across the room, and they all listened.

"His final resting place is on the eastern side of Mount Orohena, on the most inaccessible part of the giant cliff, in that cave I went to several times."

This time, they all wondered if he had become insane.

"Every morning, Taaroa will face the rising sun on the awesome sea, and every moon-cycle he will face the rising moon."

Kon paused, but they all remained silent, convinced he had lost his mind. Finally, Tamatoa broke the silence.

"How do you suggest to lift Taaroa's body to this forbidden place?"

"Oh no!" Kon replied. "It is the canoe and Taaroa's body we shall lift to the cave."

First, there was a short silence, until they correlated what they thought they had heard with what Kon had really said. Kon repeated his words, slowly.

"…The outrigger canoe and Taaroa, all the way up, on the impossible cliff of Mount Orohena, to the forbidden cave."

It was instantaneous chaos. Some were angry, some thought his words were a provocation to the spirits living in the sacred mountain. Finally, Tupua restored order, and gave Kon an angry look.

"How can you say this? We all know it is impossible. Your words are a mockery to the Maohi people."

Vana was in dismay, and felt powerless in coming to Kon's rescue.

"I gave my word to Taaroa," Kon said. "It was his idea. It is his sacred will."

"But, you pushed him to this idea," Tupua argued. "You took advantage of a poor, ill man no longer capable of judgment."

"Coward!" Hina murmured. "Is it really my father saying this?"

"I will do it alone if necessary," Kon said, disappointed.

"No, you will not!" Tamatoa replied with a thundering voice. "I will help you."

Nobody expected Tamatoa's reaction, and the matter instantly became a matter of honor. Now, it was inconceivable for other leaders not to help. Reluctantly, they all agreed they would help.

"I will help you," the tattooed giant said. "But, the idea still seems impossible. Can you explain better how you intend to do this?"

Kon stood up and raised his arms above the fire.

"With Mana's force!" he said, with a powerful voice.

"Who is Mana?" Tamatoa asked, puzzled.

"Mana is the great power sleeping in you," Kon replied, "and you don't know how to use it."

"Show us," Tamatoa said.

"Bring one of the ropes I asked you to make," Kon said, pointing a finger at Tupua.

A short time later, five men brought a long rope, and Kon told them to drop it in front of Tamatoa.

"How many men would it take to break this rope?" Kon asked.

Tamatoa inspected the rope, tested it with his powerful hands: "Five men pulling in opposite directions."

"Then try!" Kon said.

Two teams of five men pulled on the rope, which gave no sign of breaking."

"This is a good rope," Tamatoa remarked.

"Give it to me," Kon commanded. "With Mana's force, I will break it with my two hands."

Everyone clustered around Kon. Tupua asked for total silence. Kon sat cross-legged, closed his eyes and concentrated. He took the rope with both hands. Slowly, he brought his fists closer to one another, and the rope curled between his hands. Kon forgot the world. His only universe was that rope breaking. Slowly, it became inconceivable that the rope would not break.

Satisfied, he opened his eyes. Everyone noticed his eyes

were different-deeper, and confident. Suddenly, his fists moved in two opposite directions. Instantly, the rope snapped with the sound of lightning. It seemed that nothing could have resisted the tremendous power of Mana. Kon's act astonished everyone.

"Who are you?" Tamatoa asked, placing a heavy hand on Kon's shoulder.

"What is important is not who I am," Kon replied. "What is important is for you to believe you can do the same thing."

"Yet, I don't know how to use Mana," Tamatoa commented.

"It takes many moon-cycles of intense training." Kon replied. "I can teach you a lot of things before we lift Taaroa to Mount Orohena."

Tamatoa shook his head in disbelief: "Mana or no Mana, ropes or no ropes, I still think it is impossible to lift this heavy canoe to the cave."

"But we will lift the canoe all the way to the lake of the sacred ducks as requested by Taaroa," Kon said. "Then, from the lake, we will bring the canoe down, using long ropes."

"I see," Tamatoa murmured, lost in thoughts. "Not bad."

Vana stood up, restless, showing pain in his legs from sitting for too long. He was preoccupied by a thought. Kukara turned her head on Hina's lap, and smiled at the magnificent priestess.

"Mother, your time is coming."

Startled by the comment, Hina wondered what Kukara meant.

"Before we go too far in this discussion," Vana said, "I would like to address something that may greatly complicate your endeavor. It is our tradition that a young new priest shall spend one night, alone, with the sacred spirit of the dead, after the final destination is reached. So, who will volunteer to do this at the forbidden cave?"

Vana glanced around, behind the high dignitaries where many young priests were listening. For many years, they had been told the cave was the place from which nobody can return. Nobody volunteered, and Vana did not blame them.

Nevertheless, one of them had to be chosen.

"If nobody volunteers," Vana said, "I will have to select someone myself."

Everyone remained silent. Fear was evident in some eyes, when Vana looked at them. For an instant, Vana wished he had not addressed the problem. Suddenly, to everyone's surprise, Hina stood up, and walked with grace and determination toward the great priest.

"I, Hina of the Valley, will accept the challenge."

Vana was startled, and embarrassed for the young men. It never occurred to him that Hina would volunteer. Yet, he was angry at himself. He should have thought that the young woman, who challenged him so many times when she was a child, could strike again. Here she was, beautiful and in control. Vana shook his head in disbelief, and glanced at the other leaders. They were all silent, paralyzed, their mouths open.

"No!" Vana said. "The task is impossible for most men, therefore it is not the place for a woman."

"I climbed Mount Orohena; they did not," Hina replied.

"Amazing," Tamatoa murmured to himself, "you inspire me, young woman."

"Vana, oh great priest," Hina said, "you asked me to become a priestess, and I did. If I cannot volunteer for the undertaking, then I shall relinquish my rank as a priestess. For my honor and for yours, I must do this."

Tupua looked at his daughter with immense pride, yet he was frightened at the idea of losing her.

"Don't be afraid, father," Hina said. "A long time ago, my destiny was chosen on the beach of the Teauroa Point, when I saw Kon for the first time. Later on, I chose to bypass the sacred taboos protecting Mount Orohena, and I came back. Therefore, it is my duty to return to Mount Orohena, for Taaroa."

Overwhelmed by Hina's courage, Vana placed two long, red feathers from the tail of the sacred tropicbird, into Hina's hair.

"Be the selected one for this honorable function. Hina of the Valley, for one night you shall be Hina of the mountain. The sacred choice is done, and final. From now and on, everything shall be done according to Kon Tici's words."

Kon was amazed that Vana pronounced his name correctly for the first time. He glanced at Kukara, who had also noticed: They smiled at one another.

"How did you know I would do this?" Hina inquired.

"Viracocha knows everything," Kukara replied.

"You did not answer my question," Hina argued.

"I am not who you think I am," the girl replied, disappearing into the night.

Vana circled around the fire. There was unmistakable emotion in his deep black eyes, mixed with great excitement. He stopped in front of Kon and pointed a finger on his chest. "How many men do you need to lift the canoe to the cave?"

"I need twenty-four men willing to die for that cause."

"Now, the question is," Vana said, "who are these men? Obviously Kon is one of them."

Tamatoa stood up. They all thought he would tell whom he selected. Instead, he walked away saying: "I need to think for awhile, alone. I will not be long."

The great warrior reached the beach, walked in the cool sand and listened to waves pounding the shore. He thought about his empire, and his love for the awesome sea. He also thought about his sons, his daughter and his wife: He had everything. Furthermore, he had avenged his father's death. Yet, he was not happy. He knew the reasons: He was a friend by necessity. Everyone feared him, the tattooed giant. He liked Hina and Kon. He liked Tupua and Vana, but no matter how strong his empire was, the conquest of the hearts was an entirely different matter. He sat on the sand, and put his head in his hands. For an instant, he wished he was not the king, or the great warrior or the tattooed giant. He wished he could be the ordinary man. He looked up at the stars, and the stars spoke to him, immediately. A powerful beam of light entered his tormented mind. He felt someone touching his shoulder. He turned around and saw Kukara standing behind him.

"You are a good man," she said, vanishing into the night.

He stood up, and searched in vain for the girl. He smiled to himself, and looked at the stars once more: He knew exactly what he would do.

When Tamatoa came back, they were all waiting for him. He paid attention to no one, and walked straight to Hina. Then, the unthinkable event took place, stunning everyone, including Kon Tici. The great Tamatoa kneeled in front of Hina. The giant removed his royal hat.

"I Tamatoa, king of a seafaring people, king of Rarotonga, Pora-Pora, Huahine, and Havaiki, shall become an ordinary man for all the duration that it will take to prepare and lift the canoe to the cave. In the meantime, Taatamao shall be the supreme commander of my empire. Hina of the Valley, Kon Tici, from now until we enter the cave with the sacred canoe, I shall serve you."

Hina smiled at him, and placed a gentle hand on his awesome shoulder.

"Once before," Hina said, "on Mount Orohena, I found out who you really were. When your word is given, it is unambiguous, unalterable and just. Therefore, so be it, and I welcome you."

She looked at him for awhile, and found out she had admiration for him.

"From your people," Hina pursued, "whom did you select to help us, beside yourself?"

The answer came, clear, and unambiguous: "Tera, Teahu, and Mehao. They are all my sons."

Tupua could not resist any longer, congratulated Tamatoa for his words, and placed both hands on the shoulders of his former adversary. The two men looked at one another, straight in the eyes. A strange, faintly eager look flashed in their eyes: From now on, they knew they were friends.

The ceremony went on. Tupua selected Aru and three more strong men from the neighboring district, known for their climbing skills. Hotu Matua, king of Hiva, selected two men from his delegation. Taranga Tici Viracocha selected Rangi, one of Kon's best friends. Within no time, the team was complete.

Satisfied, Tupua exhaled a long sigh of contentment. Determined to share his good mood with someone, he looked around wondering who would be his prey. At first, he thought about Tamatoa, but dismissed the idea. Though, when nobody fitted what he had in mind, he came back to Tamatoa.

"After all, why not?" Tupua said with a suspicious smile. "I can teach you about Mana."

Tamatoa looked around, wondering to whom Tupua was speaking.

"I am talking to you, Tamatoa. Would you sit down, and have four young ladies take good care of you."

Perplexed, the giant glanced at Hina, Mahine, Fenua and

youg Kukara circling him.

"Now, this is going to be very interesting!" Vana said with delight, and pushing everybody some distance away.

"Now, you may start," Vana said, rubbing his hands with excitement.

"First," Tupua explained, "these two women should place two fingers under your arms, and these two women should place two fingers under your knees. Now, ladies, try to lift that heavy man."

"You are heavy yourself!" Tamatoa roared with a smile.

"This is great!" Vana chuckled nervously.

"You see," Tupua explained, "without Mana, these ladies were unable to lift you."

"I think you are heavier than father," Hina commented.

The great warrior was amused, but he was also unaware his dignity could vanish soon.

"Now," Tupua ordered, "each of you girls, put your hands on Tamatoa's head, and call Mana. Concentrate hard on what you must do. On the next attempt, Tamatoa's body must go up. Convince yourself this man is light as a feather."

Several times, Tupua repeated the three key words, slowly.

"Must...go...up! Must...go...up! Try now!"

The four women placed their fingers under Tamatoa at their respective places, and lifted him with no effort into the air.

Tamatoa opened his eyes wide, surprised to find himself flying above the girls, but Mana's effect is a very brief, transient phenomenon. Before Tamatoa even realized what had happened, he was on his way down with a crash. He fell heavily on the paved floor, raising a cloud of dust.

"Great!" Vana exploded, throwing up his hands.

Judging by the expression of his face, Tamatoa seemed

irritated and offended. Everyone glanced at one another.

"I think you made a mistake," Vana said, glancing at Tupua.

A long, uncomfortable silence took place, until Vana could no longer contain himself, and burst out laughing. Everyone glanced at Vana, then at Tamatoa, wondering if Vana's mockery would further irritate the great warrior. Vana stopped laughing, and looked at everyone: Nobody was amused. He tried to suppress a giggle, then laughter doubled in intensity, until he kneeled in pain, and pounded his fists on the ground. Slowly, more laughter joined Vana, and within an instant everyone laughed in sheer joy. Tamatoa stood up, regained his composure, looked at Vana rolling on the ground and pounding his chest with tears in his eyes. The giant looked at his daughter, Mahine, who was half laughing half crying. Slowly, a deep chuckle emanated from Tamatoa and a grin spread across his face. Finally, he threw his head back and roared with laughter.

CHAPTER 31

"In the solitude and grandeur of the mountain, we endured immense pain. Yet, we found enough pleasure for our souls to reach the world of spirits."

Kon Tici Viracocha

One moon-cycle later, at dawn of a fine day, a day everyone had waited and prepared for, Taaroa was ready to start an awesome journey. Lying among fragrant flowers, precious perfumes and majestic clothing, Taaroa was silent and all smiles. His eternal spirit floated all around. From the depth of his canoe, he contemplated a group of men and women with noble will, and unconditional commitment to their cause. Their motto was " Emotions would create ties."

For the last time, Taaroa heard the waves from the awesome sea. Then, twenty-four strong men, one daring priestess and her relatives and friends started the long lift, up to the lake of the sacred ducks. Along the way, they would follow, listen and obey Kon's command. After the sun rose, they all smelled the perfume of flower buds opening with the daylight, mixed with the first perspiration of the defenders of a dead leper's cause.

Alone and lightly dressed, Hina followed the footsteps of her heroes. Behind the village, in a damp and dark place, she glanced at the old banyan tree with its hundred majestic trunks that used to be the forbidden place where Taaroa had isolated himself for years.

"What a difference Kon has made!" she murmured.

Soon after, they passed nearby where she had met Kon for the first time, face to face. She grinned slightly, then caressed the golden condor on her chest. She recalled all the past years, the walks in the valley, the climbs to get tropicbird feathers, the journeys to Mount Orohena, the swims in the blue lagoon, the first time she made love and all the wonders she discovered with him. Tears slowly fell from her eyes. She thought Kon's life would be too short for her to learn everything he knew. They all were on a very dangerous mission. Yet, she knew there was no Viracocha possible without taking such risk.

"My lover and master," she whispered, "Mana be with you!"

As they crossed a tributary of the Papenoo River, the first incident took place. One man around the canoe slipped on a rock covered with moss. His foot went between two boulders. Unable to control his balance, and pushed by the momentum of the boat, his leg snapped like a twig. In pain, the man screamed for help.

"Bring another man!" Kon ordered. "And, let's go."

Hina was astonished at Kon's order. He, usually so considerate, acted as if the life of the man was of secondary importance. She and Vana took care of the man.

"This is not a good omen." Vana said.

"This has nothing to do with a sign." Hina argued. "The sorrow you saw in the eyes of that wounded man was not because of physical pain, but because he could not complete a journey to glory."

Hina ran uphill and quickly caught up with the canoe. She thought Taaroa's death had a new meaning. It was a commitment to achieve a deed that would remain in the Maohi oral tradition.

The time had come when she would be accountable for the success of this mission. The time had come when she would find answers at the forbidden cave.

Later in the day, they reached the Atohei plateau covered with giant ferns. The terrain became steeper and more slippery with the rain. They stopped for a moment and Hina brought them water. Kon took a cup she gently handed to him, and rested his back against the rugged trunk of a giant fern. Some distance away, Tera was struggling with dead fern splinters that had found their way deep inside his feet. Hina asked him if he wanted some assistance, but found him inexplicably irritated.

"I don't need your help, woman."

Hina laughed to cover her annoyance. Then, she noticed he was holding something between fresh, green fern fronds. She thought he was cleansing his cuts with the tender fronds, and left. Behind Kon, Tera placed his small package in the upper part of the fern tree. Nobody suspected him of preparing something cruel, though Tamatoa saw his son placing something above Kon and wondered what it could have been. However, the tattooed giant returned his attention to a man who was talking to him.

Kon took another sip. Above him, a ball of tiny fern fronds unfolded, and fell on the ground. Nobody noticed the long, black centipede crawling down on the dark, fern tree trunk. Tera sat at some distance away, and removed the splinters from his feet. Suddenly, Kon felt something on his left shoulder. At first, he thought it was a fern frond caressing him. Then, it became clear it was something else, something alive. He slowly turned his head toward his shoulder and saw the dangerous animal crawling down on his arm. Swiftly, he swept the centipede away, but it was too late. The animal had already injected its strong poison. Kon felt a deep burn on his arm, and immediately ran to Hina. She saw the two tiny red spots on his arm, and knew what caused them. She took a shark tooth, and made a small incision through Kon's skin. She sucked the poison out with her mouth. Nevertheless, swelling rapidly extended around Kon's arm.

"What Hina did will help," Tamatoa said. "But, have no illusion, you are going to be ill."

"As long as I can crawl," Kon replied, annoyed by the comment, "I will fulfill my mission. Let's go!"

Tamatoa took Hina's arm, and pulled her aside from the group.

"Where did that centipede came from?" he asked.

"I think it came from the top of the fern trunk," she replied.

She saw anger in his eyes. He looked at her for a short instant, silent. Then, he joined the other men who were waiting for him.

A burst of wind came from the sea, the air cooled off, and a heavy rain made the journey more hazardous. Powerful lightning struck the summits, followed by endless rumbling echoing across the valley. In a mysterious way, it was a reminder that Mount Orohena was alive, and inhabited by forces unknown to man. The mighty spirit of the mountain would blend with Taaroa's spirit. Each man around the canoe was taken into the gods' sacred dance. Their struggle against the forces of nature took on a new dimension. Hina stopped, and watched her companions. She saw their pain, their fear and their frustration, but she also saw their will, and their choice involved beauty. They struggled with courage, and endured with resolve. Under the storm, they seemed more vulnerable. Under the rain, they seemed more humble. In a way, she loved them more. She knew the mountain well: "The next three days will be an appalling nightmare," she murmured to herself.

Hina had always valued walking alone in the valley or the

mountain. Behind the men, she was alone, and had time to think. The rain stinging her face did not bother her. The breathtaking grandeur of the mountain, the aroma of the wet ferns, the raindrops running along the fronds, the majestic trunks and umbrellas of the fern trees, the clouds touching the sharp slopes, the smell of the decaying topsoil, everything was a tribute to life's beauty.

With no warning, lightning with devastating power struck a fern tree near the men, and reduced it to ashes. Blinded by the terrifying lightning bolt, two men lost their concentration and fell on the slippery ground. The unexpected extra weight from the canoe crushed the shoulder of another man.

Tamatoa, who was on the same side of the canoe, took all the weight. Slowly, they laid the canoe on the ground.

"Mana was with you," Kon said.

"How is your arm?" Tamatoa inquired.

"Swollen, with fever, and the pain is acceptable. But, I am getting weaker."

"May Mana be with you," Tamatoa replied.

Later in the afternoon, the rain stopped, and a spectacular double rainbow crossed the entire valley. Before sunset, they reached the selected location where they would spend the night, on a narrow plateau, near Mount Taat Hau. Kon was fighting chills, fever and joint pain. Hina saw him retch with nausea and vomiting. She was the only person allowed to cleanse the men's wounds and to talk to them. She was mostly concerned by punctures produced by sharp rocks and chips of decaying ferns. She did her best to wash them with water and protect them with a thick paste prepared by macerating coconut tree roots and sandal wood chips in coconut oil. It was a strong healing agent. She rubbed Kon's arm and shoulder, but most of the pain was around his neck.

"You are ill," she said.

"Yes, I am. Perhaps, I will be better in the morning."

Tamatoa took his son Tera aside. They disappeared in a forest of fern trees. With no warning, Tamatoa grabbed his son's shoulder, and lifted the young man as if he had been a feather.

"Did you place that centipede in the tree, above Kon?" Tamatoa roared with fury in his eyes.

"I did not," Tera replied, with his feet dangling above the ground.

Tamatoa dropped his son. "If I ever see you touching one hair of that man, I will crush your brain between my hands,… understood!"

He left Tera, expecting no answer. Then, as if he had a second thought, he went back to his son who was, this time, on the defensive. Tamatoa poked a powerful finger on his son's chest. "I expect you to respect Hina of the Valley, and be courteous to her. I shall not be disobeyed on this matter."

Tera looked at the ground, and waved with one hand in a sign of approval, but Tera was a man with no honor, a symptom of decadence in a man whose authority was given rather than won. Tera was at the wrong place, at the wrong time.

Farther down on the plateau, dignitaries settled in for the night. Mahine and Fenua built a fire around which everybody would gather, except Kon's team and Hina. Taranga came close to Kukara with four heavy bags in his hands. Tupua and Vana had wondered since early in the morning what could have been hiding in these bags, but they never asked Taranga, who was obviously secretive about it. Once, Vana asked Hotu Matua, but the king of Hiva would not tell.

"Kukara," Taranga said with a malicious smile on his wrinkled face, "help me prepare an unusual meal for our friends."

Then, he gave two bags to Kukara, and two bags to Tupua.

"This is a gift to honor you for your hospitality," Taranga said. "I know you will make wonderful use of these tubers from my world."

Always pleasantly surprised by unexpected gifts, Tupua opened one bag slowly, in a ceremonious manner. Overcome by uncontrollable curiosity, Vana tried to see what was inside the bag. Tupua stepped away with the bag. "I am the king, I shall look first."

Vana did not resist his master, and went to investigate what was inside Kukara's bags.

Sudden anger flashed in Tupua's eyes: "Vana!"

The roaring voice of the king took the high priest by surprise. Kukara who intuitively understood who should be first, kept her two bags away from Vana. She stared at the high priest with dignity in her eyes, to the amusement of everyone.

From one bag, Tupua retrieved a large sweet potato tuber. He examined it, smelled it, and took it to his mouth.

"Don't!" Taranga said. "Keep those and plant them, so they will multiply. Kukara will cook the ones in her bag."

From his second bag, Tupua retrieved a manioc rootstock: "I suppose I should save those, too."

"I planted these around my dwelling in Hiva," Hotu Matua said. "After a sun-cycle, they were everywhere. They are good to eat. You will like them."

They watched Kukara wrapping the sweet potatoes and manioc rootstocks inside several layers of banana leaves. She placed them on the fire. At regular intervals, she rotated them with a stick. At one point, as if preoccupied by something, she took one sweet potato aside on the cooler side of the fire, as if she wanted to save it for later. After she became satisfied with the texture, she took a sweet potato and a rootstock to the king.

Tupua tasted the potato first, burned his fingers, then his mouth, in obvious pain.

"I did not realize it would be that bad." Vana said.

"Shut up, and taste it yourself," Tupua yelled at him.

Everyone roared in laughter.

Soon, potatoes and manioc cooled off, and Tupua and Vana savored their precious meal, licking their fingers, and showing absolute delight on their faces.

"This is much more than a gift," the King said. "This is a way for my people to survive. We are seafaring people, and you knew how dear to us tubers are, as we can save them for a long time, at sea. I am honored beyond what words can tell. You came in peace, and became a friend. Your name, Tici, shall remain sacred forever on these islands."

Mahine sat close to Kukara, intrigued by something.

"Show me your hands."

Kukara complied, surprised by Mahine's curiosity.

"You just put your hands in the fire," Mahine said. "How come you did not burn them?"

"Because my father is the Son of Fire," Kukara replied.

Hina came, and took Kukara aside.

"Kon has been bitten by a large centipede," Hina said. "He has fever and little energy."

"Go back to him," Kukara replied, "he is ill no more. Give him this sweet potato I saved for him."

Hina complied, and left. Along the way, she stopped and reflected on Kukara's answer. Kukara's behavior was amazing as if she knew exactly what was happening inside people, even those far away.

"Who are you, Kukara Tici Viracocha?" Hina asked herself.

At some distance, Kon listened to the silent stars. Once, he heard Tamatoa yelling at his son. Once, he heard Tupua yelling at Vana, and wondered how the joyful priest could have annoyed his best friend. He felt the blood racing in his swollen arm, and the fever burning inside his body. He tried to relax and find forces inside his mind. He looked at a shiny dot in the sky, and found its light pouring through his arteries. He closed his eyes, and found himself walking in a green meadow, surrounded by cliffs of rugged rocks. He was inside the crater of a volcano, on a faraway island. He knew the place, though he had been there only in dreams. A dust devil passed nearby, and he heard his name in the whirling wind. A ghost talked to him. He could see the white robe, and the face of a familiar woman. She had long black hair, dark blue eyes, and she was of a remarkable beauty. She was his brother's wife, Kama Tici Viracocha. He talked to her, but she did not hear him. So, he simply listened to her.

"Where is everyone?" she said, with a sob in her voice. "Where am I, lost on this island, with no horizon but water, with nobody to share anything?"

She bent down and picked a wildflower.

"What is beauty for," she asked, "if I cannot share it? What is life for, if I cannot serve others? What is my family for, if I am no longer part of it?"

She walked to a pond, and looked at herself through the still water.

"How can I break my solitude? Oh, Viracocha, help me!"

She fell on the ground, with tears blinding her eyes. Kon tried to put his hand on her shoulder, but she instantly vanished. He was alone, as if nobody had been there before. Lost in the mist of the unknown island, he finally slipped into the depths of the night, during which his body made a remarkable recovery.

When Kon opened his eyes, at once he thought about Kama. Was it conceivable that she was the only survivor, somewhere on a lost island? The thought was intolerable to him. Or, was it only a bad dream? He knew too well that Viracocha mastered dreams. He knew too well everything in his dreams came true. He turned around and looked at the mountain. More than ever, he was determined to use Tamatoa's skills at sea, for a long journey to the far east. For the time being, he had to prove to the Maohi people that he was a man of honor, of trust, who gets things done as planned.

"This mission has just begun," he said to himself.

"You look better," Hina said, giving him the sweet potato and water.

"It is a good thing," Kon replied, "because look what we have to do today."

Her eyes followed the well-known fantastic ridge.

"No problem!" She smiled.

"I prefer a rough sea to this," Tamatoa said, behind them.

"Here, at least you know where the end is," Kon argued.

"Come to me," Mount Pitohiti said. "Dare bring Taaroa where no man has rested before. I am waiting for you all. Come with the sacred wind. Orhena's son, come to Pitohiti...."

"Are you listening to the wind?" Tamatoa said with a thundering voice. "From now on, listen to each of us."

Kon looked at each man, straight in the eyes. He was no longer ill, and they all knew it.

"You did well," Tamatoa said, "and recovered fast."

"Do not be afraid of the mountain," Kon said. "Instead, be afraid of yourself. If an accident happens, it is because one of us makes a mistake."

Hina distributed food and coconut milk. Shortly after, they

started the most daring adventure of their lives. At first, they followed a small trail blazed by former hikers. The men started singing a song. Then, the trail became elusive, the ground steeper and the ridge very narrow. All morning, they struggled their way forward, until they came to a stop at noon. They ate and drank. Then, they looked up. The end of their journey was obscured in clouds. Each man wrapped a short rope around his waist. At the end of each rope was an anchor that would help them to maintain their balance on each side of the ridge. The boat will remain on the ridge. Everything went as planned at first, until the slope was so steep that the boat would not remain still on the ridge. From that moment, their journey became far more difficult as they no longer could rest.

Kon was amazed by the power of his Maohi friends. On several occasions when they encountered unexpected difficulties, he was astonished by Tamatoa's strength. When the night came, they stopped on a narrow ledge.

"You did well today," Hina said.

"Maybe too well," Kon replied.

Indeed, the following day, around noon, not far from the summit, the mountain was waiting for them. Hina sat with one leg on each side of the ridge. She observed the slow progression of her companions. The cliff was barren, with only rare tiny ferns growing in cracks. The mountain resembled a giant stairway. One by one, they had to mount the huge steps. Suddenly, at the forefront a man called Tei pulled on one boulder. Behind him, Kon saw some gravel fall from under the awesome rock, a well-known and frightening sight to him.

"Careful of that rock!" Kon screamed.

It was too late. The crushing power of the boulder could be heard, and nothing could stop it. It rolled on top of another boulder, thus gained enough momentum to jump over the boat, falling on one side of the ridge. All the men there saw the horrifying vision.

Tei had been crushed under the rock. His body literally exploded, projecting blood everywhere. Another man, Lutafu, lost his balance. Tera, Tamatoa's son, tried to hold him. The canoe fell down, breaking Tera's leg. In turn, Tera lost his balance, and both men fell to the abysse. For these two men, there was no survival possible.

Hina, who was sitting at some distance below the men, saw the boulder coming straight toward her. It was a terrifying vision, and it happened so fast that she was paralyzed. Desperate, she finally jumped away from the ridge, toward a lower terrace, but it was too late. During her fall, she heard the boulder bouncing on the ridge. She saw the growing, formidable mass cover the entire sky. She closed her eyes, waiting for the last heartbeat. She wondered if she would have enough time to feel pain. She felt a swift blow to her shoulder, and whistling air around her ears. She immediately realized the boulder had missed her by inches.

She heard Kon screaming her name, but from where she was, he could not see her. She grabbed a few ferns, cutting her hands, and finally secured her feet on a narrow ledge. She felt the warmth of blood mixing with the green fronds, but did not give up her grip. She witnessed the flight of the boulder toward the valley, cutting bushes, trees, crushing ridges and disappearing inside the rain forest. Some distance below, she saw the bodies of Tera and Lutafu. She found enough energy to call Kon, and tell him she was alive. She took a quick look at her shoulder: It would be a bad bruise only, she realized.

She climbed back to the ridge, and found herself ill and shaking. She sat, felt her blood leave her brain, and vomited.

All the remaining men were frozen in fear, barely holding the canoe. Something had crossed their path at amazing speed, and they were not sure yet what it had been.

Tamatoa showed an implacable face, with no fear, no anxiety. He was perfectly aware of his son's death.

"Let's take that thing to the top…," he said, with incredible calmness.

"Now!" he added with a roaring voice.

"We need more men," Kon objected.

"I take their place!" Tamatoa replied.

Tamatoa saw Rangi at his side, more or less in his way. With one arm, the giant grabbed him and put him on the canoe. Embarrassed, Rangi glanced at Kon, while everybody lifted the canoe.

"Give him room." Kon said. "He has Mana."

At every lift, Tamatoa had more power. A wooden handle carved in the canoe broke under his astonishing pull. Ignoring the incident, he went to the next handle. There was no more coordination among the men. There was only coordination between Tamatoa and all other men. Tamatoa felt a fern tree pocking his back. As he was still holding the canoe with one hand, his other hand grabbed the fern tree, whose trunk snapped at ground level. More than ever, he was the giant, and even nature submitted under his feet. There was light in his eyes, and growing rage. When the time was right, he screamed orders to all, and no one argued. In the process, it seemed they were receiving part of his incredible energy.

Kon suddenly measured the man at his full capability: What a formidable enemy he could have been, if angered. Behind Tamatoa's shoulder, covered with Tei's blood, the mountain seemed smaller. They were very near the top of Pitohiti.

Hina witnessed Tamatoa's formidable performance, and forgot her pain. Kukara massaged Hina's wounds.

"You were lucky, mother."

"Maybe Viracocha protected me. Maybe you protected me."

The little girl smiled but did not reply.

Hina climbed slowly, keeping a respectable distance from the canoe. She worried about what Tamatoa would do after they reached the summit.

"He is a good man," Kukara said.

"I know," Hina replied. "But, he is a warrior, too."

Three more maneuvers and they would be at the summit. In a last superhuman effort, Tamatoa dragged the canoe all the way to the top, so there was no need for more maneuvers. At the summit, everyone circled the boat to make sure it was in a secure position. They had reached their goal, but there was no joy in their eyes. They all looked at Tamatoa, and he looked at them, silent. His eyes were rimmed with tears, so he left the group. Kon followed him, but was stopped when the hand of the giant told him to stay away. At some distance, the great warrior collapsed on the ground, and sobbed loudly.

Kon and three other men went to recover the bodies of their unfortunate companions. On his way, he encountered Hina and took her hands, holding them strongly, and kissing them. He did not say anything, nor did she: Words have meaning only if they improve the profoundness of silence.

Hina reached the summit. She looked at the canoe, and the rest of the crew, but she did not see Tamatoa, until someone pointed him out to her. She went to him, and sat nearby, on a cushion of green ferns. She did not say anything, and she did not touch him. Her silence drew his attention. He turned his head toward her. His eyes met hers: She was full of compassion.

"I always feared one day I would lose Tera," Tamatoa said. "Today was the day."

"He died trying to save the life of somebody else," Hina said.

"He was my terrible son. At war, he often took unreasonable risks. But, I did not lose him at war. Instead, I lost him during peacetime. How ironic things can be!"

Hina measured his extreme distress. She thought he looked more human. His hands were covered with bleeding blisters. His smell was a combination of perspiration and blood. She could not resist, and ran her friendly fingers through his hair. Then, she left without saying anything. She walked to a small waterfall, undressed and washed herself. Then, she took fresh water to the men. At this very instant, she had love for every one of them. She had pride for what they had done. With care, she cleansed their wounds. She thought all this was a small price to pay for something that would create lasting ties between Maohis.

The following day, they took the canoe about halfway between Mount Pitohiti and Mount Orohena. They carefully selected the place directly above the sacred cave that waited for Taaroa, far below. They could not see the cave, only guess where it was. Perhaps, they had only completed the easiest part of their journey. Now, they had to challenge the most inviolable wall that man could imagine. High above the valley, tropicbirds were circling. It was a no-man's land.

CHAPTER 32

"Tera's life was taken by brutal force, and deep inside I was crushed. But Kon and Hina deserved my help, and I gave it to them."

Tamatoa the great

Before the descent to the valley below, they took a one-day break. Many had already forgotten the drama of the previous day. Tamatoa himself seemed to accept the hard fact. They put to rest the remains of their companions in the cave Kon and Hina knew so well. At least, their spirits would live forever, side by side, with Mount Orohena. It was an honor to them, and to everyone else. Thereafter, in a strange way typical of Maohis, the despair of death was turned to positive joy.

Far below, the Papenoo River wound along its path through the rain forest. The wind of the cool afternoon blew in the princess of the valley's long black hair. Her thoughts wandered far away on the Viriviriterai plateau on the other side of the valley. Then, farther beyond, she could see the endless awesome sea.

"Don't worry about that trip," Tamatoa said, managing a smile. "You should be much more concerned about that descent."

"How did you know I was thinking about this mysterious Mata-Kite-Rani island?" Hina asked.

"Because, like myself, you wonder if it even exists," Tamatoa replied.

"I have no doubt about this," Hina said.

"Searching for Mate-Kite-Rani is a noble goal," Kon said. "Such exploration for a new world should inspire us all, and feed our souls with a reason for being."

"But you are only interested in finding your brother," Tamatoa said.

"Yes, I want to find my brother. But I am also looking for a resting place for what is left of the Viracocha race."

"How do you know he is on that island?" Tamatoa asked.

"With Mana I can see his family struggling for survival on Mata-Kite-Rani."

"Whatever our destiny, good or bad," Hina said, giving a slice of warm breadfruit to both men, and with a glint of humor on her face, "don't forget to live!"

Kon glanced at Tamatoa, and both burst into laughter. Once more, Hina had taken them by surprise. She walked away, feeding the other men.

Kon looked down, scrutinizing all the details of the mountain. He had all the steps well programmed in his head, but he was still searching for details he might have overlooked.

"Why are you doing all this for us?" Kon asked.

"Do you think there is malice behind my services?" Tamatoa asked.

"No, you are a man of honor," Kon replied. "But..."

"You are thinking about my son."

"Yes, I was," Kon admitted.

The giant looked Kon straight in the eyes. His face, covered with spiraling tattoos, was frightening. He put one hand on Kon's shoulder, and if he had wanted, he could have crushed it. Instead, an innocent smile spread across his face, showing wrinkles clearly attesting to his true age. To Kon, Tamatoa was a triumph of honesty over malice, and no words could have improved on his silent smile.

"Kon Tici," Tamatoa said, "you pass through our life like a shooting star. Your light reaches all of us, and I am no exception. I still don't know who you are, but I care no more. I just want to be your friend."

The deep blue eyes locked with the powerful black eyes. A deep trust took place. The two men realized at about the same time, they could make a team with unprecedented skills, strength and talents. Tamatoa looked down at the ravines, and shook his head with concern.

"Tomorrow, you should take Mehao with you in the canoe," Tamatoa suggested. "He is smart, not too heavy, and my best climber."

"I was wondering whom to choose," Kon said. "So be it, Mehao is the man!"

Tamatoa and the entire crew gathered around Kon, who explained his plan for the descent to the cave.

"We have four long ropes. One is attached at each end of the canoe, and one in the middle. The fourth rope is a spare we keep in reserve. A six-man team will slowly release each rope attached to the canoe. Tamatoa shall coordinate the three teams. Mehao and I will take our places inside the canoe, at each end. Each time Mehao and I will push the canoe away from the mountain with these bamboo poles, you must release the ropes for no more than one arm's length. Coordination and timing are critical. So, I will give the signal to Tamatoa, who will transmit it to you."

Early, at dawn, Hina sat at the edge of the incredible cliff, and watched the crew preparing for the descent. Mahine came and sat close to her.

"You are not supposed to come so close to the crew," Hina said.

"You are my best friend," Mahine said, "and you are going to descend there. I am scared. I asked permission of Vana who granted it."

"I am glad you are here," Hina said, holding her friend's hand.

"I guess it is Kon with my brother," Mahine said, amused.

"The last time it was Kon against Taatamao." Hina said. "This time you should like the combination better."

Mahine looked down, and stiffened instantly. Sheer terror swept her mind.

"Very unusual, isn't it?" Hina joked.

"How can you do such a thing?"

"Don't ask!" Hina frowned, annoyed by the question.

"I must go," Mahine said. "Oh, I almost forgot. Kukara looks forward to seeing you very soon."

Hina reflected on Mahine's last words, and wondered what Kukara really meant. She knew her words often carried subtle implications.

Kon and Mehao began their dangerous descent. At first, the coordination between those pushing the canoe away from the mountain, and Tamatoa's teams releasing the ropes by small lengths was poor at best. Brutal jolts almost threw Kon and Mehao overboard. Mehao complained, while Tamatoa started laughing. Then, the giant burst out in laughter, and so did his men.

Mehao glanced at Kon with a grin on his face: "I am not too sure about this!"

"Nor am I," Kon replied, irritated.

By midmorning, they reached the first narrow platform covered with ferns, on which they carefully secured the canoe. All the men went down. Tamatoa was the last one. He took the spare rope, made a slipknot around one of the main ropes, and sent it down. The rope crashed heavily near the canoe. He released two of the main hanging ropes, and prepared for the descent.

"Hina, it is your turn, just after I reach the canoe. Are you ready?"

"Yes,…I am excited!"

Hina descended, very slowly at first. Other than vertigo when she was looking down, she found it was easier than she had expected.

"Perhaps, I am good at this stuff!"

She stopped and looked at the abyss. It was like the deep sea, unfathomable, without end. She recalled that Kon had told her not to look down and only concentrate on her hands and feet, but for nothing in the world would she have missed the special effects of this unique moment. Purely for pleasure, she stopped, solidly bound herself to the mountain, and looked down. She did not move. She listened to the dance of the fern fronds in the breeze. She looked at tropicbirds circling. Fascinated, she kissed the rock. She looked at her fingers, and thought how wonderful was the human hand. She closed her eyes, and thought about the men below waiting for her. She thought about the cave, where she would be alone. A shiver crossed her body, like a warning that beyond the cave was another life, where dreams mix with life, where fiction mixes with reality. She opened her eyes, spat on her hands, solidly grabbed the rope and continued her descent. This time, she kept a cool head, and concentrated only on her hands, her feet and the mountain in front of her.

On the narrow ledge, near the canoe, six men struggled to drive ironwood posts inside the mountain cracks. Kon installed a rope cuff around each post. It would act as a roller, protecting ropes from too much friction damage.

As Hina reached the ledge, dark clouds encircled the mountain. Tamatoa swirled the rope, sending a loop all the way up to the top, liberating the rope from its short anchor. Now, there was no possible turning back. Down was the only way, with a slick, vertical wall against which no man had put his feet before. They were on sacred, forbidden territory.

"We should not wait long," Kon said, looking at the clouds.

The descent went without a hitch, until they reached the clouds below. Kon and Mehao felt a mist mixing with their sweat. Hina, who had nothing to do but watch, was freezing. Any communication between Kon and Tamatoa consisted of one sharp whistle to release the ropes a little, or two long whistles if the two men in the canoe encountered momentary difficulties, in which case they would stop the descent by making several loops with the ropes around the posts.

The cliff became slippery, and the soil between ferns became muddy. Furthermore, many men developed bleeding blisters in their hands.

Hina placed her back against the mountain, which was slightly warmer than the surrounding fog. She could barely see her feet. Ahead of her, she could only see the grayish mass of the clouds. She had only to take two steps forward, and would have vanished forever in a deadly fall. She fought the negative powers in her mind, and admitted her task was much easier than the one of these brave men. She could see Tamatoa, calm and confident, looking powerful, which comforted her. She looked to see how much rope was left. She thought time had stopped. It was taking too long, which was an indication of the appalling difficulties they were enduring.

Suddenly, Kon whistled twice. A shiver went through her

back. What could the problem have been? Immediately the ropes were secured several times around the posts. Tamatoa saw the fear in Hina's eyes.

"They are all right," he said. " There was no tension on the ropes, therefore the canoe was resting on the top of something."

Then, Kon whistled three times: They had reached another ledge and it was the signal for everyone to come down. Hina smiled at this fleeting moment of peace.

Tamatoa was last to leave the ledge. She saw him disappear into the clouds below, when lightning struck the valley, illuminating the thick mist all around. She felt her heart pound, and the sweat of fear on her face. She had more difficulty holding the wet and slippery rope. She panicked and looked for an anchor for her feet. She found a crack and immediately put her foot in it. It was enough to release the pressure on her hands. She tried to dry them against her garments, without much success. On her left, she saw a vacant nest, perhaps the home of a tropicbird. She went down, focusing her thoughts on the tropicbird and the wild beauty of its kingdom. Suddenly, the rope became more slippery and sticky. Hina realized it was coated with fresh blood. So, every time she saw young fern fiddleheads she collected them and placed them inside her belt. She would extract a precious liquid from them. It would heal wounds. Then, her thoughts went to the cave again. Something seemed wrong, but she could not determine what. It was like an intuition, something warning her about unknown forces. She was convinced Kon knew about them, but had chosen to remain silent. When she reached the canoe, most of the men were surrounded by ferns high enough to cover their shoulders. The ledge was much wider than she had expected.

"We shall spend the rest of the day and the night here, to

recover," Kon said.

"Thank you!" she said with a smile of contentment.

Relaxed, Hina collected more fern fiddleheads.

She pressed them to extract a precious juice with which she cleansed the wounded hands of her men. Patiently, she cut narrow strips of soft bark-cloth she had prudently taken with her, to protect the most serious wounds.

Later in the afternoon, the rain stopped and the clouds slowly vanished. Once again, Kon and Tamatoa could carefully inspect the mountain below.

"We are farther from the cave than I thought," Kon said.

"A full length of the ropes is not sufficient," Tamatoa said. "We must stop somewhere else between."

"There is no place to stop," Kon replied. "Show me your hands."

Tamatoa complied, a little puzzled.

"Do you see the few tiny pinnacles at some distance above the cave?" Kon asked.

Tamatoa carefully scrutinized the mountain: "Yes, I see them."

"Your hands are in good shape, therefore I can use your full strength."

"How?"

"There, I will fix three wooden posts."

"Then what?" Tamatoa asked.

"We will pass beyond the posts with the canoe. You will go down with the fourth rope. Then, you will lift the canoe from one side for an instant, so we can release one rope and wrap it around one post. We will repeat this operation at the other end of the canoe."

"And, how are these men going to find a place around these

pinnacles?"

"With an additional loop around each post, there will be no need for so many men."

"Can these ropes sustain the abrasion created by the second loop?"

"I hope so!" Kon replied. "We have no other option."

"You really think I can lift the canoe as you said."

"Three days ago, you showed me you could."

Tamatoa glanced at Kon. His deep black eyes seemed lost in memories. He spat on the ground, and stood up. Then, his eyes slowly brightened with passion.

"Your idea is good. So be it!" Tamatoa roared, giving a devastating blow to Kon's shoulder.

Hina chuckled at the way Kon tried to recover his composure.

Tamatoa looked once more at the pinnacles: "The journey just begins!"

When they felt the cool evening breeze, their clothes had already dried. They managed to build a small fire with the many dead ferns from the ledge. Far down in the valley, they could see several campfires from their friends watching them. Hina prepared a meal with tender fern roots grilled for a very short time. They had plenty of clean water from the many springs coming out from the mountain. They dreamed about the next day, the last day of the journey for the men, but the beginning of the unknown for Hina. She leaned back on her elbows, and watched the stars.

"What is that large star appearing first in the evening, and racing after the sun?" she asked.

"It is Viracocha's companion at both ends of the day," Kon replied.

They fell asleep, covered with green blankets made of woven

ferns. The night was chilly. The wind ululated, like the living spirit of sacred birds. Above them, there was something hovering, something that could neither be seen nor felt. It was something Maohis feared and respected, and something Viracocha's sons interacted with, and also respected. At that place, remote, strange and impossible, they all felt the grandeur of the Great Taaroa, also called the Great Viracocha. Aside from their body, quarrels and day-to-day life, they all knew there was something else to believe in, mysterious, coming from another place, far away. The wind, the silence, the stars, were all one in their souls. Birth and death were both ends of a circle, a single and same place, and a narrow ledge within the immensity of the unknown. On the narrow ledge, they were at peace, exploring territories that made them different. They were the mountain's children.

Early at dawn, they started the final assault, the final descent. The sun reflected on Mount Orohena, but they were still in the shade. Little by little, Kon and Mehao pushed the canoe away from the mountain, and Tamatoa's men released the ropes. Everything went smoothly until the canoe reached the tiny pinnacles, where Kon would have to drive three solid wooden posts into the cracks of the mountain.

Kon inspected the rotten rock, and selected three places where to anchor the posts. It took all morning for Kon and Mehao to solidly secure them into the mountain. Kon waved at Tamatoa, who visibly became impatient. Hina watched Tamatoa. His body was covered with superb tattoos. Elaborate spirals covered each arm and leg joint. Using the fourth rope, he went down, rappelling with long and powerful strokes against the mountain. He was ready and confident. She thought there was great majesty in this man, and started admiring and respecting him for who he truly was. She knew Tamatoa would never ask anyone to do something he could not do himself, but what a challenge for his men!

Solidly anchored near one post, Kon waited. Tamatoa went under him, until he could reach the canoe and grab it with one hand. He secured his feet on the mountain, and with his other hand held the spare rope with which he came.

"Are you ready?" Tamatoa asked.

"When you are," Kon replied.

Tamatoa took a deep breath, and his huge body went to work. With one hand, he raised the canoe high enough for Kon to take the loose rope and make three loops around one post. Then, far above, the other men released the rope. Kon carefully secured it around the post. Tamatoa let the canoe down, gently.

"Well done!" Kon said. "Mana was with you."

They repeated the same procedure for the rope holding the canoe at the other end.

After a few other men came down to hold the ropes around the posts, the descent continued. However, with an additional loop around the posts, the ropes were not sliding very well, making the descent much more chaotic. It did not take very long before one rope was dangerously worn, just above Kon's side. First, one fiber broke, then another one, then another one…and nobody noticed.

They were not too far from the cave, and already smiling, but once more, the mountain would decide otherwise. Once more, they would meet uncertainty, pain and fear. Once more, they would meet Mount Orohena's spirits.

The rope slid on a sharp edge. The canoe was very close to the awesome cliff, and under it was the emptiness going so far away. Then, it happened with no warning. The rope broke, and Kon's side dropped, out of balance. Suspended by the two remaining ropes, the canoe bounced away from the cliff. Kon fell over the canoe, but his safety belt kept him on the side of the hull. The mountain was coming. Kon realized his problem, and there was nothing he could do. It was happening too fast.

"Kon!… The Mountain…" Mehao screamed.

It was too late. The formidable mass of the canoe slammed Kon against the slick wall. He desperately tried to absorb the shock with his arms against the mountain. But, he was not strong enough. Kon felt sharp pain inside his chest. He looked up, and saw Hina covering her eyes with her hands. Everyone saw the accident, and they were waiting for what would happen next.

Tamatoa was the first one to recover, and went down to rescue Kon, while Mehao was trying to maintain his balance and putting his weight on the well-secured end of the boat.

"How are you feeling?" Tamatoa asked.

"Not good!" Kon murmured, blood coming out from his mouth.

Tamatoa quickly secured the boat with the spare rope, and lifted Kon into the boat, where he could lie down.

"Son, let's get to that cave quick."

Mehao complied, and the descent continued.

"Another rope is shredding." Mehao said.

Tamatoa took the hanging rope under the canoe, jumped out and landed heavily in the ferns covering the ledge where the cave was. He quickly regained control of himself, and pulled the canoe safely over the flattest part of the ledge.

Holding his ribs, some of which were broken, Kon walked out and lay in the cool ferns.

"We did it, Kon Tici," Tamatoa said.

"Thanks to you,…my friend…," Kon said.

Tamatoa gently put his hand on Kon's shoulder.

"Kon Tici, as long as I will live, I will never forget this

moment. You will recover."

"I look bad, but I think I will be all right." Kon replied.

"The life of you and Hina is sacred to me," the great warrior said with a smile, "until the day I die."

CHAPTER 33

"Taaroa told me I shall help Hina of the Valley become a great priestess. Commissioned to serve you, I long for your coming, my beloved sister."

Kama Tici Viracocha

The sacred canoe was placed inside the cave, so only the early morning light would reach Taaroa's eyes. Each man, one by one, honored the late great priest by standing at his side, silent, for a moment. One by one, they went down to the valley, using the long ropes. Tamatoa kneeled near the heavy outrigger, and stared at the great Taaroa.

"I wish I had known him a long time ago."

"But,... he is still...alive." Kon said, with difficulty.

"Perhaps," Tamatoa replied, "but the world of spirits is not mine."

The great warrior stood up, and put a friendly hand on Kon's shoulder.

"This is a place you found. Through Taaroa, you and Hina own it. I am sure you will explain this young and beautiful priestess how to make the best use of it."

Hina enveloped Kon's chest inside several layers of barkcloth, very tight, to protect him during the descent. They helped Kon to stand up.

"Keep your arms around my neck," Tamatoa said, "I will take care of the descent."

"I wish...I could stay." Kon said, kissing Hina. "But, it is a sacred place, and a sacred moment for you."

"Why for me?"

"You volunteered, you were chosen, and we all want you to be alone in this place until tomorrow evening."

"What am I supposed to do, here, all by myself? I want to be with you."

"There is a cave to explore. A surprise is waiting for you. Then, spirits will visit you."

"You better do as he said," Tamatoa said. "Down there, there are plenty of people to take care of him."

Concerned for Kon, she watched them going down, until they reached the valley. Then, she released the three ropes, and kept only the spare one. She was in total isolation, with a canoe, the great Taaroa, silence, wind and Orohena's spirits.

She walked around the cave, and found it boring. She walked several times around the canoe, perplexed and not knowing what to do. Outside the cave she went along the ledge, aware that it led nowhere. She thought the experience was a waste of time, and only a ceremony to comply with. She sat in the ferns, and looked at the incredible view across the valley. She was in the shade of Orohena, and the cool breeze caressed her naked shoulders. Suddenly, at some distance on the ledge, she noticed a tiny swirl of dust taking shape. It slowly gained momentum and became a well-shaped whirlpool coming to her.

"Here we go again," she murmured, with a chill in her spine.

For an instant, it stood still, close to Hina, then went above the rope she had stored near the entrance of the cave. One end of the rope came up slowly, and the vortex brought it to her.

Hina had never been terrified, but she seriously considered going down the cliff. The rope fail on the ground, and the vortex went to the cave, climbed into Taaroa's canoe, tearing apart a few bark-cloth strips from his mummified body. Petrified, Hina watched the vortex disappear inside the cave, and she heard a plaintive whistle.

"Shiiinaaa..."

She shook her head, convinced she had heard her name. Total silence was restored, as if the vortex had been swallowed by something. She walked inside the cave, but found nothing, and heard nothing. Slowly, she regained her confidence.

"Whatever you are, I am going to get to the bottom of this."

Determined, she went as deeply into the cave as possible, placed her back against the wall, and listened carefully by holding her breath. She heard nothing. She waited until she became accustomed to the darkness, then inspected the wall. Suddenly, she saw something darker on her left. It was not moving. She waited, until it became clear it was a narrow passage leading to another room. She climbed into it. Her body could barely fit inside it, but she managed to edge her way in. It was absolute darkness. She looked behind, and saw some light coming through the narrow channel she had just passed. She went forward, with one foot first: The ground was flat. With her hands in front of her, she tried to find the end of the new room, but found nothing. Concerned about her safety, she recalled the rope.

"The vortex showed me that rope: Was that a recommendation?" she asked herself aloud.

She smiled about the astonishing possibility, went outside, attached the rope around her waist, the other end to the boat, and went back to the cave more determined than ever.

She struggled across the narrow passage, went across the

room and bumped into some objects on the ground. She squatted and investigated them. They were long, and one of them was bulky. Blood flushed to her face, as she realized they were human bones. She had a skull in her hands. Then, she vaguely recalled Kon had told her about this, a long time ago.

"How could you have passed through that channel?" she asked incredulously.

She smiled in the darkness, looking at the small halo of light behind her, hopping the man she loved would recover from his wounds.

"Kon Tici, you are incredible!"

After she pulled all the rope attached to the canoe, into the room, she proceeded with her exploration. She reached the opposite wall. It was slick, wet and felt warmer. She took a small stone, threw it upward and immediately bumped against the ceiling: The room was not very high. With her hands, she investigated the wall carefully, until she heard something. It was the vortex, but it seemed far away, in another room. Possessed by fear once more, she stopped breathing, and listened to the faint whistle that slowly vanished. She had heard it long enough to locate its exact direction. She slowly walked to the wall, explored with her hands in the upper part, and listened. She heard her heart racing in her chest. She held her breath as long as possible. On the third attempt, she finally heard something very faint. Drops of water were falling into a pond, at long intervals. The sound came from the wall, on her right upper side. She found a narrow passage with her hands. She climbed into it, but her body was too large to move around in it. She backed off in the room, and thought for a moment. Her only chance was to undress. She removed her clothes, secured the rope around her foot, instead of her waist, and made another attempt.

This time, she went much farther, until her hands could reach the other side. She pulled hard, felt rough edges scratching her hips, but she did not care. As she emerged on the other side, she tried to feel the ground with her hands, but there was only air. How far down was the ground? She found a tiny place to stand, grabbed a stone and threw it ahead. She heard it fall on dirt, just in front of her. She untied the rope from her foot, and tied it back around her waist. Careful, she went down, until she felt the ground with one foot. She took another stone, and threw it ahead: It fell on the ground. She grabbed another stone, and threw it farther: It fell in water. A pond was ahead. She took another stone, and threw hard: It bumped into a wall across the pond and fell in the water, which gave her some kind of perspective. Suddenly, she felt something moving under her feet. She grabbed the wall for stability, and realized she was perched on the top of a boulder. She sat on it, and slid to the ground. The room was remarkably flat, too flat to be natural. Then, it sloped down gently, until she could feel the water with her feet. She backed up, and explored the room. With her hands, she could feel carvings on the walls, and wished she could have seen what they were. At both ends of the wall, she found the pond. She was surprised how warm the room was. The water was also warm, and had a terrible smell. The contact with the water was pleasant, but the smell quite unpleasant.

She walked forward one step,...a second step,...a third step,... until the water reached her knees. Then, with one foot, she could tell it was becoming steeper. She went forward. The water reached her waist, then her shoulders. Now, she was swimming. Though, she could not see anything, she went to the other side of the pond, found only a wall, with nowhere to put her feet. She secured the rope around her waist, and dived to check how deep the pond was. She went as deeply as she could, but did not reach the bottom. Surprised, she went up slowly. As she broke the surface, she noticed the bad smell had become intolerable. She swam toward the shore, but instead, bumped into a wall. She swam in the opposite direction, and also bumped into a wall. She found herself short of breath, and very uncomfortable. Thinking she had lost her sense of direction, she swam along the wall. To her stupefaction, the wall was circling all around her. Blood flushed to her face. She was in another place. She had dived into another room, one much narrower. She felt dizzy, and unable to control herself, and that smell... Suddenly, her instinct ordered her to get out. She pulled on the rope until it became taut. Then, she dived following the rope. She felt the rope going around an edge, and she went up again. The surface was too far; she swallowed some water, and finally broke the surface at the limit of consciousness. She struggled to summon enough energy to swim until the water became shallow. When she stood up, she felt dizzy and unable to walk. She sat in the water, her head barely afloat. She searched for the rope, found it and pulled on it. Slowly she came out of the pond, and lay her back on the ground. She took several deep breaths. Slowly, the dizziness went away, and she regained her strength. She realized how imprudent she had been. Something she was sure of, none had gone as far as she went inside the mountain.

She listened to the occasional drops falling into the pond. She listened for the vortex, but heard nothing besides her breath, her heart, her eyes blinking, and the drops. She pulled the long rope out of the water and rolled it neatly near the boulder she would have to climb on her way out. With her hands, she inspected the walls around the room, in more detail. She found a long, rugged surface, more like a wrinkle. Slowly, she followed it. It was like a large circle carved on the wall. Then, she realized it was not a circle, but a spiral. Her fingers reached the center, felt a strong current of energy, and she distinctively saw an ephemeral, dark purple light dancing between her fingers. Her first reaction had been to pull back her hand. She touched the center once more, but nothing happened. She continued exploring the wall, and soon found another spiral, much larger. Slowly, she moved her fingers toward the center. When she reached the last loop before the center she stopped, and focused her eyes on her hand, which she could not see. She moved her finger to the center. Instantly, a long blue-purple spark traveled along her arm, illuminating the entire wall. The beam of fire had been ephemeral. Nevertheless, she had enough time to memorize the wall details. It was a magnificent network of petroglyphs and paintings. She recalled seeing a birdman, with a human body and the head of the great wandering albatross. She was in a sacred, long forgotten place.

She searched for other spirals, but found none. She touched the center of the two familiar spirals, but nothing happened. Suddenly, she bumped against a structure, on the ground, nearby the water. She explored it with her fingers. It was a cradle long enough to contain her body. Warm water entered its lower part, where her feet would have fitted. She found the structure most interesting, and decided to lie inside it. Slowly, she entered the cradle. The warm water flowed around her feet, so she realized the water in the pond was actually coming out of the cradle. She lay down, waited silently and felt a tremendous sense of comfort she had not experienced before.

She thought about the birdman, until her mind drifted away. She heard the vortex, but it was very faint, as if in another world behind the walls. She felt a cold, misty rain falling on her. She found herself sitting on the edge of a formidable cliff surrounding a shallow lake of extraordinary beauty: Never had she dreamed of such spectacular scenery. To her left, over the cliff, she could see the awesome sea with its dark blue horizon.

She heard the vortex again. This time, she saw it coming toward her. The powerful swirl followed the edge of the cliff, and became stationary at a short distance where she could almost touch it. She stood up and went to it.

"Orohena's spirit, I want to touch you!"

To her surprise, the vortex slowly metamorphosed into a woman wrapped inside an elegant white robe, and a dark blue belt. She was tall, her hair long, straight, and black, ruffling in the evening breeze. At first, Hina could not see her face. Then, she heard the woman speak in a gentle voice.

"Hina of the Valley, you have been chosen by the Great Taaroa."

"Chosen for what?" Hina inquired, short of ideas.

The woman slowly faced Hina, who immediately opened her mouth, surprised, amazed and shaken. The woman had the most magnificent dark blue eyes she had ever seen, slightly slanted like Kon's eyes. She was a Viracocha woman. Hina touched her hair, but felt nothing: She could walk through the woman without being able to physically contact her.

She spoke again, with a friendly, but determined tone of voice.

"You have been chosen to be the heir of a lost race. One day, you will have a son. He will be Kon Tici Viracocha's son. You shall name your son Maui. After an incredible journey, you will reach this island where your spirit is now. You will name this island Mata-Kite-Rani. In your language, it means Eyes Looking at the Stars. You will grow old on Mata-Kite-Rani and will never physically return to Tahiti-nui. But you will learn to travel with your spirit alone, and you will become a great priestess and a queen. I shall be on your side serving you, my beloved sister."

The woman's smile was compelling and an irresistible attraction. Her beauty was beyond description.

"What is your name?" Hina asked.

The woman's eyes twinkled with tenderness and a touch of emotion.

"My name is Kama Tici Viracocha."

Hina was not surprised. She wanted to ask her more questions, but Kama vanished into the reappearing vortex. Hina felt heavy, dizzy and collapsed to the ground.

Hina awoke in the cradle, and she realized she had had a dream. Or, was it something else? As she attempted to exit the cradle, she heard the vortex again. This time she knew it was in this room, just behind her. She slowly turned her head, looking behind her. The vortex made of dark purple light was moving toward the pond. It came near Hina's feet. Then, it came on top of her. Hina felt dizzy, and transported to another place. She awoke on the sacred shore of Vaihiria Lake. The vortex slowly assumed a human form,…a young girl,…Kukara Tici Viracocha.

"Who are you?" Hina asked, stunned.

"Do not fear, mother." Kukara replied.

"I am not your mother. And, you are not Kukara. Where do you come from?"

"I am the Light," Kukara replied, looking at the calm surface of the lake.

"If you are so powerful, tell me what will happen to Kon. Do something to cure his wound. Can you do such things?"

"The Light does not answer questions," Kukara replied. "The Light only propagates life, improves life, in search ofr perfect beauty and harmony in everything."

"So, I am not beautiful enough! So, I am not worthy of your help."

"Do not be sad, Hina of the Valley. The Kukara you know and the Light in front of you are not the same person. I took Kukara's body to make easier on you. You have been chosen because you are beautiful, because your mind is beautiful. Therefore, I will protect everything and everyone you cherish, so you can be happy. But life shall take a different course for you, and the life you knew so far may vanish. When this will happen, do not fear, remember me, and have faith in your future. You will indeed, step by step, build and inspire a new civilization. Those are my words, and we will never meet again. Use my powers wisely."

Instantly, Kukara became a vortex. Hina awoke and looked around. To her great surprise, she saw Taaroa's canoe in front of her. She raised herself on her elbows, and suffered from a severe headache. Holding her head, she went to drink at a small outlet on the ledge. She went back to the canoe, and saw the long rope neatly piled there. Only then, she realized the rope was not attached to her waist, and she was nude. Extraordinarily confused, she tried to recall everything that had happened. She knew some of it was true, and some was just a dream. Determined to clarify a few details, she went inside the cave, then passed into the second room where she found her clothes on the ground. She went to the wall where the narrow passage to the next secret chamber was. Now, there was no passage. She listened for the dripping water. Now, there was no dripping water. Everything spun in her head. She was no longer capable of distinguishing between what could have been a dream, and what was reality. She walked outside, sat near the ledge, looking at the valley. She wondered if she was still dreaming. She closed her eyes, breathed deeply, and tried to concentrate on details she could remember.

She opened her eyes, and looked at her legs. With her fingers, she wiped a piece of dry mud, and smelled it. The odor was unmistakable. It was the same strong, terrible smell she had experienced in the secret room. So, this part could not have been a dream. Determined, she went back inside the cave, searching for the narrow passage. She did not find it. Somehow it had been sealed. Defeated, and humiliated, she exited the cave in anger. She went directly to the rope, unfolded it, then suddenly stopped. The rope was wet. The rope smelled bad.

"No, Orohena!" she screamed. "Hina is not insane. Hina knows the difference between a dream and reality. Don't try to fool me."

After several more attempts at finding a passage that did not exist, she had to admit her defeat. Reluctantly, she followed the ledge to the place where the falls poured out from the mountain. She thought the water was slightly warm, but wondered if it was her imagination. She washed herself, and smelled the water. There was no bad smell. Suddenly, she noticed an unmistakable detail. Under her nails, she could see some red paint, the same red paint covering the spirals on the walls of the secret cave. She smiled, and stared at Mount Orohena.

"Great Spirit of the mountain, forgive my temper. I understand my mission in the cave has been fulfilled. Hina of the Valley shall obey, and walk to her destiny."

She went back to Taaroa's canoe. She looked at the face of the great priest. He was smiling at her. Behind the dried, thin flesh, she could see his bones.

"Oh, Taaroa," she said kneeling, "help me to understand! If my destiny is to be a great priestess, I must understand. Don't leave me alone."

She sat, and crossed her legs, facing the valley. She closed her eyes, and meditated as Kon had taught her so many times. She went through all the details of her dream. She recalled all Kama's words, and all the Light's words. She opened her eyes and looked at the first stars in the evening. Her eyes caught an awesome shooting star falling toward the east.

"Vana would say it is a sign. Maybe there is truth in his beliefs," she admitted aloud.

She thought about Taaroa's new home. For generations, the place would be sacred, taboo. There would be no need for anyone to protect the integrity of this special place. Nature would take care of anyone who would dare to trespass here. The wind would quietly ululate at the entry of the cave, as it did now. She listened to the fascinating sound. It was the voice of the Sacred Spirit, and she found pleasure in it. At this sacred place, Taaroa would have all eternity to travel in time and space, perhaps with the Light. Every morning, Taaroa would contemplate the awesome sea. Every night, Taaroa would count the small fires in Hina's valley. At times, Taaroa would hear the voices of those who live for only a short time. Maybe Taaroa would travel to the valley inside the vortex, and scare those who are arrogant enough to believe they know everything. Then, mankind would forget Taaroa. Mankind would forget Mount Orohena. Mankind would forget the wonder of looking at the Light.

"Not as long as Hina of the Valley is alive!" Hina said, opening her eyes.

She raised her hands to reach for the stars. Never before had she looked at light with such insight, such concern and such respect. That faint light entering her eyes was alive, and intelligent. She looked down at her feet, smiled, amused by her incredible fantasy. Thus, something guided her thoughts to Mata-Kite-Rani.

Now, she knew the meaning of Eyes Looking at the Stars.

"I, Hina of the Valley, look at the stars. Humbly, I accept starlight as my spiritual food."

She was overwhelmed and happy.

"There is light everywhere life is. Then, there is the Light, the Great Taaroa, the Great Viracocha, the Great Spirit of Mount Orohena,…. It is all the same master."

Hina closed her eyes, and saw the radiant energy in her mind. For the first time, an incredible thought went through her mind, a thought she would have not considered possible a few days earlier: She did not need help from Kon Tici Viracocha anymore. She was capable. She was Princess Hina, priestess of the Valley, in touch with the Light.

All recent events provided a sudden meaning. There were no mysteries.

"It does not matter if what I saw and felt in the cave was a dream or reality. It does not matter if the woman with blue eyes exists. It does not matter if I cannot touch the stars. What matters is who I want to be."

She felt a halo of comfort, mixed with shivers. She wrapped herself snugly inside her white robe.

"Mata-Kite-Rani,…one day, I will seal that vision in sacred rocks,…one day I will make the silent look of a frozen face looking at eternity, more powerful than anything alive,…I swear!"

Content, she lay in the cool ferns, and went to sleep.

At dawn, from the moment she opened her eyes, she knew she was no longer the same Hina. A powerful force was in control of her. She walked to the canoe, felt it with her fingers and looked at Taaroa for the last time.

"You are not dead. You just left this body for an eternal journey. So long, leper of a moment! You are alive and well, and the Light is with you."

Without looking back, she started her descent. When she passed nearby the tropicbirds within their nest, they looked at her quietly, as if she had always been there. She looked down and smiled: She no longer had vertigo.

At the foot of the falls, they were all waiting for her, to conclude that long ceremony that Kon had created and directed for so long, but he was not near her father where he would have been on such an occasion. He was not there at all. She finally reached another tropicbird nest, where a long time ago, Kon had collected the sacred long feathers for her. She stepped on the narrow ledge, and watched the mother sitting on her eggs. The bird was not afraid. Hina left the bird in peace. She took the rope, twirling it all the way to the cave. The rope fell, way down into the valley. She followed the ledge until she reached the thick forest where the sacred green pigeon waited for her. Hina was, once again in her valley.

Deep inside the hot, humid and dark rain forest, she felt wrapped in a familiar world. The giant mape trees blocked the sunlight. Their intricate roots wandered on the ground like living walls as tall as she. She had to climb many of the slippery tentacles. After so many days at high altitude, she felt her body sweat more than usual. Nothing was moving in this kingdom where silence was king. Soon, she saw the ancestor of all mape trees, the first one that had been created. When she put her hands on the trunk, it was the only thing she could see. Taaroa had told her about the tree ancestor, many times. She was not sure Vana had seen it, as he had never mentioned it.

Hina heard the master of the rain forest call her: Whoo-hoo,… Whoo-hoo,… Whoo-hoo,… The call was frightening to the ordinary man, but not to Hina, who knew better. She was at home. She stopped, looked up and saw the master, right in front of her, perched on a low branch. The sacred green pigeon was staring at her. Its eyes were peaceful. She could not comprehend that such a fragile bird could be the object of so much fear in humans. The green pigeon was known to carry the evil spirits of the darkness, but Hina was Hina: different, unique and fearless concerning legends. She was the living legend. She searched around the tree, and found a small package protected by a cover of dead leaves. She opened it, and found a smaller one, beautiful, decorated with tiny cowries. It was a ceremonial bag that only the great priest would be allowed to touch.

A few days earlier, she would have hesitated to touch the bag, but now the Light was with her. Mana was with her. She had freedom to do as she pleased. She opened the bag, in which she found a dress especially made for her. Whoever had made the dress knew her well. She removed her old, dirty garments, buried them under the tree, went to a small stream nearby to wash herself, and came back to the tree. Slowly, delicately, she slipped into the dress, into the magic of a great priestess. Around her waist, she tied a belt decorated with tiny, white cowries. On her hip, she felt something inside the dress. There was a pocket she had not noticed at first, in which she found the sacred green pigeon's favorite seeds. Instantly, the bird left its perch, gliding to Hina's shoulder. One of its wings flapped on her face, and she found herself tickled by green feathers. The gentle bird started cooing. She caressed its soft back and slowly lowerd the bird to the ground, and gave it the seeds. The green pigeon was interested only in its treat.

Hina looked at herself, and found the dress most unusual. It was short on the sides. Two long tapa strips reached her feet, one in front, and one in the back. On the sides, long strips of dry grass reached her knees. As she walked, her long legs could be seen through the bouncing grass. Around her shoulders and chest, a thin strip of tiny red feathers underscored her beauty. She took the hat, inspected it, pulled her hair back and put it on her head. On the top of the hat, long white-tail tropicbird streamers made her look very tall. She encircled her wrists and calves with narrow bands covered with green feathers from the sacred pigeon of her valley. Finally, she took a long wooden staff carved in the image of Taaroa's face. She was gorgeous, and she knew it.

After eating the last seeds, the pigeon came back on her shoulder, cooed, then flew away. She looked at it for the last time. Somehow she knew she would never see it again. Now, she was ready to meet her people, and conclude what Kon had begun. She walked with dignity toward the meadow, where she could already hear the falls. She thought about the words she would say. On the return of the one who had been selected to share the ultimate night with the late great priest, it was a Maohi tradition to listen to his or her sacred words. So, Hina knew everyone had great expectations of her.

She heard people talking and laughing. Soon, she appeared at the edge of the forest, then a respectful silence fell. Only the timeless pounding of the falls could be heard. They all looked at her: She had never appeared so beautiful. She walked to her father. She saw Tamatoa, Hotu-Matua, Vana, Mato and Taranga.

"Where is Kon?" she asked.

"At Tupua's house," Taranga replied. "Because of his severe injuries, I don't want him to move too much for a few more days. He is all right."

Hina felt joy and relief. She did not answer, but a few tears ran down on her cheeks. She quickly recovered her composure. They were waiting for her words. She went to Kukara, who was near Vana.

"Are you the Light?" Hina asked with a smile.

Kukara, taken by surprise, and visibly embarrassed, struggled for an answer.

"I know who the Light is,…but I am not the Light."

"Were you aware the Light was with me in the cave?"

"Yes, mother," Kukara replied, in the voice of a shy girl.

"It is all I need to know," Hina said.

Thunder rolled with awesome power across the valley. With this powerful introduction by Mother Nature, Hina delivered the words everyone waited for.

"Oh, Tahiti-nui, inspire peace to the world! Oh, my dear valley, give food and water to Maohis! Oh, Great Orohena, provide order and make each of us respect others!"

She went to her father, and glanced at Hotu-Matua and Tamatoa.

"Rulers, make all Maohis near you happy, and those far away attracted to you. This shall be the model that was born along the way to that cave: Never forget it!"

She went to Tamatoa.

"I will be your great priestess during the long trip across the awesome sea. That is my decision."

CHAPTER 34

At times, my mother thinks I am the Light.
At times, I don't know myself who I am.
But Kon and Hina showed me who I want to be.
So, they and I, are just starting a long journey to a new world."

Kukara Tici Viracocha

Hina entered her father's house, and ran to Kon, who was lying on bamboo mats and conversing with Atea and Fenua.

"How do you feel?" Hina asked, taking his hands in hers.

"I will be all right. I feel better than yesterday. I still have problems with my tongue I badly bit during the shock against the mountain."

Two days later, on the black sand beach near Papenoo, the man who became the humble servant of a cause, was once more the king, Tamatoa the great. His steps pounded on the sand.

He turned around, swung his long, red cape, and put his powerful hand on Tupua's shoulder.

"Honorable neighbor, king of Tahiti-nui," the charismatic giant said with a thundering voice, "I shall leave. My people wait for me on Pora-Pora. But we shall meet again soon, at the great gathering of the Maohis."

Tamatoa stepped into his ship, ordered warriors to push it away from the beach. The ship gained momentum, and headed toward the sun setting behind the horizon.

Tupua walked back to the village with Vana and Hotu-Matua.

"My fear for that man is gone," Hotu-Matua said.

"He is a man of honor," Tupua said. "I forgive him for his past mistakes."

Later the same day, at the Marae of Toerau, where Kon had been transported, Hina could not stop talking to him about her experience in the cave.

"I will never see that place again," she concluded, with sadness.

"One day, we may return," Kon said, to comfort her.

"I don't think so," she replied. "I will have to learn to live on a new land, appreciate its roughness and visit my valley only in distant memories."

"Are you looking forward to that long trip after the great gathering?"

"For you, Kon Tici, I will do anything!"

One moon-cycle later, Tupua's ship entered the Te Ava Moa Pass leading to the Opoa Bay in the south part of Havaiki. Straight ahead, they would meet Maohis from many faraway islands. All the kings and priests would gather around the sacred, white monolith of the Marae of Taputapu-atea.

As the ship approached the beach, Hina and Kon recognized the massive outline of Tamatoa's ships, Hotu-Matua's and many more. Some were from Rarotonga, Pora-Pora, Huahine, Rapa and from distant places such as Mangareva and Samoa. Kon hoped to find some of his Viracocha brothers and sisters, but before the day would be over, his hopes would be dashed. They found nobody who had seen them. For Kon, it was a devastating disappointment, and more incentive to pursue his search in the far east.

Tupua inserted himself between Kon and Hina.

"Go rest, my children, tomorrow night will be an incredible event."

Later, in a guesthouse near the beach, Hina took a cupful of coconut milk to Kon, who took the beverage, and shared it with her.

"Your mind is not at peace yet," she said.

"No, I am dreaming too far ahead of myself."

Hina lighted a Tutui candle-nut and placed it on the top of a carved drum, near Kon. They both looked at the dancing shadows against the walls covered with painted tapa. A gecko came hunting fruit flies and mosquitoes around the candle-nut. The tiny lizard inspected all the carvings on the drum. At times, its shadow on the far wall looked like an incredible monster.

Hina rolled over Kon, and put her lips on his forehead.

"Easy on my chest!" he pleaded.

"I know a way to bring you back to this world," she murmured.

She stood up, and went halfway between the lamp and the opposite wall. Slowly, seductively, she undressed herself, and the shadow of her perfect body projected against the wall.

"I have never seen a woman as attractive as you are," Kon whispered.

His eyes traveled from Hina to her shadow, and he instantly succumbed to her incredible charm. Confidence shined in her black eyes. Every move of her hips, legs and arms, did not jiggle her perfectly still breasts. Her eyes gave him an invitation for loving passion. With considerate lightness and grace, she lay on Kon's side, and slowly crawled on top of his body. Her warm breasts were against his stomach, and her hair all around his wounded chest. For a long time, she explored the depth of his blue eyes in which she saw herself reflected. She caressed his lips with the tip of one finger, then she circled his eyes, and with the swift voice of a princess, she asked a most unexpected question.

"Can you transform yourself into a vortex?"

Kon smiled with a teasing grin.

"No, and if it ever happens, it would be a hallucination on your part."

"No, Kon Tici," she replied, "Hina of the Valley never hallucinates."

"So, you will never see me becoming a vortex."

She took his head in her hands, so she could look him straight in the eyes.

"Kukara can change to a vortex, and so does Kama, therefore you can."

"But it was in your dreams."

"Not so fast!" she said. "You can keep the truth from me, but never lie to me."

He was still teasing her by giving vague answers.

"The vortex is a ploy created by our ancestors…," Kon said, "nothing extraordinary."

"It is a ploy all right," she smiled, bringing her lips to his, "and I am not going to let you get away with this, Kon Tici."

She kissed him with passion, and looked in his eyes again.

"Tell me you can become a vortex," she said, kissing him before he could answer.

"Did you see many stars?" Kon whispered in her ear.

"Yes!" she replied, kissing him once more.

"Did you see spiraling wheels made of light?"

She raised her head, and frowned.

"Yes! What are they?"

"That is where the Light lives. You can see them only in your mind."

"In the cave, after the Light disappeared, one of those wheels came to me at amazing speed, and the only thing I remember is like an explosion, before all light vanished, and I found myself lying near Taaroa's canoe."

Her words surprised him. He realized she had gone much farther than he had thought. He put his hands on her head, caressed her neck, her shoulders and her back. He was no longer teasing. He could not believe how beautiful she was, and now, capable.

"Now, you can travel with your mind," Kon said.

"How?"

"This is something you will have to learn by yourself, through meditation with the Light."

A cool breeze blew through the room and extinguished the candle-nut, as if something had been listening at what they were saying. It was dark, with no moon visible that night. Their bodies became one. They felt each other glide in the emptiness of black space, and they went to places only they knew.

The following day, late in the afternoon, they went near the huge fire that had been prepared for days, at the Marae. Many dignitaries were already waiting there. When they saw Kon Tici and Taranga Tici, they were astonished at how different they looked. When Taranga sat near the white monolith, they noticed even more his white robe, white hair, and white beard: He seemed to be at the right place. Then, they noticed the extraordinary length of his fingernails, which almost doubled the length of his fingers. Cross-legged, Taranga faced the kings, the priests and their relatives. He laid his hands on his lap, glanced at everyone. He invited Kon to sit at his side. Then, he called Hina and Kukara, and told them to sit at his side as well. The priests marveled at the Rongo-Rongo tablets hanging around

Kukara's neck. The young girl kept her calm and distinguished manners. They all noticed her maturity for her young age. Then, the attention shifted to Hina's gold necklace, and Kon's gold earplugs and bracelets. Never before had they seen such a magnificent, glittering material. All these details with majestic attire captured their attention, and there was no doubt in their minds that the small group seated in front of them was the most important feature of the great gathering. They were excited with anticipation, and they prepared many questions.

The Havaiki high priest, stepped forth and gave the command that questions could be asked to Taranga, the most honored guest.

"Why did you came to Tahiti-nui?" Vana asked.

"To learn from Taaroa, and take him to a sacred resting place," Taranga replied.

All the dignitaries agreed it was a wise answer. With respect to the late Taaroa, silence ensured, deeper and deeper, until the waves pounding on the distant coral reef could be heard. It was the most important moment of the gathering, a time when the most honored guest would speak, a time when Taranga would have to explain who the Viracocha people were. He knew it was of the utmost importance not to disappoint the Maohi dignitaries with his choice of words.

"Who are the Viracocha people?" Mato asked, emphasizing every word.

Taranga looked at Tupua, Tamatoa and his friend Hotu-Matua: They all waited for his answer.

"Many of you are amused by our long, thin noses, and our long ears."

Several dignitaries laughed. Instantly, the sound of drums rolled slightly, reminding them that absolute silence was requested out of respect for the honored speaker.

"See, I told you!" Taranga said with a smile.

This time, all dignitaries roared in laughter. After an appropriate interval, a slow rolling of the drums restored complete silence. Taranga's face became solemn. His slanted blue eyes looked at the stars.

"Many generations ago, the Viracocha people lived on a cold land, far away in the north of the continent we came from. We were fishermen, and like you, great navigators. We built heavy stone structures that withstood the forces of nature. We always lived peacefully. We chose to locate our villages where the Earth's scenery was an inspiration to our soul. We were ordinary people, with humble needs, but inquisitive intellect."

"How did you learn so much?" Mato asked.

Taranga searched in his memory.

"Our lives are ruled by six factors," Taranga replied, showing six fingers: "stars, the sea, mountains, birds, peace and daring."

Taranga paused for a moment, and pointed at one star.

"No matter how many times I look at them, shivers travel through my entire body when I do so. Stars talk to us, if you learn how to listen."

He paused again, raised his arms as high as he could, looking Mato straight in the eyes, and coming closer to him.

"Mata-Kite-Rani!" Taranga exploded, taking everyone by surprise. Hina felt her pulse pounding in her temples. For her, they were the magic words. His words reverberated against the white monolith, and flew to the sea.

"Never forget these words. If your life is full of trouble, walk alone on the hills, and look at them. Take their sacred Light with you, and your pitiful worries will shrink to manageable burdens. Then, your life will proceed with serenity."

Taranga's eyes searched for Tamatoa.

"The perfect silence of an infinite force," he said, pointing a long finger at the tattooed giant. "Does it mean anything to you?"

"This is a question for a priest," Tamatoa roared.

"You may be right!" Taranga smiled. "But, on one condition: The ruling king shall listen to the creative wisdom of his priest."

A radiant smile of satisfaction spread across old Mato's face. And, at some distance, Mahine started listening to the words she knew could irritate her fierce father.

"Are you telling me the king is an instrument with which the priest reaches his goals?" Tamatoa asked.

"No, I shall not annoy you," Taranga replied. "I suggested the king should have a friendly relationship with someone well trained on positive thinking."

"I must admit I should have listened to Mato's words in the past," Tamatoa said.

"You are a great man," Taranga said. "You fought, you conquered, you had your revenge and you built an empire. But, do you know what could be the greatest empire?"

"A clean island," Tamatoa replied with no hesitation, "a clean lagoon, and people respecting others."

"Not bad!" Taranga said, with a touch of surprise. "Not bad at all!"

Taranga went to the giant, and put one hand on his muscular shoulder. Mahine had tears in her eyes. Her father had passed a difficult test. Then, Taranga went to Mahine.

"I am going to tell you what is the greatest empire of all," Taranga said. "It is a tear of happiness in the eyes of a child…. It is the tear of happiness in the eyes of an elder…. It is a tear of happiness in the eyes of someone dear to you."

"There is no weakness in humbleness," Taranga continued. "You can be strong, and be humble. You can command, and be humble. You can dare, and be humble. You can do all that if you search for inspiration among starlight."

A long shooting star crossed the entire sky, and everyone saw it. Everyone listened to the sea, continually pounding on the reef.

"Why is the awesome sea so important to us?" Taranga asked. "You, Tamatoa, know the answer better than anyone. Listen to it. You, who are born seafarers either by choice or necessity, what would you do without the sea? The sea gives us the clouds, the rain, the rivers, the forest and our food. Yet, the sea is brutal, and its fury often unpredictable. We like its usual calmness, and the harmony it brings to our shores. So, as Tamatoa the great said: Keep the sea clean, always."

A cool breeze from the mountain passed over the fire and sent red embers among the audience.

"Why is the mountain so important to us?" Taranga asked.

Nobody answered.

"This man is the great master of the mountain," Taranga said, pointing at his grandson Kon Tici. "He shall give you the answer."

Kon stood up, typically charismatic. Many travelers who did not know him, marveled at his blue garments, embroidered red belt, rising suns on the headband, long, black hair attached above his head with a gold pin and falling around his shoulders, deep blue eyes and, above all, the glittering gold bracelets and earplugs. He had an imposing mien, in a special way. It was not physical power: Kon was no match for the Maohis in that regard. It was something else, about his personality, something no one could describe. It was Mana's unmistakable magic.

"The mountain is a bond between men and birds," Kon said. "In the mountain, I feel like a birdman."

Hina opened her eyes wide, as she recalled the painted

birdman in the cave.

"During daylight on a summit," Kon continued, "you hear animals and man from great distances. At night, you can explore another world, out there. The higher you go, the more mysterious the mountain is, and the more you feel the reality and presence of spirits."

Vana raised his hand, asking permission to make a comment, to which Kon agreed.

"We are seafarers. We spend our lives near the lagoon. For us, the mountain is the domain of the dead only, like Taaroa, where he can be at peace forever."

"You know by now there is much more to this," Kon replied. "High in the mountain, I discovered the charm of an outstanding princess, I gave my hand to an adversary in trouble, and I found a friend."

"With him," Kon continued, pointing at Tamatoa, "I accomplished the unforgettable, and earned the respect and admiration of our fellow followers. Because of the mountain, today, we have no enemy. Only meditation in the mountain can provide the necessary inspiration to overcome our conflicts. Furthermore, because of the mountain, there is a valley, there is Hina's valley, with its rivers, water, the rain forest and food. So, we shall keep the mountain clean, as a perpetual sanctuary where everything we need begins."

"Why are the birds so important?" Taranga asked, carefully removing the sacred green pigeon feather from Hina's chest. "Because they fly, and therefore they are closer to starlight, and they travel faster and farther than we can. They attract us with their beauty. They direct our course at sea. They clean the environment. And, they please our ears with lovely melodies. But, above all, they soar higher than the clouds and the mountain."

Taranga placed the feather back on Hina's chest. She felt a forceful current of energy penetrating her, as an unmistakable signal Taranga expected much from her, later in the evening. She understood the message.

"Why is peace so important?" Taranga asked, taking Kukara's hands. "This young girl should tell us."

Kukara stood up, surprised. Unprepared, she searched for answers on the Rongo-Rongo tablets.

With his hands, Taranga asked everyone to be patient, but Kukara was quick. She took Kon's hand.

"Kon is not my father, yet he is acting as a good father. Hina is not my mother, yet she loves me as if my real mother. Hotu-Matua is not the same blood, yet he is my best friend. Taranga is not my real great-grandfather, yet I love him."

Then, with a contagious effect on the audience, the young girl showed hot tears on her cheeks, illuminating her large, dark blue eyes.

"If peace could have reached the heart of our adversaries," she continued, "most members of my real family would still be alive."

She sobbed. Her eyelids trembled. She fell on her knees. "When I look at starlight, at the sea, at the mountain, or at birds, I find peace. When I look at men and women, I fear for peace. Yet, I trust my beloved family members did not die in vain."

In a surprising move, she went to Tamatoa. She looked him in the eyes. Near the giant, she looked like a tiny, fragile morning flower. She laid her hands on his thick wrists, and with victory in her eyes she said Mana's magic words: "Yet, I trust there is good in each of us."

Incredibly touched, Tamatoa grabbed the sobbing girl in his arms and hugged her against his massive chest. A long silence followed. Additional words from anyone on the subject of peace would have been futile. Waves could be heard, far away, on the reef.

Taranga went back to Hina of the Valley.

"Daring! Why is daring so important? Take a close look at this magnificent young woman. As a child, she dared to argue with the great priest. As a woman, she dared to climb Mount Orohena. As a princess, she dared to bend the kingdom rules. As a priestess, she dared to face death at sea to save a few men. As an accomplished priestess, she dared to explore the territory of spirits. Every time, she was right. As a result, she has no fear, she inspires us, she is lovable, and she is happy and makes others happy. Today, she is the most inspiring Maohi legend because every day of her life, she accepted a new challenge at dawn, and would humbly savor her achievement at sunset with the one she loves. She lives well!"

"We still don't know who you are," Tamatoa said, still holding Kukara. "There are too many things missing in your explanations."

"You may be right!" Taranga replied. "May be I don't know all the answers myself. Who we are does not matter. Maohis and Viracochas are all the same people racing with time, and struggling to live well. My people with long ears and blue eyes will fade away, mixed with the noble Maohi blood. In a distant future, Maohis will also fade away, mixed with the blood of navigators coming from the other side of the world. What counts is not the race you belong to. What counts is not what you may do. What counts is the kind of person you are, ought to be and the sort of life you ought to live. In this respect, Hina of the Valley and you are doing superbly well. With audacity we must dare, then look at our achievements with modesty. The sacred alliance between daring and modesty shall forever help us to erase arrogance, so in peace, we may master who we want to be."

Taranga sat down on a massive ironwood bench, drank some coconut milk and stared at Hina. She did not notice right away the deep blue eyes of the old Viracocha. She thought she had heard Taranga's words before, from Kon's mouth, on Mount Orohena. When she came out of her dream, she saw Taranga staring at her. She looked at Kon: He was staring at her. She looked at Kukara: She was staring at her, and so did everybody else. She felt a shiver down her spine as if everyone was invading her privacy. She was supposed to do something, but she did not have a clue what it was.

Hina felt a powerful command. She stood up, looked at her friend Mahine and at her sister, Fenua. They both obeyed the young priestess without any word being said. The three women disappeared into the night, and prepared for a sacred dance, or at least, it was what Hina thought they should do.

The sound of drums reminded everyone to remain silent, as the three women came back. They took their place between the audience and the sacred fire that had been burning for several days. They wore white skirts made of long grass, a belt made of red feathers and shiny, brown cowries. Their long and loose black hair covered their well-shaped breasts. They wore a tall, white hat made of bark-cloth and feathers. Three rows of small golden-ringed cowries circled their heads at the base of the hats. On each side of the hat, long garlands of tiny sea snails fell to their hips. At the very top of the hat, long, white grass fibers made their heads look like the rising sun. Their beautiful, dark bodies were in sharp contrast to their white costumes. In each hand, they held a whisk made of grass fibers.

Hina looked different. She was taller and slender, and wore

two long, white tropicbird streamers in the middle of her belt, covering her stomach, passing between her breasts, and attached to one another behind her neck. Above all, the gold condor hanging on her chest fascinated the entire audience.

The drums rolled gently. The three women waited for the signal to start the sacred dance, but no signal came. They were not supposed to dance. Confused, Hina looked at Taranga with interrogative eyes. Once more, she felt a shiver down her back, then a new command, then the fright of a daring and impossible mission.

She heard the rolling waves on the beach. She vaguely saw her father come to her, and attach the feather of the sacred green pigeon on her forehead. She instantly felt a great peace invading her. She heard the green pigeon cooing, as if it was in her head. At that point, Hina knew Viracocha's force was at work, up to something no one had done before. The wind became stronger, stirring the fire. Dark red embers became bright red, almost white. Tiny embers flew away between trees and hit the huge walls of the sacred Marae. Hina's mind traveled in space. She smiled at the incredible scenery she had already seen before in the cave. Rivers of shiny stars spiraled into gigantic wheels. One wheel approached her at incredible speed, until the entire sky became evenly blue with heat. Before she could raise her arms to protect herself, a colossal explosion blinded her eyes: She was in touch with the Light.

When she awoke she was covered with perspiration, squeezing Mahine's and Fenua's hands.

"What happened to you?" Mahine asked.

"I will never be able to describe what I saw in my mind," Hina replied. "But, now I am sure it is safe for me to perform what I am supposed to do."

"What is it?" Fenua asked.

"You will know soon."

The fire, made in a long pit, was covered by flat stones, heated for so long that they were white-hot. Hina watched the glowing stones for a moment, then called a few servants.

"Spread the hot stones evenly, into a flat bed, then remove all the burning wood. I want no flames in the fire, only the white-hot stones."

Puzzled, the crowd whispered. Something out of the ordinary would take place. Tupua glanced at his daughter with concern in his eyes.

"Hina," Tupua said, "what do you want to do?"

"I want to walk across the fire," Hina replied, with incredible serenity and no fear.

Tupua remained silent for awhile. Then, anger flashed in his eyes.

"Walk across the fire!… She wants to walk across the fire!…"

Kon put one hand on Tupua's shoulder, but the monarch did not welcome the gesture.

"Do not worry," Kon said, "nothing bad will happen to Hina. Trust me!"

Not totally convinced, Tupua sat on the royal ironwood bench, and Atea came close to him with fear in her eyes. Kon held her hands.

"You better be sure about this," Tupua whispered, "because I will make the Viracocha people accountable for anything that would hurt Hina."

Slowly, Hina walked barefooted toward the fire. Everyone was stunned at her audacity. As she reached the first white-hot stones, she raised her head in Maohi pride, closed her eyes and proceeded.

"Mana is with me," she said.

Very slowly, she walked atop the fire. She found the contact with the stones very smooth, almost slippery. It was like walking on a thick carpet of rain forest moss, but she thought there was something missing in her comparison. Then, she recalled what it felt like walking barefooted on the tiny heads of a brain coral. It was rough, yet smooth enough to be quite pleasant. Everyone was absolutely startled when they saw her smile, and take her time. She finally reached the other side of the fire. She looked at her feet: There was no trace of a burn. Astonished and filled with fear, the crowd dispersed into the night. Only the high priests, the kings, and her close friends forced themselves to remain in their respective places. Then, a long silence ensued. At some distance, all drums were abandoned.

Taranga, followed by Kon, then Kukara, walked across the fire.

"I can do this, too," Tupua said.

The overweight monarch walked away from the fire, faced it on the narrowest side, ran as fast as he could, and jumped across the fire without touching a single stone. In the process, his clothes covering his buttocks caught on fire. Embarrassed, the king swiftly extinguished the flames with his hands. Everyone laughed. Vana dropped to his knees. Laughter came up from deep inside his throat. He turned red and choked so badly that Tupua himself started laughing.

"The only new thing I experienced tonight, is new heights," Tupua said, chuckling.

"And hot buttocks!" Vana added, lying on the ground and holding his chest, ready to burst into laughter again.

"Oh it hurts! I cannot laugh," Kon chuckled, holding his healing chest.

Then, Hina approached the fire a second time.

"Cross the fire no more," Kon said, taking her hand. "Unless, you are sure you are under the Light's command."

"I am!" Hina replied.

Kon let her go.

Slowly, she proceeded across the first stones. Then, she felt extreme heat, and realized she had been arrogant and made a monumental mistake. It was too late; smoke came out from her feet. She had only one escape. Under the gaze of stunned friends and relatives, she transformed herself into a purple vortex with incredible energy. Hot stones flew away from the fire. The vortex climbed to the top of the white monolith, and slowly faded. Hina was gone.

CHAPTER 35

"I am the Light. I am the Mighty, and created everything from pure energy. Rulers thirsty for power ruin this world. They make it impossible for the cosmic quarantine, in which I placed them, to stop. They should be replaced by carefully appointed facilitators. I shall give these humble and kind gifted ones special power in their hearts. Liberated from arrogance, ambition and prejudice, they shall protect the ones nearby, and inspire the ones far away."

Hina opened her eyes, and stared at the vegetable roof above her. It was enough to alert her that she was no longer at the gathering. She looked around, and recognized familiar objects. She had been sleeping on bamboo mats, in her father's house, in Papenoo, in Tahiti-nui. She recalled the fire burning her feet. She touched her toes: They were fine. She recalled the ceremonial clothes she was wearing. She looked at herself, and noticed only casual clothes she had long forgotten. Something was very wrong. She looked at her hands: They seemed smaller than usual. She grabbed her breasts: They were almost nonexistent. Blood flushed to her head at the intolerable implication of her observations. She searched for the gold necklace around her neck: There was nothing. She was a twelve-sun-cycle-old girl. She ran out of the house like a tornado, rushed to her father, who was napping among the many flowers of his royal garden.

"Where is Kon?" she asked, with dilated eyes.

"Where is who?" Tupua inquired.

"Kon Tici!" she screamed.

"Calm down! I have never heard of such a name."

With no further attempt, she ran to Vana's dwelling, and entered with no warning, scaring the old priest.

"Where is Kon?"

"Who is Kan?" Vana asked. "What is wrong with you?"

"Kon Tici Viracocha!"

"Kan Teke Chaco…ravi…? Who is that?

She left, very angry. She went to her Marae of Toerau, across the Papenoo River. There was no Marae. She found only wilderness. She sat on the ground, listened to the waves pounding the bottom of the cliff, then she put her head in her hands, and tried to recollect her memories. She rejected the devastating idea that she may have been dreaming the amazing saga that ruled her life for several sun-cycles. At this moment, she would not even consider the remote possibility of such a hypothesis.

"I am dreaming right now," she murmured.

Just to make sure, she went swimming in the cold water of the river, and stayed until she was shivering. Then, and only then, she slowly realized that she might not be dreaming at all. She went to the valley, to the great falls, looked up and saw the tropicbirds soaring to the clouds. She went inside the forest, to the great mape tree, and searched for the clothes she had buried one moon-cycle earlier. She found nothing, and she did not see the sacred green pigeon.

On her way back to the village, she went near the forbidden banyan tree, under which she saw the pitiful leper telling her to go away. She did.

She went to the place where she had met Kon for the first

time, and searched for evidence of his presence. She found only places where man had never been. She cried... Crushed, she desperately called Mana's force.

"There is no way I am going to let this happen," she murmured, "I would rather die."

Angry at what was happening, she went back to the village, and saw her father giving orders to prepare for the coming storm. She recalled in her memories that such a thing was supposed to take place the day before she met Kon. The thought gave her hope. She did not mind reliving the past, as long as it would be with the man she loved.

She attended the evening ceremony, listening to Vana's legends, and especially the breadfruit legend. She tried her best to act like the original twelve-sun-cycle-old girl, and seemed to be successful at it: Vana was indeed impressed by her knowledge.

The next day, she helped her mother and sister to restore order after the storm, as she always did, but the next morning, she prepared for the long walk to the Teauroa Point, along which she would search for rare shells brought to the beach by the angry sea. She went to her father, as she always did, asking permission to leave.

"Please father, let me go to the Teauroa Point, so I can be the first one to collect the most beautiful shells."

"Of course, little girl, be back at sunset."

Hina went to the beach, ran to the Teauroa Point, in no mood to look for shells. Nevertheless, along the way, she found two nautilus shells she knew well. She took them: She wanted everything to be as the first time.

At the point, she sat on the black sand, and watched the reef barrier, searching for the remains of Kon's raft. She saw nothing.

Then, she recalled an important detail she had long forgotten.

At this precise moment, she was supposed to see a vortex of black sand climbing the beach, and coming toward her. She looked around, waited, but saw nothing. She realized that long ago, when she was a young girl, she had been in contact with the most powerful spirit of all. At that time, she had never suspected the full significance of that contact, until now.

"How blind and naïve I have been!" she declared aloud.

She knew that if there were no vortex, there would be no Kon Tici as well. In doubt, she waited,…until midday,…until sunset.

Nobody came to the cool Vaipopoo River, behind the sand dune. No raft came from behind the reef. She went to the tiare bushes, took a white flower, and placed it above her left ear. The fragrance was so strong, so familiar and pleasant, that she managed a fleeting smile.

She knew the reason why she was back as a young girl. Prior to walking on the fire a second time, she recalled having been arrogant in the name of the Light. It was her punishment to be here, far away from the man she loved.

"But, it was a game! I did not commit a crime," she said defensively.

Indeed, it was not Hina's nature to be arrogant, and it had been precisely because of this exceptional quality that she had been chosen by the Supreme Being. So, the lesson was clear: Hina will live, Hina will be a priestess, but she will never forget the lesson.

She walked down the beach with one nautilus in each hand and looked at the sunset behind Moorea.

"Oh, Viracocha, I am not a mean person," she groaned and wept. "Why did you abandon me? I was learning. I was innocent of your power. I meant well…"

She fell on her knees.

"I want to be your servant. Please, give me another chance."

Only the hissing sound of the receding waves on the beach answered her prayer. At some distance, she saw a sandpiper running away from her: She knew it was the end.

"Wherever you are, my love, be in peace."

Then, Hina recalled the Light's recommendation: "Use the power I have given you wisely."

She started drawing a spiral on the wet sand. Circles came closer to the center slowly. At one point, there was no place for another circle, so she stopped. She knew that when she would complete the spiral something would happen. Humbled, she completed the spiral with her finger.

"I am your servant, and I believe in You, immensely."

At some distance from the Marae of Taputapu-atea Kon walked on the beach, his thoughts far away at sea. At his side, Taranga was silent. Nearby, Tamatoa and Hotu-Matua were planning the great trip to the far east.

"One moon-cycle from now, I will leave with three ships, toward the Rapa-iti direction," Tamatoa said. "I know that area well. Kon, you will come with me."

"I will go toward the Tuamotu Arch direction, with five ships," Hotu-Matoa said. "I will take Taranga and Rangi with me."

They went back to their quarters, and gathered around Hina, who was sleeping on a blanket of coconut fronds. She had been asleep for two days, after they rescued her from the fire where she had mysteriously vanished for an instant.

"She is lucky; her burns are only superficial and already healing well," Vana said. "She was talking in her sleep a moment ago. But her words did not make sense."

Taranga took Kon's hand.

"Do you realize what you have done?" The old Viracocha said. "I am sure she went far beyond everything you had imagined."

"She overwhelmed me," Kon said. "We are a doomed race, but she and the Maohis are not. They have the duty to inspire the world with beauty, kindness and peaceful hearts."

"Yet, behind this lovely woman," Taranga said, "Maohis will show there is no impossible undertaking for correctly focused mankind."

"Wake up Hina of the Valley," Kon said, "we need to prepare for the trip to Mata Kite Rani!"

The priestess opened her eyes. She looked intently at Kon, not too sure if she knew him. Finally, she gave him a smile. She looked at her feet wrapped in light bark-cloth. She stood on her feet, felt a twinge of pain, and managed to walk to the white monolith a short distance away. She touched it, and turned around, facing everyone staring at her.

"Forgive me," she said, "I have a terrible headache!"

Wiping her forehead with her arm, she quickly recovered her full awareness.

"For you, Kon Tici, my name is Hina of the Valley," she said with a charismatic voice. "But, for Maohis, my name is Hina-tu-a-uta."

On her chest, the gold condor was glittering brightly. She climbed on the white, sacred monolith, and invited all her loved ones and friends to circle around her, joining hands. They did.

"Kon Tici, you named this faraway, mysterious island "Mata Kite Rani," It means "Eyes Looking at the Stars". It is a beautiful, inspiring name. But we also need a Maohi name for this place where so many of us will settle, with you."

Tupua's face saddened at her last word.

"I have a name for that place," Hina said, looking at Tamatoa. "We shall name it Rapa-nui!"

****

END

It was the dawn of the Rapa-nui civilization (i.e., The astonishing, mysterious settlement of Easter Island).